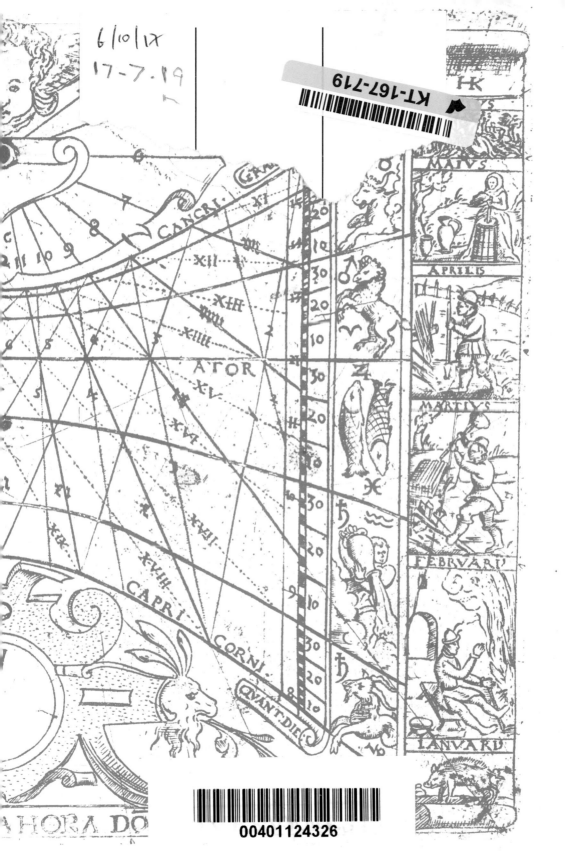

1588
A CALENDAR
of CRIME

By the same author

HEW CULLAN MYSTERIES

Hue & Cry
Fate & Fortune
Time & Tide
Friend & Foe
Queen & Country

1588
A CALENDAR
of CRIME

A Novel in Five Books

SHIRLEY McKAY

Polygon

This edition published in Great Britain in 2016 by
Polygon, an imprint of Birlinn Ltd
West Newington House
10 Newington Road
Edinburgh
EH9 1QS

www.polygonbooks.co.uk

9 8 7 6 5 4 3 2 1

ISBN 978 1 84697 363 5

The five individual books in this novel are published separately as eBooks

British Library Cataloguing-in-Publication Data
A catalogue record for this book is available on request from the British Library

Text design by Studio Monachino
Printed and bound by Scandbook AB, Falun, Sweden

Endpapers: Calendar, Monogrammist HK (engraver), Rijksmuseum,
The Netherlands. *Page 298:* From Jost Amman's Stände und Handwerker
mit Versen von Han Sachs (1884), Wellcome Library, London.

CONTENTS

BOOK I

Candlemas

Now diverse secret agues breed
Be choice of food, beware of cold:
Abstain from milk, no vein let bleed
In taking medicines be not bold

RICHARD GRAFTON'S ALMANACK,
A brief treatise, conteinyng many proper tables
and easie rules... (1571–1611)

I

The candlemaker's boy was thankful for the moon. Without its friendly glare, he would have to make his way through darkness down the path adjacent to the cliff, perilous by day, let alone at night. And no one but a lunatic would care to take that chance.

A crowd of yellow pinpricks clustered at the Swallowgate, where lanterns cast a dimly well-intentioned light, but over to the west the darkness pooled and chasmed, blacking out the cliff top and the gulf beyond. And westward was the crackling house, set back from the town, where the salt winds might snatch the rank air, and the sea water carry it off.

In the year of plague, the dead had been laid down to rest in this place. So much that was noxious was settled in the wind. The candlemaker's boy muttered out a prayer, and shuddered as he passed. He thanked God when he came upon the low flame of the crackling house, swinging at the door as the law required. A slender skelp of taper guttered in the draught; the candlemaker grudged to spare the smallest light.

The boy entered the crackling house, pulling off his hat. 'I have done what you asked.'

The candlemaker, bent over his great greasy pot, did not look up. 'Is that a fact?'

'I went to a' they houses, all the ones you said. The auld wife at the last one wasnae best pleased. She wis not pleased at all.'

'No? And why was that?'

'She said ye had not sent her all that she had asked for. And she did not like the candles that you sent. She said that the tallow was filled full o cack.'

'That guid wife is a lady. She did not say that.'

'No. She said – ' the candlemaker's boy assumed a high-pitched plaintive voice, pinching at his nose, 'Please to tell your master, there is offal in it. Oh, but it does stink!'

'You do the lady wrong, to mock at her like that,' the candlemaker warned.

'She is not so gentle, as you seem to think. She says she will not pay you the prices you demand. She says you have extortioned her. She says she will report on it to the burgh magistrates.'

'She will not do that. And she will pay the price. For we ken what it is that she does with her candles.'

'Do we?' the boy asked, unsure.

'Of course we do, you loun. What did she gie to you, to thank you for your pains?'

'Nothing. I telt you, she wasnae pleased.' The boy stamped his feet. 'Three miles through the dark, and the wind was fierce.' He did not tell the fear, the horror he had felt, to shiver in the great hall of that wifie's house, where, he was quite certain, there had been a ghost.

'Cold are ye? Come by the fire.'

'Nah, I'm a'right.'

'Did you no hear me, son? Come by the fire.' The candlemaker left his post to slide a helping hand around his servant's shoulder. He grasped the boy's ear, and twisted it sharply. The boy gave a yelp. 'Whit was that for?'

'What did she gie ye, ye wee sack of shite?'

'Nothing. I telt you,' the prentice boy whimpered, wrenched by his ear to the rim of the pot. 'For pity, you will hae ma lug off.'

'Aye, and I might.' The candlemaker let go of the ear, that was throbbing fiercely, radiant and red, but before the boy could cup it in a cooling hand he felt the candlemaker's fingers strangled in his hair, forcing him down to the filth of the bath.

'Mammie!' He could say no more, for the fumes from the tallow filled his eyes and lungs, and his legs beneath him buckled at the stench. A little of his forelock flopped into the fat, and began to stiffen as his master pulled him up. 'Why wad ye do that?' he wailed.

'For that you are a liar, and an idle sot.'

'I did not lie. She gied me naught. I telt you. She was cross.' The boy was snivelling now. Perhaps it was the fumes. He could not help the streaming from his nose and eyes. He ought to be inured to them. He ought to be inured to the candlemaker's wrath. It was not the force of the fury that disarmed him, and caught him off his guard – fearful though it was – it was that the moment for it could not be foretold. The candlemaker's boy could seldom see it coming; he had not that kind of wit. And, when it came, it knocked him from his feet.

'Mebbe that is true,' the candlemaker said, and the boy felt his nerves shiver to a twang, 'but that does not excuse your fault in your craft. What do you say to this?' From their place upon the rack he pulled down a rod of limp tallow candles, all of them shrunken and spoiled. 'What do you say?'

'They were too early dipped.'

'And what limmar dipped them?'

It struck the boy, quite forcefully, that it had not been him. Perhaps it had been the candlemaker's wife. He gathered to his service what he had of wits, and managed not to say so. 'Ah dinna ken,' was what he spluttered out.

'You do not ken?' The candlemaker raised his arm, and paused, to rub at it.

The candlemaker's boy took courage from the pause. 'I heard the surgeon say, ye must not strain yourself.'

'Not strain mysel'?' The candlemaker glowered, and let his sore arm drop. 'I'll show you strain.' But something in him slackened, and appeared to slip.

'Will I do the work again?' the boy suggested then.

'I'll see to it mysel'. You will pay for the waste, out of your wages. Awa with you, now. Hame to your lass. Look at ye blubber. Ye greet like a bairn.'

The candlemaker's boy rubbed his nose on his sleeve. 'Ah dinna greet.'

It was the odour of the grease pot that had caused his eyes to stream. Surely it was that. He could feel the tallow drying in his hair, the tufted strands of sheep fat pricking up on end. His master could see it, and his humour changed. 'Tell your lassie I have dipped for her a scunner of a candle. She may put her flame to it, if she can stand the stink.'

The boy's wit as always was slow to ignite. 'Whit candle is that?'

'You, you lubber, *you*.'

It was not for kindness, nor from common charity, that he sent the lad away. Charity would be to give the boy a light. Instead, he let him flounder, on the dark path home. And if the candlemaker stayed to work on through the night, in spite of his sore arm, then he had a purpose for it that was all his own. There were certain kinds of business played out in the darkness, and best prospered there; business of that sort had no business with the boy.

At nine of the clock, or a little before, a visitor came. He had brought with him his own little lantern, in a sliver of parchment, like the ones the small boys bound up on to sticks, to carry back from school on winter afternoons. The candlemaker thought it would not last the wind, to see the bearer home.

The visitor was well wrapped up. Perhaps against the wind; perhaps against the flavour of the candlemaker's shop – the crackling had a savour not to everybody's taste; perhaps because he did not wish to show the world his face. He wore a kind of cowl, a long and shapeless gown, a hood up round his head. His muffler could not mask the feeling in his eyes, which were pale and agitated. He looked about, and back, as though the shadows of the night might engulf him on his way. His words, when he spoke, were low and unwilling. 'So. I have come. As you said.'

The candlemaker lifted out a row of candles from the pot. He stood awhile, considering. Then he placed them carefully to dry upon the rack, and took up another row, preparing them to dip. 'A moment, if you will.'

'Yes.' The visitor accepted, and remained politely, while the row was dipped. It was not until a third descended his impatience showed itself. 'I cannot stay so long. If you do not have what I want —.'

The candlemaker showed no flicker of concern. 'I have what you want. But this is a business that cannot be rushed. If it is rushed, it will spoil, do you see?'

'I see that.' The visitor was courteous, conciliatory, even. The candlemaker sensed that he would not put up a fight. 'But, I think you said to be here before nine. And it is nine now.'

To confirm this, the St Salvator's clock at that moment could be heard to strike the hour.

'I believe, sir, it was you that fixed upon the time,' the candlemaker said.

The visitor conceded, 'Ah, perhaps it was. My pardon to you, sir. But since you are still occupied, and I may not stay long, I shall come again. Tomorrow, if you will.'

The candlemaker smiled. 'Aye, just as you like. Though I must warn you, sir, that I cannot promise I will have tomorrow all that ye require.'

'But surely... since you say you have it now...' The visitor, plainly, was baffled by this.

'I have it for ye now. And, sir, I have kept it for you, at some trouble to myself, when the commodity you look for is very dear and scarce. If you will not take it now, I cannot be expected to have it still the morn.'

'But I will take it now, if you will only give it to me!' the visitor exclaimed.

'Very good. I will. When the rack is done.' And the candlemaker, blandly, went on with his work.

The candlemaker dipped, for such a length of time as he could see the patience of his customer last out; he judged it very fine, like the grains of sand running through a glass; and when he saw that the great mass of sand, all in a rush, was about to flood out, he straightened up quickly, and said, 'If you will take it now, sir, I will fetch the stuff.' And from a shelf in the shop, where it opened to the street, he produced a slender box. This he opened up. 'Fine, is it not?'

'It is less substantial than I had supposed. That is, for the price...'

'As to that,' the candlemaker intercepted smoothly, 'it comes in at two pounds, six shillings and sixpence. And, I suppose, you would also like the box. A shilling for the box and the paper in it. I will not count a penny for the scrap of string.'

The visitor blinked at him. 'Two Scots pounds, we said.'

'So much had I hoped for. I do not set the price. And, as I have said, it was hard to find. But the profit to you is, I ask nor answer questions. Whatever you will do with it, is your own affair.'

'I understand you, sir. The pity of it is, I cannot pay that much,' the visitor confessed. 'This is all I have.' And, to prove his point, he emptied out his purse.

The candlemaker hesitated. 'I do not always do this. But, as I believe, you have an honest face' – so little of that face as was left to view. 'Give me the two pounds. And you can owe the rest. Can you write your name? Then put it in this book.' He took out from the counter a fat leather notebook, and opened to a page, on which the date was written: *First of Feberwerrie*. 'That makes, in all, seven shillings and sixpence.'

The visitor glanced at the book. He squinted at the figures. But he did not seem convinced. 'Seven and sixpence? What are your terms?'

'Pay the money on account by the first of March, and the debt will be cleared, without further cost. If you cannot pay, interest will accrue, but we need not speak of that until the debt is due. Sign for it now, this very day, and you may have the stuff to take away with you. Or, if you will not, I must offer it for sale.'

The visitor agreed. He signed his name and left, the burden of his dealings bundled in his cloak. He fled the crackling house, as though the devil's spur and pitchfork pricked behind him. He did not look back. And the candlemaker's prophecy was proven to be right, for his sliver of a lantern did not last the wind.

The candlemaker meanwhile worked on through the night. Though he had made a profit he did not feel quite satisfied. He felt a deeper sense that something was not right. And he did not feel well. His legs were weak and tired. His forehead and his forearm had both begun to throb. The bandage on his arm was bulging, hot and tight. He sat down in his chair and loosened it a little, letting out the cord. He let his dull eyes close, and soon he was asleep, so shuttered to the world, he did not hear the latch.

¶

Frances had not slept. For a while she shifted, soundlessly sought rest, before she slipped the shackles of the heavy quilt and found solace in the shadows by the window sill. Hew felt the coolness of her absence in the bed, and woke to find her gazing out upon the moon. 'Is there aught amiss?'

'Nothing is amiss.'

'Will you come to bed?' He felt for the tinder box, striking a flame. Frances said, '*Don't.*'

Bewilderment clutched at him still. 'Do not light the candle,' Frances said. 'So little have we left, of the purest wax. Bella says tis hard to come by, at this time of year.'

'Tomorrow, I will fetch you some.'

'I would not have you trouble, for my own indulgence.'

'It is not indulgence. You shall have the best.'

Frances had developed an aversion to tallow, in candles of the common sort, as to the scent of flesh, and fat of any kind. It was parcel of a change in her that mystified and baffled Hew, though his sister Meg assured him it should not be feared. He had done what he could to keep her in comfort, over the last seven months. Now the store of beeswax, apparently exhausted, caused him some concern. The cost of the candle meant little to him; yet scarceness was a thing he could not help but count. The town trade in wax had been stifled at the plague, where the sweet balm of the wax-maker's craft had conspired, drop by drop, to draw him to his death.

'Besides,' Frances said, 'there is light enough. Tomorrow night, I doubt, the moon will be quite full.'

There was truth in that. At this time of year, on a cloudless night, there was more light to be had in the glancing of the moon than in the laggard day, when the sun struggled blearily across the sullen sky. So it seemed to Hew, as he rode out in the blinking of a bloodshot dawn, to fulfil his obligations at the university.

The porter at St Salvator's hailed him at the gate. 'Good day to you, professor. Doctor Locke is called out, urgent, to a casualty. He asks if you can read for him his early morning lecture, on the chiels, an such.'

De caelo et mundo, Hew interpreted. 'Certainly I could. He did not, I suppose, report the nature of the accident?'

'Only that it was a most woeful and perplexing one.'

Casualty, Hew thought, was a curious word, and no doubt one the porter had not thought up by himself. Hew's closest friend, Giles Locke, was Visitor for Fife, reporting to the Crown on unexpected deaths. Hew was accustomed often to assist him, and, in legal cases, to assume the lead. Where there was a *casualty* he felt an interest too, and a little piqued to be left behind.

'He will be obliged to you. For he was afeart the students will revolt, and take it for a holiday. They may not have a holiday, though they will entreat for one, on account of Candlemas.'

The old tradition was, in grammar schools at Candlemas, the scholars gave their masters silver as a gift to fund the cost of lighting in the schoolroom for the year. The schoolmaster would grant them a play day in return. And college students hankered still for such small indulgences.

'The wind is, we shall have a royal visitation, in the Whitsun term. Wherefore, says the doctor, keep them to their books. And the student Johannes Blick is keen to speak with you,' the porter went on.

Hew smiled at that. 'No danger, I suppose, that he is pleading for a holiday?'

'None at all, I fear.'

Johannes was the son of a Flemish merchant, in his final year. In age in advance of his fellow magistrands by a year or two, he outstripped them by a score in intellect and aptitude. And there was no doubt, when the king's commissioners came to make their inspection, Johannes would stand out among them as a shining star. Yet day to day, his brightness was a strain. When his tutor could not fathom to the bottom of his questions, he had turned his attentions devotedly to Hew, an attachment which occasioned as much mirth among the college, as it did relief. Hew had done his best. He had lent him books, and given many hours to hearing out his arguments. He liked Johannes well. Yet still there were days when he would sigh and sink to hear the fatal words, If I might for a moment, sir, intrude upon your time. Then time would run like sand, and never be enough.

'Forewarned is forearmed. I thank you, Will, for that. Then all is well, besides? No more that I should know?'

'Naught else, of note, except you have a visitor. I left him in the cloister, where he can do no harm. I did not care to think what Doctor Locke would say,' Will concluded cryptically.

Barely had Hew entered through the archway to the square when Johannes fell behind him, matching step for step. '*Salve*, Master Hew. I trust you are quite well. If I may intrude a moment on your time…' Johannes spoke in perfect Latin, well-tuned and precise. His clear pedantic sounding filled Hew with dismay.

'*Salve*, Johannes. I am quite well. You find me in some haste.'

'Then I shall not detain you, sir. I wanted, simply, to thank you for the help you were kind enough to give me, and to return your books.'

'But surely,' Hew, despite himself, could not help but say, 'you have not read them yet?'

'I have, sir, read them all. If you have a moment, I will fetch them now. I have made some notes, of the principal matters contained in the books, and the principal questions, and objections, arising therein, which I should very much like to discuss with you.'

'*Facile*. Of course. But, alas, not now. Speak with me after the lecture,' Hew suggested, desperately.

'What lecture, sir, is that?'

'Aristotle, *De caelo*, which I must give in place of Professor Locke.'

'I have heard Professor Locke, on the movement of the spheres, and of the elements. Most illuminating. I should like to hear, indeed, your own interpretation of it.'

'The lecture is no more than a reading of the text. Trust me, Johannes, I shall not deviate at all, from the version you have heard before from Doctor Locke.'

Johannes smiled the gentle smile that so rarely broke upon his solemn bright blue eyes, transforming his face from a paragon of seriousness. 'Now that is a thing that I very much doubt.'

The student was disarmed, evaded for the while, and Hew came to the cloister, to confront the visitor, whose purpose had been pressing on his mind. For here was Roger Cunningham, who once had set his wits so fiercely against Hew. A student at the college, Roger had withdrawn, in a fine show of arrogance and supercilious pride, before he was expelled, and bound himself apprentice to a barber-surgeon. Giles Locke in particular was hurt by his deception, and found his dereliction hardest to forgive.

Roger faced him boldly. 'Well, you took your time.'

Hew did not rise to this. He sensed, behind the swagger and display, a current of uneasiness. Roger was not comfortable, or brave as he appeared. In the corner of the square, and at the chapel door, a group of students gathered, pausing there to stare, at one whom they no longer counted as their friend. Roger was unnerved. And that was rare enough.

Hew saw the students off, a brusque wave of his hands, to scatter them like birds. They would not fly far. 'What is your business here?'

'There has been a death,' said Roger, 'in the crackling house. John Blair the candlemaker. Please, will you come?'

There was meekness in his tone, and in his demeanour, which astonished Hew. 'Did Doctor Locke send you to fetch me?'

'No, sir, he did not. *I* am asking you. My master is suspected as complicit in his death. Occasion and the circumstances do inform against him. I wish you to defend him,' Roger answered simply. 'For it is not true.' What did it cost him, to put such a case?

'Why would you ask me?'

'I know of no one else.'

That much was honest, thought Hew. 'Suppose that it *is* true?' he asked Roger softly.

'Then, I suppose, you will find it out.'

'Understand, I make no promise. I will come and see.'

Johannes saw them pass, and called out in astonishment. 'Are you going out, now? Will there be no lecture? What about the students, waiting in the hall?'

Roger grinned at him. 'Tell them it is Candlemas, and they have a holiday. They never liked you half as much, as they will like you now. Close your mouth, Johannes, it is dropping to the floor.'

Johannes said, reprovingly, 'I know this Roger, sir, that was a student here. I cannot find in him an honest heart or pure. I pray to God you do not place your trust in him.'

'Before the year of plague, there were three or four candlemakers working at the crackling house. John Blair was the last,' Roger had explained. 'He leaves behind a wife and a prentice boy. At Martinmas, at slaughter time, he took on extra hands. But for the most part, he worked on his own. He liked it like that. His journeyman Tam Cruik, when he had served his time, found work as a straggler, travelling to the manors and the country farms to make their candle for them when they kill their lambs. Perhaps he comes to yours.'

Hew did not reply. They had come upon the place. And his answer had been swallowed, stifled by the smell. The stench of the tallow had the curious effect of dulling down the image that appeared before his eyes, stripping it of force, as though the strength of the assault on that most sensitive of senses dampened down the rest.

The crackling house was narrow, eight foot wide at most. A window on a working day opened to the street, a counter folding down to hold a small display of the candlemaker's wares, for any who were stout enough to seek them out at source. Most would be content to wait till market day, when the candlemaker's boy would go forth with his creel to cry them by the cross. The shutters now were closed, the counter folded in. In the chimney a large pot of fat hung suspended, cloaked in a sooty black smoke. Someone had dampened the flames of the fire, in time to save the house from burning to a crisp, the tallow having caught a little as the pan boiled dry. The silt that smouldered still explained the acrid smell. On a board beside were several moulds of copper and a metal trough, where melted grease was poured, and the candles dipped, while a rusting pail oozed tallow fat unrinded, marbled and veined with pale pink and blue, to which the rank rumour of sheep flesh had stuck. Two small windows, barred, looked out on a yard, to allow the smoke a pitiful retreat, and in this yard, come fair or foul, the candlemaker rendered down the raw slabs of the tallow, polluting the fresh air for a mile around.

Hew allowed his eyes to rest a moment on these things, to fix them in his mind. The gross slab of sheep fat left so much of an impression there, it came back to him when he next closed his eyes; and when he fell asleep, it merged, indistinct and irresistible, with the vision of the candlemaker – which he turned to next – and they became so blurred, his waking mind could scarcely tell the two apart. The figure of the man dissolved into the tallow, sallow, slick and bloodless, sundered from the flesh.

The candlemaker sat, or somehow had been stuffed, stiff among the cushions of a single settle seat; so broad was his beam he filled its girth completely, packed close as a candle poured into its mould, with no gap for air. It would take a timmerman to prise his carcase out. He was stripped down to his shirt, a loose tent of flax flowing over his breeks. His points were undone, and his sleeves were rolled up. Both palms lay open, slack, in his lap, his elbows constrained by the sides of the chair. From his forearm to the right, a little past the joint, a bandage had been pushed, loosened from its place and very lightly flecked. The arm below was drenched with rivulets of blood, that streaming from the place they first had found a pulse had coursed the long way down through woollen breek and hose and pooled upon the floor, coming to a close at the candlemaker's shoe, where they had discoloured to a sympathetic brown. A second stream had cupped in the candlemaker's hand, thick and darkly red.

Standing on each side, attendant on the corpse, were, to its right, Sam Sturrock the surgeon, and to the left the physician Giles Locke. Between them a lad, of eighteen or twenty, fiddled with his cap and hopped from foot to foot, the one small anomalous flutter of life.

Giles was first to speak. His presence in a crisis, circumspect and steady, always reassured. But Hew could read no comfort in the voice that said, 'What brings you, Hew? Is there something amiss at the college?'

'Nothing is amiss. Roger came to call for me, and brought me here to help.'

'Then, as I suppose, there will be no lecture,' Giles concluded bleakly, more resigned than vexed. 'And it is hard to fathom how you hope to help. Still, since you are here, you must now bear witness to this sad affair.'

Hew understood, at once, that he should not have come, that Giles Locke had a purpose, in trying to ensure that he was otherwise engaged. As witness, he was bound to give evidence in court. And if he were to be called to serve upon the jury – since jury members always had an interest in the case – he could not be allowed to speak for the defence. The white face of the surgeon, whose misery was plain, who looked as sick at heart as the candlemaker's corpse, convinced Hew a defence was soon to be required. But since he had quite wittingly intruded on the fact, it was now too late to offer to withdraw. He had made himself a witness, willingly or not. In which case, someone else would have to speak for Sam.

'The defunct is John Blair,' Giles went on. 'You knew him, perhaps. His friends called him Jock. He was sometime the beadle, at the town kirk.'

Naming him had humanised the carcase in the chair, assigning it a pathos Hew did not like to admit. The candlemaker's head had fallen to one side, slipping from its pillow as its owner fell asleep, and – Hew thanked the Lord – the eyes were closed. He forced himself to look upon the candlemaker's face, and forced himself to see, though the features slipped and shrank upon the bone, as though the lifeless flesh had melted in the fire, that there was something there he dimly recognised. He remembered one John Blair, beadle in the kirk, bustling through the town with prurient efficiency. Was it not John Blair, had turned out the young Dyer bairns for fidgeting in kirk, when their da had died? And the same John Blair, that took a throaty pleasure in the stripping of a whore, exposed for all to jeer at in the market place? And when Agnes Ford was taken for a witch, was it not John Blair had kept her from her sleep, and applied her torments keenly and assiduously?

'Sam Sturrock, the surgeon, ye ken,' the doctor continued, relentless. 'And this lad here is John Blair's prentice, Alexander Forgan.'

Alexander Forgan said 'Eck,' unused to, and recoiling from, the full force of his name, which woke in him a kind of fearful superstition.

'Eck,' conceded Giles, 'tell to Master Hew here all that you told me, that he may be a witness to your true account.'

Eck surpassed himself, with a flush of pride, for despite his squeamish pity at the scene, and a vague suspicion things did not bode well for him, a thrilling kind of horror bubbled in the boy, and he was brimming over with the tale he had to tell. 'It was I that found him. Ah *fund* him, d'ye see?'

The matter amounted to this. He had last seen his master, alive, between eight and nine of the clock, the night before. He thought it must be closer to the nine, for he minded that the bell had rung, to mark the college curfew, just as he reached home; he lived landward, with his mother, half a mile away.

He had spent the day, and the evening after dark, making some deliveries of candles through the town, and some way beyond. It was a busy time. And it did not surprise him that his master lingered on, working through the night. He had known him work all the night before, to see the orders done. When he was tired, he would sleep in his chair. His wife was forewarned not to expect him.

At the mention of a wife Hew's stout heart sank a little. Sam Sturrock stood and listened all the while, saying not a word, as Eck babbled on.

The master was not well. He took very bad headaches, and sick with it too, that hampered him cruel in his work. He consulted with the surgeon for it, and, on Saturday, went to him to be bled. The surgeon said to rest. And he had rested, properly, on the Sabbath day. On Monday – yesterday – he said he was recovered, and came back to work. He had a deal of work, since today was Candlemas.

'Is Candlemas observed still?' questioned Hew. He did not think that Andrew Melville, kneeling on the flagstones of his college cloisters, would call for many candles to illuminate his prayers. The reformed kirk was dead to such whims.

'For certain, sir, hereby. For it will ay be Candlemas. Though they reform the kirk, they can't reform the calendar.'

Here Hew and Giles exchanged a glance, and Giles informed him wryly, that the pope in Rome had done that very thing.

'Oh, the pope in Rome,' Eck repeated scornfully, with the blithe contempt of a true bairn of reform, too young to have an inkling where his world was formed, or what fuelled the superstitions to which he succumbed. 'We do not keep it, mark you, in the popish way. But guid folk want new candles, as they always will.'

'You do not, I suppose,' Hew could not help but say, 'have any made of wax?'

'We are not wax merchants, sir. We sell tallow candles, and soap. We have, if you will, some very fine soap,' Eck replied, mechanically. Hew shook his head. He could not bear to think of the candlemaker's soap, moulded from the scum of tallow in the vat, against Frances's white skin.

'But my master, perchance, may procure some to order, if you desire …' Here Eck tailed off. The horror of the fact had dawned on him in full; his master would not order anything again. 'Oh, sirs, he is dead.' Recognition wrung from him a solitary tear.

Giles said kindly, 'There. You have done quite well. Perhaps you should go home.'

'Oh, but I cannot,' wailed Eck, 'while there is work to be done.' He looked about him hopelessly, for want of a direction, which at last was settled in the pail of fat. 'That should not be there. If you do not mind, I will tak it outside.'

'Do, if it will please you,' Giles encouraged him. They watched as the prentice boy shouldered the pail, and carried the tallow fat out to the yard. He set down his load, and stood scratching his head, the impulse to action apparently fled, quite at a loss as to what to do next.

Sam Sturrock, all this while, had spoken not a word. Giles turned to him now. 'Will you speak to us, Sam?'

The surgeon said, tonelessly, 'I have telt you all I can. There is nothing more to add.'

'Please, will you tell it to Hew?'

Sam did not respond. It struck Hew that the man was in a state of shock. And in his shock he was in no fit state to answer to such questions, no matter in what gentle manner they were put to him, and by so kind an inquisitor; perhaps, especially in that case. Giles Locke saw it too, for he proceeded patiently, 'Sam, you must go home. I will visit you there, before I submit my report, and put the question again. In the meantime, you must give me your word you will desist from practice.'

The surgeon nodded merely, staring at the corpse.

'There is nothing, now, that you wish to add? You say that John

Blair consulted you, about recurring headaches. That on Saturday, you opened up a vein for him, and told him he should rest?'

'That is what I said.'

'And you will not explain, why you chose this course, at such an inauspicious time, that nature, sense and physic all were ranged against it?'

Sam Sturrock whispered then, 'He wanted it that way.'

'He wanted it that way? And did you not tell him the danger?'

'I telt to him the danger. But he was not deterred. He professed himself in such an agony and heat, the most extreme and violent measures were required.'

'And did you never think to consult with a physician, what remedy was best in this exceptional case?'

The surgeon bowed his head, and answered not at all.

Roger exclaimed, 'This is not right. It cannot be right.'

Giles turned his gaze on him. 'Were you with your master when he cut the vein?'

Roger faltered then. 'No, he sent me out.'

'Therefore, you have no purpose here, no place to speak for him. But it seems strange that he sent you away. Did someone else assist you, Sam?' Giles persisted quietly.

'There was no one else.'

'And is this the cut to the vein that you made?'

The surgeon answered, carefully, 'That is the place.'

'It cannot be. Tell them,' Roger implored. 'Will you not speak?' When the surgeon would not, Roger attempted to walk the man home, but this was repelled.

'Cease, Roger. Stay. Accept what must come. What has been done cannot be undone. There is no hope.'

On this grim command, Sam departed alone, and Hew placed a hand upon Roger to hold him. 'There is a boy, in the yard outside, in want of a strong drink.'

'And what is that to me?' Roger answered rudely.

'Apposite,' said Hew. 'That boy has a tale to spill. And when he is over his dread – which he will be quite presently – he is like to spill it to the first friend at hand. That friend will be you. He will trust you best, for you are most alike.'

'We are nothing alike,' Roger retorted, his superfluous pride spilling over at this. 'How can you think so? He is an ignorant loun.'

'And you a presumptuous one. Yet you have more in common than you may suppose. You are close to him in age. You are prentices, both, and both, for want of a master, as likely to be cast adrift. If you cannot in your conscience relate to his predicament, then he has the wit to relate to yours.'

His own situation so forcefully brought home to him, Roger said sulkily, 'What should I ask him?'

'Use your own intelligence to find out what he knows. Since you are so clever, that will not be hard.'

'Aye, but he stinks.' There was such a fit of childishness beneath his stubborn pride, despite his pompous posturing, that Hew was moved to smile. He felt, inexplicably, a fondness for Roger, who was not as worldly as he liked to think.

'Of course he will stink. He is a candlemaker's boy. But I have seen you carve your way through gobbets of green flesh, and hold your knife and nerve. Surely, as a surgeon's page, you have not grown fastidious.'

'Mebbe,' Roger scowled, 'I like my foul flesh dead. Well then, for Sam Sturrock's sake I'll take him for a drink. Since we are puir bairns both, we'll charge the drinks to you.'

'What are you about, Hew?' Giles asked his friend, when the two of them were left together in the room, with no matter still between them but the candlemaker's corpse.

'Roger asked me to investigate the candlemaker's death. He cannot comprehend that his master is at fault.'

'He will, quite naturally, not want to comprehend it, in view of its consequence, not least for himself.'

'Doubtless,' Hew agreed. 'You do not think, at all, there may be some hope in it?'

Giles was quiet for a moment. Then he shook his head. 'Do you mean for Sam? I wish I thought there was. I like Sam Sturrock well. I have always believed him an honest, a credible surgeon. It grieves me in my heart to find him brought so low. And yet, I cannot help but find he is at fault, and gravely so. His conduct has led, quite directly, to this poor man's death, through negligence, or worse. You saw his demeanour: he is quite aware of it. He offers no defence, for there is none to give. For every kind of fool that ever read an almanack can tell you, clear as day, there never was a time of month less apt for letting blood, nor season less auspicious for it, than the present one.'

'As any fool might say,' said Hew. 'But men of physic make exception, surely, for a special case.'

Giles favoured his old friend with a narrow look. Presently, he said, '*Men of physic* do. And if you have the will to browse among my books, you will find recorded there whatever such exceptions may be safely made. I do not have the time just now to go through them with you, for I must tell a guid wife she is now a widow. I will see you at the college when that heavy work is done.'

In Giles Locke's turret tower, Hew had spent the best hours of the afternoon reading on phlebotomy. 'Let not blood at any time,' the book began oppressively, 'unless there is great cause.' Hew wrote in a column all the arguments against: the weather, the season, the phases of the moon. In addition to the warnings set out in the almanacks – the present moon in Leo was especially inauspicious – there were impediments most pressing to the candlemaker's case: the foulness of the air, the nature of his work, the severity of pain of which he had complained, the wobble in his wam, with vomiting and flux, his agitated state, his want of rest and sleep, his corpulence and indolence, the diet he had kept. In the column 'for,' he could write but one, and that he did not find in any kind of book. It was the surgeon's own and only explanation: 'Because he asked me to.' And it was clear to Hew that made no kind of sense.

He was sitting hopelessly, chewing at his pen, when he was distracted by Johannes at the door. '*Salve*, Master Hew. I was told by the porter that you might be here. I have no wish to disturb you.'

'Don't then,' muttered Hew. He had not intended that it should be heard; he spoke it in the Scots, but Johannes was a student of extraordinary faculties. He looked a little hurt, but not at all deterred. 'What I have to say will not detain you long. You have been so good, to help me with my work. If you can say a time, that is most convenient to you, I would like to thank you, and return your books.'

'Johannes,' Hew said wearily, 'there is no need to thank me. Please, keep the books. They may profit further study.'

'As to that,' Johannes said, 'I have made some notes.'

Hew stood up, exasperated. He took from the shelf the first book to hand. 'Here is a book that you have not yet read. It will profit you well to turn it into Latin' – he glanced upon it quickly – 'ah, to turn it *from* the Latin, into native Scots. That I think is somewhere where you lack experience.'

Johannes said, baffled, 'It is a book about bees.'

'And bees are, indeed, a very fine exemplar. You may come and see me, when the work is done.'

Had Hew been left for longer to his own devices, he might well have repented of this treatment of Johannes. But barely had he turned back to the case in hand, when Doctor Locke returned, with Roger at his heels, and both of them brought news that chased it from his mind.

II

It was chance alone that brought the two together; they had met on the turret stair, where Giles overcame his antipathy to Roger, sufficient to allow him access up to Hew. Roger spoke first. 'You were right enough about the prentice boy. He had a tale to tell. His master, it seems, was a hard man to work for. He was little liked. There were many people might have wished him harm.'

'It matters not,' Giles pointed out, 'how many may have wished him harm. One man harmed him. That was Sam. And if you mean to say he had a reason for it, that hardly helps his case.'

Roger said, 'Hear me, for there is more. The boy's last commission on the eve of Candlemas was to deliver candles to a guid wife out of town. That woman was by no means well disposed towards his master. The boy believes she put a curse on him. He is quite convinced, that she is a witch. He saw a spirit in her house. Perhaps it was that wife that killed the candlemaker, caused his vein to burst by the casting of a charm.'

Giles retorted, 'Pah!' an expression of disgust which he did not clarify, by gracing it with words. But Hew, more circumspect, inquired of Roger if he knew the woman's name.

'She is, I understand, some relation to the Balfour family. She is aged, far beyond the common course of life, and she lives in a coven, by the Poffle of Strathkinness, two or three miles from the town.'

Giles corrected, with a snort, 'She is a distant cousin of the Balfours. She has lived in seclusion now for many years, in a house she rents from them. Her given name is Ann. She is a lady, though a very poor one. And she is by no means a witch.'

'Do you know her?' asked Hew.

'She is a patient of mine. And if you will libel her, with this vile lie, I will take it much amiss.'

'Who says,' Roger countered, 'that it is a lie?'

The doctor turned on him. 'There speaks the boy, who has no faith in God! You do not for a moment take her for a witch, for you do not believe in them. And yet you will not hesitate to propagate the slander, for the sake of Sam. It is not just, nor honest. It is vicious, cruel and foul.'

Roger coloured at his words, but would not be cowed. 'Is it, though? Are you so very sure, that it cannot be witchcraft? When will you admit, that there is something in this case your physic and your science cannot yet explain, and recognize the evidence right before your eyes? Do not pretend you did not see it too. I know you did.'

'What evidence?' asked Hew.

'Aye, *tell* him,' Roger urged.

'Roger here believes he has the cunning of a surgeon, when he has been employed by one no more than seven months. That is not so strange. For when he was a student here, he knew himself to be so fully a philosopher, he did not need to trouble taking his degree,' Giles remarked, evasively.

'*What* evidence?' said Hew, again, until his friend replied. 'As I understand, he is referring to the fact that the incision seems too deep. The vein was severed through. It is Roger's contention, that if his master's blade had buried in so far, the wound could not be stopped, and John Blair would have died of it, *statim*, there and then.'

'And is there any truth to it?' It was rare enough that Giles was unequivocal, and it was clear to Hew that he was not so now. His antipathy to Roger made manifest, perhaps, his own internal doubt.

Giles answered honestly. 'It is, to be sure, an exaggeration. A man may cut his arm off, and survive, with proper care. But, I will confess, it gave me some concern. I come to the conclusion, that John Blair's exertions on the night he died caused the vein to tear, severing completely the place that had been cut. Roger is correct that it does not satisfy, and yet it seems to me the only explanation. The fatal error was in bloodletting at all.'

'It is not an explanation,' Roger argued, 'that has any credence, more than witchcraft does. You will not deny, whatever else you think of me, that I am an expert in using knives on flesh, from long years of experiment.'

'That is true enough.' Hew supported him.

'Therefore, I ken its properties. Am I not to judge, how the thing was done? And I would chance my life, my master had no hand in that savage piece of butchery. That was not his work.'

'The pity then,' said Giles, and the sadness in his voice revealed no relish for the argument, 'is that he says it was.' And Roger had no answer to this final word.

'Well,' reflected Hew, 'whatever is the cause, I think that I must talk to Ann Balfour. For if the boy accused her for a witch, then it must be proved, or the rumour quelled, before it can take hold. I will call on her tomorrow.'

Giles consented, 'Aye, it grieves me that you must. Be conscious of her age, and gentle with her, Hew. Meanwhile, you should go to see the candlemaker's wife. The body has been taken to their house, which is on the North Street very close to here. She is most indignant at her husband's death, for which she holds the surgeon firmly to account. I telt her we were looking into it most properly, and you would likely come by to investigate. Which seemed to ease her mind.'

'Then I shall go now, before I leave for home.'

'Will you not come, first, to talk to Sam?' Roger begged. 'Allow him the chance, the better to explain himself. Or else you will have her damn a man unheard.'

'Tsk,' objected Giles. 'We will not have that.'

But Hew responded coldly; he needed to be certain Roger

understood. 'I will talk to him. But you should be aware, whatever happens next is likely to have consequence. There is no turning back, if you do not like the truth. I cannot promise things will turn out well for Sam. They may well be worse.'

The surgeon's house was situated in the Market Street, conveniently close to the apothecary. A small consulting chamber opened to the street, scarcely out of place among the other shops, where the nature of its business was exposed to public scrutiny, and passers-by could judge the surgeon by his wares. Here, a man might watch the pulling out of teeth, and in the balmy shadows of an afternoon in spring, when the wind was warm and the weather temperate, a crowd would form outside, spilling down the street, for the pleasures of phlebotomy. On fair days, it surpassed all other entertainments.

It was in this chamber Roger had left Hew, while he went inside to fetch the barber-surgeon. The house behind was small, a single room in width. Roger slept above, in a narrow loft, a modest home enough for a man to lose, when all his future hopes had been invested there. The chamber now was dark, the shutters closed defensively against the craning street. Roger had left Hew the light of a lantern, and its shadows lit upon the metal glow of instruments, stacked upon shelves and hanging from the wall. The box chair, disconcertingly, was bound with leather straps. It was not a place where Hew could find comfort, with or without the presence of the surgeon, and he jumped a little at the opening of the door. There he saw not Sam, but Isabel, his wife.

She was loosely, but modestly, dressed, in a grey kirtle and gown, and a little lace cap, to cover her hair. In the light of the lantern she looked very pale. Her voice, when she spoke, was serious and strained. 'Roger says that you have come to help. How I wish you could. But my husband will not talk to you. It is hopeless, I fear.'

'Come,' he encouraged her, 'nothing can be hopeless. What has he told you?'

'That he is responsible for a poor man's death, and fears that he may hang for it.'

Could it come to that? Hew believed it could. For surgeons had been hanged for recklessness before, where they endangered life. 'He telt you he felt himself to blame for it? Did he tell you why?'

'He will not say, at all. And reason cannot move him to confide.'

From above them came the cry, tremulous and shrill, of an infant child. Unconsciously, her hand was drawn towards her breast. 'That is my bairn. I must go.'

'You have a new-born child?'

'She is ten days old. I should not have come, to show myself to you. I have not been kirked.' The taint of her childbirth was fresh still upon her, she meant. She had not been cleansed. She smiled at him. 'This day is Candlemas, the feast of the purification. I find that sad, and strange. But we do not count it now.'

It occurred to Hew that Roger had arranged for this. He did not reappear. But doubtless, he had hoped to provoke Hew into pity for the surgeon's wife. If that was his intention, he had calculated well. For Hew could not dispute that the design had worked.

He told himself the candlemaker also had a wife, and reset the balance, calling on her next. She had rebounded from the horror of her husband's death with a strange resilience. 'I expect,' she said, 'that ye have come to see himself.'

He echoed her, 'Himself?'

'My husband, Jock,' she returned complacently, 'in the nether hall.'

'I saw him at the shop.' And that had been enough. He would not look again.

'Aye, not like this. Come away and see. It will ease your mind.' She took him by the hand, as though he were a child, and led him to a room at the back of the house, where the candlemaker lay, flat upon a board, with a strange, seraphic wonder staring from his face. His cheeks were soft and plump, coloured with red lead, and his hair was tinted yellow, neatly trimmed and combed. He was stripped of his clothes, but his nakedness was bound in acres of white cloth, sprinkled with fresh herbs.

He asked her, 'Did you wash him yourself?'

'Why would I not?' There was fondness in her smile. 'Would you have me leave him to a stranger?'

'No, by no means. But it must have been hard for you.'

'Not hard at all. Look at him, now. Handsome is he not? He was a stubborn man, and not, some wid say, an awfy pliant one. But he bent, good as gold, quiet as a lamb. And never did I see a more bonny- looking corpse.'

Bonny though he was, Hew could not stomach Jock for long, and he edged her back into the other room. There she was boiling something greasy in a pot. It was all, she declared, Sam Sturrock's fault. 'He never should have opened up that vein.'

'Did you advise your husband against it?'

'Advise?' She laughed at that. 'There was no advising, wi' Jock. He wasna one for advice. And he would not be turned, from where he set his mind. His headaches plagued him cruel, and he got it in his head that the cure was letting blood. I cannot tell you why. But it was the surgeon's job to free him of the fallacy, if that is what it was. Wha should ken but he?'

'Were you in the crackling house, on the day he died?' he asked.

'For a while, I was. Then he sent me hame, for to make the soap. We did not rub along, together in the shop. I do not like the stew. He said I did things wrong. I had a thought, to put a drop of perfume in the tallow, so to scent it sweet. Jock said it was daft.'

'Perhaps you could try it, now that he is gone?'

She was pleased with that. 'Mebbe, then, I will. I am going now, to give a hand to Eck. He has orders to fill.'

'But what of your husband?' Hew wondered.

'He will not gainsay it,' she said.

¶

Frances, sitting shadowed in the warm light of the fire, had a
kind of glow to her, that served to reassure Hew of her spark and
strength. And there was nothing in the least about her petted or
indulged, for when he told her that he had not brought the candles,
she cried out at once, he should not spare a thought to fret upon
her foolishness, which made him wish he had them, all the same.
Instead, he brought her wine, and sweet white almond cakes, and
settled by her side he told to her the story of the candlemaker,
while she listened carefully, and did not turn her face from his
until the tale was done. And he could not imagine a world where
coming from the cold to sit before the fire he should not find her
there, and share with her the weight of matter on his mind.

When he paused at last, she said, 'A new-born infant, too. I
cannot help but feel for them.'

It sobered him to hear her light at once on that. He had not,
deliberately, skewed the tale to Sam. But then, he considered,
it was natural enough, that the surgeon's circumstances played
upon her sympathy. Had they coloured his?

'And tomorrow,' she had smiled, 'you must go to see the
witch. I wish you would be careful, Hew. For I should not like
it if she cast a charm on you.'

He rode west towards the Poffle at Strathkinness, until he came
to a dilapidated farmhouse, nestled in a clearing in a copse of
trees. Outside in the yard, a female of great age drew water from
the well, while her ancient counterpart split firewood into logs, a
test of strength and vigour for which both were ill equipped. The
old man left his work as soon as Hew approached, but buckled
at the knees, and could not straighten up. 'Can I help you, sir?'

Hew asked if he might speak with the mistress of the house, on business that concerned her and the candlemaker. The woman was despatched to take the message in, while the old man offered stabling for his horse, which comfort was a fencepost, where the mare was tethered, in a thistle patch. Hew occupied his time in filling up the guid wife's buckets from the well, to her man's disgust. 'You will mak her soft.'

The woman reappeared, to whisper an instruction in the old man's ear. She gazed upon the buckets with a blank astonishment, fearful of the magic that had taken place. The old man shuffled off, and beckoned Hew to follow, entering the house. Hew found himself inside a dark-oak coloured hall, a single draughty chamber partitioned at one end to form a sleeping place. The furnishings were sombre, heavy and ornate, and held within their finery an odour of decay. In a pewter chandler, and in sockets round the wall, a score of tallow candles lit among the dust yellowed to obscurity the fleeting strains of daylight, spilling out a sweaty, faintly fetid smell. Beyond them clung the last notes of a heavy kind of perfume, darkly sweet and sinuous. He felt its tendrils quiver, fragile, in the air.

The old man said a word to someone in the room. He motioned to a figure sitting by the fire, and quietly withdrew. And presently Hew heard, distant in the fog, the splintering of wood as he went about his work.

'Have you brought the candles that are owing to me still? The ones you sent were foul,' spoke the figure by the fire. Her voice was high and fine, and quavered clear and light like a hollow reed sharpened to a quill, a delicate thin flute. It had a foreign tone to it, that savoured of antiquity.

Hew responded, 'Madam, I am not the candlemaker.'

'I hear that from your voice. Nor are you his boy. Then my servant Adam has been caught in a deception.' She reached out to the hearth place, where was set a bell.

Hew countered hurriedly, 'I think your servant Adam has not understood. There was no attempt nor intention to deceive. My name is Hew Cullan, and I am come to ask some questions, concerning the man who sold to you your candles. I make no claim to be that man himself.'

'Then it is more likely Adam has misheard. He has grown quite deaf. Come to me, close. For you will apprehend I cannot see you well.'

As Hew came to the fire, he saw that her eyes were covered with a film, a thick, milky cloud through which no image pierced, and wondered if the candlelight could penetrate at all. She was dressed in a gown of old-fashioned silk, whose fugitive colour had fled from the folds of a rich lavish blackness to a dull brown and blue.

'If you come on behalf of the burgh council, then it is high time you dealt with my complaint. The candlemaker Blair adulterates his wares. Because I cannot see, he thinks I cannot smell. He fills them up with filth. Because I was a lady, once, he thinks that I am rich, and he inflates his prices far above the statute rates. I do not hear you writing, sir. Do you take this down?' the lady said.

'I am not from the council,' answered Hew. 'I am a lawyer, from the college of St Salvator, called in to investigate the candlemaker's death.'

'Do you say, then, that the man has died? I cannot understand wherefore such an event would require you to investigate.' The lady showed no sign of pity or surprise, for she was at an age where death occasioned none.

'His death was not a natural one.'

'All deaths are natural, are they not?' She answered him clear, and sure in her response. Hew had the sense that somewhere, someone watched, beyond the steady remit of her sightless eyes. He listened to the rhythm of the old man at the woodpile, the thudding of the axe, a rustling somewhere near. 'Is someone in the house? Are we quite alone?'

'We are never quite alone. But the servants are outside. Adam and his wife. They have been with me for more than sixty years. There is no one else.'

He listened for the sound, heard nothing but the wind.

'Perhaps,' the lady said, 'it was a rat you heard. Hew Cullan, did you say? I knew a boy called Cullan once, who grew to be an advocate.'

'My father was an advocate at the justice court.'

'Then you are Matthew's son. Your father was a good man. And you have a sister, married to the doctor. He wrote me a letter, to the Holy Trinity, to say I was not well enough to walk down to the kirk. For which I was obliged to him. They are good men, both. And what of you, Hew Cullan? Are you a good man too?'

Then he understood, and knew what she was asking him. 'I do not believe that you will count me so.'

'Ah. That is a pity. Should I be afraid of you?'

He told her softly, 'No, you should not be afraid.'

'Then I will believe that you are better than you think. Why have you come?'

'To tell you that because of the candlemaker's death, there will be no more candles for a while.'

'Aye, that is a pity. The candles here are blessed. And I cannot tell you the comfort that they bring.'

'Your pardon, mistress, but...?'

'Can I see their flame? My dear, of course I can. And I can feel its flicker lighting up my face. It is an old face now. Many years ago, I was at the Court. The candles there were wax, and each one weighed a pound. These feeble drips of tallow burn through in an hour. But they are precious to me still. You were kind to come. Let us light a candle for your candlemaker, though I cannot think he will profit from it now. When you depart, I shall light one for you.'

¶

'Well,' said Giles Locke, 'Are you done with your witch?'

'She is not a witch, as you are aware. She is a Catholic woman, harbouring a priest.' Hew was gratified to see his friend's look of alarm. It was not that he thought the doctor was to blame, but since his hopes were frustrated, he was feeling cross, and sought to vent his mood. His investigations all had come to naught.

'What makes you say that? Did you see the man?'

'Smelt the incense from his censer, heard the rustle of his robe. What more need be said?'

'Seeing is believing.'

'I have met a lady who would disagree with you. You need not look like that. I have not set the hounds upon her and her Jesuit.'

'Not Jesuit, Hew! Friar John was never yet a Jesuit,' Giles objected. 'He is a Franciscan, of the mildest kind.'

'Friar John, is it now? You could have telt me, Giles.'

'I could not have told you. The trust between a patient and her own physician should be sacred as the trust between her and her God.'

'And surer to maintain, when you share a faith. I do not like you well, when you are sanctimonious.'

'I do not like you well when you are savage, Hew. The friar blessed her candles for her, at the Candlemas. That was all he did. And you cannot conceive of the comfort it brought her.'

'What manner is this priest? Whence has he come?'

'He has lived among us, quiet all the while. You have met him, too. He was at your father's funeral.'

Hew spluttered, '*That* man? God help us!'

Giles answered patiently, 'That is the point.'

Hew's indignation did not last for long. 'They were holy candles, then, however much they stank. Pity the poor friar! Do you have wax candles, Giles? Ours are all but done.'

'None to spare, alas. So dark and dreich has this winter been. We have bees, though. Did I tell you, we have bred a colony of bees, in our garden on the South Street? They are wondrous creatures. And I have, somewhere here, an illuminating book.' Giles poked about the shelf. 'It seems I have misplaced it. Else I could inform you, when we will have wax enough for Meg to make you some.'

Hew cleared his throat. 'Ah, never mind. Tis pity, all the same. Frances is averse, still, to the tallow kind.'

'Indeed. Is she, still? And to flesh and fish too?' the doctor said glumly. 'What a sad board you must keep.'

'Should the loathing have abated?' Hew pursued.

'As to that,' said Giles, 'I ken no kind of pattern for a perfect progress. I knew a woman once, with the opposite complaint. She had a taste for tallow, and would eat the candles. Her husband was most grieved at it. Nor was it resolved, until she had the child. Yet it did no harm. With Frances, her aversion is like to last to term. Which is some weeks yet. Is she well, besides?'

'She is well enough. Yet I do perceive in her a certain sort of restlessness. She did not sleep last night.'

'That is common too. If you are concerned, I will send to Meg, and ask her to call in on her. This afternoon, perhaps. Meanwhile, I must settle down to write, for pity that it is, it cannot be put off,' the doctor sighed.

'Aye? What will you say?' Hew asked, reassured.

'That the candlemaker's strain as he went about his work caused the vein to burst, and sever through entirely, once he was asleep. You can be sure, his weakness would ensure the flood would never wake him. So much is the substance I will write in my report. He died through the surgeon's negligence. And I see no alternative, except it were the surgeon snuffed his life deliberately, and that is something I do not like to suppose.'

Hew could find no argument to turn him from his course. For surely, there was none. Sam's silence on the matter signed and sealed his guilt. He retreated, hopelessly, to mope about his room, where his depth of misery was mercifully plumbed by a timid knocking on the chamber door. Johannes Blick appeared. 'Your pardon, sir,' he said. 'I know that my appearance is abhorrent to you. But, by your leave, I will not keep you a moment. I wanted only to return your books to you, and express my gratitude, for all that you have done.'

Johannes was encumbered by a wooden box, as well as all the books, and Hew succumbed at once to the pricking of remorse. 'Johannes, by no means am I dismayed to see you. I am sorry, indeed, if I gave you that impression. Come in, I pray, and sit down.'

Johannes, pinkly gratified, perched on the edge of an oak caquetoire, the box and the books balanced in his lap. 'I hope I do not keep you from your present work.'

'Not at all,' said Hew. 'The truth is that you keep me from my present self, and for that I find myself grateful.'

Johannes blinked at this. His Latin was impeccable, and yet he found this sentence hard to fathom out. He dismissed it in the end, as some perversion in the Scots. 'I am ashamed to say,' he said, 'I have not made much progress with the book of bees.'

His guilt compounded, Hew confessed, 'The truth is, I may have overstated the importance of that work.'

'Indeed, not at all,' Johannes said politely. 'For so far as I have read, it has been most illuminating. I have learned a great deal of the life of bees I did not know before. I would dare to say, I may go into beekeeping. It seems to me more lucrative than scholarship.' He ventured forth a smile, to signify a jest, which coming from Johannes was a thing so rare, it required a finger-post, 'And it is strangely pertinent, to this box in hand. I have brought a gift, to thank you for the time and patience you bestowed, upon me and my work.'

'Johannes, that is kind. But there is no need.'

'Indeed, there is need. It is my wish, and my father's also.

He is a rich man. I have prospered here at the university, and that is thanks to you. You were meant to have it for the Candlemas; that is the tradition, as I understand. But circumstance dictated I could not present it then.'

Johannes, rising up, offered up his present with a formal bow. Hew set down the box, and opened up the lid. In paper wrapped inside he found two dozen candles, of the finest wax. For a moment he stood staring, could not find the words. 'Johannes,' he began.

'Alas, you are not pleased,' the student sighed. 'My father believed you would not be offended. He felt the choice of gift was adequate and apt. But if it was misjudged, then we meant no ill by it.'

'Johannes, the gift is a perfect one. Nothing you could give me could have pleased me more. But your generosity awakes a shame in me. I do not deserve this. It is far too much.' Hew took one of the candles up from the box, and admired the sweet ripple of beeswax as though it were something of great worth and wonder, which at that moment it was.

'It is a mote, in the eye of the kind exertions, that you have expended on my poor behalf,' was what Hew understood Johannes to have said. When he had made such sense of the Latin as he could, he was warm in his reply.

'Well, you could not have chosen for me a more delightful gift. However did you find them?'

'They were ordered for me, by that poor man who used to make candles here. As I have heard, he has recently died.'

Hew's attention was captive, at once. 'When did you buy them?' he asked.

Johannes hesitated. This most innocent of questions caused him some distress. His answer was careful. 'On Candlemas eve.'

'The very day,' concluded Hew, 'he met with his death.'

'I had heard that. Indeed.' Johannes was quite deeply, openly unhappy now. 'Sir, I have to say, that though he was undoubtedly accomplished at his work, I do not think that he was a very good man. He did not deal fairly with me.'

'I am sorry to hear that, Johannes.'

Hew knew better than to press Johannes at this point. His patience was rewarded when the student blurted out, 'I cannot, in all conscience, keep my secret to myself. I must confess to you.'

Surely not Johannes, Hew thought, but his brief sense of dismay was readily displaced. He steadied his excitement in a sympathetic face.

'The candlemaker promised he would have my order ready early in the day. I called, several times, only to be told I had come too soon, and I must call again. As I believe, he had them all the time. His notion was to hold them from me, so that I should want them more, and then increase the price. That is what he did.'

'I am sorry,' Hew said, 'that you went to that trouble, for me.' But his thoughts ran ahead, and his heart was not sorry at all.

'I told him, in the end, that I would come in good time to collect them by nine, and I must have them then, or else not at all. You will understand, that I was mindful of the curfew in the college, though my fears on that I did not share with *him*. I hope you understand, sir, that I minded that.'

Hew nodded his encouragement, 'I am sure you did.'

'It was never my intention, to remain out past the hour. But he kept me waiting there, almost with a purpose to it, so that I was late. And when I returned, I found the gate was locked.'

'Is that your confession? That you missed the bell?' Hew could not help but smile. Flooded with relief, amusement, and, he recognised, a certain disappointment, he controlled himself. 'How did you get in?'

Johannes answered coyly, 'Ah, there is a place.'

'Ah. There always is.'

'You will require, of course, to report on the transgression to Professor Locke. He will doubtless want me to reveal the place. I say now, that whatever kinds of torments may be heaped upon me, I will never do so. I owe a debt of silence to my fellow students. In this I will not break. I am quite resolute. My family has endured much hardship on the way here. And I am strong enough to bear a good deal more.'

Hew burst out laughing then. 'I will tell Professor Locke to bear that in mind when he puts you to the rack. I do not think, Johannes, it will come to that. But it grieves me you were vexed by it, and on my account. I hope the candlemaker did not rob you blind?'

'He did the best he could, to inflate the price. And when I told him I could pay no more, he claimed the difference to him as a debt, and made me put my name into a book.'

'What kind of book?'

'A fat one. Into which he entered those who owed him debts, and the interest paid. Of both, I will affirm, a great deal had accrued. The interest was extortionate, beyond the rate of law, and should the same conditions have applied to me, I should not have agreed to them. For my part, it was several shillings, owing on account. My feeling is, he let the debts start small, and slowly reeled them in. For that, my father said, is how the thing is done. Not that he takes part in such shameful practices. Yet he is a man of business, and he must be wise to them.'

'Most excellent Johannes! And you saw this book?'

'He let me see it, freely. Because I am a stranger here, he did not believe I had the wit to read. It may surprise you, sir, to learn, since we share our converse in the Latin tongue, I am not so fluent when it comes to Scots.'

Hew suppressed a smile. 'I should not have known. But was he not aware you were a student here?'

'I did not reveal it, and he did not ask. More pertinent than that, I am my father's son. And nothing holds my interest more than other men's accounts.'

'You are, beyond a doubt, a paragon of virtue. Can you now remember where he kept his book?'

'He kept it locked away. But I recall the place.'

Hew leapt up at once. 'Go, fetch your coat. We are going out.'

'Out?' Johannes stared at him. 'I cannot go out, sir. The philosophy class is about to begin.'

'Johannes,' Hew insisted, 'you can miss your class. You have quite flagrantly stayed out past the curfew, compounding the fault by breaking through the gate; you are determined to be stubborn in the face of correction, and you cannot be redeemed. Set conscience aside, for your case is hopeless. Besides, you have a debt a pay.' Since his tone was too cheerful to occasion much dismay, Johannes went bewildered to find his hat and cloak. He was not so much disturbed. For he would have gone with Hew to the far end of the earth.

The candlemaker's boy was working in the yard, rinding the tallow in a massive pot. He scooped out the refuse rising to the top – 'that is the crackling, d'ye see?' – working with a wit and will he had not shown before. The candlemaker's wife, standing at the counter, presented to the world the fair face of the shop. She had set out her chandlery in a fine display: rows of dipped candles, hanging up in pairs, soaps, oils and unguents, rush lights and spills. 'New tallow candles, two shillings the pound. What will you buy?' A pair of candle-snuffers, gilded and ornate, was given pride of place, and Hew could not help but covet them for Frances.

'Bonny, are they not?' said the candlemaker's wife. 'And the scissor blade so keen, for snipping through a wick. Would you like to try them, sir?'

'By all means,' said Hew. 'But first I have a young man here, come to pay his debts. He owed your late husband – how much was it, Johannes?'

'Seven shillings and sixpence,' Johannes confided.

'And here is a ten shilling piece. You make keep the change.'

'That is very honest of you, sir.' The guid wife's action proved how faithless were her words, as she tested out the mettle of the coin against her teeth. 'Not many folk, in truth, would honour such a debt, and I am much obliged to you.'

'Now, by your leave, we shall strike it from the book.'

'What book is that?' It was plain that the secret had been hidden from the wife. And the candlemaker's boy, called in from the yard, could throw no further light on it.

'If I may?' Johannes said. He came inside the shop, and began to clear the counter of its wares.

'Whatever do you do, sirs?' the candle-wife protested. Johannes did not falter, but turned the counter down, and opened up a panel in its outer edge. 'It is hollow inside.' He slipped in his hand, and pulled out a book.

'Well, fancy that,' said the candlemaker's wife. 'All that was his must now be mine.'

Hew had his hand on it. 'I think you will find it belongs to the Crown. Unless you are prepared to pay the price for usury.' He opened up the book. And though both wife and boy strained to see it too, their efforts were in vain, for they could not read.

The book was filled with names, and dates, that went back years. One name in particular, seeming to recur, came to Hew's attention, for it last appeared on the same page as Johannes. 'Who is David Doig?'

'That man wis a thorn in my husband's side. A thorn in his flesh, and a flesher,' said the wife. 'The fleshers are no more than renegats and thieves. The lot of them are rogues.'

The prentice boy explained. 'The fleshers' and the candlemakers' work is closely linked. The law is, that the flesher cannot sell his tallow, but that he has it show it to the candlemaker first, and he must offer it to him, at the lowest price. That is a law that the fleshers try to cheat.'

'Your master has written that David Doig was to bring him a bucket of fresh tallow on Candlemas Eve,' Hew remarked aloud. And tallow was not all, he noted privately.

'Aye, that wis right. There was a big row about it. My master had heard that Davy had some dead sheep – that is not common at the Candlemas – and he demanded fat from him, such as was his due.'

'Yet it is not marked off.'

'It widna be marked off. For when Davy brought it, it was full o trash. He had made the weight up, with a' kinds of filth. My master telt him plain, to tak the stuff away, and he would rue it hard, if he did not bring fresh. And Davy swore at him, that he could go to hell for it.'

'There was tallow in the shop, the morning that we found him,' Hew pointed out. 'Sitting in a pail, there by the board.'

'Aye, sir, so there was, ye mind me of it now. He must have repented of it, and come back again, while I did my rounds. I took it to the yard, where it did belong.' Eck screwed up his face. 'I cannot tell you rightly when I saw it first.'

'There was no pail,' said Johannes, 'when I came at nine o'clock.'

Hew asked, 'Are you sure?' He felt in his bones a shiver of excitement.

'I am quite certain. He made me stand and watch him while he did his work. And I have, sir, as you know, a retentive sort of mind.'

'God bless you, sweet Johannes,' Hew said with a cry, astonishing the student with the present of a kiss.

Once Johannes was returned to the safety of the college, Hew made his way to the surgeon's house, where he insisted he must speak to Sam. 'It makes no matter if he will not speak to me. But I would be heard.'

The surgeon came at last, to hear what he supposed would be an indictment; no man looked more miserable who went to face his doom. Hew, in his excitement, had a strong desire to shake him.

'I will put a case to you. You may find it fantastical, but listen, if you will.'

And as he told the surgeon what was in his mind, he saw the storm clouds lift, and his face transform. 'Do you mean to say,' Sam cried, 'that I am not to blame?'

'I warn you now,' said Hew, 'it will be hard to prove.'

'It does not matter, if I know in my heart, that I am not to blame; I did not kill that man.'

'Will you tell me now,' Hew asked, 'what hold he had on you? For you were not in debt to him. I did not find your name recorded in his book.'

The surgeon hesitated. 'It was money, all the same. Well, I will tell you. It is a matter which gives me no pride. The business of embalming. It has lately been adopted by the candlemaker's wife. She is very good at it. By tradition it is done by the wax-makers; that was their downfall in the plague. But in many places it is bread and butter to the barber-surgeon. I have felt the loss. You see, I have a wife, and a new-born bairn. I have – though Roger is an asset I do not deny – an expensive and demanding prentice boy, who must have new knives, and the sharpest saw. I do not grudge him that. But there is a balance to be made. And the candlemaker, acting out of greed, has taken from the pockets of the other trades – the fleshers and apothecars – with his pots of grease, his unguents, soaps and spice – and forces those in debt to buy their wares from him; the money that he makes is the money that he lends. He cares not where he deals. Did you ken that he was beadle once, in the parish kirk? He lost that place, for selling Catholics candles for the Mass.

'So when he came to me, and begged me to let blood, I for once could bargain at the better end. At first, I refused. I telt him of the facts. But he implored and wept, his headaches were so bad he could not do his work, and nothing else, he telt me, could assuage the pain of it, but I would let his blood. He forswore the danger of it. And so I made a bargain with him. I would go to his house, and open the vein, and he would be sure to rest, and not exert himself. And in return, he would see that a half of the corpses he was offered for embalming would be sent my way. I did not take Roger, for I did not want the boy to be tainted with bad practice, but I can assure you, I took every care and skill with the phlebotomy. If he had rested on the second day he would have been well. And I swear to God, I did not mean to cut so deep.'

'I don't believe you did.' It was, considered Hew, a grim little tale, and one that did small credit to the surgeon. 'Why do you suppose he went against your word? Why was he convinced phlebotomy would help him?' For, as any fool who had an almanack must know, it was no time of year to be letting blood.

'He said it was phlebotomy had cured his pain before. But it was more than that. He had once consulted with a very fine physician, and had paid that man to draw his horoscope. He was told that he had a superfluity of blood, and a sanguine disposition, that had to be assuaged. He had a full repletion, and a red choking surplus, bulging at each vein. So much he had had from the great man's mouth. What would a barber-surgeon know? But I swear to you, I never did imagine it would bleed him to his death.'

Hew had one last visit to make, before he put the case to Giles. On this occasion, he allowed Roger to accompany him, though he warned him he must wait outside. Roger objected to this. 'I know that man. I bought blood from him. And a lamb's bladder once.'

'Aye, you are two of a kind. Stand out of earshot, but where you can see.'

'Why should I not hear? It was I provoked you to investigation.'

'You provoked me, certainly. He will not speak as freely, if he thinks you hear. Conversely, he is less likely to stick his knife into me, if he thinks you will see it. Comfort yourself. If he does, you will have the pleasure of observing it.'

'What comfort is that, if I do not have the pleasure of hearing you squeal?'

The flesher was outside his shop, butchering a pig. Roger wandered off a yard or so, where the gutter had been stopped to stem the flow of blood. He squatted like a child before a rock pool full of crabs, and began to poke about in the debris with a stick. The flesher scowled at Hew. 'Is that your boy?' he asked. 'Uncouth kind, he is. Likes to cut things up.'

'He is not my boy, mercifully,' Hew retorted pleasantly. 'He is prentice to a surgeon, where his love for cutting stands him in good stead. Sadly, the surgeon is suspected of killing a candlemaker, and Roger is therefore at a loose end. That is not a place where it is good for him to be.'

'Is that so,' the flesher said, returning to his pig.

'It seems late in the year, for the slaughter of a pig. It will soon be Lent,' Hew observed.

'It is a private pig, that met a sudden end.'

'I am sorry to hear it. I hope it did not belong to the miller's boy.'

'What?'

'The miller's boy keeps pigs. I hope it is not one of his. Some people disdain to eat pork. I am not one of them.'

'I ken no miller's boy. The pig is not for sale.'

'A pity, then.' Hew stood in silence a moment, to watch the butcher slide his knife into the carcase at his side. He removed from the wam a large slab of fat, and slapped it on a board.

'Is that tallow for candles?' Hew asked.

'You do not get tallow from pigs. That is lard.'

'What is the difference, then?'

'Lard is soft.' The flesher muttered, 'Not unlike yerself.'

'Then what kind of flesh has the best fat for candles?'

'Sheep fat is best. Cow, at a pinch. Why do you ask about candles?'

'But it must be hard to find that at this time of year. No flock will be slaughtered, when it's near to Lent. There would not be time for the flesh to hang.'

The flesher straightened up again. 'Are you asking me, to sell you meat in Lent?'

'I suppose I might be. But I had always thought that very hard to get.'

'Then you have never looked for it in the proper places. Whatever you may hear, there is always flesh in Lent, though the markets may be closed for it. You only have to ask.'

'Well, bless me,' Hew exclaimed, 'but I did not know that.'

'It seems to me – your pardon, sir – that you do not ken much.'

'I fear you may be right. I lead a sheltered life. I am a scholar at the university.'

'Then that explains it, sir. The scholars at the college never get much meat, for fear it heats their blood.'

'One thing that I ken,' Hew said unexpectedly, 'is that animals were butchered on the eve of Candlemas, for you took a pail of tallow to the candlemaker's shop. Was it cow, or sheep?'

'How would you know that?' The flesher turned, suspiciously.

'Because you left it there. And you mark your pails, as the farmer marks his sheep, to distinguish you from any other fleshers in the town. You need not answer, though. I know that it was sheep.' So much Hew had learned from the candlemaker's boy.

'So what if I did? What devil are you, then, to come and question me?'

Roger looked back, at the sound of the flesher's raised voice. There were other people in the street, though most had kept their distance from the flesher's courtyard, which was far from clean.

Hew answered very softly, 'Was John Blair asleep, when you brought the pail?'

The butcher hesitated. The fact he paused to think suggested what he said would most likely be a lie. But he could not decide. Finally he said, 'He was dipping candles. He was not asleep.'

'Yet it was very late.'

'He required the tallow to complete his work. I brought him what I had.'

'You brought him what you had earlier in the day. But he had refused it. He said it was foul.'

'That is true. I wanted to oblige him. But I had no better in the shop. I had to find more sheep.' The flesher answered easily. He had fallen for the trap, and did not wonder why; it was a relief to tell the simple truth.

'That was a great length to go to. It must have been quite inconvenient,' Hew said sympathetically.

'That is what we do. There is no separate deacon of the candlemakers' gild, so they look to ours, for help and benefit. The fleshers have always worked closely with them. Our interests are tied. They use our mort cloth, when one of them dies.'

The mort cloth covered coffins on their way to burial. 'Apt, don't you think?' Hew remarked. 'You shared other interests too. Did you ken he kept a book, in which he wrote your debts? Your interest was substantial. In that book he kept, he wrote down everything. He wrote down what was owed and he wrote down what was paid. And, as I suppose, he gave out a receipt. On the day he died, he had written that you owed a pail of tallow, and the sum of seven pounds. Neither was crossed off. I wonder why that was.'

'He mentioned no receipt. But he was very tired. No doubt he fell asleep,' the flesher answered stubbornly, 'before he had got round to it.'

'That is it, perhaps. But shall I tell what I rather think? I think you came with your tallow, and you found him fast asleep. Did you have the money, also, in your purse? Or did you have a tale that you had spent it on the sheep? In either case, you saw a short reprieve. You put the tallow down, and turned to go. You did not leave the money, for we found none in the house. But then, you looked at him. And he was really very sound asleep. The force of his exertions, his want of proper rest, the letting of his blood, that left him worn and weak, conspired to reassure you he would not awake. He had opened out the binding and offered up the vein, as though it were a gift. How could you refuse? How simple it would be to take the sharpest blade you carried in your belt and open up the wound; what surgeon's art more supple than the butcher's knife.'

'This is slander, sir, and I will not hear it! If I killed him, if, why would I leave behind the bucket with my mark on it? Ha? Ha! Answer me that!' It was plain that the flesher had rehearsed this many times; it was almost a relief to him to play the part at last.

'You ask a pertinent question, sir, and that you ask it quickly undermines your words. I expect you have asked it over and again, ever since you saw that it was a mistake. To your credit, I suppose the killing was an impulse, one you did not have in mind when you first set out. A novice, after all, cannot think of everything.'

The flesher said boldly, 'That is a lie, and cannot be proved.'

'I grant it will be hard. But there is in our college a fine anatomist, who is especially skilled in identifying wounds. He has a kind of glass, that will tell him at a glance, if the flesh was torn by a single blade or two. And if there is a smear of sheep fat in a vein, or the smallest scrap of wool, he is sure to find it out.'

'You are the devil!' The flesher lunged at Hew, and Hew knocked the boning knife deftly from his hand. As it clattered to the ground, Roger wandered up, a pig snout in his hand. 'How much is this?' he inquired.

'A glass, in which a man can see the matter in a wound? Whoever would believe in such a thing?' demanded Giles.

They were sitting in the safety of the turret tower, where Hew had spilled his tale. 'There are people who believe a corpse can name its killer,' he replied.

'As often, in a certain sense, it can. Your logic is fantastical. How I wish I had that kind of glass.'

'It matters not,' said Hew, 'since he did not confess. The case cannot be proved.'

'But doubtless, if the flesher is indicted for the crime, you will be a witness, and must serve upon the jury,' Giles pointed out.

'I suppose I must. Yet what justice can there be, when the jury is selected from such men as ken the evidence, and the panel too. It has always struck me as skewed,' objected Hew.

'None the less, if I accuse the flesher in my own report, and the sheriff is disposed to issue an indictment, you are the witness central to the case. You will not find it hard to convince the rest. As juror, you will have more sway upon them than the king's own advocate. A magic glass, indeed.'

Hew was silent for a moment, for he had not thought of that.

'If the man has sense,' said Giles, 'he will not wait around to hear you stand against him, but even as we speak will be packing up his bags. Whatever is the outcome, it is not a happy one.'

'Yet for Sam,' insisted Hew, 'there is justice of a sort. He is rid of the horror that he caused John Blair's death. And relief has made of him a different sort of man.'

'It does not help me much in writing my report. For the truth is, Sam did practise phlebotomy, when his inclination and the season spoke against it, and his judgement was impaired by interests of his own. Though I do not indict him on a murder charge, can I recommend to the deacon of his gild that such a barber-surgeon should not be struck off?'

'I understand your qualms. Yet I believe you should. For

Sam, in this case, did everything he could to ensure that Blair was safe. He warned him of the danger, and took every care, to keep him in good health. His instruments were clean, and he told him to rest. If John Blair had followed his surgeon's sound advice, he would still be well. But he was adamant, quite adamant, that he must be bled. And we must wonder why.'

'I do wonder it,' said Giles. 'It is not common practice in a patient.'

'In the first place, he did not take heed of his surgeon's words as keenly as he should. He believed, wrongly, that Sam Sturrock was refusing him the treatment he required because he had encroached upon the surgeon's trade; therefore, he was well disposed to disregard his sound advice. And, in the second place, he had it on the highest, most impeccable authority that bleeding was the proper course in his state of health. He had it from the mouth of the finest of physicians. Whose opinion, for sure, he valued over Sam's.'

'What physician?' murmured Giles. 'I understood that none was called.'

'Nor was there, at the time. But the candlemaker Blair had paid to have a horoscope, that telt to him the details of his disposition. And what was written there he followed to his end.'

'A horoscope?' Giles groaned. 'Dear God, the beadle Blair! I drew up his horoscope! But that was years ago. He came to see me when I first came to the town.'

'And did you tell him that he should be bled?'

'I may have done. As I seem to recall, he had the most unbalanced disposition, I have ever come across. There was undoubtedly a superfluity of blood. But Hew, I did not mean to say, whatever was the time, for any kind of ill, I should prescribe phlebotomy, as an essential cure.'

'Whatever else you meant, he took you at your word. And never had forgotten it.'

'Dear God. Then I am to blame, quite as much as Sam.'

'Neither of you caused the candlemaker's death. And though it may be true the time was out of joint, the season was most pertinent, most poignantly, for him.'

'Well,' reflected Giles. 'I will write that we both did act in honest faith, and that Sam's actions, surely, did the man no harm, save that they sparked off a sad train of events, which could have taken place at any other time. And yet, I count it strange it came to him at Candlemas. There is a kind of fate we cannot understand, and are powerless to control. Still, this tragic tale could well have been averted, if the surgeons and physicians were on better terms, and more like to trust each other. I will write that too.'

'I believe it true. Balance in all things,' said Hew. 'Is not that the principle, on which your art is based?'

He returned to Kenly Green, with a light and steady heart, and with Johannes's candles safely in his hands. The house was strange and dark. 'Where are you, my love?' he cried out to the hall. 'I have brought a gift will light you to a smile.'

A servant came out from the kitchen, an elderly woman he had thought long retired. 'Peace to you, sir, do not be alarmed.' Never had such words impressed on him more violently, the opposite effect.

'Where is my wife?'

'Mistress Meg is here, and the midwife too. All is in hand.'

'What midwife here?'

'The labour has begun.'

He stared at her. 'It cannot have begun. It is far too soon. I must go to Frances.'

'Whisht, will you sir, you cannot see her now. Leave them to their work. She is in good hands. Come to the kitchen. There is a fire, and a warming drink.'

'I do not want your fire,' Hew protested peevishly, 'I want

to see my wife.' His house rebelled against him, thwarted and distorted his will at every turn. Gavan Baird appeared, with his crumpled coat and foolish ruffled hair, grinning from the library. 'Come and sit with me. For there is a book I want to share with you. We need not interrupt the ladies at their work. They will be some while.'

Hew was consumed with a wild dislike of him. 'Have you gone quite mad? I want to see my wife!'

'Now is not the time.'

Hew pushed Gavan Baird, and his simpering, away, and leapt upon the stair. He had not reached the landing place upon the second floor when Robert Lachlan came, welcome as an ogre rising in a dream, a nightmarish attempt to keep him from his task. Lachlan, unlike Baird, would not be pushed aside, and he was quite prepared to match Hew blow for blow, if ever Hew were fool enough to attempt to fight. Finding his way blocked and further progress barred, Hew assailed him fiercely, 'Is this friendship, Robert? To deny me the entrance to my own house?'

'Dinna disport like a bairn. You don't want to go there, and the women do not want you. She is well provided for, with Meg and Bella too. Whit wad they want with you? Leave it to a lass.'

'But what can I do, Robert? How can I help?'

'I recommend strong liquor. It will make the time pass, wondrously. When Bella lay in with wee Billy, the whole thing went by in a flash.'

'When Billy was born,' Hew corrected, 'you were out cold for three days.'

'What did I say to ye? Done in a flash. And a grand bonny babby is he.'

His sister Meg appeared, the calmest voice of reason in this frantic world, coming down the stair. 'Keep your voice low, Hew. You make too much noise.'

'What has happened, Meg? How does Frances do? Why have you left her?' he cried.

'Did I not just tell you to keep down your voice? Frances is quite safe, for now, with Bella Frew. Her labour has begun. It cannot be of help to her to hear you rage and shout.'

'But Meg, it is too soon.'

'It is early, yes. But babies do not mark the days off on the calendar. They come when they will come. Trust her with us, Hew. I came out for a moment, to find one of your servants. For I think the time has come, to send a man for Giles.'

A panic came upon him, gripping at his bowel. Physicians were not called upon, never were they called upon, until there was a real and present threat of death. 'Why would you do that?'

'Why, then, should I not? He is my husband, and your dearest friend.' Meg's response was bright. But she could not conceal the shadow in her face.

Bewildered, he whispered, 'It cannot be now. I have brought candles for her.'

BOOK II

Whitsunday

Now is the month of Maying,
When merry lads are playing.
Fa la la la la la la la la.
Fa la la la la la la.

Of Thomas Morley the first booke
of balletts to fiue voyces, 1595

I

In St Leonard's College on the South Street of St Andrews, a
boy of fourteen lay half the night awake. His name was Robin
Grubb, and he was the smallest of the poor scholar clerks, who
paid for their degrees by completing menial tasks. It was Robin's
turn on Tuesdays to ring the bell to call the college from its sleep,
to light the fires and fetch the water from the well, and introduce
his colleagues briskly to a day which they were more inclined to
take their time to meet. Robin was a country boy, and natural
instinct told him when he ought to rise. And yet, on Tuesday last,
his country sense had failed. He had overslept. It was already
a quarter to six when the sun had streaked into the dust of his
room and spilled on his white face to wake him, and it was six
o'clock before the bell was rung. The shame of it engulfed him
now, and kept him from his sleep. For when he closed his eyes he
could hear again the censure of the college principal, magnificent,
benign, and measured in reproof. He had not called Robin to
account for his fault, nor shown his disapproval of him in a word
or look. Instead, he had preached a sermon against sloth, taking
as his theme 'the sluggard will not plough by reason of the cold,
therefore shall he beg in harvest', and hot blood had flown to fill
Robin's cheeks, as surely as though he had slapped them.

Tonight there was no moon, and Robin could not quell,
through the dim dead hours, the fear that the daylight somehow
might escape him. He left his bed at last to look out on the
darkness where the lanterns hung, hoping for a glimpse of the
college clock. He gasped at what he saw, rubbing at his eyes,
uncertain for a moment if he was awake.

The wind of Robin's gasp, blowing through his dreams,
caused the fellow student who shared a bed with him to mutter
in his sleep, turning on his back and flinging out a foot, beyond
the blanket's grip. It was only this, a foot more stout and

ominous than either of his own, that stamped on Robin's will to rush across and wake him. He gathered up his breeks about his slender hips, and flimsily protected, tiptoed from the room.

He paused at the door of the regent, Robert Black, believing it was safest to report to him. Robert was in charge of the third year class. He had been a regent a dozen years or more, without promotion to professor or a living at the kirk, and nothing could surprise him in this weary world. His most withering reproach was a cynical disdain. He was also quite sharp in his wits, once the whiff of a crisis had prised him awake. This had been tested the previous term, when the snuff of a candle, carelessly flicked, had threatened to burn them alive in their beds.

Robin gave a knock, and when there was no answer entered Robert's room. The master was asleep in a truckle bed. It was rumoured at the college that the masters dreamt in Latin, save for at St Mary's, where they dreamt in Greek. Robin did not choose to put this to the test, for though the students were constrained to speak Latin at all times, it felt to him a leaden and unwieldy instrument. He could read it well enough – it was for that reason that the minister of his parish kirk had recommended him to the university – but he found it cumbersome and foreign on his tongue. It lacked the sense of urgency that was wanted here – how could he be adamant, fishing for a verb? And so he spoke in Scots. 'Sir, sir, ye maun wake up now, sir,' lifting up the sheet to pull at Robert's shirt. And Robert Black confirmed his intuitions were correct, for he sat bolt upright, wild-eyed and bright as a ghost in a tale, and answered him at once.

'What is the matter, child?'

Words in no language were adequate enough. 'Ye maun come an' look.' Robin tugged at him. 'Is that no the gentleman that was here the day?'

The window to the chamber opened to the south. Robert Black looked out. 'Upon my soul,' he said, 'I believe it is.'

'He is, ah, he is—'

Robert answered gently, 'I can see that too. You did well to wake me. And I would like to think you have shown no one else.'

'Wha would I show? They are all asleep.'

'That is to the good. But you must fetch the principal.'

'Must I?' Robin said.

'Certainly you must. Run and wake him now. I will deal with this.'

The boy set off reluctantly, while the master dressed. And Robert kept an eye on the dancer in the square, who did not seem to know or care that he was watched.

The dance was grave and strange, the dancer with his head inclined, as though he were attuning to a distant sound, too rare and faint a melody to touch the common ear. His trunk and neck were still, the movement of his feet at first quite slow and stately, turned to skip and lilt, to sway upon the ball, and finally to leap, spinning in the air with a speed and grace surprising in a man so fleshly in his form, light upon the toes that did not miss a beat. The slender limbs that bore the full force of his gravity maintained his bulk aloft, and held it proud and stern, as Atlas bore the weight upon him of the world. The dancer entranced, as though he cast a spell. The more, since he was dressed in not a stitch of clothes.

The regent Robert Black made his way outside and approached the dancer, holding out in front of him his folded scholar's gown. 'Your honour, are you well? The night air is cold. Will you take my robe?'

The dancer paused his flight, and turned to stare at him. His eyes were dazed and dark. The principal appeared, in his shirt and pantofills, with little Robin Grubb close upon his heels. 'How now, my lord,' he said. 'This will not do at all.'

The dancer held their gaze, and did not seem to hear. He answered not a word, but as his dance was paused, it seemed as though the sound to which he harked had stopped, the music that had worked him coming to a close, and there and then, he dropped, lifeless as a puppet broken at the strings, reflecting in the shimmer of his sightless eyes the sliver of a light that he would not see again.

From the solace of his slumbers in a tavern loft, the student Henry Balfour was wakened with a grin and a warning from its landlord: 'It will soon be light. You had best be off.'

Henry kissed his lass, once upon each breast, and once upon that place kept sacred just for him, to console her loss. 'When will you be back?' she protested sleepily.

'Tomorrow, if you will.' Already he was up, threading through his points.

'Promise me,' she said.

'Barring death or accident.'

He gave the man a shilling, for good manners' sake, no more than a fraction of his mounting debt. A young man's pleasures paled when his purse strings were constrained, and Henry was aware that his would soon run out. For this, he blamed his father, who requited poor performance in examinations with a pitiless assault upon his son's allowance. That was cruel indeed, and Henry thought illogical, to vent upon a body that had never served him ill; what hurt had the allowance ever done to him? The punishment would fall upon the pillars of the town – the fleshers, cooks, and tavern keepers to whom it was pledged – and they would be the poorer for it. Old man Balfour, doubtless, had not thought of that, and Henry had more practice in his father's moods to care to point it out. It would be plain enough, when the bills came in. His fair-day friends, no doubt, would all be gone by then.

He did not count Mary in this. Mary was convinced she was in love with him, and bestowed her goods most willingly in kind. And on a day like this, in the lovers' month of May, with the dawning promise of a rose-pink sky, he could be persuaded that he loved her too. He would write a poem to her, that morning in his ethics class, if he stayed awake.

He expected to meet no one on his way back to St Leonard's, unless it was the baxter coming with the bread, little Robin Grubb or the college cook, all of whom he counted close among his friends. The porter on that day was taken ill in bed, which had stripped the hazard from an opportunity. Henry was light in his heart when he climbed the wall and swung down from the tree, well placed to offer access to the college court. He did not expect to drop squarely into such an incident, almost in the lap of the college principal. Nor did he expect to come upon a corpse. Cornered as he was, he let slip a profanity to make his masters flinch and little Robin blush. No young man of decency should swear before a clergyman. And Henry understood that he was properly at fault. The principal said, in a terrible voice, 'Stand where you are, sir, right there.'

Henry was a young man of considerable resource, and while he was aware of the pickle he was in – he had never once before, in his four years at the college, been spoken to emphatically in such a dreadful voice – he could see at once that at least one other person present at the scene was in a worse predicament. And so he took his chance, deflecting the attention deftly from himself. 'Lord, sirs! Is he deid?'

'We wonder that ourselves,' Robert Black said mildly. 'Though we fear he is.'

'Here is a feather.' Henry, nothing daunted, plucked it from the ground. 'Shall we make a trial of it?' Receiving no objection, he placed the feather carefully across the dead man's face, where it did not quiver by the whisper of a breath. 'Aye, no doubt of it. And bless me, if it is not the Lord Justice Bumbaise – Sempill, I mean.'

Young Balfour showed no feeling but an honest interest, for he felt no pang of pity for the man. He had come across Lord Sempill several weeks before, where he had a part to play in Henry's present woes. Sempill was inspecting, on the king's behalf, the standards that were held at St Andrews University. He was present at the time that Henry was examined for his bachelor's degree. And on that occasion, he had professed himself baffled – bumbaised, he repeated, as his favourite word – that a student could put up so brave a show of ignorance. Nor was he content with humiliating Henry on a public stage. He had followed with a letter of bumbaisment to Lord Balfour, who Henry had made certain would be absent on the day. And the public inquisition had been superseded swiftly by a painful private one. Though he was not disposed to bear a man a grudge, Henry marked his fate with cheerful curiosity. 'What happened to him, then? And why has he no clothes?'

The simplicity with which his student phrased the question brought home to the principal the horror of the sight. 'Cover him,' he said. 'Cover his poor face.'

Robert Black obliged with his college gown, which covering the face, did not extend quite far enough to reach down to the toes. Two spindle shins, of bare skin and bone, were left sticking out. Robin Grubb admired them. 'What little feet he has!'

'Mebbe we should send for Doctor Locke,' Robert said, 'His house is close to here.'

The principal said heavily, 'We must, of course, send out for him, to find the cause of death. There will be questions, perhaps also a trial. Lord Sempill is a man of importance at the court. He was lately here with us on business of the Crown. The answers that we gave him failed to satisfy. Therefore, we must brace ourselves for further inquisition. Giles Locke will bring Hew Cullan with him to investigate. And Hew will turn our college upside down.'

Robert said, 'No doubt. He always does. We may pray for their discretion. But we dare not hope for it.'

The four of them stood silent, looking at the corpse, and though they were agreed upon a course of action, no one made a move to put it to effect.

'It is a pity,' Henry said, putting into words what was in their minds, 'that whatever happened to him, had to happen here. The New College, after all, is so very close. How much more convenient had it happened there.'

'Since it did not happen there, your comment is not helpful,' Robert Black rebuked him.

'I mention by the by,' Henry went on undeterred, 'that there is a handcart over by the wall – a barrow of a sort – left there by the man who comes to prune our trees.'

'That is an irrelevance.' The principal glared at him. 'And I do not understand what can be meant by such impertinence.'

'I mean nothing by it, sir. I merely point it out, as an observation. I have noticed too that there is a path which is not overlooked, running through the woods that overlap our lands and those belonging to the New College, leading to a gate on their south side by the burn. Tomorrow is the day – I should say, this morning, for it is but an hour away – the college gardener comes, and enters through that port.'

'Speak plainly to me, sir, what is it you say?'

'Nothing more than this. Master Andrew Melville, the master of that college, is an honest Christian man, who does not shirk his duty with a shy dismay. He is accustomed to controversy. Some might say he welcomes it.'

The principal turned pale. 'What you propose,' he hissed, 'what I do infer, to be your foul proposal, since you are not brave enough to dare to spell it out, is an abomination that will not be borne. An abomination, is it not, Master Black?'

'An abomination,' Robert Black agreed. They stood there

side by side, staring at the feet that peeped out from Robert's gown, as though young Balfour's impudence had left them lost for words. Then Robert asked, quietly, 'Is it?' When he was not repelled, he added in the form of a tentative aside, 'What he says of Andrew is quite true, of course.'

The principal said, in no more than a whisper, 'Do you think at all, Robert, that it might be possible?'

The colleges were rivals at the best of times. There was a proximity, largely geographical, between St Leonard's and the 'New' college of St Mary, and a proximity in faith that was nominal at least; it did not mean the principals were friends. James Wilkie at St Leonard's liked a quiet life. Andrew Melville, the reformer who was provost at St Mary's, did not flinch before a storm, and would not be perplexed to come upon a corpse; more fitting then by far that he should have to deal with it. Sempill would be treated to a quiet funeral, without a song and dance, sending off his spirit to its final resting place. Which might as well be Faerie land, for all the college kenned.

Giles Locke, the medicinar, and principal of the 'Auld' college of St Salvator, further on the North Street, was a proposition quite apart. He was well kent for a Catholic, in outlook if not in his observance at the kirk, attending to a faith that foolishly believed it had some subtle influence upon a dead man's fate. Which was not the case. Giles Locke was the Visitor, appointed by the Crown to look into the cause of unexpected deaths; and his interest in their outcomes was not called for here. For now was not the best of times, but counted with the worst.

These considerations, and others of their kind, convinced the college principal to set aside his qualms and send Henry for the barrow he had noticed by the wall. Wilkie went himself to fetch the curtains from his bed, which were put out to be aired. In these, he now proposed, they should wrap the corpse. 'For it will not do to wheel a body bare. Mind and bring them back.

No scrap nor thread of ours can be left to cling to him.'

Lord Sempill was rolled up and hoisted in the cloth, and, anchored by his buttocks safe inside the wheelbarrow, soon was firmly lodged, while Robert Black ensured that all was well tucked in. It took the boys the best part of the hour to trundle through the wood, taking it in turns to hold aloft the lamp that lit them on their way, the shortest journey stalled with many starts and stops. When at last they came to the back lands of St Mary's, their lantern was extinguished in the rising sun. They found a sheltered spot close to the college gate. Lord Sempill, tumbled out, and shaken from his bonds, fell naturally at ease to find a resting place. The grass on which he lay was damp with morning dew.

'It does not seem right,' Robin said, 'to leave him there, unclaithed.'

'He had no clothes when he came,' Henry said, 'and he shall have none when he goes.' And whether he had meant his passing through St Leonard's or his passage through the world, it was all the same a fitting epitaph.

Henry gave Robin sixpence from the bottom of his purse to take the barrow back to the college on his own. The morning's work had wearied him, and he retired to bed.

The bell that morning did not ring till sometime after six. And though the scholars who enjoyed an extra hour of sleep observed that Robin Grubb was quiet and subdued, James Wilkie made no mention of it in the morning prayers. Henry Balfour slept, quite righteously, till noon. There could be no question of recrimination; he had played his part. They were conspirators, all four. Five, if Lord Sempill was included in the count. And why should he not be? It was his secret they kept.

The principal experienced a murmuring regret for little Robin Grubb, who was green and young. It did not run deep, and it did not last long. He stopped short of suspecting Robin of the kind of innocence for which there was no precedent established in his kirk. Yet he was not, by any means, untouched. He developed a dislike for the curtains round his bed, and when the laundress came he asked her to dispose of them. 'They are full of moths.'

The laundress stroked the cloth. 'That is fine silk velvet. And there are no holes.'

Conscience had betrayed him; he did not lie well. 'The truth is, I am mindit now to do away with vanities.'

'Bed curtains are a vanity?'

'They are,' he iterated, 'an unnecessary thing. And I am resolved to keep nothing in my house that is not essential. Have them for yourself.'

'I thank ye, then. I will,' she said. 'Is this to do wi' they men, who wanted to see the accounts?'

His answer sounded hoarse. 'It is to do with them.'

'Then is there nothing ither you would be without?'

Helpless, he had promised her to see what could be found. So when she came across the clothes, puddled in a doorway next to the latrine, she thought he kept his word, and took them for her own. The linen and the shoes would do her youngest son. The coat and the breeks were of very good stuff, and, if she kept canny, would fetch a high price.

II

The servants were asleep when Hew Cullan left for town. The silence in the house retained a quiet melancholy, but, he was aware, the trouble in his heart had settled there and stilled. No longer did he fear to close the gate behind him, no longer did he feel the plummet of his heart, the clenching fist of dread, on lifting up the latch to open it again. And in the first faint shadow of the morning sun he found a peace in solitude, and an understanding; felt, at last, content.

That content was transitory, he was well aware. For the past three months, he had not felt like this. Then he had been thrawn, and had not dared to hope. Still, the world went on. He could scarcely fathom how the world went on, though he saw it did. Already it was May, the rose burst from its bud, the haar began to clear, the hawthorn was in flower.

It was early still. He was riding to St Andrews, four miles to the north, where he was professor at the college of St Salvator. His absence had been felt there over the last term. Now he was returning to take up his place again, to assist his friend the principal Giles Locke. The college was preparing to receive the king's commissioners, who were making an inspection of the university. Their commission had begun a month ago in April, examining all three of the colleges in turn. St Salvator's had satisfied: a student called Johannes Blick had proved himself exemplary, and all the rest appeared at least sufficient to the task. St Mary's had protested mitigating circumstances, while St Leonard's, in particular, had failed to show its best. This second visit purposed to examine the accounts, which none of the three colleges intended to supply. The commissioners were led by the Lord Justice Sempill – depute in his time to the crown justiciar – who put many intricate questions, and wrote down a flurry of notes in a niggardly, quivering hand. At the very first trial that Hew had defended, seven years before, Judge Sempill had presided at the high court bar. Sempill had been ponderous, difficult, and dim, frequently objecting that the case perplexed him. It was to the good if he had since forgotten it.

Giles had tidied up. He had removed from the turret tower some of his more personal and peculiar effects – exploratory instruments and pickled body parts – and many of his books, which were rare and singular, concealing them from inventory. It troubled Hew to come upon this bare and barren place, the spirt of his friend dilute if not dissolved. He looked for reassurance in familiar things. 'Will there be trouble?' he asked.

'Not in the least,' Giles assured him. 'We shall be civil, and the meeting will be brief. I have excused Master Wilson from attending. He does not feel up to it.'

'Will they not expect him? Since he is economus, in charge of our accounts?'

'It matters not a whit whether they expect him. He will not be here. I have explained, also, that you have no interest in accounting at the college, since you live outside the compass of the town. You are here solely as my witness.'

'And I hope, your friend.'

'Dear Hew, always that. You look well. It lifts my heart to see you looking well.'

'Have I not always looked well?'

'To speak plainly, you have not. The turbulence since Candlemas has wrought its worst in you; you became a ghost. Yet, I am thankful, that storm seems to have passed.'

'Because of you and Meg,' Hew said, awkward at the flood of feeling it released in him.

'Now, none of that. God present your strength. Did I tell you, I heard some sad news? Alison Pearson, of Boarhills, has been taken for a witch. She will come to trial at Edinburgh at the end of this month. Archbishop Patrick Adamson has sworn a writ against her.'

The turn towards a subject dark enough to cover him was almost a relief. 'For the physic that she gave him? That was years ago,' Hew said. Alison had been a tenant on his land. And obliquely he believed his fate was linked with hers.

'Five, to be exact. She escaped them this long while. But they have flushed her out.'

'Then I do pity her.'

'Pity her, indeed. The trial has provoked a relish in the town

that I fear is symptom of a general ignorance. Involvement of
a man as notorious as Patrick is was bound to cause a stir. Yet
I cannot help but think that this crying of a witch is louder,
more persistent, than it was some years ago. Then a witch was
rare, and her fate remarkable; now I seem to hear it murmured
everywhere I go. It is an unwelcome advance.'

'Is that why you have hidden half your books?' Hew asked.

'I confess it is, in part. But for the most part it was economical.
I would not have accompted in the college revenue assets of my
own.'

Hew made no reply, for they were interrupted by a sharp rap
on the door, and the appearance of the king's commissioners, a
little in advance of their appointed time. They numbered in their
ranks David Carnegie, laird of Colluthie; Master Philip Clench,
and a servant William Soutar, who fulfilled the role of clerk.
The laird of Lundie and the provost of Dundee were absent by
design. Lord Sempill, their president, was absent by default.

The laird of Colluthie launched at them abruptly, 'Good
morning to you, sirs. Where are your accounts?'

'Where is Lord Sempill?' Giles Locke returned.

Philip Clench was hesitant, glancing at his colleague. 'We had
supposed that he had come ahead of us. What can have become
of him?'

Colluthie said, 'No matter whether he is present here or not,
we three are sufficient to attend upon the business.'

'Ah, but, you know,' Giles contradicted him, 'it matters quite
a lot. Lord Sempill is in charge of the king's commission. He
has the right to put to us the question. In his absence, I am
not persuaded you have that authority. Indeed, I am persuaded
you do not. I remark, also, that it is unlike him to miss an
appointment.'

Master Clench agreed. 'It is most unlike, and cause for some
disquiet, sir. The last time that we saw him, he was not himself.'

'In what way?' Giles asked, drawn to a distraction which Philip Clench provided somewhat indiscreetly.

'We had come lately from St Leonard's College, where he had not been satisfied with the principal's account of affairs conducted there. He accused him of shifting answers, swore if he kept secrets, he would find him out. Nor would he let lie, but it possessed his mind.'

Hew asked, 'When was this?'

'Last night, at suppertime. We have not seen him since.'

The laird of Colluthie cut his colleague short. 'That is not pertinent here. The likelihood is he has returned to St Leonard's to resume his inquiries. There we shall go next, and oblige him with the records we bring with us from St Salvator's.'

'That will not be possible,' said Giles. 'Quite apart from the matter of your ain authority, which is in dispute, we do not have them here.'

'You were warned, were you not, that they were expected?' That Colluthie was vexed at the challenge to his state was plain in his expression and the tone of voice he took.

'Aye, indeed we were,' Giles answered patiently. 'And as I explained to Lord Sempill at the time, the charters were interred in the college grounds, many years ago. So says our economus, who oversaw the planting of them, buried in a kist, long before my time. The pity is, despite his best intentions, he has been unable to remember where he put them. As to the accounts, some were in the keeping of a man called Cranston, who left us at the plague. And some, as I believe, are kept here at his house.'

'Then send to his house, and have the man fetch them, with no more ado.'

'That I would gladly do, on Lord Sempill's authority. But Master Wilson, our economus, has not been well today, and must not be disturbed. He is of an age that does not well accommodate. It is, you will allow, a reasonable position.'

'It is not reasonable at all.' But Colluthie understood that no progress could be made without the aid of Sempill. He called a retreat, if only for the while. 'Expect our soon return, when you will assist us in a thorough search. Whosoever digs a pit may find he falls into it,' he warned.

Giles replied, 'Indeed. We must hope such hazard has not happened to Lord Sempill.'

'Is it true?' Hew asked, once the coast was clear. 'Were the papers really buried in the grounds?'

Giles said, 'Master Wilson says so. And who are we to question the word of our economus? He promises to look for them. I cannot help but find Lord Sempill's absence strange. It is not like him at all. Still, it buys us time.'

'There is little love between him and Colluthie,' Hew observed.

'As I imagine, none at all. We may have our troubles, Hew. But they are small, and pale before those of the world.'

At St Leonard's, the commissioners had no more success. Lord Sempill, it turned out, was nowhere to be found. 'We have not seen him this day,' the principal said carefully. 'Not this day, indeed.' Without Lord Sempill's sanction, he was not prepared to admit them to his college. On no account at all would he show up his books. The commissioners were obliged to continue to St Mary's, where they met a welcome of a carping kind. Master James Melville, in the absence of his uncle, proved willing to invite them in and to show them round. He took them on a tour of dilapidated walls, stinking drains and sinks and saturated lavatories, unsanitary kitchens and schoolrooms that were damp, the students forced to bide in a debilitating poverty, injurious to health. There was, of course, no question of accounts. The troubles Andrew Melville had struggled to contend with over the last years had meant that none were kept.

As James was sure Lord Sempill would fully understand. His submission was affecting; Philip Clench was moved to slip a shilling to the poorest clerk when Colluthie's back was turned. But they left the college with no document to show for it.

The St Leonard's college principal, from his stronghold further down the South Street, kept an eye on the proceedings all the while. When he saw that the commissioners had concluded with St Mary's, and were returning to the West Port for their dinner break, he was much alarmed. He summoned Henry Balfour, shaken from his sleep, and the bursar Robin Grubb to meet him at his house.

'I telt you to leave him where he would be found.'

'We did,' Henry said. 'By the garden gate, where the gardener could not help but come upon him.'

'It is remarkable, I doubt, you claim to ken so much. Yet you were deceived. Lord Sempill is not found. That is a terrible thing. I never meant for him to lie alone for hours.'

'I do not think,' said Robin, meaning it for kindness, ''tis likely he will mind.'

'I mind,' the principal snapped. 'There is only one recourse. You boys will have to find him. You ken where he is. Go now. You shall say – what shall you say – say I have sent you to complain about their doves. They have been marauding through our corn again. They are ever doing that. Say I sent you to speak of it to the gardener, and that you came upon Lord Sempill lying in the grass. Make sure it is St Mary's where you raise the cry – run straight to the Melvilles – and on no account return it here to us.'

'May I say something, sir?' Henry requested.

'If it is pertinent.'

''Twas only to applaud the cunning of your lie.'

'You may not say that. You are a wicked boy. And were it not for the extraordinary circumstances – *extremis malis extrema remedia* . . . Go. Go at once. And do not return until Lord Sempill has been found.'

Once the boys had gone, the principal knelt down upon his bare stone floor, and portioned for himself an hour of serious prayer. But his devotions – his contentions with himself and God – were not advanced so long when he was disturbed by a knocking on his door, and Robert Black appeared. 'I do not want to put you to alarm,' he said, in the kind of voice disposed to do just that, 'but I have something here that you will want to see. A student found it, in the college jakes. And as luck would have it, handed it to me.' He showed up a pocket, tied with a string.

The principal felt sick. His tongue clung claggy, thick, filling up his mouth, so it was a struggle to enunciate the words. He managed only, 'His?'

'I imagine so. You had better see what he kept inside.' Robert opened it, and taking out the contents with delicate distaste, placed them on the desk where the master read his books, where he cut his pens, and, worst of all, where he wrote the sermons he delivered in the kirk. Wilkie shuddered at the thought. 'What horror have we here?' he said. When Robert Black did not reply, he gathered up the things and returned them to the pocket, which he locked at once inside his writing slope. 'Do you suppose there is anything more?'

Robert shook his head. 'I made a proper search. No trace of his clothes, nor other note was left. Let us believe that this was the last of him.'

'Ah, that I could!' the principal cried. 'God help us, Robert! What have we done?'

The boys took no great hurry on their journey through the woods. A feeling for the delicate, not earlier in evidence, appeared to hold them back. 'He was barely cauld when we left

him,' Robin said. His country childhood taught him certain facts
of life he felt it was his duty to report. 'He may not be as hale, or
wholesome as he was. There may be birds or beasts have come
to make a feast of him.' He cast his mind upon a sheep that he
had once found in a ditch. 'Not all of him, of course.'

Henry felt the lurching of a sudden squeamishness, rising in
a wave from his belly to his throat. He did his best to brace
himself. 'Wild beasts or not, he will be altered. He must be
altered. A dead man is not fresh for long.'

But when they arrived at the place they had left him, he was
not so much altered as gone.

Henry knelt down in the space. 'This is where he was, where
the grass lies flat.' The college gate was open, and they could
hear the gardener singing at his work. There was no stir behind
him but the buzzing of the bees. 'He was dead, though. He was.
Properly dead. Was he not?'

Robin said, 'He was. And, if he were not, why is he not found?'

'Have ye lost something, lads?'

The gardener appeared, coming through the gate, and Robin
stammered, 'Doves.' But Henry leapt up, telling him to shush,
and answered cheerfully, 'Good morrow to you, Jock.'

The gardener pulled off his hat. 'Your pardon, good my
master, I did not ken you then. Who is your young friend?'

'This is Robin Grubb. You do not need to mind him. He kens
to haud his tongue. I came to thank you for your posy. It has
won the lady's heart.'

'Ah, tis good to hear. I hope it brought you profit, sir.'

'Indeed, it did that.' And there followed an exchange of
nudging and guffaws, bewildering to Robin, who was looking
up a tree. He tugged at Henry's sleeve.

'Whisht a while,' Henry said. But Robin stuttered 'Bird', and
pointed to a hawthorn branch, high above the spot where they
had left the corpse.

'Aye, son, tis a rook,' the gardener explained to him, in a kindly voice, as though he were a fool, which given Robin's gaping mouth and staring eyes and stammering did not seem off the mark. 'He lives in that tree. There is his nest, the rookery above. He has a mistress, and a clutch of eggs. An insolent limmar, he is. Well, sirs, I will leave you to it, there is leeks and parsley wanted for the pot. If ye could find your way,' he appealed to Henry, 'to settle your account, then I would be grateful. Tis some while now, I doubt. It vexes me to mention it, but I heard a rumour that you were not good for it. Tis slander, says I, for I ken for a fact his faither, Lord Balfour, is a rich man.'

'Quite right,' Henry said. 'I will look to it today.'

'I thank ye for it, sir.' The gardener retreated through the college gate.

Robin said, 'This is a terrible thing.'

'Terrible,' Henry agreed. 'I do not have the money to pay him.'

'I do not mean that. The bird. Do you not see? It is *him*.'

Henry stared at him. 'Do you mean to say you think Lord Sempill is the rook?'

'Of course he is. He has transfigured himself. It is plain to see. There can be no other explanation. And – and – there was a feather left beside him on the ground. A black feather,' Robin said.

'That is true. There was.' Henry gave some thought to this. It was well known that witches were able to transform themselves into the likeness of birds. They applied magic ointments so that they could fly. 'But still,' he said judiciously, 'there is no certain proof.'

'You did not see him, though. Naked in the courtyard, leaping in the air. Like he was trying to fly. Like this, an' this, an' this.' Little Robin Grubb, who had never heard of a galliard or pavane, nor ever learned to dance, began to cut a caper underneath the tree. The rook became alarmed, letting out a squawk and swooping at his face before retreating smartly to the safety of its branch, where it cawed again.

This terrifying outcome served to settle it. Robin ceased to prance, shaken to the core. And Henry said, 'Tis true, he has the look of Bumbaise. The beadiness of eye, the beakiness of neb. I fancy there is something also in the coat; his black silk shot with shades of emerald and blue. Come, now let us go. I do not like it here.'

'The principal said do not come back till the lord is found,' Robin pointed out.

'Well, we have found him. What can we do? We cannot catch him.'

Robin said, 'I can. I know how tis done. We must come at dusk, and you must shine a light, a lantern, in his eyes. That will make him blind, and I will shoot him down with a little pellet I have in my sling. It will not hurt him much. Then when he is captured they will make him turn back into himself, and everyone will see that he is a witch.'

'Are you not afeart of him?' Henry Balfour marvelled. For he had reached the limit of his own thirst for adventure.

'Na, I am not feart. I have a stone my grandame gave to me, protective against charms. You may haud it, if you like.'

'Wondrous Robin Grubb! When I quit the college, as I am afraid I may do very soon, will you come with me? You can be my page.'

Robin answered frankly. 'I do not think I will. For fear I won't be paid.'

III

The commissioners were lodged in an inn by the West Port, the newly built triumphal entrance to the South Street. All three had stayed the night. Colluthie's house was close, but he would not go home, determined to remain wherever Sempill was. The stranger was it then that he did not complain when Sempill disappeared. Nothing but his dinner taxed Colluthie now. He had declined the ordinary at the common board, of bannock, beer and broth, asking for a tray to be sent up to the room he shared with Philip Clench. Lord Sempill had reserved a chamber to himself, though no one could establish whether he had slept in it; his servant William Soutar had been quartered in the barn. Soutar was intelligent, an honest, gentle clerk who Philip hoped would join them; Colluthie disagreed. 'Discretion now is all. We must talk alone. We cannot be attended, vexing though that is,' he said. But he did not seem vexed, nor disposed to talk of any kind at all, as he ate his meal. He had called for capon, roasted on a spit, rabbits in a pie and a jug of wine, chewing over carefully the matter on his mind.

Philip Clench ate sparingly. And it was Philip who was first to break off from rumination. 'What should we do, then?' he asked.

Colluthie dabbed a napkin on a spot of gravy that had settled in his beard. 'I will write a letter to the king, this after-dinner time, asking him to grant me charge of the commission. When I have his answer, then we shall proceed. These colleges, ye see, are obdurate and obstinate. But we shall bow and bend them, supple to our will. Meanwhile, we maun wait, and bide his Grace's time. Send to the cook if there is some cheese, and mebbe a pippin or two. Won't you have some pie? The flesh is soft and sweet.'

Philip stared at him. 'No, I thank you. What of Lord Sempill?' he said.

'I shall make report that he deserts his post.'

'Deserts? What cause have you to say that he deserts his post? He has disappeared.'

'Call it what you will,' Colluthie wiped his fingers, sticky from a bone, 'ye ken as well as I do he was in a dudgeon with St Leonard's yesterday. They played him for a fool.'

'Nor did we fare better,' Philip pointed out.

'Aye, that is true,' Colluthie allowed. 'But for the reason, solely, that we lacked the authority. Our president is weak, therefore we are weak. While he is our president, that cannot be helped. But when I am in charge, there will be a change. These scholars at the colleges will sing out loud and shrill. And they will rue the day they led us such a dance.'

'It seems to me,' said Philip, troubled at his tone, 'his absence does not stir in you a proper true dismay.'

'Aye? And why should it?' his colleague replied. 'Sempill is done. He is spent. His word is worthless here. He kens as much himself, wherefore has he slunk off hameward in his shame, as the whipped dug creeps, cringing to its kennel.'

Philip shook his head. 'He has not gone home. His horse is still here in the stable.'

'Oh. Is it?' For a moment, Colluthie was taken aback. 'You have looked into that?'

'William Soutar has. 'Tis wonder to me now, that you have not yourself. A man who did not ken you better, as an honoured laird, might suspect you had a part in Lord Sempill's disappearance, so little do the reasons for it seem to give you trouble.'

'An honoured laird indeed. Consider, *Master* Clench, and mind who ye are talking to.' Colluthie was amused, rather than incensed. He did not count Philip Clench, or anything he said, of importance to his cause.

It was Philip who appeared to be itching for a fight. 'I would rather be kent for a master of arts, than for the proud possessor of a poke of land. Colluthie, are ye called fer? Where the Deil is that? A man might be a laird perforce of his inheritance, or upon the favour of a fickle king, as quickly lost as won. But my good name was worked for, at the university, and my honours earned,' he cried.

Colluthie answered with a smile, sour enough to wither him. 'Ah, there it is,' he said, 'Now it all comes out. I wonder that you kept your sly tongue still so long. You are one of them. Where was it, then, St Leonard's? You are of their camp, cut from their same cloth. No wonder you would side with the doltish Sempill. It is your intent to collude in their concealment. Now I see it all.'

'As it happens,' Philip said, sorely stung by this, 'it was not St Andrews. It was Aberdeen. But that is not the point.'

'The point is,' said Colluthie, 'where your loyalty lies.'

'That is not in question. I will report, impartially, the facts. But those facts include the absence of Lord Sempill, missing from his charge, which alarms me somewhat, more than it does you. We cannot proceed until he is found.'

'Aye, very well,' Colluthie said at last, weary of the feud. 'If it will appease you, send Soutar out to look for him.'

'He has gone already, of his ain accord. Which ye would ken,' said Philip, 'if ye cared at all.'

The servant William Soutar had sacrificed his dinner to the search. He began his inquiries at the kirk of Holy Trinity, the centre of all commerce and conversation, from the most exalted to the carnal kind, and discovered that Lord Sempill had no dealings there. Next, he tried the taverns, with the same result. At the town house, he reported him as missing to the clerk, who pinned up a notice of it at the mercat cross. It was quiet in the tolbooth, and in the street itself, for it was not market day; his lordship, to be sure, was not lost among a crowd. Therefore was his absence all the more remarkable. Lord Sempill had not been seen in any place that day, though several folk had spoken with him on the day before. How could a man have vanished so completely in so close and circumspect and quisitive a town? William widened his search, southward to the Kinness burn,

and lands that lay beyond the South Street colleges. Here he
saw the gardener scattering some seed, and two truant students
fleeing through the trees, guiltily returning to the books they
shirked. He continued west, as far as the new mill, where the
farmers congregated with their sacks of grain, and returned
along a path that circumscribed the town, following the course
of the mill lade to the harbour. He considered whether Sempill
could have fallen in the lade, somehow slipped and drowned,
but concluded that an obstruction of Sempill's bulk and weight
would have stopped the flow of the chain of mills that churned
the millstream on, seamlessly and smoothly. No sound more
alarming than the water's rush, the singing of the blackbird,
the mistle thrush or lark, coming at the beck of an early
summer day, broke upon the peace. At the harbour, he found
fishermen, and asked if any stranger had chanced to hire a boat,
or if some ship had lately put out from the port. When they
answered not, he walked along the sands some distance to the
east before returning to the pier to climb up the Kirk Heugh,
surveying through an archway the grounds of the cathedral,
and exploring to the north the rocks below the cliffs, extending
from the harbour to the castle beach. The castle was closed up,
and he passed its precincts, calling at the cook shop, through
the Swallow Port and up on to a precipice, from which vantage
point he scoured the white peaks of the waves, where nothing
dipped and floated but the shrieking gulls. He continued west,
past the guid wife's crackling house, where the candle tallow
carried on the wind, to the golf links and the coning warrens
kept to feed the town, but found nothing but a rabbit kitten,
keeking through the grass.

Having now concluded his circuit of the town, with neither
hide nor hair, William took up camp in an alehouse on the North
Street, to consider his next move, and to slake his thirst with
a welcome pint. A friendly lass looked out a hunk of bannock

too, a herring and a cheese, and he made good a dinner for the time that he had lost.

The alehouse was quiet, for those who had the time could ill afford to drink, at this hour of the day. In the one public room, where William pulled a stool up to the common board, a solitary drinker drained his worth away, already in his cups. 'Good morrow to ye, man. Will ye share a drink with me? For I am celebratin',' he invited William.

William answered, 'That is civil o ye. I will not say no. For I have had the devil of a futless chase today. What cause have ye to celebrate? Is it a holy day?' The celebrant he judged to be twenty-eight or thirty, weathered in his face and in his ragged hands, leathered hard with work. There was something else about him, sorely out of place.

'Haly as a wedding day,' he answered enigmatically, 'for my auld master's deid.'

William sympathised. 'Tyrannical, was he? I have had the luck to work for men like that.'

'No bit of it, ye ken. He was no so bad. He was guid eno' to leave to me a legacy. An' when I am done here, cheerful and fu', I will treat with my sweetheart to make her my wife. Prithee, drink to that!'

The friendly lass returning with a stoup of liquor filled up William's cup. 'If the lassie has sense, she will refuse him,' she said.

'Aw, crowdie mowdie, dinna be like that.' The drunken suitor pawed her. She slapped his hand away.

William Soutar caught it, grasping firm his wrist. 'Away now, whit are ye, her faither?' his captive protested.

'That coat that you wear is some very fine stuff. I wonder that a loun like you could manage to afford it,' William Soutar said. He recognised the cloth. How could he not, when Lord Sempill himself had asked him only yesterday to replace the button that was missing from the cuff? The pity was, his lordship had not left it for repair when he took it off. If he had taken it off.

'What do you mean?' said the man who wore it now. 'Did I no say the noo I had come into guid fortune?'

'So I doubt, ye did. An' awbody kens, fortune is a wench that brings muckle good to some. Yet I marvel she should bring ye Lord Sempill's coat.'

To the scuffle that ensued, the magistrates were called, and the drinker was taken to be questioned at the tolbooth, suspected of the robbery, and probably the murder, of the missing man. He was locked up overnight for the attention of the coroner, who had means at his disposal to elucidate the corpse, which he had doubtless hidden somewhere in his coat.

When the laird of Colluthie heard of these events, he put aside the letter he was writing to the king to see how they turned out. The thought that Lord Sempill might be lying in a ditch, murdered by a stranger, was sufficient to provoke in him a rumble of alarm, not least for himself. The commissioners kept together, for safety, in the inn, while a search was made. The excitement occupied them through the afternoon. At the close of day, they heard that no further trace of Sempill had been found, and sat down to a plate of beef and buttered bannock, restorative to spirits that were chopped and churned. Yet no sooner had they settled than their supper was disturbed by the coming of a boy with a live bird in a bag. When they saw what he brought, and listened to his tale, all three men were amazed. Philip Clench could see, in Colluthie's face, the gamut of emotion ranging through his mind: a gargoyle of dismay, bafflement and fear, of horror and disgust, and incredulous delight.

Hew Cullan, riding home, had not heard the news. He saw the men returning from their searches through their fields, unaware that they were looking for a corpse. Night began to settle, grey upon the waters ebbing from the shore, and on the path ahead. He came back through the gardens, heavy with the scent of rose and hawthorn blossom, and through the shadowed hall, closed off to the sun, where someone had left out a little pot of violets on a window sill. He took the violets up to Frances in her room.

She was sitting by the window with a candle at her elbow and a letter in her hand. There was a little colour, fragile but perceptible, in the cheek she turned to him, patiently, to be kissed. Her eyes were bright with tears.

'You have been crying,' he said. Fear began, again, to close upon his heart.

'It is nothing,' she said. 'I had a letter from my cousin Mary Phelippes. She has sent some things.'

She showed him: a lace cap, a napkin, a white infant's smock. He looked at her blankly, closed in a grip that dulled understanding. Frances read the look of terror in his face. 'No, it is not that. See, Flora sleeps.' She made him turn his head to look into the crib, where he saw his child, temperate and still, pink inside her swaddling clothes, that might have been a shroud. 'Mary lost a child, and cannot have another,' she explained. 'Therefore did it touch my heart that she sends Flora clothes.'

'I recall. Tis sad,' he said, foolishly, and numbed.

'We are so lucky, Hew.'

It had not felt like luck to him. He remembered still – remembering was not the word, he could not cleanse the stain of it completely from his consciousness, no matter how he tried – when his bairn was born, lifeless in a tide of so much silt and blood he could not comprehend how Frances had clung on. She had been ill for months. His sister Meg had brought the infant back to life, by what he understood to be some secret form of magic. What else could it be? The child was small and frail, born before its time, wrestled to the world translucent in its skin, its first cry weak and tremulous. Flora had been nursed for weeks by Bella Frew, along with her boy Billy, while Frances recovered her strength. Now there was a life, a colour in the cheek of both his wife and his daughter, timid as a shoot that felt its way out tentatively from the barren earth, tender to the frosts and the scorching sun.

'What does she say in her letter?' he asked, careful to conceal the turmoil of his mind.

'That she has been helping Thomas in his work.'

'With the ciphers?' Phelippes was perhaps the principal cryptographer to the English Crown. Hew had worked with him, under Secretary Walsingham, at a time and place that seemed a world away.

'That is not unlikely. But she does not say. She says that he is exercised at present with despatches that concern the war with Spain – for it is a war, whatever men may think. There is a present terror and a danger to the queen, for the stand she has taken in the Netherlands.'

'There is always that.'

'True. But Mary thinks that it grows graver by the day. How far away it seems,' Frances said.

'Aye, thank God.'

But Frances did not look on it like that. 'How was your commission?' she asked.

'Not quite as expected. Lord Sempill, who has the charge of it, has disappeared.'

'How exciting. Will they want you to find him?'

'I do not suppose so.'

'They should. No one is as good at finding things as you.'

He laughed at that. 'Perhaps. But I would rather be at home.'

Frances let slip the smallest of sighs. She folded Mary's letter, handing it to him. 'Read it, if you like. There is a kind of life in it that makes me miss the world.'

'What? The war with Spain?' he teased.

'Not that.' She considered. 'Perhaps, even that. London seems so far.'

'Do you miss your aunt?'

She could not explain how she felt confined and closed within the house. She answered carefully. 'We were at the mill today. The maids have dressed it up with flowers, in honour of the May. The air was fresh and cool. Tomorrow, if the day breaks fair, I thought of going to the town, with Flora, to see Meg.'

'With Flora? Is that wise?' He could not quell the fear. She sensed it in his voice, although he tried to steady it. It welled up like the wind, and all but overwhelmed.

'Bella Frew walks often through the fields with Billy on her back, tied up in a shawl,' she reasoned quietly. 'Or in a little basket, riding at the horse.'

'That does not sound safe.' For Frances was not Bella Frew, and Flora was not Billy. He felt himself adrift, helpless to protect them.

'Gavan Baird has books to take to Matthew Locke. He will walk with us, he says. If you think it well. He will not do so else. So, what do you think?' Frances looked at him.

The colour in her cheek, the brightness in her eyes, which had been lost a while, returned to hold and still the beating of his heart. 'I think it will be well,' he said, 'if the day is fair. But Gavan need not walk with you. I will go myself.'

When morning broke, he walked with her, and led her horse on foot with Flora in a basket carried at her side, where a gentle sunlight welcomed his small child to blossom in the breeze. When at last he left them in the leafy South Street, in his sister's house, he felt light at heart, returning to St Salvator's more settled and at ease than he had been since Candlemas.

IV

Giles was in a humour that was brittle and capricious, quite unlike his usual one. 'There have been advancements,' he announced. 'Lord Sempill has been found. And a man has been arrested, on suspicion of his murder.'

'Then I am sorry to hear it,' said Hew. 'Have you examined the corpse?'

'What corpse? Did I say, at all, that there was a corpse?'

'You said he had been found,' Hew pointed out, confused.

'Aye, and so he has. He is in this room. I wonder, exceedingly, that you do not see him. He was brought to me this morning in a bag. I found for him the comfort of a cage.'

The injured rook was in a cage of wire, suspended from the ceiling by a hook. 'You do not mean—' Hew said.

Giles circumvented him. 'I do not mean at all. Wherefore should I mean,' he said, 'when all the world is mad? What is meaning for? This, I am assured, is the spirit of Lord Sempill transfigured in a bird. It was brought to me this morning by Carnegie of Colluthie, who had it from a boy who brought it him last night. The boy is a bursar in the first class at St Leonard's. He has sworn, by all that is holy and much that is not, that Lord Sempill turned into this creature yesterday, sometime in the night.'

'And Colluthie believed him?'

'Of course he believed him. He wanted to believe. His terror at the thing I cannot overstate; it is equalled only by his joy in it.'

'Why, then,' wondered Hew, 'has he brought it here?'

'Because he is too cowardly to keep it in the house. He says he hears that we are good at solving mysteries. I telt him it was death we dealt in. He was not deterred. He expects that in due course Lord Sempill must revert to his habitual form, relying on us then to cry him for a witch.'

The bird began to flutter feebly at the bars. 'I do not think Lord Sempill will fit inside this cage. It may prove an impediment,' Hew said.

Giles conceded dryly, 'That is a concern. Sad wretch. No doubt there is a mistress rook, and chicks.'

Hew did not like to think of that. He turned his mind instead to the man who was arrested, asking how the thing had come about.

'That may be more serious,' said Giles. 'He was found in a tavern, wearing Sempill's coat.'

'Then,' Hew concluded, 'Sempill may be dead; we cannot rule it out.'

'I fear that is the case. I hoped you might investigate. The suspect is held at the tolbooth. He claims he bought the jacket from the laundress at St Leonard's, not kenning whose it was. The woman has denied it all, of course.'

'St Leonard's once again,' said Hew, for whom investigation was already under way, taken up as easily as slipping on a coat. 'Then that would seem to me a likely place to start.'

James Wilkie at St Leonard's had spent a restless night. He did not regret sending Robin Grubb to Colluthie at the West Port, without Henry Balfour to second his report. Robin, he believed, had an air of innocence that was pure and credible, almost a simplicity, for clever boys – and Robin was a clever boy – were sometimes also fools. Lord Balfour's son was clever of a different kind, worldly and sophisticate, in no way a sop. Robin was the safest choice to offer up the bird; the pity was that he had told a partial truth. Robin had borne witness that he had seen Lord Sempill transform into the rook, between St Mary's gate and St Leonard's wood. But if he told a lie, it was only of the place, and if he had stopped short, in his natural modesty, of speaking of the dance, or of Sempill's nakedness, which details would provoke a further stream of questions, it was to the good. As to the transformation, Robin Grubb believed – honestly believed – that this was what they all had witnessed in the college courtyard. This was no wonder at all, for Wilkie believed it himself. He had further evidence, beyond that of his eyes and unbeknownst to Robin, that cemented that belief. And Colluthie had believed it, on less compelling evidence, because he wanted to. None of that concerned him. Sempill had been caught, and the exact location where he had transfigured was an incidental in the grander scheme.

It was the washerwoman who had pricked at Wilkie's conscience, and had ruined his sleep. She had found Sempill's clothes, lying in a place where they had not thought to look, and had sold them on. Now the man that bought them was lawfully detained, accused of Sempill's death. The laundress had quite sensibly denied the part she played, which had left James Wilkie standing in a quandary. If he did not speak out, then it was quite likely that a man would hang because he bought a coat. But if he gave support to his story of the laundress, they might hang her too, as complicit in the act. If he told the truth, the whole truth must come out – for that the clothes were Sempill's could not be denied – and then the college and its principal were folded in as deep as a body lapped in the curtains from his bed. He shuddered to imagine where those curtains might be now.

Wilkie saw one straw, one slender chance to extricate the college from the horror that pursued. There was one man had the skill to break into the truth, and that man doubtless also had the cunning to conceal it. That man was Hew Cullan. Hew Cullan was a graduate and master of St Leonard's; he had been a regent there, a friend of Robert Black's. He held in his heart certain loves and loyalties, from before Wilkie's time, which could be worked on now. More recently than that, he had been married, to his English bride, in the college kirk; and more closely still, Wilkie had gone on a frost-ridden night to deliver the sacrament to his first child, when no one had believed the infant would survive. Hew Cullan was the man who was wanted now; the principal received his intervention gladly, which once he had anticipated with a sense of dread. Desperate times called for dark measures, he consoled himself.

And so, when Hew arrived, he did not have to trouble to expose the lie. Wilkie laid all bare before him – astonishingly bare – before he had to ask.

'If you can find a way,' said Wilkie, once the tale was told, 'to free the man who had the luck to buy Lord Sempill's coat without reference to the college, I would be obliged to you.' His story had acquired an air of indignation, as though St Leonard's College was the injured party, not the man himself. Sempill was the villain, on whatever count.

'And how might I do that?' said Hew, struggling to move on from the picture of the dance, which Wilkie had been painting vivid in his mind.

'It will not be hard. You need only prove that Sempill is the bird, and all will be resolved. The matter of his clothes is an accidental. If Sempill is the rook, then he is not dead. And if he is not dead, then he has not been killed.'

'If Sempill is the rook,' said Hew, whose echo had no hint in it of Wilkie's own conviction, 'how do you propose I prove that is the case?'

Wilkie said, 'With this. The same bag of tricks with which he was disfigured.' He unlocked his desk, and took out Sempill's purse. 'You need not say, of course, where you came upon it. Can you find a way to put this matter right,' he begged, as Hew stood up to leave.

'I will not let a man be damned without a fight, who has done no wrong,' Hew returned ambiguously. Wilkie seized upon it, single in his purpose.

'So did I believe. Our hopes depend in you.'

Returning through the Market Street, Hew called at the tolbooth, where he asked to see the prisoner. Here he was well known for assistance he had given to the crownar, Andrew Wood. Sir Andrew Wood was absent still, on business in Dundee, where he had bought a house. He was in the process of retiring from his office, and had not yet found the time, through his most attentive and exacting methods, to determine if the suspect should be sent for trial. Hew spoke in his absence to a burgh magistrate, who had the delinquent safely in his charge.

'See him, if you like. Talk to him, if you will. And if you can stop his greetin' I will be obliged to you,' the magistrate replied. 'He has been wailing half the night.'

The drunken man had woken to a sober melancholy, and his face was mottled heavily with tears. His mouth and throat were dry, and it cost Hew fourpence to procure a drink for him, before he could determine what it was he said. He had been a journeyman for nine years to a carpenter, a timmerman at sea. His master had passed on and left to him a legacy, with which he was intending now to settle down, and take a wife on land. He had in his mind a lassie from the town, whom he had had his eye on for a while. He had not thought, before, that she would stoop to look at him. But with his newfound wealth, he hoped he had a chance with her. He had bought the coat to build upon that chance, for it was such a coat a gentleman would have; by wearing it, he hoped, the lass might think him one. He had it from a friend, whose mother did the washing for St Leonard's College, and claimed it was a gift from the college principal, a gentleman, that was. And it was dear enough, he sniffed, without the devil took him also for the price of it; he had no idea it was a dead man's coat. 'They kenned it was, I doubt. And doubtless they had set upon and killed that man the gither, for baith of them deny they ever saw it now. And now,' the timmerman concluded his distressing tale, 'the crownar is to come and bring wi' him the pilliewinks, an' I am meant to tell him where the corpse is put. And how will I dae that, when I do not ken?'

'Is that what they have telt you?' Hew said sympathetically. 'I would not give it heed. I know the crownar well, and to my kenning he does not resort to torments like the pilliewinks; his methods are more subtle, though they are as keen. Tell him, when he comes, that you have Hew Cullan now to speak in your defence, and he must come to me. He will not like it much. We are combaters of old. But he will hear your plea.'

'Combaters, you say?' The word held out no hope. The timmerman would have preferred it if they had been friends.

'Trust in it,' said Hew. He asked the burgh magistrate if he might borrow Sempill's coat, to help in his inquiries. The man did not seem sure.

'Evidence, that is. Tis here to show the crownar.'

'I do not mean to take it further than St Salvator's, where Doctor Locke will look at it for any trace of blood. It will help your case,' Hew promised.

'Aye, then, very well. You maun sign your name for it,' the magistrate agreed. 'What news from Doctor Locke? Has he found the body?'

Hew said enigmatically, 'Though some believe he may have done, I am persuaded not.'

He took Lord Sempill's coat with him to St Salvator's, to hang up on a peg not far from the rook. 'For when he wants to change,' he said.

Giles raised an eyebrow. 'Seriously?'

'Not seriously, in truth. Ah, I do not know. The truth is that, whatever is the truth, Lord Sempill is not found, and I have no inkling where he is.' Hew told Giles the tale he brought back from St Leonard's, ending with the pocket that was found in the latrines, which he opened up to show what was inside: a stub of tallow candle and a pot of cream. 'What do you make of that? Wilkie is convinced it is the flying ointment Sempill used to transform himself. The candle he believes was lit to cast the charm. Why he chose St Leonard's to effect this transformation, Wilkie cannot tell. What do you think? Is it flying cream?'

Giles sniffed at the contents of the pot. 'Meg is better placed than I am to tell you.'

'Because she is a witch?' Hew inquired facetiously. It struck, none the less, a bitter kind of note, which Giles was quick to blow away.

'Because she is an expert in the herbal medicines of the natural world. She may ken what is in it. James Wilkie is not wrong when he supposes that magicians deal in diverse strange and secret ointments. Some such are composed of arsenic and antimony. They may cause a man to think that he can fly. He cannot fly, of course. And as to turning him into a bird – well, we see where such illusions sow their seed, and propagate,' he said.

Hew turned to the rook. 'What say you, my lord? Shall we dip your feathers in this fantastic ointment, to see if you turn back? For God knows how to find you by another scheme.'

The bird did not fare well in captivity. After several hours, it had ceased to beat its wings against the bars of the cage, and sank into a corner, dazed at the futility. It refused to countenance the smallest scrap of food, or to drink the water that was offered in a cup. It had plucked three feathers from its broken breast, allowing them to flutter plaintive to the ground. Hew picked them up, and returned them to the cage.

'Poor prisoned creature,' murmured Giles. 'We should let it out.'

'No.'

'No? That is not like you, Hew.'

'If Lord Sempill is found, if he is alive, then the bird in its cage is the one thing that might save him. We must keep it there, and its refuse too. No matter if it dies. No particle nor part should be suffered to escape.'

'Ah, I see your mind. Nature is not kind. But how much more upsetting is our work upon her world.' Giles stripped from its sinews a morsel of meat, and dangled it close to the bird. 'Feed, little rook. Look to your strength.'

'There is a man had a coat that did not belong to him, wants your compassion too,' Hew advised him grimly. 'Lord Sempill must be found, and both poor wretches freed.'

He took the ointment for his sister to examine in her South Street still room. If Frances was dismayed to see him back so soon, she was reassured to find he would not stay. He kissed his wife and child. 'Lord Sempill must be left to find himself awhile, for I have I promised Giles to read the second lecture,' he said. 'I will return at dinner time to learn what you have found.'

'You ask a lot,' said Meg.

'But not too much, of you.'

He departed then, to lecture to the second class, a lightness in his step. Frances said, 'Tis good to see him occupied. He has not been himself.'

'He is in his element,' said Meg. 'I think he has not been there for a while. The last months have been hard on you both.'

'He is attentive.' Frances sighed. 'He would protect us, sometimes, from imagined threat.'

'He believes it is his duty to keep you and Flora safe. And he has not the faintest notion how to go about it. He is terrified. Nor can he believe in his good fortune. He does not think that he deserves it. But he will accept it, over time. Now he is content, because he has a crime to solve, and the one thing he is sure of is that you are safe with us. Can I ask you to watch Martha while I take this ointment to examine at the still?'

Frances said, 'Of course. But can you really tell what compound is inside?'

'The chance is small, I think. For I am no magician. I will not be long.'

Though Frances gave no sign, the task of watching Martha filled her with disquietude. The servant, Canny Bett, had taken Martha's brother Matthew to his class with Gavan Baird, and she was left alone. The child was playing outside in the garden; from time to time she ran into its wilds, returning with a leaf, a pebble or a flower. Meg's gardens stretched out far off to the fields, and were filled with hazards: water butts and bees, thistle clumps and thorns, and enough poison to see off a city. Giles had built a wall around the physic garden, but was there not a space through which a child might slip, as resolutely fey as Martha was? The place was ripe and full of danger; it astonished Frances Hew supposed it safe.

Now and then the child would disappear from sight, and Frances was alarmed. She was caught at a cross; Flora lay asleep in a basket on the floor, and she did not like to leave her daughter in the house, or Martha in the garden, unattended. She called out to the child, and was relieved when Martha Locke came running, with her streaming tangled hair and bare beggar's feet, for Meg allowed her children to run wild. She tried to settle Martha in her lap, but Martha would not have it, wriggling herself free. She was all limbs a-flailing, like a windmill in the wind, while Flora was lapped up tightly in a package, neat and straight and stiff, with a little placket for her placid face, primly peeping out. Martha was prattling all the while, some fantastic folly of imagination; she lived half her life in an imaginary world. Her brother Matthew Locke was a solid, studious child. But Martha was a creature entirely of her own; her parents had indulged and encouraged her wild flights, and had not taught her that such fantasies were dangerous and wrong. Frances hoped and prayed that Flora would not follow by example; she pictured Flora peaceful at her books or stitching at embroideries, sitting on a cushion on the grass at Kenly Green, underneath the apple trees. She would play the lute, and learn to sing, as Frances did, and they would sing for Hew on winter afternoons, when the lamps were lit, settled by the fire. Here, at home with Meg, she found that she could hope, daring to look forward to that future life, believing in her heart that Flora would grow strong; and understanding Meg had saved the baby's life, Frances felt ashamed for thinking her at fault. She turned back to the child. 'Tell me what you play.'

Martha's play involved the story of a bear that was 'bitten by the bees'. There were hives at the far end of the garden out of sight, and Frances felt it fell upon her to inform the child, 'You must not stir the bees. For it is the May, and they are apt to swarm.' Martha prattled on. She did not want to sit, to suffer to be kissed, or to admire the baby sleeping in her crib, and Frances made small sense of the substance of her talk, a convolute confusion of question and delight. 'What a lovely tale,' she said, glad when Meg appeared, to ruffle with her hand through Martha's tangled locks, that Frances longed to comb and fetter in a cap.

'Have you been good for your aunt?'

'She has told me,' Frances said, 'the most illuminating story of a bear.'

Meg laughed at that. 'I have never fathomed what lies in her head. There are no bears in Scotland. I suppose she has seen one in a picture from a book.'

Giles Locke had many books that were supplied with pictures. Sometimes, he would cut one out, and give it to his children to colour in with chalks. The boy filled his minutely, keeping to the lines, with every little detail carefully preserved. But Martha would scrub with her fat little fist, round and round with the stub of the chalk, till the paper was riddled and riven to dust, while her father stood by with a smile. Frances trusted Hew would be less reckless with his own books, which were very fine. 'There are bear pits in London, on the south bank of the Thames. They give the bears names of the poor folk at Bedlam,' she said.

'That is not kindness,' said Meg.

'I suppose not. But the bears when they are shackled have the same sprawling gait. They lumber like madmen.'

This image left a strong impression working in Meg's mind. She pondered it a while. 'You do not suppose—'

The question on her lips was settled by the child, coming from the press with her father's shirt.

'Where do you go with that? Is it for the bear? Bears do not wear clothes,' her mother called to her.

'Not bear, Mamma. Barc. The barc man is cold. And sore,' Martha said, at last relieved of news that she had been attempting to deliver for some time.

V

Returning at the dinner hour, Hew was astonished to discover 'Bumbaise' Sempill, propped up at the board in the doctor's cap and gown, finishing a bowl of his sister's barley broth.

Frances confirmed, 'Lord Sempill is here.' She whispered, 'He has not been well.'

Lord Sempill set down his spoon. 'I have been set upon by a band of renegats. They did me grievous harm; the hurts are plain to see. All of them must hang.'

'The renegats were bees,' said Meg. 'I do not think it likely you will hang the bees. Besides, the ones that stung you are already dead. Giles will mourn their loss. Frances will attend you, while I fetch a salve to take away their sting. Come and help me, Hew.' She drew her brother quietly aside. 'Martha found him naked in the garden. There is a kind of den, where the children play. It seems he spent the night there. He does not remember much; he is very flustered and confused. But I believe he suffers the effects of physic, taken in excess. The cream he has been using was a compound of henbane.'

'I knew that you would know,' said Hew.

'I did not know,' said Meg, 'until he told me what was in it. It is very hard to take apart a compound. What he has not told me is what he used it for. However, I can hazard that it was not witchcraft. The poor man is distracted by the burden of his shame. Wherefore I will not intrude upon his misery. If you must know the reason for it, you will have to ask him.'

'Could henbane have reduced him to this parlous state?' asked Hew.

'I believe it could.' Meg spoke a little more about the workings of such physic on a feeble body. 'He is lucky,' she concluded, 'that he is not dead. But now the worst is past, the drug is wearing off.'

Hew said, 'I will talk to him. What shall I tell him? Not the whole, I think.'

He returned to the hall where Lord Sempill sat, and the women with their children quietly withdrew, leaving them to talk. Then Lord Sempill crumbled, all his bluster gone. 'My pardon to you, sir, but can we speak in confidence? For as I believe, you are an honest man. Your good wife and sister have cared for me with uncommon kindness. I am in your debt.'

'Not mine,' answered Hew.

'No. Perhaps not. Forgive me my manners, if they seem rude. I have had, do you see, the most bumbaising day. I must ask your help.'

How can I help you?'

'You think I do not ken you, but I do. I mind a green young advocate who spoke before my court. The circumstances were extraordinary. Your argument was curious, exact, and convolute. In parts, it was exasperating, tending to the tedious. And yet there was a brilliance in it I will not forget. You could well have risen to a most prodigious course. It is to your credit you did not.'

'I had not supposed that you remembered that,' said Hew, both flattered and astonished.

'Ah, indeed, why not? Do you now assume a girlish sort of modesty? Or is it, in fact, that you believe old Sempill is wanting in his wits? That because I profess myself so frequently perplexed, I do not understand the working of the world? You are not the first to come to that conclusion. But it is a mistake. I seek for truth, and clarity. Confusion in such cases is a powerful tool. It forces men to look again for ways they may express themselves. The more they must revise, and revisit their accounts, the greater is the hazard they will lose and trip themselves, and inadvertently reveal their secret truths. Do you understand?'

Hew said, 'I begin to.'

'You begin to. Good. Then let me tell you this. I have had a life. When I was a bairn, I was first a page, at the court of James the fifth. When I was full grown, I studied for the law. For years, I was first depute in the justice court, second only to the lord justiciar. I saw many trials, and many men were hanged, at my word of command. I am not a fool.'

'I understand you, sir. How then may I help you?'

To Hew's dismay, Lord Sempill's eyes began to dim with tears. 'The trouble now is this. For the first time in my life, I find myself afeart. I woke up in a field, naked to the skin, and I have no notion how I came to be there. I have stolen honey from a guid wife's hive, and startled her small child. I have been stung by some scores of bees, and I cannot tell you why. And I am afraid that I may lose my mind. There is a man at my back, on the king's commission, who will do all he can to oust me from my place. He must not learn of this.'

'That is Colluthie,' Hew supposed.

'Colluthie, aye. What have you heard?'

'He thinks you are a witch, transfigured to a bird.'

'Oh, my dear Lord,' Sempill groaned.

'We shall prove him wrong. Your clothes have been found, in the place where you had left them. The woman who found them chose to sell them on. The man who bought them from her is suspected of your murder.'

'What, so much wrong?' Lord Sempill dropped his face into his hands.

'There may yet be worse. But we shall put it right. You must tell me this. The potion in your pocket. What do you use it for?'

Lord Sempill whimpered, 'Trust me, that it is not what you think.'

'You cannot know what I think. But it is imperative that you answer honestly.'

'Then I see no help but to tell the truth. The pot continues an ointment for a sore affliction, of which I am ashamed. I bought it from a guid wife in the Canongate, who assured me of discretion. She is not, I may say, my usual practitioner.'

Hew asked, 'What affliction?'

'I prefer not to say.'

'And I prefer some hope of making out a case for you.'

'Ah, very well. It is an ointment prescribed for griefs of the fundament. The candle stub is instrumental in its application,' Lord Sempill answered wretchedly. 'The truth is that the woman warned me not to use so much. But I have been cruelly afflicted. It was a long ride from Edinburgh.'

Hew said, a little grimly, 'Aye, no doubt it was. My sister is acquainted with medicinal herbs. She tells me that the henbane active in your ointment, taken in excess, can lead to fits of frenzy and paralysis. Therein is explained your lapse in sensibility.'

'Then I am not mad! I thank God for that. Yet am I ashamed.

What happened,' Sempill whispered, fearful in relief, 'in those desperate hours that I cannot recall? What happened to my clothes? And why should Colluthie take me for a witch?'

'As I believe,' said Hew, 'you went to St Leonard's to find out what secrets they kept hidden from you. The physic you had applied had already done its work, else I do not think you would have ventured out at night. Whatever was the purpose foremost in your mind, while you were there, you made use of the latrines. And there applied more of your ointment, which already you were using to excess. It tipped you to the brink of a strange delirium. A fever perhaps, for you took off your clothes. There it was you left them; there were they found. You ran back through the woods.'

Here Hew chose to edit, straying from a truth that Sempill, he was certain, would not care to hear. He would never learn it from the four men at St Leonard's, who were sworn to secrecy; their interests mirrored his. What purpose was in truth, if the humiliation of it was too hard to bear? The version Hew presented now caused Sempill pain enough. 'At St Mary's,' he improvised, 'you collapsed, insensible. A student saw you there. He took you for dead – henbane can disguise any sign of life – and went to call for help. He came back with a friend, and found the corpse was gone, and in its place a bird. You had woken up, and meanwhile wandered off, coming to Meg's garden, where you found a bed. The silly boys believed that you had been transformed.'

Lord Sempill was too vexed to dwell upon this foolishness. 'A student saw me bared? Then I am undone. No more. A laughing stock. The butt of rude boys' jests.'

'It is not as bad as you think. The student was too delicate – or perhaps too feart – to recount your nakedness. He is very young.'

'Aye, but the clothes?' Sempill moaned.

'The man who is accused has nothing but a coat. You need only find a reason why you left it there.'

'Then, can it be possible? Something can be saved?'

'All can be saved. I will take you back, washed and dressed and salved, and we shall both flesh out the bones of your account. Your appearance will restore and set the thing to rights. And the man and the bird who are imprisoned will be freed.'

'Then I thank you, sir, from the bottom of my heart. For reputation, though tis hard to win, is very quickly lost.'

'I will fetch some clothes from your baggage at the inn. It will not do, I think, to dress like Doctor Locke.'

'I am much obliged to you. The student who observed me – how long was the grass?'

'Exceedingly, no doubt. For we are now in May.'

'And you are sure, you say, that there was no one else but your sister and her bairn, confronted with my nakedness?'

'If anyone comes forth to lay a claim to that,' Hew chose his words with care, 'I will eat my hat.'

He turned back at the door. 'When you were at the court, when you were a bairn, did you use to dance?'

Lord Sempill's eyes lit up with a kind of wonder. 'To dance? Why, then, we did. You mind me of a thing I have not done for years. Why do you ask that?'

'It is a matter, now, of no consequence at all.'

The commissioners at the West Port were flustered to receive a letter from Lord Sempill, requiring their attendance at the college of St Salvator at three o'clock, 'to conclude that business that was there left off'. 'He has turned,' said Colluthie, 'just as I telt ye. What did I say? A witch cannot keep the shape it takes for long.'

'But if he has turned,' objected Philip Clench, 'how is he at large, to send to us a letter? Surely Doctor Locke has not set him free again?'

'He could not send a letter,' Colluthie reasoned carefully, 'if he was a bird.'

'The feather of a bird,' William Soutar said, 'is, properly, a pen.' Both men stared at him. 'Perhaps,' he ventured timidly, 'we should go and see.'

They found Lord Sempill whole, in the figure of himself and in his own black coat, together with the rook, still huddled in its cage. Giles Locke and Hew Cullan stood on either side. Colluthie was the first to speak. 'Where have you been to, my lord?'

Sempill answered, 'I have not been well. I was tended, in my sickness, by Doctor Locke's wife, who is a woman of outstanding virtue. Now I have recovered.'

Colluthie shot the doctor an accusing look. 'Why did ye not say?'

'I did not know,' said Giles.

Philip Clench observed, 'He does not look well. You do not look well, my lord. Are those pustules on your face? God forbid it is infecting.'

'Sadly, it is not,' said Giles, who was bitter still about the damage to his bees. 'The danger has passed.'

'Aye, I am well. And restored to health, yet have I been vexed by strange, fantastic tales. A man has been detained for picking up my coat, which I left off in haste. He has been released, and the coat returned,' said Sempill.

Philip said uneasily, 'Good, then, no harm done.'

'No? Then what is this?' Sempill picked up the rook in its cage and allowed it to swing close to his face. The effect, Hew saw, was terrifying. In private, he applauded the performance.

'A boy brought it to us. He telt us – well, he was mistaken,' Philip said. 'It does not matter what he telt us.'

Giles said, 'Sirs, your sport is done. Let the creature go.'

But Colluthie was not easily distracted from his mark. He

opened up the cage, and lifted out the bird, which fluttered faint and feebly in his hand. He held it aloft, to show to it the window, and for a moment Hew believed he meant to let it go. Then, with a snap of his figures, he broke the bird's neck. His eyes, all the while, had remained fixed on Sempill. He let the rook fall, a loose sack of feathers, soft, to the ground.

Giles gave a small cry of disgust. Hew asked, 'Why do that?' But it was Sempill who replied.

'I can tell you why. He did it because he thought – because he hoped – that it would hurt me. He looks to cause me pain. Is that not the pith of it, David?'

The laird of Colluthie rubbed his hand upon his coat, as though the place was sore. 'A witch may have a familiar,' he said. His eyes were dark with doubt.

William Soutar said, looking at the coat, 'There is a mark that may not come out.'

'And the rook is my familiar? Is that it?' Lord Sempill said, in a terrible voice. He towered above them then, sober, sharp and scornful. And Hew could see the ghosts of all the desperate men that he had once condemned and sentenced to their deaths, gathered in Colluthie, trembling and perplexed.

'I think, I think,' Colluthie said, 'we may have been misled. But ye will apprehend, there are questions to be answered,' he concluded weakly.

'Aye, there are, indeed,' Sempill said, returning to his normal self. 'There is, first and foremost, our commission in the college, and the question of accounts.'

'I can help you there,' Giles said unexpectedly. 'It is an extraordinary thing. But this morning, our gardener was digging up some radishes, and he found a box.'

He lifted down the box from a shelf behind him and placed it on the board. The four men gathered round. 'It is, as you can see, a thing of great antiquity. And there is no doubt that we will find inside it the ancient college charters.' A hush descended as he opened up the lid, and Hew, who craned behind him to see inside its vaults, saw nothing there but dust.

Colluthie said, 'What? Have we more of your tricks?'

But Sempill said benignly, 'Thank you, Doctor Locke. William, take this down: The Report of The Auld College, on the ninth of May, 1588: "There is no complete inventory of their documents, the provost alleging that Master William Cranston has the great part of the same documents" – you did say that, Doctor Locke? – "and that the rest was put in a kist under the earth and long thereafter found there by chance, but that the documents were altogether consumed therein." That will do nicely, I think.'

'It will not do,' Colluthie said. 'What of the accounts?'

Sempill fixed him with a look. 'Peace, I come to that. Do you have accounts?' He returned to Giles.

'They are not complete.'

'Excellent. Write, "There is no perfect account this nine years bygone." We shall return, Doctor Locke, on the twentieth of May, which will give you time to gather what accounts you have. Hew tells me your economus is ill. Please tell him he is held in my regard. We go now to St Leonard's, in hope they make amendment for their previous faults.' He swept his men before him, with a clear command.

'He is magnificent,' said Hew. 'And yet he holds on by a skin. Do you think it possible that he has got away with it?'

The doctor shook his head. 'It is hard to say. The taint of witchcraft may not ever leave him. Tis difficult to shift. And those who persecute it have long memories. Look at Alison Pearson.'

They were silent for a moment, thinking of a woman who prepared to tell the world of her travels into Faerie land in the hope to save her soul, knowing that her body would be given to the flame.

'Colluthie will be always at his back,' said Hew. 'It is a long ride home.'

Though St Leonard's College did not show up their accounts, Lord Sempill did not seem to be concerned. 'We shall come again, when you are prepared for us,' he said. 'For now, we are done here.'

'We are not done. I wish to see the boy who brought to us the bird,' Colluthie said.

Lord Sempill said, 'I see no need for that,' and Wilkie at the same time answered, 'That will not be possible.'

'That boy,' Colluthie said, 'swore to us he saw this man transformed. He must now account for it.'

'He believed it,' Wilkie said. 'And he meant no malice by it. Now he sees his fault. It was an honest mistake. He is, in truth, a little simple-minded.'

Colluthie leapt at him, picking at his words. 'Simple, do you say? Yet he is a bursar at the university!'

'Indeed. He is here by charity. And charity is the cornerstone of our institution. Your clerk may make a note of that, to put in his report,' Wilkie suggested, with a nod to Soutar, who did not write it down.

Sempill said, 'Quite right. No matter if the bairn believed it. You believed it too.'

'We believed it,' said Colluthie, 'because the bairn telt us he had seen his lordship changing, right before his eyes.'

'Now, then,' Wilkie countered, 'did he tell you so? Did he say that, precisely, in so many words?'

Colluthie hesitated. He appealed to Philip Clench.

'The truth is,' Philip said, 'that none of us remembers exactly what he said. We were caught up in the strength of the moment. We were distracted.'

'Bumbaised,' said Sempill.

'Indeed.'

'Then there is no purpose in demanding of him now what it was he said, since he has retracted it. Let us proceed with the business in hand. We note, Master Wilkie, that you do not have accounts. We give you ten more days in order in prepare them. You gentlemen go on, and I will meet you at the New College. Meanwhile, nature calls.'

Sempill stayed behind, on the pretext of latrines, for a word with Wilkie. The two men, left alone, eyed one another warily, neither knowing what was on the other's mind. In Sempill's case, a hazy recollection, troubling and confused, had begun to filter through; on Wilkie's side, he would prefer it to remain forgotten. 'I do not suppose,' Sempill said, and hesitated, 'someone in your college found a pair of breeks?'

Wilkie fixed on him his smooth and placid face, the one he wore in kirk, to answer him impassively, 'I do not believe so, my lord.'

Lord Sempill left St Leonard's with a vague sense of unease. He came upon some students loitering at the gate, shuffling with some counters he believed were dice. The counters disappeared before he could be sure of it. But one of the four students he recalled by name, and he called him out. 'Young Balfour, is it?'

Henry Balfour bowed in a way that seemed extravagant. 'Aye. Your servant, sir.'

'I trust you have applied yourself since we last did meet. And that your father has impressed on you the merit of hard work.'

'He has done so, my lord.'

'I am glad to hear it. It grieves me to think of a young promise wasted, gone to the bad, in a profligate son. I hope he was severe, and that you were not spared. And yet I see you smile. Are my hopes in vain?'

'They are not, my lord. My father's education is most careful and exact. Forgive the foolish face that causes you offence; it is my natural one.'

'Do you mock me, sir?'

'Not for the world. I take your words to heart.'

'Well, see that you do. Go back to your books, and do not dally here.'

A friend of Henry's whispered, 'You have quite a face, to sport with him like that. Are you not afeart?'

'Nevermore, of him. Someone telt me once that if a great man daunts ye, you should try to see him naked in your head. With Bumbaise, I find it conjures up quite easily.'

His friend was not so sure. 'There is your father, still. He will clype to him.'

Henry found the dice he had hidden up his sleeve and threw them in the air. 'For that,' he said. 'I have a compass. I will not go home.'

Henry Balfour consulted his regent, Robert Black, in the Latin tongue, which had been instilled in him when he was small and tractable, and which he spoke with ease, and a certain charm. 'Suppose,' he said, 'I wanted to excel in my examination. How might it be done?'

'With work,' said Robert Black.

'So had I feared. There is, I must suppose, no more convenient way?'

'No other way at all. But, if you are prepared to put your heart in it, then I am prepared to offer you my help.'

'*Spiritus quidem promptus, caro vero infirma*. The heart is not the trouble, as you see,' Henry sighed. 'Yet I am resolved. Hard work it must be. How will you help?'

'I can hear your practice sometimes after hours.'

'That is kind, indeed. But you must understand – for I would not for the world endeavour to deceive you – at this present time, I cannot pay you for it.'

'Do you imagine,' Robert asked him, 'I do it for my gain?'

'I imagine you do not. Why do you do it, then?'

And Robert found he did not have an answer to the question, so long had he mouldered there, without hope or cause. If there was a purpose in it, he had long forgotten it. He had been a regent for a dozen years, with no ambition to advance to the place of a professor, and as little interest in the outside world.

'My father,' Henry said, 'may reward you handsomely, if I should succeed. Or, there again, he may not. It is hard to tell. There will be, of course, the usual gift of gloves.'

'Gloves are, of course, always welcome,' Robert said. At the last laureation, when seventeen of his students had passed at the black stane, he had been given seventeen pairs.

'I should like,' Henry said, 'to become a magistrand, and to graduate next year, with all kinds of honour, as Master of Arts. Is that likely, do you think?'

'Likely is a word I hesitate to say. Yet it may be possible.'

'Possible is music to my ears. Good Master Robert, you lift up my heart. I am resolved to prove my worth, both to the college and to my father. To show that I am true in my intent, I propose to stay here pending the vacances, and spend the hours in study. I shall board with you.'

'With me?' Robert echoed, baffled at this turn. 'Why would you do that?'

'So that you can steer me to a steady course. My father would approve it. You could write to him.'

'You presume too much. I may have made arrangements. I may depart upon a walking tour. Hew Cullan has told me of a place called Buckstanes, in Derbyshire, where people go to rest and to take the waters. Perhaps I will go there.'

This unlikely proposal failed to impress even Robert himself, and Henry said, sceptical, 'Do you intend to go to that place?'

Robert said, 'Probably not.' The thought of a world beyond the college gates awoke in him the sense of a sick alarm, before he began to consider public baths. 'But why do you wish to stay here through the summer? Do not pretend, I pray you, that it is to learn. A girl, I suppose. When is it ever not?'

'Not just a girl. You must remember what that feeling is.'

Robert Black, no more than five and thirty, answered this aloofly. 'Must I, indeed? Shall I tell you the last time I was in love? At no time at all.'

Henry thought this one of the most tragic stories he had ever heard. 'Your pardon, sir, if I have offended you. I had no right to ask.'

His petition touched a chord. Robert told him, 'Not at all. And if I am not absent during the vacation – I think we may presume that I will not be absent – you may board with me, providing that you work. I will write to your father. When shall I tell him the arrangement will begin?'

'At Lammas,' Henry said, owning to it cheerfully, 'for I have promised Mary I will take her to the fair.'

POSTSCRIPT

Visitatioun of the Colleges of Sanctandrois Anno 1588

The Second Visitatioun of the Universite of Sanctandrois, be Commissioners appointit be his Majestie 9 Maij 1588

Report of the New College
In the New College thair was na comptis perfyttit, nor copeis reddy to be schawin to the counsall, becaus, as the Maisteris allegit, Mr David Auchmutie, Iconomus, had maid nane.

Report of Sanct Leonardis
They refuse to deliver the copie of the inventor of thair evidentis upoun suspitioun, becaus thair land is not fewit.

Report of the Auld College
Imprimis, Thair na inventair of thair evidentis perfyttit. The Provest allegeand, that Mr. William Cranstoun hes ane greit part of the saidis evidentis. And that the rest was put in ane kist under the erth, and thairefter found be chance, but that the evidentis was altogidder consumed thairin.

Thair is na perfytit compt this nyne yeiris bygane.

(Extract from Report of Visitation to St Andrews University in 1588, published as Appendix to Great Britain Commission for Visiting the Universities and Colleges of Scotland: University of St Andrews. Printed by W. Clowes and Sons for H.M. Stationery Office, 1837. Curiously, Lord Sempill's name is absent from the source. We can only suppose that the record was buried.)

BOOK III

Lammas

And if thou wilt but come vnto our greene,
on Lammas day when as we haue our feast,
Thou shalt sit next vnto our summer Queene,
and thou shalt be the onely welcome guest.

MICHAEL DRAYTON, *The Shepheards Garland*, 1593

AUGUST 1

I

Elspet left the sweepings for the tide to take out. There were ships, three or four, coming to the fair. 'Look out for Spaniards,' Sliddershanks had said, and she could not help but glance across the bay, though she did not really think the fleet would come. It was just his play.

She had belonged to Sliddershanks – she looked on it like that – for almost six years now. She had been fifteen, in service to Maude Benet at the harbour inn, when they first had met. She had woken in her bed one cruel December night to find that Maude had gone, with her daftie daughter and the cat. The lass who worked beside her had not lingered long. 'I have expectations, d'ye see?'

Elspet herself had had no expectations, no other refuge or friends. She had stayed for three days alone at the inn, and when the sailors came to drink she had telt them bluntly that the house was closed, stopping up the doors and her ears against their oaths, mindful that Maude Benet would not let them curse. She had swept the floors and scrubbed the stools and boards, and, when a mouse appeared, caught it in a trap and left the carcase out as a warning to the rest. She had made pottage and broth with the pulled roots and herbs in the kitchen, and bread from the barley and oats. She had returned to the loft, to her old sleeping place, when the sun had set and had woken again as it rose. On the fourth day, Sliddershanks had come, with a paper from the council, forcing her to open up the locks. He had told her that his name was Walter Bone – though in her head she thought of him as Sliddershanks, for he was slow and crippled in his legs – and he was now the owner of the harbour inn.

Sliddershanks had looked her up and down. 'Whit age are ye? Ten?'

She had telt him, indignant, 'I am not ten.'

'No? An uncomely twattle, are ye no?'

'A twattle?' she had said.

'A mimmerkin. A dwarf.'

'I am not a dwarf.'

Maude Benet had been stern. Sometimes even sharp. But she had not called folk names. Elspet had telt him, as Maude would have done. And he had laughed at her.

'Ye are a hichty wee quean. But ye will not do here. Ye are the wrang sort.'

She had asked him, 'What is my sort?'

'A pin-hippit runt. Not the sort that men like, that will bring in the drinkers. That has something to hing to, up here, and an arse.' He had placed his hands on the offending parts, and told her in a way that was kinder than his words, 'Flat as a board. Now if ye were a wean, the chance is ye wid sprout. But sin ye are full grown, there is little hope. What man wid want you?'

'Oh,' she had said. 'What will I do, then?'

'Have you nowhere to go? No family?'

Elspet had shaken her head. Maude and the daftie she had thought were her family. Now they had left her alone. It was not strictly true. Maude Benet had remembered, when she went to flit, that Elspet had a mammie living still at Crail. Mebbe she forgot she had a faither too, and what that father did. She would not go to them.

Sliddershanks, with his withered smile and his crooked bones, had not looked like a man who was heavy with his fists. He had looked around him, taking in the room that was swept and scrubbed, the savour of the broth and the carcase of the mouse, and he had nodded. 'Well. Stay, if ye will. But keep out from the tap. That ploukie-facit mow of yours is sure to sour the ale.'

His name for her was Mimmerkin. And she returned his taunts. The first day she had dared to use his name of Sliddershanks he had turned to gawp at her, and she had been feart that she had gone too far. Then his crooked face had split into a smile. 'You are an impudent quean.'

She was not bonny, he telt her. No man would want her. But he had been wrong about that.

Sliddershanks did not allow her to mix with the men. For that, he brought in the sort of lass he liked, buxom and broad-hipped. All of them, he telt her, were comelier than she. Only when the inn was full, and the heaving bosoms buckled at the strain, would he let her go out with a cup or tray. 'The hope is that the drinkers do not spy you in the crush, foulsum as ye are. The help is you are slight enough to slip among a crowd.'

'More help than you are, with your futless leg.'

'I had a foot once,' he said.

She gave him as good as she got. But sometimes in the night, when she was in her bed, she felt beneath the sheet her slender hips and thighs, the sweet bud of her breasts, and wondered if she was so foul that she could not be loved.

By day, she kept the house. And when the drinkers came she sent out broth and bannock, herrings, bread and cheese from the kitchen larder she now thought of as her own. The lassies in the front room she saw come and go, Alys and Isobel, Jonet and Em. All were of a kind, and none of them stayed long. Some went off with sailors who had come across the sea. Some of them were married. Some of them went wrong. She saw Jonet on a Sunday, stripped down to her shirt, weeping at the kirk. They had cut her hair. Not long after that, a council from the kirk had come to talk to Sliddershanks. The minister himself was there – for that was before he was taken at the plague – and Elspet had heard his censure, strenuous and stern. Sliddershanks had called her in, and she had been afraid.

'This is Elspet Bell,' Sliddershanks had said, 'who has worked for me since the day I came. She lives in this house. There is nothing here that she does not ken. Ask her what she sees that is not clean or seemly.'

The four men from the kirk had seemed to be discomfited. It had seemed to Elspet that they did not like to look at her. Perhaps it was her kirtle they found unbecoming, or they were offended at the plainness of her face. Was she yet so foul, they could not meet her gaze?

The minister had cleared his throat. 'I know Elspet well. She is a communicant of conscience in the kirk. A guid kind of girl,' he had telt them.

Encouraged, she had looked at him. But he had not looked back. 'I have to ask you, Elspet, if you have been privy to uncleanness in this house.'

'I keep the house clean,' she had said.

'I can see that you do. That is not what I meant. Have you been attendant, while men have conversed?'

'I do not listen, sir.'

'I refer to converse of the carnal kind.'

And she had answered, 'Oh. I have heard of that. But only at the kirk. I have not seen it done.'

'You are a fine lass,' Sliddershanks had said, once the men had left. 'Foul in the face, but fine none the less. I have a mind to marry you.'

He had not seemed, at that moment, to intend a jest, and Elspet for her part was not displeased with him. Sliddershanks was old – forty if a day – and with his ravaged body was unlikely to live long. She, at that time, had just turned seventeen. She could see a day when she would be like Maude, hostess and proprietor of the harbour inn, and hoped for it to come. But Sliddershanks had married someone else. He had chosen for his bride the kind of lass he liked – Maggie from the inn – the plumpest and most fetching of the slutherouns. 'She trapped him,' the others had said, and Elspet had not understood. She had pictured Sliddershanks, clamped in Maggie's thighs.

And that was not far from the truth. For they were not married a month when Maggie gave birth to a child, a lusty bawling boy. The infant had been given up to Elspet to look after, and she had not liked it much. It was red and round, all of it of Maggie, nought of Sliddershanks. She had not been sorry when the bairn and mother both were sent away, to escape the plague. She had not been very sorry when they died.

The plague had been bad, and a good year for her. The harbour had been closed, but she had stayed with Sliddershanks when the rest were gone. And they had come accustomed to each other's ways. Their words were not kinder, or fonder. They had not had between them enough to eat and drink, and Elspet had grown thinner, Sliddershanks more frail; he had not spared to tell her quite how ill she looked. He grieved his wife and bairn. Yet they had been content enough to keep each other company.

If he had asked her then to marry him, she thought, she would have accepted, not to have the inn, but for the sake of Sliddershanks, for him. He had not asked again. Maggie Mauchlin's vice had squeezed out all his marrying, and none of it was left.

That, she thought, was then. Things were different now. She was twenty-one. Far too old, said Sliddershanks, for any man to want her. 'You are a guid lass. But ugly as sin.' But Sliddershanks was wrong. And he had told a lie to her that she could not forgive.

Michael was a labourer, who had come at seedtime. When the seeds were planted, he had gone away. And Elspet had believed her hope of him was gone. Sometimes she believed that he had not been real. That she had thought him up. But she did not forget. How could she forget, when he was in the ale?

Elspet hugged herself. Sliddershanks would say that she had lost her mind. But Sliddershanks told lies. She must not think of him.

At seedtime, he had waited for her outside at the pier, where she poured the slops. She had heard her name, and took it for the gulls, mewling in the froth. But then she had seen that it was a man, with fair tousled hair like tufts of ripe corn and a face coloured dark from the sun.

Elspet had asked him, 'How do you ken me?'

'You are the girl from the inn. Will you fetch me a drink?' Michael had said. Though she had not kent he was Michael then.

She had shaken her head. 'I canna. We are closed.'

'Oh, but I am thirsty, Elspet Bell.'

She had fallen for him then, right at those words, as though the saying of her name had cast a kind of spell. But she had not liked to show it. 'You should have come before.'

Michael had telt her, 'I did. I was turned away. The landlord said I'd rue it if I ever came again.'

'That does not sound like him. Why would he do that?'

'Because I asked your name. Because I never saw another lass as lovely. And when he would not tell me, I asked your friend Marie.'

Elspet had answered with 'Oh'. She did not like it that Marie had a part to play. If she had made it up – and sometimes she believed that she had made it up – that part would be left out.

'Your master must be fond of you, to keep you to himself.' He had winked at her.

Elspet had felt a flood of confusion. 'Mebbe,' she had said, 'I could fetch a drink for you. Just one.'

When she had returned to the inn, Sliddershanks had gone already to his bed. Elspet had been thankful not to face him then. She had poured the ale and taken it outside. She had half expected Michael to have gone. She thought she had imagined him. But he was waiting still. He had drunk the ale in a single draught. He had been as thirsty as he said. When the drink was done, he had bent and kissed her, covering her mouth with a spray of foam that was bitter-sweet and frothy in its breath.

Marie had been waiting when she took the cup back. She sensed
that Marie knew, and could not look at her. She could hardly
speak. She was trembling with such violence that she feared to
waken Sliddershanks, shaken from his sleep. Her teeth were
chattering too. Yet when Marie asked her why she had the cup
she answered her quite easily. 'One of the fishermen left it outside.
I was bringin it in.' The lie had astonished her, but no more than
the truth. Michael had been planted, sprung up like a seed.

Marie was not fooled. 'Oh, aye?' she had said. 'You had
better mind that he does not find out.'

Michael made a promise that he would return for her when
the harvest came. She had not believed it then. She did not tell
Marie. But Michael kept his word. He came on Lammas eve, to
find her by the pier and claim her for his own. She would be his
sweetheart at the Lammas fair. Lammas was today. And Elspet
kept her secret close and safe from Sliddershanks, knowing that
her friend would not be welcome here. Michael had been kind
to him. 'You cannot blame a man that wants ye for himself.' Yet
that could not be right. For Sliddershanks, she knew, had never
wanted her.

II

The colleges were closed on Lammas day. For Hew Cullan of
St Salvator's, the start of the vacation came as a relief. The last
days of the term had been stormy ones. Giles Locke had spent
the dog days of July – canicular, he called them – bearding the
apocalypse. According to the compass of the ancient almanacs,
the world was set to end in 1588. Giles had proved them
wrong, with endless sheets of sums and logic so abstruse that it
had baffled Hew. The storms were summer squalls, with fairer
winds on course for 1589.

Hew was pleased to hear it. 'I have planted trees, and would be annoyed if the world should end before the grove is grown.'

'The world is good,' said Giles, 'for a few years yet.'

The lightness of their words concealed a present threat, which Hew took very seriously indeed. There were wild reports that the Spanish army had landed on the coast, and the town was placed on perpetual alert. Giles had drawn a chart of the British Isles, on which he marked the progress of the Spanish fleet. The Spanish made no secret of their ships; rather, they had leaked their lists and inventories, the powder kegs and armoury of thirty thousand men, the ripple of their forces gripping at the sea. The lists had been enhanced with varying accounts of the types of torture that were taught on board, with their end effects. The students were distraught. Their spare hours were wrung out in practice at the butts, where their summer contests ceased to be a sport, and they sparred and squabbled over the results. Some were eager to be out and fighting for their faith, frustrated at the college that had penned them in. Others were afraid, and spent their days in prayer, fearful that a way of life to which they were attuned might soon become unstrung, their brittle futures plucked from them before they were begun. Most were ill and fretful by the end of term.

Giles had marked on his map the place in Flanders where the fleet had mustered, following its course into the English Channel. Hew remarked his interest with a deep unease. The Spanish had, officially, no quarrel with the Scots. But if England were occupied, and her queen overthrown, how likely was it then the Scottish king would treat with them, to gain the English throne? Or, if he did not, would join her fight with them, and sacrifice his people to the English cause? Nor was the Spanish army like to rest content while there were reformers on adjacent shores. The king in betwixt them, to serve his own ends, could scarcely stay neutral for long. There were open spies, willing to assist the Spanish in their aim, and though the king had taken measures to deter them, some had found his efforts feeble and lukewarm.

Hew, who had witnessed at first hand the devastation caused by Spanish troops abroad, did not underestimate the truth of the reports. He consulted with the spy and soldier Robert Lachlan how they should prepare themselves for the event of war. They had served together in the Netherlands. The substance of their talks he kept secret from his wife, for he had no wish to add to her alarm. For his sister and her husband he reserved a cool discretion, hiding from them both the matter in his mind. For sometimes, when he came into the tower where Giles was at his work, he saw his old friend start, and cover up his charts. Nowhere in his heart did Hew believe his friend – a Catholic through and through – colluded with the fleet, or opened up the passage for the Spanish force. Indeed, he was aware that such suspicions pandered to the enemy, opened up a door by driving through divisions in his native land. Still, he used a trick that he had learned from Walsingham, placing all his trust upon a single man, so that if a man betrayed him, he knew who it was. That one man, for now, would not be Giles Locke.

With so much to distract him, he was glad enough when the term was done. On Lammas eve, he sat with Robert, making lists of arms and working out a course of action late into the night. They resolved to go together to the fair, not for any pleasure of their own, but to hire a sturdy band of men, ostensibly for working on the land, but secretly to form a fighting force. Such was Hew's intention when he went to bed. He found he could not rest, but lay alert and fretting through the early hours. At last, he fell asleep, and when he next awoke the day was well advanced, heavy with a squalid, listless kind of heat. When he called for water, Frances came.

'Were you up with Giles last night? You were very late.'

'Robert,' Hew replied.

'Bella did not say.' Frances was surprised. 'She said that you and Robert would be going to the fair, to look for hiring men.

But since you slept so late, he has gone ahead. He will meet you there, and I will come with you.'

'You?' Hew's wits were not awoken yet. 'Why would you do that?'

'How strange you are today. Wherefore would I not? I want to call on Meg. There are certain matters I want to discuss with her, and some things I need to buy.'

'Lammas is no place for you. Tis filthy, loud and lewd. You will not like it there,' Hew said.

She fixed him with a look. 'Do you suppose I have not been to fairs at Leadenhall?'

'That is what I mean,' he countered desperately. 'It is not like London. It will disappoint you. There are no good stalls.'

Frances was intent, and would not let it lie. 'How will it be different from the other fairs? I have been to those.'

'Because the town is different now. The colleges are closed. Lammas is the harvest fair, for those who work the land.' It was, he recognised, the worst thing he could say. For Frances was involved as closely in the land as he was in the law and the university. She kept a close surveillance over his estates.

The paradox had not escaped her. 'And when were you so bound up in the land you oversaw yourself the hiring of your hands? Robert Lachlan might. But you? What are you about? Bella says it is a coupling fair.'

'You cannot think—' said Hew.

'What am I to think, when you will not say? I do not like it when you are so shifting, Hew. Do not look so stricken, for I know full well what it is you do. There is one reason only why you look to Robert Lachlan, and it is not for the wenches or the drinking games. Robert is a fighting man, and we are at war.'

'You have seen my mind. But we are not at war. I seek but to defend against that possibility. I did not want to frighten you,' he said.

'You cannot frighten me by telling me the truth. My country is at war, in peril as we stand. I feel it all the time.'

'Forgive me, then. I did not think.'

'No,' Frances said. 'You did think. You have been thinking of us, while I was thinking of them. Tis like you.'

'Does Bella ken too?'

'Bella does not ken. She does not know Robert quite as well as I know you.'

'Perhaps she does,' said Hew.

Frances kissed him fondly. 'Ah, perhaps she does. Now you must wash and dress, and come with me to Meg's; I cannot go alone, and I must speak with her.'

'Why today?' asked Hew.

'You should know that women have their secrets too.'

As soon as he was dressed, they set out to walk together to the town. His spirits lifted then, to see the carts and crowds in all their coloured finery, the fields of ripening corn that lined the country way. Hew felt like a boy again, with his English bride, among the lads and lasses in their play day clothes. They left the infant Flora home with Bella Frew, who had told them that she felt her coupling days were done. 'And if ye see that man of mine, up to his old tricks, tell him that his coupling will be over too.' Hew, for all her fears, doubted Rob would stray. For though he was red-blooded with a belly fu', he was milk-and-wattir when it came to Bella.

III

There were four strangers staying at the inn, come for the fair. One was a chapman, with a great pack full of trinkets and toys. Two of them were tumblers, young Egyptian brothers, who could walk on ropes and stilts that made them giants, tottering and tall. The last was a juglar, expert in legerdemain. Marie liked the juglar best. He had cut an apple open with a knife, and placed the cut side down upon the board, where it had spun round without any touch; the drinkers marvelled at it.

For Marie, he had turned the apple on its back, showing the black beetle that was trapped inside. He had shown no one else. At first she had thought that he had found it in his bed, and was making a complaint. The beds were none too clean, though Marie shook them out. The tumbling brothers shared, and as she imagined, woke up from their dreams tangled in the sheets, while the juglar had been quartered with the chapman and his wares. But the juglar had not come to complain. He showed her a box where he kept the beetle and a little frog, and clinging to the lid, no bigger than a mouse, a creeping blind-eyed bat. He showed her a goose egg blown and sucked out, and put the bat inside, curled up in its wings. Then he covered up the place where the shell was cracked with paper and paste, smoothing it out until the crack was gone, and no one would guess that there had been a hole. He had given her the mended egg to hold. And she had felt it solid in her hand. Its weight was anchored still, as though the yellow yolk was still inside its bowl, and Marie had wondered if the bat was dead. The juglar had told her that it was asleep. When it was dusk, the bat would wake up, and the egg would fly up in the air. Probably. It was a trick that did not always work.

There were other marvels that he would not show her, saying she must come and see them for herself. He had taught her a trick, and he asked her to show her secrets in return, giving her a shiny English shilling on account.

She let him have a kiss, promising her secrets if the egg should fly. She did not think it would. When he first arrived, he had had a boy with him, enchanted with a charm. The boy had gone *bow wow*, running on all fours, like a little dog, and everyone had laughed. He had done a dance, and when the juglar telt him to take off his clothes he had stripped them off, right down to his hose. But when he was telt to take them off too, he took it in great snuff, bursting into tears. He said that if his pintle must be bared for all to see, he would want to have another half a crown. The crowd had roared at that. The juglar then was sad, though she did not see why. When the morning came, the juglar's boy was gone. 'He was my confederate,' he confided in her. Marie liked the word. 'But he was nae good.'

She had served the men breakfast early that morning, of bannock and butter and ale. All four of them were going to the fair. And Marie wanted badly to be going too. The shilling she had won was squirrelled in her purse. But Walter had determined it was not to be. He had made Joan and Marie draw a straw to see which one of them should go, and it was Joan who won. Elspet had leave to go out as well. She did not even have to pick one of the straws.

Marie said, 'It's no fair. You always favour her.'

'Ach,' Walter said, 'Elspet is no use to us on a day like this. Her face is so sour it turns men awa'. The drinkers want a bonny one, like yours.'

He always spoke like that, no word of truth in it, and Marie was put out.

'You are a fool for her,' she said. 'Ye widnae be so fond if ye *kent*.'

She had the devil in her then. For Elspet's sake, she ought to haud her tongue. But she felt in her throat a kernel of spite, a tight angry knot she could not swallow down. Venting it afforded her a vicious kind of pride. 'Oh, you think her chastely. I tell you, she is not. She is flesh, like us. And the first lusty laddie comes laiking with her, she is up and efter in the twinkling of an ee.'

'Aye? What lad is that?' He humoured her. Marie saw he did. He thought that Elspet, precious as she was, kept no secret from him. He took her for his own. Marie thought the spark between them an uncanny thing; they were like brother and sister, twin scrapping bairns, or a husband and wife, who long ago had lost all front before the other, mellowed to a comfort that was closed to her. Marie would not dare to flyte with him like that. She was jealous of the favour Elspet had from him, swaddled as it was in a loose contempt; their casual warmth of humour made her feel shut out, excluded from the jest.

'He came at the seedtime, and now he has come back. His lustrous blue een and bright yellow hair have spun sic a charm upon your ain pet lass that it will be seedtime, for sure. Elspet is ripe. He is reaping her now, at the fair.'

She stopped then, aware that she went too far. The hard little knot that gathered in her mouth was suddenly undone, at the pricking of remorse. Yet the words were said; she could not take them back. Walter said nothing at all. And the longer he went without making reply, the more ashamed she felt. Finally, she challenged him. 'Have ye nought to say?'

'You have a foulsum tongue,' was all he said, and mild, as though he did not mind. Perhaps, after all, he kenned it all along; it was a part of the game that they played.

She told herself that, consoling her conscience, a sharp little thing that was pointed and sore. She liked Elspet too, did she not?

Walter worked on for an hour, drawing up the barrels from the cellar down below, preparing for the influx later on that day. At the close of the fair, the business would transfer to the inns and taverns, and, if the night stayed dry, spill out on the sands and the harbour shore. The merchants from the market would be ready for their drink. The house was quiet in the meantime; one or two stray creel men, who had sold their crabs, came to slake their thirst; most fishermen were absent, with the herring fleet. Noon trade would be slow, for people took their dinner at the fair. By twelve o'clock, the place was bare, but for one old man, too old and deaf to traffic with the crowd, who drank his solitary pint on a stool outside, sipping in the quiet of an August sun.

Walter Bone took off his apron. 'I maun go out for a while.'

'Where will ye go?' Marie asked, alarmed.

'I have rin out o physic I take for my back. It is hurting me sair.'

It was true enough that he did not look well. He had shifted half a dozen kegs that day, and the crates of wine. It was easy to forget that Walter was not strong. He rarely made complaint of it. 'I can go,' she said.

Walter shook his head. He saw through her tricks. The disappointment soured her. 'Ye will not leave me here, to labour on ma ain? Suppose there is a crowd?'

She knew as well as he did that there would not be a crowd, until four or five. But it took her by surprise when Walter Bone replied, 'Give poor Geordie there another stoup of ale, and ye may go till four. Close the door when ye gang. I will be back in an hour.'

She could not believe her good fortune. 'Go to the fair?'

'Did I not say so? Here.' He gave her two bright pennies from the counter cash box. 'Buy a wee treat to yerself.'

It was her due, was it not? The money no more than her worth. Her pleasure in the fee eclipsed all sense of guilt. Marie smiled at Geordie as she filled his cup.

Walter Bone made his way up Kirk Heugh. He did not go at once to the house on the South Street where the woman was who made up his pills. She might be at the fair. He hoped that she was not. He might find her at the market close to the apothecar, stocking up on spices, sugarloaf and herbs. He would not purchase physic she did not prescribe; he trusted her. The medicines she distilled for the torment in his bones brought him some relief. They could not yet dispel the underlying cause. Relief was transitory. And, when it returned, the hurt was sharper, crueller than before. He had not telt a lie to Marie about the pain. But for Elspet, he could have borne it, he thought. He could have borne much more.

It strained him to walk up the hill. The market was in full thrang, in the mercat place. But at the west sands, by the golf links, there were sports and games, and races on the shore, while the tide was low. In mid-water, there were horses chasing through the spray. And up at the butts were archery contests, for young boys and men in all stages of life. Walter Bone had never taken part. The gripping in his banes had afflicted him since childhood. Yet he was a sharp man, no less; it had not afflicted his mind.

IV

Henry Balfour too was going to the fair. He had left his college at the end of term, and moved across the street with the regent Robert Black. He looked forward to a summer of adventure and excess. If the Spanish came, he would take up arms, and place himself where practical upon the winning side. Meanwhile he would ride and spend time with his lass. The future augured well, despite prognostications that the world would end. Breakfast had been served. Henry had an egg, herrings and a cheese, while Robert's interest in his bread and ale was watered by the tone of the letter in his hand, which he read aloud with increasing gloom. 'Your father's word is clear. And though I find the manner of it somewhat strict and strained, I cannot in good conscience let you go against it, while you are in my care,' he said.

Henry took advantage of his tutor's loss of appetite to relieve him of the best part of his bread. He was not at all dismayed by the thunder of a father who was far away, when he had a summer's day in hand. He pointed out simply, 'He does not prohibit the fair.'

'Not,' conceded Robert, 'in so many words.'

'When there *are* so many words, you can be quite certain that his silence is assent.'

Robert hesitated. He suspected Henry's father would make short work of that argument. 'Does he even ken there is a fair today?'

Henry said, 'He has sent a present of a bow. At Lammas there are always contests at the butts. Therefore he must mean that I should try it there. I am sure to win.'

The bow was a reward for passing the black stane, where Henry had received, on his third attempt, his bachelor's degree. Henry had shown promise through the years in archery, the only distraction which his parent had approved. And it was more than likely he would take the prize.

'Well, you may go,' Robert Black agreed, 'if you give your word to me that you will not converse or meddle with your lass in any secret place. Though she is free and willing, please remember this. Your father will not furnish you a fart for buttock-mail.' Lord Balfour knew his son, perhaps a little better than his son knew him, and a full page of his letter was devoted to a case which, should it arise, would not be well received.

'I noticed he said that,' Henry took a pat of butter on his knife, and smeared in on the bread, 'and wondered what he meant. What is buttock-mail? Is it like a flankart, armour for the arse?'

'It is the penalty you pay for the sin of fornication, as no doubt you ken,' Robert answered grimly. 'The wages of sin. But that is futling in respect of the cost to you, if you are found out. Your father will disown you, and the college too. It will be the ruin of you, and me as well, no doubt. I make no mention of the lass, for her welfare must fall to your conscience, as yours does to mine.'

Henry had not looked for, and had not expected, so severe a lecture on the first day of his holiday, and Robert was encouraged when he looked a bit abashed. Less so, when he said, 'Oh, but we are careful.'

'Careful not to sin, or that you are not caught?'

Henry answered vaguely, 'Aye, for certain, that.'

'To that end,' Robert said, 'come back here by nine. I will not have you prey to the evils of the night. Otherwise, you have my blessing and my trust.'

'I thank you for your kindness, sir. I will keep your trust,' Henry said.

He showed he had a gentle heart, and Robert Black was pleased, for he believed that with a steady hand, Henry would be set upon a constant path, naturally inclined to follow what was right. The father was at fault. Savage yet indulgent, both severe and lax, he had set a course designed to ruin the boy.

Henry, nothing daunted, went to meet his lass. His converse with her secret place was fairly well advanced, a fluency which he thought wise to hide from Robert Black. But he supposed that Robert meant they should not leave the crowd.

Dozens of young men were gathered in the market place, looking for employment from the factors and the farmers who judged them on experience, provenance and strength. Bargains were made quickly, and were sealed with drink, before the chosen ones took their pick themselves of the giggling lassies waiting in the ranks. Henry found the company, of country lads and lasses let loose from their bounds, a rough and rowdy one. He looked for Mary through the crowd, and found her with her baskets by the butter tron. Beside her was a woman who was full with child, and a little boy with a filthy face. Mary caught his eye, and left the woman's side, taking up the small boy by the hand. Henry sensed a straining in her smile. Perhaps she felt, like him, uneasy at the herd. She did not offer up a kiss. Instead she whispered to him, 'What have ye got on?'

'Do you like it?' Henry said. Mary had not seen him out of scholar's weeds. He had dressed that morning in a dark green hunting coat his father had sent up. It was made of fair fine cloth, and cut to flatter him, with a trail of ivy quilted in the sleeve. Lord Balfour had devoted far more thought to choosing it than Henry had that morning when he put it on. The king would be at Falkland for the summer months, and Henry might be called upon to join him at the hunt. The colour of the coat would show off his dark looks, with no thread of gold to cause the king offence. Then Henry might look forward to a place at court. They were close in age.

Though Henry was aware of his father's hopes, he did not care for them. He lived for the day, and took chance where it came. The moment was the fair, and he wore the coat because the cut allowed him to move freely with his bow. He thought it good but plain. It perplexed him to find Mary fingering the cuff, tracing with her fingers through the fine relief, as though she had not come across such delicate embroidery. 'It's awfy fine,' she answered him, uncertainly.

'Fine it is,' he said. 'But who is this?' He gestured to the bairn, a squat, stolid child, who stared back, unsmiling.

'This is wee Jock, my sister's boy. Big Jock is my daddie,' Mary said.

The naming of Big Jock caused Henry some alarm. Mary had not mentioned him by name before. He wondered, fleetingly, just how big he was. 'Has your father come here to the fair?' he asked.

Mary shook her head. 'He disnae like to, since my mother died. It was here they met.'

Henry answered, 'Oh,' conscious his relief ought not to be expressed. There were complications here he had not met before, and he felt, for the moment, out of his depth.

'Jockie has been hoping he will see the puppet play.'

Mary's meaning dawned on Henry, showing in his face. She anticipated quickly, 'Tis only for a while, until the eggs are gone. They're sure to sell today. My sister had been guid enough to take the stand till then.'

Henry glanced back at the sister by the butter tron. The eyes she returned to him were shadowed and unfriendly. Mary's sister served her as both mother and a friend. She had taught her all that Mary knew of men. Which was quite a lot. Henry was obliged to her. Yet he found no warmth of welcome in her face. He could easily have bought the whole stock of her eggs, freeing her to see the puppets with her son. The thought occurred at once, and he almost acted on it. Good sense held him back. For it would have seemed that he was buying Mary, and he would not for the world have it look like that. The eggs he had no want of would be left to lie, snatched up by the gulls or splattered at the stocks. For Mary and her hens, they were of some worth, and Henry did not care to cheapen her, or them. And so he took the bairn on with a gracious nod, to trail them in their pleasures like a spectre at the feast.

There were no puppet players at the fair that day. But Jockie saw a monkey in a velvet coat, and two Egyptian tumblers burling over hoops. He saw a juglar slice off his own nose and restore it whole again. Henry had once seen a pickpocket cropped of his nose at the cross, with a less happy result, and did not find the magic quite so entertaining. He yawned when the juglar brought out yards of silk, in every rainbow colour, streaming from his mouth, and when he fished a groat out of Jockie's ear. Jockie gulped and gawped, but did not speak a word.

'Can the bairn not talk?' Henry asked.

'He is five years old. Of course he can,' Mary said.

Jock was like no bairn that Henry was acquainted with, of the gentle sort. His flat, sullen face, like the face of the monkey he had prodded with a stick, had the fixed expression of a hardened labourer. Nothing could effect in him a movement of excitement. He was gloomy as a butcher at the start of Lent. Henry bought a whistle for him, and some sooking candy twisted in a poke. Jockie sucked on both, adamantly grim.

The fair was sweaty, foul and raucous. Henry smelt around him the ripeness of the crowd, rancid flesh and fish blackened over coals, sickly fruits and sweetmeats curdled in the sun. The shows were surrounded by stalls, spilling from the market square to the wynds and lanes and further to the South Street. A ballad singer sang a song against the Pope, pleasing to the kirk in whose yard he stood. The fiddle and the drums and the pipes were played. Chapmen cried their wares: ribbons, tinsels, lace. Mary paused to look.

'Let me buy you something. Ribands, or a handkerchief. A hat,' Henry said, uncertain what might please her, in amongst the trash.

Mary shook her head.

'Well then, a book.'

Mary hesitated. She liked to hear him read to her, for she had not had the chance to learn to read herself. His voice was fine, and grand, she said. It was part of the pattern of the nights they spent together. She asked him to speak Latin once, but Henry had refused. He had enough of that at the university. She had wanted to attend his last examinations, to cheer him in the schools. 'If they are public, why can't I?'

'Because you are a lass,' Henry had explained. He found a stall with books and pamphlets. 'Here is one for you. *A Thousand Things of Note*.' To last a thousand nights, he thought, a thousand conversations, written in the sheets.

'A thousand,' Mary said, 'sounds an awfy lot.'

'Not near enough, for you.' He bought the book and gave it to her, as the piper in the square broke off, announcing that the games on the sands would soon begin. 'Now I will try my bow, and win you a prize.'

Coming to the links in a fresh sea breeze Henry felt relaxed and once more in his element. He had shot and hunted since he was a child, on horseback and on foot, and had long refined and tuned his natural skill. He was sure and strong, both in hand and foot. The targets where he practised each week during term were bairns' play to him. He could spear a bird or a sprinting hind, delicate in flight. The farmhands and cowherds, surpassing him in strength, wanted his finesse, the sureness of his eye, his cool and steady hand, his confidence and nerve. It did not exercise him to secure the prize. He had it closed in sight, when a voice behind him said, 'A braw bow, is that. '

Henry straightened up, and turned to face his foe. He saw a fair young man, older by some years and taller than himself, glaring at his back. He answered pleasantly. 'Aye, indeed it is.'

'Awbody might win, wi a bow like that,' the challenger complained.

'Would you like to try?' Henry smiled at him. He offered up the bow in his gracious hand. 'Three shots at the papingo. Whoever hits the eye, he shall take the prize.'

The other man backed off. 'The contest isnae fair, for you are used to it.'

'Then you shall have your pick, and I will take my chance with any bow you like.' Henry looked around. The course was well equipped with racks of common bows, for anyone to use who had not brought his own. Henry was accustomed to the college armoury, and could well adapt. His own bow, on the other hand, had been made for him, and worked to best advantage solely in his hands. When he picked it up, he blessed his father's gift, and was overcome with filial love and sympathy. There could be no way to make this contest fair, as his opponent knew. For Henry had the privilege of birth.

His opponent's pride was spared by the lass beside him, clutching at his sleeve. 'Michael, will you come? We are going to miss the races on the shore. You promised you would run for me.'

'Aye, my love, I will. You shall have a ribbon for to pin upon your sleeve. Will you come race, then?' Michael asked Henry.

Henry said grandly, 'With my horse, gladly; by no means on foot.' He collected his prize, of a silver pin, and gave it to his lass. But he was disappointed when she passed it to the bairn.

'Who was that?' she asked.

'Some presumptuous loun, who thought to snatch your prize. I have seen the lassie at the harbour inn. I do not ken her name.'

Mary pulled a face. 'At the harbour inn? Why do you go there? It is a filthsum place. No better than a bordal-house, so my sister says.'

Henry said, 'I don't. I went once last year, to play a game of dice. The company was low. I did not go again. But I'm sure I saw her there. She has the sort of face a man does not forget.'

Mary snorted, 'Face. For sure it was her face.'

'Do not be that like. You know that I have eyes for no one else but you. I only caught a glimpse of her.'

'You were lucky then, if that was all you caught.'

He liked that she was jealous. He had felt her cooling to him, on this summer's day. He yearned to be alone with her, in some secret spot. 'This bairn must want his mother now,' he said. 'And you and I shall find a place quiet from the crowd.'

Mary nodded. 'Aye, we should.' Her answer gave him hope. They took her nephew back to his mother at the tron. All the eggs were sold. Mary spoke a word, and listened, to her sister. Henry heard her promise her, 'I will not be long.' The sister glanced at Henry, heavy with mistrust. Jockie's hands were sticky, and she wiped them on her skirt.

'Succar candie,' Henry said. 'If his teeth are rotten, I have several cures.' She did not meet his smile.

'Where will we go?' Mary asked. 'Not to the inn, at this hour?'

'Walk with me,' said Henry. 'I know of a place.'

He took her by the hand, landward through the South Street to St Leonard's fields.

'Suppose someone sees us?' she said.

'It belongs to the college. But the college is closed up, and the principal away. There is no one but the farmer and the tenants of the land. And all of them are absent at the Lammas fair. Come, lie down with me. No one can see us in amongst the rigs.'

They were in a barley field, a shiver of green stalks that shimmered in the sun. Henry spread his coat between the rows of corn. 'Lie with me,' he said.

'I cannot,' Mary said. 'I have not come prepared.'

There were herbs she used, and pessaries of wax. Henry did not know how it was she came by them, and had never asked. It fell to a woman not to get with child. Some women chose to snare a man, and caught him in a trap. But Henry knew that Mary was not of that sort.

He lay down on his back and looked up at the sky. Mary sat beside him.

'Lie with me awhile,' he said. 'For there are other ways. I can show restraint.'

She laughed at that. 'You? You never can.'

It was true enough. He rolled on to his front to disguise it from her. 'I will read to you. From the notable things. One fact for a kiss. Four facts for a—'

'You are bad,' Mary said. It was a compliment that she had paid before. But now her voice was sad. And Henry at that moment was quite certain what he felt for her. It was more than lust, though he ached with that. It was more than the delusion of a tender boy, scribbled in the margins of his copy book. *At Martinmas, I met a lass, At Candlemas I kissed her, At Whitsuntide, I lay with her, At Lammas tide, I loved her.* It was deep and true.

To still the rush of blood, in heart as well as groin, he opened up the book. 'Here is one. Stop both your ears with your fingers, and the hiccup will go away within a while after.'

'How long is a while?' Mary asked.

'He does not say. But he swears tis proved. Now you owe me a kiss.'

Henry broke a wisp of barley from its stalk and fell to tickling her. She wriggled from his grasp. 'I do love you,' she said.

He sensed, unthinking then, the cloud behind the words. He knew there was a *but*. He fell back in the grass, and looked up at the blue of a cloudless summer sky. He felt at once, instinctively, what she had to say. He closed his eyes and tried to block it out, to feel the sun, the breath of barley graze him on the cheek, to hear the mellow doves, the murmur of the bees.

'Henry, don't. Look at me,' she said. 'I have to talk to you.'

He opened up his eyes, and found her looking down. She spoke the words he did not want to hear. 'I cannot see you again.'

She told him that there was a man, who had asked for her to be his wife.

'It will no be for a while. He is prentice to a blacksmith, and he cannot marry till his time is up. My sister says I should. He is a guid man, she says.'

'How long must you wait, then?' he asked her.

'Four years, near enough.'

Four years was a lifetime, Henry thought. He could not conceive what it was to wait. In a year's time, he would leave the university. He would be at court, in service to the king. Or fighting overseas, in a foreign war. Life was short and swift. It could not be put off.

'Mary, stay with me. I will have left here long before then.'

'I cannot,' she said, 'or he will not have me.'

'I love you.'

'I believe that you do. But ye ken full well that you will not marry me.'

'I never telt you that.' It was true, of course.

'You did not have to say it, for I always knew. Look at you down there, with your books and bow, and your brave new coat. How could you marry me? I do not blame you for it. But my sister says I have to take this chance, or no one else will want me, once my lord has gone.'

'I bought the book for you,' he said, bewildered at her words.

She kissed him on the cheek. 'I owe you for the fact. And I will not forget. When I have the hiccups, I will think of you. But you must keep the book. I have no use for it.'

V

Hew and Frances reached the town a little after twelve. They watched the races at the links, and met with Robert Lachlan there. The men that Robert had engaged showed themselves as fleet and strong, and Hew approved his choice.

'Ye canna tell the mettle of a man till he is tested,' Robert said. 'And strength is not itself a mark of courage. Still, it is a start.'

'When do they begin?' asked Hew. 'The barley is not ripe for reaping yet.'

'Then we shall have a week or twa to break them in. I have telt them they should show at eleven on the morn, and every morning after that at dawn. They will be drunk tonight.'

'Do they know what they come for?' Frances asked. Robert glanced at Hew, who answered in his place.

'Their labour on the land is all we ask, for now. They will be here till Michaelmas. And after that – God knows. Robert, is there news?'

'Rumour is all. The country hauds its breath. There are beacons set, all around the coast, but none of them yet lit. The harbour is the place for news. Folk will gather at the inn there when the fair is done. I will move among them.'

'If you hear aught, come find me. We may be at my sister's house,' Hew said.

Robert left them then, to begin his reconnaissance in the taverns of the town.

'Bella does not like him going to that inn,' Frances pointed out.

'He will be at work. He goes to spy for us.'

'That will not stop him drinking.'

'It should not stop him drinking. He must fit the part.'

'He fits it far too well.' Frances sighed. 'Was he not married, once, to the woman there?'

'For another purpose, in another world.'

Hew steered his wife gently from the subject back into the town and through the market place. There they met Giles Locke, giddy with his bairns, buying gingerbreads. 'Meg is expecting you,' Giles said to Frances. 'She sent us with a list, which we have fulfilled. Fair winds for the morrow. Everything is set.'

'What is tomorrow?' asked Hew.

'The harvest, I suppose.' Frances said. 'We should have a goose for the men at Michaelmas. What do you think?'

Meg was with a patient. But she came out at once when they arrived. 'Your coming is fortunate, Hew. I have someone here who has been asking for you. He is not a man given to impose or to press himself in any way. He is modest and restrained. And yet I have the sense his need is urgent. He would like to speak with you. His name is Walter Bone.'

'Walter.' The name was not unknown to Hew, and yet he could not place it.

'He owns the harbour inn,' Meg said. 'He says you handled the conveyance, when he took it on from Maude.'

Hew said slowly, 'Aye, I did.' The mention of it caused in him a prickle of foreboding, which he did not understand.

Perhaps it was coincidence, for Robert had but lately spoken of the harbour as a place for news. That news they looked for, endlessly, in dread. Robert and Maude Benet at the harbour inn. A life, a world away. No good could come from there.

'I will see him,' he said.

'I hoped you would. He is in my still house, where he came for medicines. Canny Bett is with him. Send her out to us. Frances, I have something for you in the kitchen. And Giles has promised . . .'

Hew left them to their talk. Meg dispensed medicines from the small house in her garden, stilled from the flowers and herbs she grew. Here, there was no wind, the garden seemed to hang in the heavy heat, yet the air inside remained fresh and cool. As Hew came to the door, he felt a shadow fall. There is nothing here to fear, he told himself.

It was Canny Bett, full of smiles and bluster, on her way back out. 'Did you not want to go to the fair?' he asked her.

'Fairs are for lovers and bairns, and I am fair trauchled wi both,' Canny said. 'The doctor has gone wi the weans, to gie us a moment of peace. We maun mak shift for the morn.'

'What happens then?'

'If you dinna ken, then I surely don't.'

Walter Bone was sitting in Meg's chair. He stood up when Hew came in, though he did not do so rapidly, or easily. He was not a man of an open disposition. But there was no mistaking the emotion in his face. It was made up quite plainly of relief. But the relief was a mask upon a deeper kind of feeling. That feeling was not physical pain, though the physical pain might be read as an expression of it. The pain was acute. But it could not reflect the depth of feeling that lay underneath. It distracted from it. It was not its expression, but another kind of mask.

Walter said, 'It is fortune that brings you here. I hoped to see you in the town today. But I did not expect it. I ken that the college where you work is closed.'

At the same time, Hew thought, whatever fate has brought me here, whatever fortune is, it cannot be good. This is an ill wind. He said simply, politely, 'It happened that we came to watch the races at the links.'

Walter shifted, as through pain. 'I was there myself. Not long. But long enough.'

'How can I help you?' asked Hew.

'I want to make a will,' Walter said.

So simple a request was not what Hew expected, and he almost laughed at it, or rather at himself, for fearing so much worse. He answered readily, 'There is a man in the mercat place will draw that up for you. He is very sound. I use him myself. If you like, I will make the recommendation.'

But Walter shook his head. 'It is you I want. The will is not straightforward. It will be hard to prove. There is a guid chance that it will be contested. I need a man who can ensure that the terms will still stand, however untoward or difficult the circumstance. We do not have long. I may die very soon. Tomorrow perhaps, or the next day.'

'I am sorry to hear that,' said Hew. 'Are you so very unwell?'

'I am not well. But that is not the point. There is a possibility that later on today I may kill a man. And, if I do, I expect to hang for it.' His words were careful, clear. They were not the product of a seething of emotion, but carefully thought out.

This is my fortune, thought Hew. It was never simple, from the start. It was not meant to be. He was sent to me, and I cannot refuse him. He took a breath, and seemed to launch himself headlong from a precipice, airless, dizzy, blind. And yet when he spoke he was completely in control. He said simply, 'As your man of law, that is not a course of action that I should advise.'

'I do not propose it lightly,' Walter said. 'And yet I am persuaded that it cannot be escaped.'

'If I were you,' said Hew, 'I would put my mind to making my escape from it. For if you proceed with it, the testament you make will be null and void. You will be indicted for murder, of forethocht felony, which is a plea of the Crown. When you are convicted for it, your goods will be forfeit.'

'It is for that,' Walter said, 'that I require a lawyer who is subtle and distinct. But it will not be forethocht felony. It will be melee chaussee. I will swing for the sheriff, not for the king.'

'That might be so,' said Hew, 'had you not telt me plain what were your intentions. That is malice aforethought, beyond a doubt.'

'I have told them to you,' Walter said, 'and to no one else. And, as your client, I spoke to you in confidence.'

The consequence of this was difficult for Hew, and he did not choose to address it now. Instead, he pointed out, 'Suppose you kill a man in hot blood, and come before the sheriff court. The likelihood is that the dead man's dependants will seek reparation, and that they will be granted it, and will seize your goods. Again, your will is void.'

'That,' Walter said, 'is what I expect to happen. I rely on you to see that it will stand. For the fact is that the person the crime may hurt the most is the person I intend to make my heir. Your role is to speak out and defend that case if any other person tries to make a claim.'

'This is a pursuit,' said Hew, 'I cannot recommend. Nor can I see a way to bring it easily about. Yet I am prepared to help to make your will.'

When the will had been drawn, and a passing clerk called in to witness it, he attempted to dissuade his client once again.

'If it can be helped, then it will be helped,' Walter said. 'This is a precaution against a last resort.'

'You will not tell me, I suppose, who it is you want to kill?'

But Walter's trust in him did not extend so far.

'Whatever is the grudge, put it from your mind,' Hew urged. 'No good ever comes from a vengeful death. I have known murderers. And the wrongs they did have lived long, on and on, a blight upon the lives of all those they had loved. No goods in this world are worth the hurt of that.'

'You are right, of course. I thank you for your counsel,' Walter said. 'God willing, and the world, it will never come to pass.'

They parted at the house, and Hew watched Walter make his way, painfully and slowly, to the mill port and the harbour where he kept his inn. Hew took comfort from the fact that Robert would be watching there. He doubted whether Walter had the strength to kill a man. But he did not doubt his mind. He returned to Meg. 'What ails him?' he asked her. 'What have you prescribed?'

'You know I cannot tell you that,' said Meg. 'What did he ask of you?'

'You know I cannot tell you that,' he said.

VI

Elspet had returned before the clock struck four. Sliddershanks appeared surprised. 'You came back,' he said.

'Why would I not?'

'For tis early yet. Was the fair no guid?'

Elspet said, 'It was the best.'

'That is guid, then. I see it. You have a light,' he said oddly.

'A light?' Elspet was reckless in her happiness. It was spilling over, and she could not keep it in. It was a dancing inside her.

'As though you caught the sun.'

'It is warm today.' Elspet looked round. 'What do you want me to do now?'

'See to the kitchins. We will be busy tonight.'

Already, she was tying on her apron, to cover her blue gown. She wore Michael's ribbons pinned up on her breast. Her hand went instinctively to keep them in their place. Sliddershanks was watching her. 'Bonny, that,' he said. 'Silver and blue. The colours of the sea.'

'The colours of the town,' Elspet said.

'Oh, aye. I suppose you won it for a prize. What did you have to dae for it?'

'Dae for it?' Elspet faltered, frowned. 'Someone must have won it, but it wasnae me. I fund it in the sand.'

Sliddershanks looked sad. 'Some lassie will be missing it,' he said.

Elspet remained in the kitchen as he had telt her. At intervals, he came with crockery to wash, and left with bowls of broth and plates of bread and cheese. After a time he did not come back. She could hear a tumult in the public room, and somewhere further off, the braying of the pipes. She went through to the house, and found it filled with men, calling to be served. Empty trays and cups were piled up on the counter. She heard Joan complaining 'Wheesht, wait yer turn'. Elspet called out to her, 'Have you no help?'

'Marie is outside. The spelairs are starting a show. They are playing on the pier, and bring with them a crowd. All of them want drink.'

'Where is Sliddershanks?'

'Walter is resting. His banes are sair, he says. Manners, sirs, and mind! I only hae one pair o' hands.'

Elspet fought her way through the drinkers and looked out. She saw Marie weave herself in and out of the crowd, carrying a tray. Closer to the inn, folk were sitting down, with hogsheads and cags for tables and chairs. Others had begun to gather on the front and the north end of the quay, leading to the pier. The

pier was wrought of timber, lined with slabs of stone, weather-
blown and rickety. At its far end, she saw the Egyptian boy
making fast his rope, a slender figure braced against the sea and
sky. Across the bay an outcrop shaped the harbour basin, filling
with the tide. The second tumbler, kneeling on this outcrop,
pulled taut and anchored deep the other end of the cord. Surely,
Elspet thought, they do not mean to cross the water. She went
back into the house.

She was not afraid to go into his sleeping-place. Sliddershanks
had been her master long enough for that. The sleeping-place
was dark. 'Are you not well, then?' she said.

His voice, when it came, sounded queer in the darkness. 'I
have taken physic. It will be better soon.'

'The house is full. And there are folk outside. A show on the
pier. There is music,' she said. 'Can you hear?'

The strains of the fiddle and the flute, the piper and the drum,
persisted, even here. 'I hear it,' he said. A catch to his voice, like
a sob.

'Folk want to drink. Marie and Joan cannot serve them all. I
will help them,' she said.

'Ye *maunna*.' His voice was insistent and hard now. 'You
shall stay back. The willow will work soon, and I will come up.
Till then, they maun shift as they can.'

Elspet said, 'Sleep for a while.' She felt a little pity for him
still. The secret she was keeping made her kind. She could hear
the music on the quay; the gladness in her heart quickened at
the beat. Puir crippled Sliddershanks could never learn to dance.

'Do as I say. Tell them,' he said.

Elspet said, 'I will.'

She went back to the house, where Joan had placed a row of
trays upon the bar for Marie to take out. Elspet took a tray, and
went among the crowd. Between them they fulfilled the demand
for drink, while Marie took the money in a leather pouch she

wore beneath her skirt. The tumblers were performing on the quay. The rope walk, the finale of their show, they promised to perform when their hat was filled. The drinkers jeered and roared, but gradually, and grudgingly, the money was amassed, won by the tumble and turn of the delicate, muscular boys. The fiddler was playing their tune. The music was swaying the crowd.

A young man called to Elspet, 'Mistress maiden, pardon, may I have more wine?'

'It looks to me,' she telt him, 'you have had enough.'

He looked like a nobleman's son, one not accustomed to holding his drink. A bonny doe-eyed boy, tearful in his cups. She wondered what had brought him to the harbour inn. Not as she supposed the tumblers on the quay, for he had his back to them.

'Ah, dinna be like that,' he said. 'I am thirsty still.'

'Wait there, then.' He was drinking good white wine, the most expensive kind, and Sliddershanks would want to have the sale. She filled another flask, from the coolness of the cellar, and brought it back to him.

'Drink with me.'

'I cannae do that, I am working,' she said.

'Sit with me, then. Tell me what to dae for a broken heart. For a lassie as lovely as you has broken a few hearts, I doubt.'

She laughed at his charm. The boy was quite fu', and ought to go home. Where were his friends?

Elspet glanced around. Marie was working the crowd, in the way that she did, a squeeze and a kiss and a slap. Her apron was fat with her purse. And all of her clients had drinks. She caught Elspet looking and winked. Elspet sat down. Her legs had grown tired, yet her heart brimmed with gladness and kindness. 'Just for a moment,' she said.

She recognised his face; he was the lad who had clashed with

Michael at the butts. He was lucky Michael was not here among the crowd. Michael was a man, and could hold his drink. He would have made mince of this boy.

The thought of Michael made her strong and proud. She asked the boy, 'Where is your lass?'

He stared at her, mournful. 'She left me.'

'Why did she do that?'

'Because I will not marry her.'

'Do you not love her?'

'I love her,' he said, 'with all of my heart. You cannot fathom how much.'

She felt that she could. 'Marry her, then.'

'Marry her, aye. It is not as simple as that.'

The piper struck a tune.

'Dance with me,' the boy said.

'I cannot.'

'I will teach you. I once saw a justice dancing naked in a court. Do you believe that?'

'I believe you saw it in a dream.'

The young man stood up, finding his balance and dancing a jig, folding his limbs at her feet in an extravagant courtesy, making her laugh. 'Jackanapes.'

'Ah, mistress cruelty, be kind.'

'Why won't you marry her, then?' Elspet asked.

'I cannot.'

'Why can't you?'

The question seemed to sober him, or else he did not to wish to take the matter further, for he turned his back. 'Why are those people crowding at the pier?'

'The tumblers are going to walk across on ropes.'

'That is not so hard, with the basin filled with water. More hazardous to walk above the rocks.'

'It is harder than you think. The distance is quite far. And though the water here looks still, they walk close to the tide, and the current as it turns may catch and drag them out.'

'Piffle. For a fellow who has poise, as a fencer or a dancer, it is easily done. I could do it myself.'

'I'd like to see you try it,' Elspet said.

'Well then, you shall. Send a man for Mary. She shall see it too.'

The young man took off, with unexpected speed, making for the pier. Elspet cried, 'Wait! Dinna be daft. What are ye thinking of, now?'

She followed as well as she could, forcing her way through the crowd. She did not have to fear, for he had not travelled far when his stomach failed him. His limbs had buckled too, and he sat down on a stone. 'I dinna feel well.'

Elspet said, 'Sit there, you loun, and drink in the air.' She left him to feel sorry for himself, following the line to the far end of the pier. The balladeer was singing *Quhy sowld not Allane honorit be?* 'Quhen he wes yung and cled in greene, haifand his air abowt his een.' Surely, Elspet thought, that is Michael's song.

The crowd was urgent now. The young Egyptian boy had taken off his shirt, and his feet were bare. He wore a kind of hose, tight against the skin, with no flap or fold for the wind to catch, knotted round the waist with a piece of string. He was sweating, just a little, from his tumbles on the quay. Or maybe it was fear. The drummer had begun to rap upon his drum, a beat for the boy at the bending of a knee, a beat for the boy at the flexing of his feet.

Marie stood listening to the piper on the quay. Her foot began to tap. She wondered if a lad would ask her for a dance, a handsome one like Elspet had. She shook out her skirts and began to sway, hands upon her hips, provocative and plump.

She felt a blaze of happiness.

The tumblers had finished their somersaults, and bowing in submission to the crowd, prepared to make their rope walk. The older boy was kneeling on the outcrop, testing the tautness of the rope. His younger brother went into the inn, and came out with a sack. The crowd swarmed behind him to the pier. Marie preferred to watch from the safety of the shore. The pier was old and worn, and would not bear the weight of all those bodies in a storm. The tide was at its peak, and swelled upon it fiercely, clamouring to reach the pool of limpid water sheltered in its bowl. And Marie had lived by the sea long enough to ken the full fetch of its waves.

Elspet's young man was caught up in the crowd carried to the pier, and Elspet came too, calling after him. Marie smiled and waved at her, but she did not wave back. Bold piece she was, chasing him like that, for all the world but Walter Bone to see. The strumpet held her own worth higher than the rest.

Marie shifted place, to feel a sudden absence, a hollow want of weight somewhere in her skirt. Her happiness evaporated to a sick dismay. She could not find her purse. She felt beneath her apron, her kirtle and her shirt, and scrabbled in the folds to find her dread was justified; her pocket was no longer fastened at her waist, the cord that held it cut. She looked around her blindly through the crowd. She could not recall when she had it last, when she had last felt the warmth of its weight, as comfortable and close as a body part. Was it the drinker who had squeezed past her, the one who called to her for a sly kiss, the one who had pulled her to sit on his knee? Was there not one who had plucked at her sleeve, tipping the tray and slopping out ale? Were the afternoon's takings spilled with the drink? She was afraid of what Walter would say. He had never been a violent kind of man. He would not raise his hand to her. But his tongue was cruel. He could rain on words, just as sore as stripes. Maybe for her carelessness she would lose her place. Maybe he would keep her, at his beck and call, in a bitter servitude until the debt was paid. Marie was not sure which would be the worse. Elspet all the while would remain his pet, queening over her. Marie would be spit, for cleaning Elspet's shoes.

She felt something at her back, and spun round to find her friend, the juglar from the fair. He tipped his hat to her. 'Is it too late for a drink, before the rope walk starts? I dinna want for you to miss the show.'

She stared at him, blank for a moment, before she stuttered, 'Oh. Joan is at the house. She will gie you one.'

'Then I will hae to ask Joan. The pity is,' he smiled at her, 'she isnae as bonny as you.'

She liked the juglar still. He had merry eyes. But she was too upset to stop to flirt with him.

'I would fetch it for ye, gladly. But there is something I must look for, somewhere in the crowd. Please excuse me, sir.' She tried to squeeze past him.

'Something you have lost? Mebbe tis this.' To Marie's amazement, he held out her purse. She snatched at it, dazed in relief. 'How did you?'

'I saw the piker who cut it frae your shirt, and trailed him through the crowd.'

'Thank ye, sir, thank ye. I cannot thank you enough.' Marie looked around. 'Where is the piker now? Will they clip his lugs, and put him in the jougs?' There was a court, just for the fair, that made short shrift of a thief. She would find a cabbage that was rotten for to throw at him, a cabbage or a neep. But she hoped Walter Bone would not hear what he had done.

The juglar told her, 'He is far from here, crowing at his luck. He will be quite baffled when he finds his spoils have gone.'

'But does he not ken he is caught?' Marie said. 'How can that be?'

'Pardon,' said the juglar, 'but there is a wasp, crawling on your cap. If you stand quite still, I will flick it off, for I should not like you to be stung.' Marie felt his hand brush against her cheek, the lightness of a breeze, and shivered with an unexpected pleasure at his touch.

'There. All peril past. You are now quite safe, and can dry your tears.' He handed her a handkerchief.

And if she was ashamed to find her eyes were wet with them, her neb running too, for she was overcome with fear and gratitude, these feelings were eclipsed by a new astonishment. The handkerchief was hers. And there was her name, still in the corner, where her wee sister had worked it, for Marie to take when she found her first place. She knew that the thief had not snatched it with the purse, for she had found it safe in the place she kept it, tucked between her breasts.

'How did you get that?' she whispered. 'I never felt.' Her gown was tight, her breasts were full. It could not have been lifted, so close to her skin.

'It is done by distraction,' he said. 'You were thinking of a wasp, whether it would sting. You felt my hand,' Marie blushed at that, 'only in the place where you were expecting it.'

'And that is how you robbed the piker of my purse?'

'It is not theft to deprive a thief. It is sleight of hand. I think you are not pleased. Would you rather that the thief wis hanged?' he teased.

Marie shook her head. She whispered, 'I do not want my master to ken.'

'We will not tell him, then. Tis well you have it safe. I see him coming now.'

The juglar had a knack to know when there was danger, to catch it on the wind. Now she saw him too, coming from the inn. His sore leg dragged a little as he crossed the quay. She became afraid that somehow Walter knew, that he saw the cords were cut, underneath her shirt. She clutched at the purse. But he barely looked at her. 'Where is Elspet?' he said. 'She isnae is the house,' a queer, rasping tremor in his voice.

'Oh,' Marie said, 'she is on the pier. She went there wi a laddie she was dancing with. The tumblers are for putting on a show.'

Walter Bone had such a dark and glowering look, Marie was relieved it was not meant for her. 'I will swing for that limmar,' he said. She felt at his back a glad prick of spite as he hobbled off. Let Elspet be troubled for once.

The juglar took her hand. 'I will stand by you, while you watch the show. No one will come near.'

He helped her to hide the pocket underneath her skirt, and showed her a way that she could loop the cord, so that she could catch it if ever it was pulled. Then he stood close at her side, and the weight of the purse resting in her lap, and the weight of his hand resting on her hip, made her feel wanted and safe.

The tumbler on the pier had stripped down to his hose. Each piece of clothing he took off was greeted by a rolling of the drum, and a rumble in the crowd, grumbling at the boy to hurry himself up. The boy took his time. He opened up his sack. Inside were two metal balls that looked like cannon shot. The juglar told Marie that the balls were weights. The boy would hold one in each hand, as he walked the rope, and they would keep him straight, like the balance of a scale.

'What if he should drop one?' Marie said.

'Then he will fall in, and the crowd will roar. They will stamp and jeer, and like it all the more.'

Marie thought it likely that was true. Most people watching would prefer it if he fell. The juglar sounded sad, and Marie wondered if he was feeling sorry for the boy. But when she asked him, he telt her he was not. He believed that the show would outshine his own, which he was hoping to perform in the inn that night.

'The one with the egg and the bat?' Marie asked.

He telt her that he thought the bat had died. That was no matter, for he had another trick. But he could not do it without help.

Marie said, 'What help?'

'The help of a lass who has the kind of face to keep a man transfixed. A sonsie face like yours.'

Marie was flattered then. 'What is the trick?' she asked.

'A disappearing one.'

Her eyes opened wide. 'What will you disappear?'

'Anything you like. Any kind of thing can be made to disappear. The trick is distraction,' he replied.

Elspet stepped back. She could no longer bear to look at the boy's face, caught in concentration, in a clasp so powerful that it frightened her. The boy's face turned to stone, still and sculpted, strange. He listened to the wind. He did not hear the crowd.

Elspet had drifted to the far side of the pier, where the water rose and broke upon the rocks, showering her with spray. She looked on a sun that was sultry and dark, heavy with heat, in an indigo sky. The rush of the water had drowned out the crowd; the rush of the crowd had drowned out the drum; the beat of the drum had drowned out the sea, lulled to a hush as the rattle came quick, tight on its surface like sweet Lammas rain. Elspet looking back to hear the drumroll's rush saw the boy step out, taut above a pool so dark and smooth and still it seemed to hold its breath. Elspet turned again, and Sliddershanks was there. His face was grained and grey, desolate with grief. The rushing of the water took away his words, and cast them to the wind.

VII

Andrew Wood, the crownar and sheriff for Fife, held no jurisdiction at the fair. He had come to town to collect the rents for his brother's mill, and was at the tolbooth on that day by chance. So when a witness came to report a crime he referred the matter to the powder court. The bailies, when they heard the case, referred it back to him. According to the witness's account, a woman had been thrown from the pier, in full view of her friends, a slaughter with intent, which was his concern, and no concern of theirs.

A death at a fair was a rare and grave thing, and unlawful killing counted with the worst. Fairs took place on ancient soil, on what had once been sacred days, and blood spilled there could tarnish and corrupt the spirit of the fair itself. Such superstitions, never now expressed, none the less were felt, and the bailies did their best to distance these events. The woman had been taken by the sea, therefore her destruction had not happened in the town.

Sir Andrew gave the order for the building of a gallows in the market place, before the sun went down. The penalty for slaughter was plain and unequivocal. But when he came to the harbour to make his arrest, he found that the report did not reflect the facts. The case was far from clear.

In the first place, there was no sign of a corpse. The person in question had gone missing from the fair. Sir Andrew made a last attempt to refer the matter back to the powder court, but with no success: the witnesses were certain that the lass was dead. The witnesses, he found, were nothing of the sort. The girl had fallen from the pier, they said, but none of them could swear they saw her fall. Her body had been taken by the tide, but none of them had seen it swept away; the tide had turned before they thought to search. They showed a plaid, found on the rocks. No one could confirm it was the missing girl's.

'There is nothing, then, to prove that she was pushed, or even that she fell,' he pointed out.

As witness to the fact, they brought to him a slattern, racked with sighs and sobs, and a student so drunk that he could hardly stand. The student had danced with the missing lass. He was on the pier, and she ran after him. There he had passed out. He had not seen her since.

The girl had more to say, though none of it coherent, in between her wails. Elspet was her friend. She was very dear to her. They had worked together at the harbour inn. Their master was a man called Walter Bone. Elspet had a sweetheart, and Walter had found out. He had flown into a rage, and said that he would kill her.

'What were his words?' Andrew Wood said, for the words made a difference to the fact.

'He would swing for the limmar, he said.'

'By which he meant that he would kill Elspet?'

'I didna understand him at the time,' Marie said, 'but he went to do it all the same. He went to push her aff the pier.'

'And did you see him do it?' Andrew asked her patiently. He was a patient man. His patience in the past had been a shrewd relentlessness, tenacious in pursuit until he got his man. Now it was resigned; he was weary of a post he was close to giving up, called forever back to attend to one last crime. This might be the last man he would have to hang. He would not be sorry if it was.

'Ah didna *see* him,' Marie said. 'But she wis on the pier, and he went rinning efter, and ainly he com back.' She blurted out the rest.

The tumblers had been walking on a rope across the water, and everyone had watched. When the walk was done, they came back to the inn, where there was going to be a magic show.

The magician who intended to put on the show stood by Marie's side. He offered her the comfort of a string of coloured handkerchiefs, on which to blow her nose. The crownar took an urgent and immediate dislike to him. He belonged to a class of man Sir Andrew had no wish to see about the town, or any town in Fife. On any other day, when there was no fair, he would have him whipped. He was no more than a beggar and a thief. What was a juglar, but a common trickster? What was a trickster, but he ought to hang? No word of his, or this foolish girl's, had any scrap of worth.

Marie said that she had looked for Elspet at the inn. She had not found her there. But she had found Walter Bone, in the lassies' sleeping chamber, sitting on the bed that she and Elspet shared. When she tried to speak with him, he was wild and strange. Then she had seen the ribands in his hand, that Elspet had been wearing at her breast. That was when she screamed.

To illustrate the point, she began to scream again. 'Mak the wench whisht, or I will,' Andrew warned, and the juglar took the lassie in his filthy clasp. Sir Andrew turned, disgusted, to examine Walter Bone.

Walter had the ribbons still, the single piece of evidence with any substance to it. He said that the girl had given them to him.

'And why would she do that?'

'I dinna ken,' Walter said.

'Where is she now?'

'I have nae idea.'

The crownar scratched his head. He was still undecided what he should do next when he saw Robert Lachlan coming through the mill port, with Hew Cullan by his side. Robert Lachlan he disliked intensely. His feelings for Hew were a good deal more ambivalent. Hew was an expert in resolving mysteries, and rooting out the source of anomalies like these. Yet while he was adept in solving certain problems, he caused as many problems as he solved. His involvement was not likely to simplify the case. Therefore Andrew's welcome to him was at best lukewarm.

'This man is my client,' Hew told him.

'Your client,' the crownar said. 'Why does that not surprise me? You may speak to him here, in my hearing. I will not wait while you play with words, nor would I have you put an answer in his mind that was not founded there.'

This was not what Hew had hoped for. But Robert had primed him with the essential facts, and he asked Walter straight, 'Have you hurt the lass? Did you kill her, or anyone else?'

'I did not,' Walter said.

'Then,' Hew said to the crownar, 'I urge you to take him into ward, and keep him under guard until the girl is found.'

Sir Andrew Wood had not expected such a straight response. 'You believe him guilty, then?'

'On the contrary,' said Hew. 'I am convinced he is telling the truth. He has committed no crime.'

'He has committed no crime. Yet you would have me lock him up. This man is your lawyer, sir. How do you like that?' Sir Andrew put to Walter, who replied simply, 'I did no wrong.'

Hew urged the crownar, 'You ken me. Then trust me. I cannot tell you more, for it is a matter of the closest confidence. Evil will be done if you do not lock him up.'

'Will I hang him too, an it please your grace?'

'That is the conclusion I am trying to avoid.'

'Aye, very well. Let the bailies take him.' Sir Andrew had grown tired of the game. He returned to Henry Balfour. 'This student too, who was on the pier. The hussy says she saw him with the lass. Therefore I must count him also for a suspect, if a crime is done. Which is far from clear.'

'By no means,' said Hew, intervening quickly. 'This is Lord Balfour's son.' He knew Henry from his efforts in the public examinations, where he had presented several days before. 'He cannot be allowed to influence your witness. Much more will be gained be keeping them apart. And since he is too drunk to speak with reason now, I will take him home.'

A voice was heard to murmur somewhere in the crowd. 'Rich laws for the rich, and that's a fact.'

Henry had revived his wits sufficiently to say, 'I am lodging in the South Street, with Professor Black.'

'Are you now?' said Hew. 'Then God help you both.'

Robert Lachlan helped him to take Henry home. 'Ye maunna fault a man that cannot haud his drink, when he is but young. He has yet to learn. You scholars at the college havna taucht him richt.' He slapped Henry hard between the shoulder blades, a gesture of collegiate conviviality, which Henry threw straight back, in a spurt of spew. Robert sidestepped swiftly 'Manners of a whore, for aw that.'

Robert Black turned ashen when they brought him to the door. 'How can he be so drunk? Tis not gone eight o'clock! What devil have you done to him?' he asked.

'Nought but saved his skin,' said Hew. 'You will not believe the trouble he is in. He has no idea of it himself. If you value his life, lock him in his room, and do not let him out before I come again.'

'What do you say? His life is in danger?' The regent wrung his hands. 'What will I tell his father? What am I do? He is in my charge for the next two months.'

Robert Lachlan grinned at him. 'Aye? Good luck wi that.'

Walter Bone was locked in the tolbooth for the night. He had no more to say. He kept Elspet's ribbons tightly in his grasp. The crownar made no attempt to wrest them from him. He took no interest in the case. In the morning, early, he went back to the harbour, and established that the incoming tide had recovered no trace of the girl. He spoke to several of the fishermen, who had taken their boats out at night, and concluded that there was no charge to answer. He returned to the tolbooth, and set Walter free. He was not going to hang a man for a scrap of thread.

AUGUST 2

I

Elspet had woken up naked and cold. She looked about for clothes, and finding Michael's shirt the closest thing to hand, she put it on. It held her in his scent, bloody and deep like the scent of a calf. Michael lay still fast asleep. He was naked too, his hair like crumpled corn rigs, tousled tufts of gold, his bare limbs flung carelessly over the fleece. Their bed was a sheepskin, spread out on the floor. Elspet felt his body on her skin, in every part of her.

He woke and rose at once, instantly alert. 'Why would you no wake me?'

'I was sleeping too,' Elspet said. 'It is early still.'

Michael said, 'Tis late. Gie me back ma sark.'

He is fearful for his work, Elspet thought. Michael had been hired by Robert Lachlan at the Lammas fair. It was good work, he telt her. Honest and well paid. At Michaelmas, when it was done, there would be a feast. They might kill a pig, and the drink would flow. Elspet could come too. She would be his guest.

He stood above her, supple and awake; every part of him had woken strong and proud, and Elspet felt inside her a hollow kind of longing, aching to be filled. How could she be empty, still? He opened up a gulf in her. She drew up her knees, and tucked the shirt under her. 'Take it, then,' she said.

Michael laughed fondly. 'I could. God kens, I *would*. But I hae to work.'

He thought if he was late he would lose his place. But it was early yet. Elspet did not like Robert Lachlan. He had gone away with Maude, and come back on his own. Elspet had supposed that meant that Maude was dead. But Robert had not said. He drank, sometimes, at the harbour inn, as though what happened there was of no consequence. She did not like that Michael worked for him.

'Not till eleven, you said.'

Michael looked out at the sky. 'It must be after ten. Sliddershanks will miss you at the inn. You will have to think a lie to tell him. That you couldna sleep, and went out for a walk, before the sun was up.'

She had been supposed to slip out after dark, when the inn was closed, with everyone asleep. But Elspet had not kept to the letter of their tryst. She had slipped away while the show was on.

She had come to the place that Michael called his own, a ruined shepherd's hut. For door it had a scrap of cloth. Its roof was open to the skies, where Michael pitched a canvas up, to shelter from the rain. The rain that promised did not fall, and they had lain all night together underneath the stars, his jewels for her, he said. Michael had been drinking in the town, and he had not appeared until it was quite dark, and Elspet was afraid. Then his touch had found her, waking every place she had not known she harboured there, asleep.

'He kens,' Elspet said.

Michael was already pulling up his breeks, tying round the leather cord that served him for a belt, taming, tying down, the rising of his love. He stopped to stare at her. 'What?'

'He saw us at the fair. He telt me at the pier. When you won the race and gied the ribbons to me. Sliddershanks was there.'

Elspet had not cared. When he had accused her, she had plucked the ribbons from her breast and taunted, 'Take them, then. Have them for yersel'! What kind o creature are ye, peeping, spying on us?' Now she felt a pang, to think how hurt he looked.

Michael cursed, a long stream of profanities, spilling out like seed. Elspet shrank from it. 'Why does it matter now? Now that we are handfast, and will soon be wed.'

'Elspet.' Michael sighed. He squatted down beside her, and cupped his hand around her face, turning it to his, so she could see his seriousness. She shivered at his touch.

'It is Lammastide. And you ken full well that that is coupling time. You are the bonniest thing. The loveliest lass that I ever went with. Ripe and yielding. Sweet.'

'You said that last night.'

'I meant it. But, Elspet, tis harvest time. The harvest will be done. And when the corn is gone, then I will be too.'

'Where will you go?' Elspet said.

'Far away. Over the hills. Ach, dinna be sad. It will not be a while yet. And you can come again. Now you must go awa and mak your peace wi Sliddershanks. He will take you back. He likes you.'

'But am I not your wife?'

'Whisht, no more of wives. It was Lammas play, and no more meant than that. Wipe your face. I cannot abide to see a lass greet.'

She did not think that she was greeting. It could not be tears, but dew on her cheeks. She could not be crying, for she felt nothing inside her but coldness and dark, as though a door opened had let in a draught, and filled up the chasm with nothing but ash.

'You can come again, if you will not cry, on another night. I will stay till Michaelmas. You liked it, did you no? You will not tell me no. For I ken you did.'

He kissed her on the lips before he let her go, standing up

again. 'I have to go and piss. While I am gone, you should get dressed.'

Michael went outside, to the back of the hut, and presently she heard a sound that streaming on and on chilled and emptied her. She hugged her knees close, wondered how they felt so solid, when she was a husk, with nothing inside.

A shadow crossed the door, and someone spoke her name, in a voice so filled with sorrow and with tenderness she knew it was not his. Elspet looked up, and was not surprised to see that it was Sliddershanks. She thought she could not bear the sadness in his eyes. She wanted to tell him not to look at her. *For I am nothing now.* She spoke to him instead as she might have done on any other day. 'How are your sair bancs?'

He thanked her. 'No sae bad, the day.'

'I am glad of that. For you have come some way to see us,' Elspet said. 'How did you find the place?'

Careful and polite, as if she might get up, and offer him a cup of something cool to drink, a bannock on a plate, to thank him for his pains. But there was nothing here that lent to hospitality.

'Jonet telt me. Jonet has a wean, with hair like crumpled corn, the image of its da, and she got him here. You did not think,' said Sliddershanks, 'that you were the first?'

She knew that she was not. 'Why did you let me?' she said.

'They thought I had hurt you. They kept me away.'

'Who could think that? You never would. You should have telt them.'

'And shamed you?' he said. 'I would never dae that.'

She let slip a sigh. 'I am shamed now.'

'No. You will not be. I will make certain of that.'

'Well, if it isnae Widdershins.' Michael was behind them at the door.

Elspet said, 'His name is Walter Bone.' She wished she had not said to Michael that she called him Sliddershanks. Now

Sliddershanks would think she had been mocking him. That was not it, at all.

Michael grinned at him. 'Your timing is braw, if you seek your lass. She is ready to come home.'

To Elspet he said, 'Are you no dressed, yet? Tak off the shirt.'

Elspet blinked at him. Would he have her bare, in front of Sliddershanks? She shivered, and hugged herself close.

'Nae mair o your piddling,' Michael said, 'I am late for work.' He would have stripped it from her there and then, had Walter not been standing in his way.

Walter accused him, 'You have defiled her.'

'Defilit is she? Do you hear that?' Michael said. 'Widdershins thinks ye are foul.'

'She never was foul, nor is she now. You have deflowered her,' Sliddershanks said.

'Deflowered her? There is a word. Ah, but she was ripe for it! Tell the cripple, Elspet, how much you were longing for it, thirsty as the blossom drooping for the rain. What kind of man are you, that kept her locked away, too feeble and too dry to pluck her for yourself? I brought her to the light. It was what she craved.'

Sliddershanks did not reply. Instead he looked at Elspet. 'Is this what you want?'

She could not look at him. 'I do not know,' she said. 'I wanted to be loved.'

'You did not ken you were?' He shook his head, heavy with the sorrow of it. 'Well, the thing is done. And you must marry now.'

'Marry? I will marry her, at latter Lammas time,' Michael said. That was a time that never came. 'Elspet understands. Ask her, she will tell you. Oh, but she was ready for it! Luscious, sweet and ripe. You should hae had her, Widdershins, while you had the chance. But you can hae her now. I opened her for you.'

Walter took the knife he carried from his belt. 'Marry her, or die,' he suggested simply.

'Dinnae,' Elspet cried.

Michael laughed at them. 'Threaten me, auld man? Ah dinna think you could.' As Walter came at him, he struck out with his foot, to topple him as easily as he might trip a child. Walter's crooked bones were racked and twisted under him. He crumpled with a whimper. Michael squatted over him, grappling for the blade. He wrenched the knife from Sliddershanks, and waved it, dark with blood. 'Oh, Jesus Christ!' He pleaded to Elspet. 'I didnae dae that. He did it to hi'self. You saw that, did ye no?'

Sliddershanks was clutching at his thigh. And blood was showering Michael, splattering his face.

Elspet ran to Sliddershanks, pushing her hands in the place he had cut. The wound was too deep or her hands were too small, for the blood pumped out still, drowning her fingers. 'Tie your belt round him,' she cried.

But Michael stood gawping. 'He came at me, Elspet, you saw.'

Walter's eyes were closed. And Elspet felt his spirit pumping out. Her shirt was drenched with blood. Then the bleeding stopped, abrupt as it began. His eyes fluttered open. Elspet held him close.

'Look at you,' she said, 'you silly, futless cripple. See now what you've done.'

He telt her, 'Dinna girn. I will not hae you greet. Your face is foul enough.'

'Is that a fact?' she said. 'Well, ye wad ken. For ye are such a foulsum wreck yersel.'

His eyes had closed again. And Elspet felt her heart so heavy and so sore that she could not speak. When she found the words, she turned them on Michael. 'We have killt him,' she said.

And Michael did not stay to see that he was dead, but fled across the fields, cowering from her grief.

II

The sturdy men who gathered to survey the barley rigs, Robert Lachlan's band, were astonished at the sight of a man, naked to the waist, and showering flakes of blood, rising from the corn. It did not take them long to trap and bring him down, writhing like a fish. They traced back the trail to the bloody hut where Elspet cradled Sliddershanks. Hew was called, and came, bringing Bella Frew, to see what could be done. It was Bella who helped Elspet out of Michael's shirt and into her own clothes, and showed to her a rough and understanding kindness Elspet had not come across since Maude, while Walter's body, prised from her, was carried to the town. Then they made a slow procession following the corpse.

The crownar Andrew Wood was returning home when his horse was caught and halted by the messenger, who telt him that his gallows might be wanted after all. Reluctantly, he turned. A grim show was set out to greet him at the tolbooth: the corpse of Walter Bone, straddled on a board, bathed in its own blood. Michael stood shivering, cowed, naked and ashamed as Adam at the Fall. Elspet stood apart, in a solemn sadness. Nothing that was said or done appeared to reach her there.

Giles Locke was in attendance. He bore witness that Michael's account of events was not contradicted by the facts. Nor did the facts confirm it. Facts were simply facts. And the facts, as he saw them, were that the knife had entered Walter's thigh, and severed both the vein and the artery. It could have been by accident. It could have been intent. A sure, but unlikely, way to kill a man.

He believed, in the event of accident, there was very little that could have been done to save the victim's life. If Michael had remained, then the pressure of his hands, with Elspet's, could have staunched the flow. But that was not a thing a common man might ken, and Michael was not culpable if he had in mind to run off for the surgeon, as he said he did. That was yet a hopeless cause; no surgeon could have come in time. By his estimation, it took Walter Bone a little over four and a little under five minutes to bleed out, until his life was drained.

Elspet spoke at that, wondering aloud. 'Four minutes! And no more!' It felt to her a lifetime she had held him in her hands, while his life slipped out, and no time at all.

Sir Andrew made a note of it and dismissed the doctor. He looked upon the others with disdain. He had no interest in the life or death of Walter Bone, who had few fine friends to press the crownar to avenge him. Nor was he concerned with Michael or with Elspet, whose squalid love affair might trouble the kirk's courts, but did not trouble his. What caught his interest more, in all of this, was Hew. Hew stood by, white-faced. And the crownar was intent on finding out his part, to hold him to account.

'You telt me,' he said, 'to keep this man locked up, or evil would be done. Now he is a corpse. Perhaps you can explain to me how such things jump together as to be coincident, in this place and time.'

'He would not be a corpse,' Hew said, 'if you had kept your word, and kept him under lock until the girl was found.'

Sir Andrew said, '*My* word? No word of mine, but yours. This is strange work, sir. What was it? Did you have a premonition that he would be killed? Speak, or I will take your silence for a darker kind of magic. What was in your mind?'

Hew was forced to say, for Michael's sake if not his own, that Walter had confessed to him he meant to take a life. Therefore he corroborated Michael's self-defence, that Walter had attacked him.

'He slipped and fell on his ain blade. That is all I ken,' Michael said. He looked at Hew. 'I had no reason to expect it.'

Hew said, 'I did not ken the life he meant was yours. I see now that it was. But I did not know it at the time.'

The crownar stared at him. 'You heard this yesterday. And yet you did not think it worthy of report?'

'No. I will not report a man's intent as truth, when it is telt in confidence. Besides, if I had told you, you might have hanged him then, taking as confirmed what Marie said.'

The crownar said, 'I should have done. But that does not excuse you, nor should it clear your conscience. If you had but spoken, these sad events would not have come about.'

'What? If you had hanged him, he would not now be dead?' Hew asked. 'Strange reason, that.'

'Chop logic as you will, I see your hand in this. You set yourself above the law, and fortune too. This fortune has caught up with you and Walter Bone. The law can watch and wait, and bide the time when it will catch you too. When it does, understand, I will come for you. No one hangs today. You three are free to go.'

Sir Andrew turned his back on them and left. These small lives, this death, disgusted him. His pledge to serve his king and to keep the peace had exhausted him, draining his estates, and he had grown indifferent to the part. There would come a time, he hoped not far away, when he would put the rope around his last man's neck. If that man was Hew Cullan he would rest content. It would bring his service to a satisfying end.

Michael knelt to Hew. 'Master, you have saved my life.'

'I am not your master,' answered Hew. He looked across at Elspet. 'Do you want this man?'

Elspet answered clearly, 'Not ever in my life. Whatever is the law, I ken it in my heart that he killed Sliddershanks. I will not have him die for it. But I can never bear to look on him again.'

Michael swore to Hew, 'Your man, Robert Lachlan, hired me for the harvest. Wherefore I am yours, and will serve you gladly. I am strong and true.'

Hew told him, 'Did you not hear? You are set free. You are no man of Elspet's, and no man of mine. Give thanks for your good fortune, that though your life was sought you did not die today. Fortune smiles on you. Go freely where you will. But let it not be here, nor ever on my land. I have no place for you.'

He took Elspet home to the harbour inn, where he explained the terms of Walter's will. Walter had left everything to her. Elspet listened quietly. 'I can help you sell it, if you like,' Hew said. He was surprised when she said that she would remain. She would run the inn herself, as Maude had done. She asked him if he could write a sign for her. The sign was to say that the inn would be closed from now until the day that Walter Bone was buried. On the day of his funeral, it would open again, in the afternoon, for those who were his friends to come and drink to him. From then on, they must ken that Elspet was in charge. 'I will want a pot boy and a serving lass. Put that in the note. The boy must be strong and the lass must be clean.'

When the sign was done she fixed it to the door.

'How many of the drinkers here can read?' wondered Hew.

'None of them,' she said. 'But letters are a thing that they will mark and fear, who do not heed my word. If a thing is written then it is the law.'

She asked him the cost of his fee. He said there was no charge. But Elspet insisted. He was Walter's man of law; before that, he was Maude's. Now he must be hers. She would not let him go until he had been paid, and so he earned a shilling as a writer's clerk.

Marie left at once. 'I wis leavin' onyway. I never cared for Walter much. And I will not work for you. Nae offence.'

Elspet took none. She said simply, 'Where will you go?'

'To Falkland, wi Clem, for next Thursday's fair. And to Dundee for Lady Day.'

Clem was the juglar, who had asked Marie to marry him. 'Marry me, Marie.' They had laughed at that. He said her supple fingers would be fine for sleight of hand, her pert bonny breasts would pull in the crowd. Marie thought her life with him would be an endless fair day. She would live on gingerbread, sugarloaf and plums. She would be his queen.

'Mebbe I will see you here again at Michaelmas.'

Elspet said, 'Mebbe you will.'

Hew left her there with Joan, and what comfort she could find in the shadows of the house. He found none for himself. Before returning home, he called on Robert Black to tell him Henry Balfour was no longer under threat. 'I made a mistake,' he explained. 'I thought it was Henry Walter meant to harm. But it was someone else. Henry is quite safe, and you can let him go.'

Robert was not settled by the news. 'Safe! I wish he were. I know not how to keep him from the harm he does himself, never mind the harm the world may do to him. This morning, he avows he is determined to elope with some country lass; or if she refuse him, he will throw himself precipitate into the Spanish wars, for he does not care if he should live or die, if it be not with her, and so, and on, and on. And he is pale and faint, and weeping like a girl. He was sick, too, in his psalter, which I take for a very bad sign. I wish to God I had not taken him in charge.'

'Why did you, then?' asked Hew.

'For I was vain enough to think I might have shown him, by my good example, how he should behave. I thought that he would blossom, in more gentle hands. His father is severe on him. Now I see his mind. The boy is loose and reckless, and abuses liberty. You are used to trouble, Hew, whereas I am not. You will not take him, I suppose? He is lively company.'

Hew laughed at that. 'Aye, no doubt. I will not take him, though. Here is my advice. Tell him that to marry is all well and good, but that he should wait till he is twenty-one. He should finish his degree, so he can provide for her. For his father will no doubt deprive him of his wealth. This threat to his inheritance will help to fix his mind. First love is fierce, but does not last long. To fight it will simply add fuel to its fire. But let it run its course, and the wind may blow it out. Courage, Robert. Henry is your lot. You will make a man of him, or he a man of you, before the harvest's done.'

III

Hew had no will to take on Robert's troubles, for he had sufficient of his own. He went to look for Giles, but Giles was not at home. The house was closed and dark. He crossed over to the kirk, and on to Market Street. The market was long done. Crumpled flowers and fly-blown fruit were left to blow about the dust. The wind picked listless over all, snatching at a twist of paper or a withered leaf, and dropping it again.

The North Street, too, was still. The doors to the chapel and the college court were locked. But Hew saw a window at the top of Giles Locke's tower, where often he had sat and looked out on the street, open to the sun. Giles was in his room. And the welcome in his smile as he caught sight of Hew helped to lift his heart.

Now the Whitsun visitors were gone, Giles had filled his shelves again with instruments and books. In the circle at the top of the spiral stair, he had placed an astrolabe, so bright and broad in girth its compass seemed to mark the centre of the world.

Hew said, 'Still at your charts?'

'In effect,' said Giles, 'the essential one is done. But I have just been told some grave, unsettling news, and I came to mark it on the map. I met a man just now who came up from the coast, who saw a lighted beacon over from Fife Ness; Spanish ships are sighted in the Firth of Forth.'

'Can it be true? Why would they come there?'

'Such rumours often may be underpinned by truth. Perhaps they have been driven back, by the English fleet.'

'Or the threat of storm.'

'Fiddle. Did I not tell ye there will be no storms? Have ye no faith in my forecasts?'

Hew replied, 'Not much. It is a concern, if they approach our coasts. There are some here preparing to encourage and receive them.'

Giles said, enigmatically, 'So I have been told.'

'You are not among them, I suppose?'

The doctor looked startled, and hurt. 'I? You cannot think that I would chance the lives that I hold dear, your own life, and Meg's? My hope is that a man might live in peace and faith, whatever that may be, without fear or force, which comfort we had here before this present threat. You call me traitor, now? The foe that makes that rift between us has achieved his end before he ever sets a foot upon this soil.'

The passion in his words made Hew ashamed. 'I spoke ill. Forgive me,' he said.

'Ill words may be forgiven, Hew, but that ye thought them, no.'

'I never, on my life, thought any ill of you. But I am out of humour, thrawn, and ken not what to think.'

Giles did not sulk long. He looked his close friend over with a doctor's eye. 'Your spirits are thrown thwart, and your temper, too. You are pale and cross. What is the matter, Hew? Is it Walter Bone, the man who died today?'

Hew flung himself into the doctor's gossip chair, where often in the past he had sought for resolution, spilling out the trouble on his mind. 'I cannot help but think that it was all my fault.'

Giles belonged to a faith that believed in absolution, but Hew did not want to be absolved. He wanted to be showered with bitter words and blamed.

Giles did not indulge him in his wish. He listened to his words, before concluding reasonably and quietly, 'You were not to blame.'

It was rare enough that Giles was unequivocal, and Hew had not expected it. 'I foresaw the tragedy, and I should have diverted it. I tried to, Giles. Because I was mistaken, I brought the thing about. If I had not insisted Walter was locked up, he might have found the lass before she came to Michael, then Walter would have had nothing to avenge, and he would not be killed,' he said.

The doctor shook his head. 'You may not determine what things might have been. Walter telt you clearly his intent: he meant to kill a man. That one fact alone is clear and certain here. You moved to prevent it. But you were like a man with only half a map, who tries to steer a ship upon a different course when fortune has determined it must strike the rocks. Your action may deflect it for the while, but cannot keep it safe, for the cross winds blind you to the way ahead.'

'Then you believe all this was written in the stars?' asked Hew.

'Aye, to some extent. There are other forces at work upon them too, as human will, and God's.'

'But is my intervention not the devil's work? Walter came to me when he would make his will. He came to me because I was involved with all that went before at the harbour inn. I helped to make the sale. And all that went before – Elspet was the relict of it,' Hew persisted.

'And so you think that you were instrumental in her fate?' Giles raised an eyebrow, sceptically, which his friend ignored.

'She was *left behind*. I did not think of her.'

'And you believe you should have done?' asked Giles.

'Aye, I should have done. My actions then did shape what now becomes of her.'

'We cannot see the future. It were pride and folly to suppose we can,' Giles said. 'Those sorcerers who seek to ken what it is to come are damned, and see their own destruction in their crystal balls.'

'You say that, with your charts?'

'The charts are dispositions, Hew, and are not set in stone. They cannot tell us all that is to come, they merely tell us where the wind will blow. I may ken that certain physic suits a man at certain times and serve it to him at those times, to increase his chance. The man may yet depart upon a different course, and he may harm himself, but God alone decides if he will survive. Walter, I believe, was disposed to die. You did not have the power to turn him from that end. But I do not believe that you were fortune's instrument, nor that he was driven blindly to his fate. The proof is in his words when he came to you, 'to make his *will*,' he said. That will was his, not yours. You served him as his man of law. Elspet too. And there is nothing in that worthy of reproach. In this, for once, I count you not to blame.'

Hew smiled at that. 'Your kind words are welcome, though not yet deserved.'

'Not kind, but honest, Hew. Trust me to remind you when you are at fault. But not upon this day. Today, if any day, you should set aside your quarrels with the world.'

'Why, what is today?'

'You do not ken?' The doctor laughed. 'I have it on authority I do not dare to doubt – your sister's and your wife's – that this day is your birthday. Please do not deny it, for you are found out.'

'I suppose it is,' said Hew, who kept no note of it. 'But such days do not count, except for bairns and kings.'

'Do not tell that to your wife, who prepares a banquet for you. Meg is with her now, and you and I expected. It is a surprise.'

'It is,' said Hew. 'Or was.'

'I thought I should forewarn you, in your present state. Or

you would ruin the feast, with your baleful looks.'

'My birthday is no cause for feasting,' Hew replied.

'Frances thinks it is. God will you do not show to her your cold ungrateful face. Calvin himself permits a man good cheer to thank the Lord for life. We are not like pharaohs, gorging to excess. The lapin that you like, in a mustard sauce, pippins in a pie, a jug of claret wine, will do well for us. The bairns have brought you honey from our bees. And I have here a gift for you that I prepared myself. It is your horoscope.'

'My horoscope,' Hew whispered. 'Why would you do that?'

He felt a clutch, a tremor in his heart, though he did not believe, never had believed, in horoscopes. But now he understood that Giles had worked on his, through the sultry days when he was close and secretive, he was half afraid, and fascinated too, as though his friend had cast a charm that he could not resist.

'You looked to see my future there?' he said.

'Not your future, Hew. That I cannot do. And would not, if I could. Rather, I have here your native disposition, according to the motions and disposal of the planets at the moment you were born. Would you like to see it?' Giles unfurled the scroll, and showed to him a paper filled with charts and scribblings he could scarcely read.

'I know not what it means.'

'Here, to make it plain to you, I have put the sum.' The doctor smiled. 'It says you are a scholar and a true philosopher, subtle and ingenious, tending to a fault to recklessness and stubbornness, but always and essentially a searcher after truth. There, we must allow for a small degree of error. Tis possible the stubbornness is more advanced and dominant, while scholarship recedes.'

'Now I know,' said Hew, 'that this must be a fraud. You have made it up.'

'I assure you, not. Tis written in the stars.' Giles rolled up the paper. 'Later, after supper, I will show the science. For now, I have a prophecy for you.'

Hew said, 'A prophecy! You promised you had not!'

'It is very short, and not at all obscure. The prophecy is this: you will leave for home, and meet me on the path. We will walk together through the fields. And coming to your house, you will find your wife has made a birthday feast for you, which you will receive with wonder and delight.'

'So much you suppose.' Hew smiled. 'How can you be sure that it will come about? Frances knows me well. My feigning may not fool her.'

'Then you will have to practise on the way. It must turn out, precisely, as I now predict. Or I will never hear the last of it from Meg.'

They walked together through the fields, just as Giles had said. And Hew looked out upon the shore, a wash of white and watered blues. He looked upon the fields of ripening corn, the slender stalks that shivered in a veil of green, and thought, How fragile all this is. The harvest in the last three years had failed. A sudden gust, a blast of wind, could blow the barley from its course. Even as it caught its colour from the sun, it could still be crushed, as Spanish ships could light upon an undefended coast. But when they reached the gate, and came to Kenly Green through a bank of trees, he let himself be led off by the laughing bairns, blindfold, to the house. And when the doors were closed, and they were safe inside, he did not see the corn rigs bristling in the breeze, or the rain that swept them, falling soft at first.

BOOK IV

Martinmas

And when the cold of death is come
and body voyd remanes
Each where my haunting spirit shall
pursue thee to thy paines

Lewes Lavater, *Of Ghosts and Spirits*, 1596

I

CROWE

'Melancholike persons ... imagine many things'

Martinmas term blew in with a storm. The students of St Salvator's, returning to St Andrews on the first day of October, were buffeted by winds that blasted from the sea. At night, they lay awake to the rattle of the rain. They found it hard to settle after the excitements of the summer months. The vacation had been dominated by the threat from Spain. In August, the Armada had been sighted in the Forth, and many of the students had resolved to fight, some prepared to die, for their way of life. Before they had a chance to put their courage to the test, the ships were blown off course and broken on the rocks by the raft of storms that battered at the coast. The wreckage left unspent a furious pent-up force. The students did not bow down meekly to their books but brought with them an energy that the restless elements did little to disperse.

The master William Cranston, who taught the entrant year, complained to his colleagues that his class comprised 'the most fidging, kittil pack of bairns' that he had ever come across. 'It is not,' he said, 'that they want for brains. But they cannot settle to the smallest task.'

'This fretful disposition does not augur well,' said the principal Giles Locke. 'There is mischief brewing. Can you smell it, Hew?' He appealed to Hew Cullan, as professor in the law. Since Hew lived out of town, and since he did not lecture to the first year class, he could be relied upon to remain detached, his appraisals cool and practical.

'There is something growing, certainly,' Hew said. 'A fustiness and mould, where the roof slates leak. As to the smell, the college reeks of kale, and of adolescence, as it always did. Worse now, I think, because the students are confined. This is the third week that the weather has prevented them from going to the links, or to practise at the butts. They have had no exercise.'

'That is very true.' Giles proposed a remedy: a tournament of golf, 'to be held, come what may, on Wednesday next week. It will give their passions purpose and a vent. Golf is a game that stands up well to wind. I do not propose an argument for archery.'

Hew said, 'God forbid.'

On Wednesday, October 26, the day broke dull but dry. The students from St Salvator's were taken to the sands, to play a round of golf. St Leonard's too turned out. The hot and fettered spirits, recklessly released, broke out into a football match, with a hundred students grappling for the ball, some of them with golf clubs flailing in their hands, their ardour barely dampened by the showers of spray thrown up in their faces by the fractious sea. At the close of play, when the regents gathered in their drenched and bloodied ranks, the students judged the 'golf' to be a great success. Their masters were dismayed to find them more enflamed than when they had set out.

One young boy hung back, reluctant, from the rest. The student Thomas Crowe had not enjoyed the game. He did not like St Salvator's, the structures it imposed upon his daily life, or the other students in his class.

The students who returned hungry from the links jostled past him to the place where supper was set out. Thomas did not join them, for he did not like it there. A man had been strung up, or perhaps had hanged himself, in the dinner hall. An older boy had told them that when they first arrived. And Death had come to supper once or twice before. Professor Bartie Groat had perished in the plague. His sniffing could be heard in the upper cloister, when a bitter wind was blowing from the north. This was sworn as true, by students who came after Bartie Groat was dead. He had been professor of mathematics. His Euclid had been burnt to ashes in the kiln, for fear it carried in it traces of the peste.

Thomas Crowe knew death. He knew that it had a way of insinuating itself deep inside the stone, the fabric of a place. Once it had a grip, it did not let go. It left behind it grief. Thomas understood the depth to which it plunged. There was sickness in his family that afflicted the bairns in his father's house. His mother was bereft. Her children were born dead, or too malformed to live. Some said it was caused by a witch's curse. His father sought advice, and whatever the answer, it had seemed to work, for his mother had delivered two healthy sons, Thomas and his brother, older by a year. His mother's strength had failed, and she was never well enough to bear a bairn again. His father loved his boys, and taught them both at home. When Thomas was twelve, and Patrick thirteen, he engaged a tutor to prepare them to matriculate at the university. Then Thomas had awoken, restless, in the night, to find Patrick dead beside him in the truckle bed where they had slept together almost all their lives. They were close as twins. But Patrick, lately, had begun to change. His slender limbs had thickened and his voice grew hoarse, a fluff of down appearing on his cheek and chin. He had begun to grow into a man, leaving his brother still a bairn behind him. Thomas had awoken to the weight of Patrick's arm, carelessly flung out on to his side of the bed. He had thrown it off, and felt it stiff and cold. Death had come in the night, to take Patrick as he slept.

Patrick had not been unwell. His long, ranging body did not show a mark. The broad hand that dropped where Thomas had pushed it lay open, the palm facing up to the sky. The fingers that curled there did not flex again.

Patrick's body lay beside him in the bed. But there was nothing left of Patrick in it. Death had stripped it bare.

His mother was not well enough to understand the news. But his father had uttered a terrible cry. 'I have lost God,' he had said.

'No, no, no, no, no,' the minister who came to bury Patrick said. 'God has not forsaken you. He puts you to the test. Why should he test one who might not be saved? Ye mauna gie up hope.'

Patrick was not in the corpse that was put in the ground. He came to see his brother three times after that. The first and the second time it was in a dream, the hairs on his arm, the laughter in his voice as clearly defined as they had been in life, and nothing like the shadow he had left in death. The third was in the garden of their father's house, where he came to Thomas in a copse of trees. He was insubstantial then, but Patrick all the same. His presence was a comfort, and Thomas spoke to him. But when he told his tutor Patrick had appeared – his father at that time was distracted and remote – the tutor had explained it was the devil's work. It was not Patrick's spirit that had come to him, for the souls of the dead did not roam the earth. It was the devil that had taken Patrick's shape; that was a thing that the devil liked to do, and an easy trick for him, to lead a man astray. The tutor had made Thomas pray, hard on his knees till he was stiff and sore, and the devil went away. The tutor said, 'Give thanks, that God has seen it fit to put you to this test,' a sour note to his voice, as though he envied him. Thomas was confused. 'I thought it was the devil?' he had said.

Thomas turned thirteen. He had grown to the age that Patrick had been, and beyond it. Yet he had not thrown off the trappings of a child. He was small and bairnlike, and his skin was smooth. His voice, when he sang the psalms, was as faint and feeble as a boy of nine's, rising sweet and tremulous. Only now had it begun to creak and crack, as though it were the devil mocking at God's word. His tutor said he should not fight what was a natural thing. But Thomas did not like that he had no control of it.

His father had enrolled him at St Andrews University. At fourteen, he was ready to depart. His brother, had he lived, would be there before him, in his second year. Now Thomas was advised that he must go alone. His tutor had instilled in him the Latin he would need. He had instilled in him, besides, a fear of the devil and a deep mistrust in God, which Thomas had been wise enough to hide. He spent much of his time praying on his knees, with his tutor by his side, to force the devil out. The tutor had been doubtful that they would succeed.

His father did not ken of their struggles with the devil. He had retreated to a torment of his own. But he emerged from it long enough to tell his son that he would be going to the College of St Salvator. 'They call it the Auld College. You will like it there. You will have the company of bairns your ain age. Young men, I mean.'

Thomas had telt him that he did not want to go. 'Let me stay with you.' He had had no company but the tutor's since his brother's death, and he wanted none. His father had turned, so that Thomas could not see the expression on his face. 'It is for the best.'

The tutor was dismayed at the father's choice. He had taken his own degree at St Leonard's, and after at St Mary's had studied for the Kirk. It was no fault of his own that he found no living there, and had to tutor boys. (It was not, Thomas thought, for the want of prayer). St Leonard's was a fount of religion, and a solid rock of the Reformation. The college of St Salvator was a place apart. The principal was kent to have some Catholic sympathies. He held certain views. Discipline was lax, and heresies advanced.

The father had stood fast. He had been a student at St Salvator's himself, and he had no reason to suspect its present principal. Giles Locke was a doctor of physick. He had saved lives.

'Lives, aye,' the tutor had retorted. Though it was plain he hinted 'at the cost of souls', the father would not move. So this was the place where Thomas was sent.

'You will have to try especially hard,' the tutor said to him. 'See it as a test.' His pouting made it plain enough he did not hold out hope.

The night before they left, Thomas had gone in to take leave of his mother, lying in her bed in the place where she was kept. 'Minnie,' he had told her, 'I maun gang awa', to the university.'

She had turned her smile to him, hesitant and sweet. 'Patrick, is it you?'

'Aye, Minnie, Patrick,' he had said.

His father had not travelled with them to St Andrews, but sent Thomas with the tutor, who was embarking on a project there. He was on a mission to discover Jesuits. It was not clear if the mission came from the Kirk, or from God himself, but he was very pleased at it. It filled him full of zeal. It was more deserving than tutoring a boy, even one that had the devil at his back.

At matriculation, the tutor disappeared. He did not recommend him to the college principal, or to the professor who was master of the law, whom he seemed to hold in a high contempt. When Thomas took the test in proficiency in Latin, he kept back from the crowd. When Thomas was accepted, he was nowhere to be found.

The regent for the year was Master William Cranston, a placid, earnest man. He did not work himself up to such a frenzy of zeal as the tutor did, but he was more particular on small points of grammar. His methods of instruction were thorough and pedantic, tending to the dull. Besides the Latin grammar he lectured on Isocrates.

There were twelve other entrants in the first year class. 'We are thirteen,' said a boy called Crabbe. Malcolm Crabbe was loud, and irrepressibly profane. He was the sort of boy the tutor warned against. He came with an impressive cache of contraband, including a collection of the latest pamphlets, which he rented nightly to the students in his year. Crabbe knew a trick to reignite a candle when the lights were out. His library was popular. And though Thomas did not choose to subscribe to it, he heard the highlights broadcast in the twilight hours. Most prized were accounts of the Spanish fleet, together with the torments of the Inquisition, which the boys elaborated with their own effects. When the master's back was turned, they would act them out. Sometimes, they complained, 'Crowe does not pay into the fund. Why should he be privy to the play?' Then Crabbe would smile. 'Ah, leave him be.' He was wise, like Solomon. The rest deferred to him. They called him Cancer, the Latin word for Crabbe. A canker was a thing that ought to be cut out. Thomas had no doubt he was the devil in disguise.

Thomas felt confined by the college crowd. He liked the chapel best, which looked out on the street. The neglected kirk was often damp and dark, and few went there from choice. Thomas entered now, assured of peace and solitude, and found his favourite place to kneel and say his prayers. The reformers had relieved the chapel of its vanities, and made a gaudy shrine a clean and wholesome place. They had stripped the windows of their painted glass. But there were fragments still, shards that had remained embedded in the frames, like a blink of blueness in a glowering sky. Sometimes, when the sun was out, it would light upon them, scattering the motes of colour on the floor, trailing clouds of dust. Thomas had discovered how to catch the light, squinting through his fingers as he knelt to pray, playing with the prism of the dancing sun. It was like a rainbow, and the play of God, coming from the place where Patrick was. He had lit upon it on the first day of the term, when the college was assembled in the chapel vaults. He kept it to himself, a secret thing, and rare, for in the weeks that followed there was little sun.

There was none today. And though he knelt in the line of the red and yellow glass nothing filtered through to the earth around his feet, which was desolate and bare.

He closed his eyes and prayed for his mother and father to be well, and to be brought to a certain sort of lightness, though he was not certain what that light might be. For his mother, it was kindness that she was unwell. But what was kindness now might not be in the end. He prayed to God to rid his heart of sin and doubt. He asked him for courage, when the devil came. But he felt no conviction in the words he spoke, without the force of his tutor, praying at his side. 'I too have lost God,' he thought. 'I am abandoned, and can have no hope.'

Opening his eyes, he was not dismayed to see another ghost. It brought a kind of comfort, though he was afraid. The tutor said the spirits were a test. If he was tested still, then he was not yet damned. He was only sorry that it was not Patrick now. And though he prayed again, he could not find the words to make it go away.

This ghost was a man with a small pointed beard and sallow-coloured skin, of a saturnine complexion while he was alive. The curling locks of hair once luxuriantly dark were matted and unkempt. The ruff round his neck was blackened with blood, from a slack cut to his cheek. But the wound that had killed him was spilling from his side, where his fingers laced to hold the innards in. His doublet and hose were tattered to strips, ribbons of yellow and red. That he had been a soldier with the Spanish fleet, Thomas knew at once. He matched the descriptions Malcolm Crabbe had read. He was standing in the place where the altar would have been, back when the chapel was a Catholic church. He looked straight at Thomas, and let out a groan. He spoke an imprecation, in a foreign tongue, holding out his hands. 'He is Catholic,' Thomas thought, 'and will ken Latin.' He supposed the devil was restricted to the form he took, and that it must inhibit how he shaped his words. But he knew better than to speak to him. The tutor had succeeded in curing him of that.

William Cranston, in the dinner hall, observed that his charges were particularly loud. The golf had not been an unqualified success. Rather than allowing them to exhaust their passions, it had set them free; once unleashed they seemed even harder to contain. Wednesday was fish day, and the substance of the supper was a bowl of wattir-kail. Even this did not serve to suppress their spirits. Hew Cullan and Giles Locke, as extraordinary professors, lived outside the college, and they took their meals at home. Cranston envied them. At the plague in 1585, he had lost his class. Not that, God forbid, they had been carried off, but the closing of the college meant a year had dropped out, and no more than three regents were required. He had filled in the time teaching grammar to the son of the earl of Cassilis and enjoyed the table there. Now he was returned, he found that common living did not taste as sweet.

He sighed as he listened to the chatter in the hall, and tried to prevent its breaking out in Scots. Malcolm Crabbe's golf ball had been 'goited' in the sand. 'Immissa est pila in arenam', he corrected. Malcolm said, 'Et tu, magister?' and his colleagues sniggered. This will be a long year, William Cranston thought. Is it possible, just possible, I have grown too old for it? But what is the alternative? Eking out a living at some far-flung kirk?

He felt a draught from the opening door, and looked across

for someone to call upon to close it, the servant, perhaps, with a stoup of ale, of the weakest, watered kind. Instead he saw a student, one of his own, late to the board. He felt a prick of conscience, for he had not noticed that the boy was absent, and he should have done. He responded crossly, 'Why have you come late?'

The boy was Thomas Crowe, the smallest and most timid student in his class. He had shown up nothing, in the last few weeks, suggesting he had character or a spark of spirit. It was not surprising he had not been missed. William noticed now that he was deathly pale. The play at the golf had not improved his colour, as it had his friends'. William Cranston sometimes saw that look on the fourth year students in their final term, as they were preparing for examination. They were hunched and hollow, starved of air and light, withered from long days of work and endless sleepless nights. That numbness he had seen upon the faces of some who mounted the black stane as wretched as a felon taken to the block. He had not seen it in a first year at the start of term. 'This boy is not well,' William thought. He recalled some dark shadow in the boy's family, a kind of consumption, perhaps. He must consult with Giles Locke.

Thomas had crossed to the place where he sat. He looked at him, wraithlike. William said, 'Well?'

The boy's eyes were trusting. His young voice was brittle and childlike, to cut through the laughter of men. His Latin came clear, and was heard through the hall. 'Master, and it please you, will you pray with me? I have seen the devil in the college kirk. He has taken up the corpus of a Spaniard for his ghost. And I do not have the courage to confront him by myself.'

Giles Locke said, 'I blame the storms.'

'As I recall,' said Hew, 'you predicted there would be no storms.'

'Did I not tell you, too, that prophecy can never be exact? I did not pretend to know the mind of God.'

'Then when you said the words "there will be no storms" you forgot,' Hew teased, 'to take account of God?'

Giles retorted huffily, 'I never made a claim to perfect science. God kens; so should you. This quarrel does not help us, Hew. It is a plain truth that a storm can play havoc with the mind. Young imaginations are yet more subjectable. Bairns are more rebellious when there is a wind. But Thomas Crowe insists he saw a ghost. Whatever else is put to him, he will not be swayed. He does not believe that he imagined it.'

'If he believes he saw a ghost,' said Hew, 'then perhaps he did.'

Giles Locke raised an eyebrow. 'I have heard you say such things do not exist.'

'A searching eye sees all, and rules nothing out,' Hew said. 'But I believe that what he saw owes more to human mischief than the devil's kind. To put it plainly, now, I do not believe that spirits walk the earth. Where is Thomas Crowe? I will talk to him.'

'Ah, I hoped you would. He is in the fermary, where he is treated for his melancholy.'

'Is he melancholic?'

'I imagine so,' Giles said. 'What man would not be, who has seen a ghost? If not before, then after. A ghost is cold and dry, to the last degree. Whether there is malice in it I will leave to you. For I have no doubt that you will find it out.'

The fermary, as Giles Locke called it, was a small, separate building to the north side of the college, which the doctor had established following the plague, to contain infection. Here students were confined who showed sign of fever, or suffered from the flux. The servant Kennocht Cutler acted as the fermer,

tending to their needs, and putting into practice what the doctor
had prescribed.

Today, there were two patients in his ward. George Robertson,
a tertian, had a tertian fever, brought on by excitement at the
golf. Following his breakfast of a pat of butter (loosening), on a
hunk of bread (absorbing) and a roasted egg (binding), George
would be discharged; his symptoms had subsided in the night.

The second patient, Thomas Crowe, did not have a fever. His
pulse was slow and strong, and his piss was clear. His bowels
were brought to flux through the doctor's clysters, while it was
the vomitaries left him limp and pale, wringing out the flush
of colour from his cheeks. He had been thoroughly purged.
And yet he was not cured. The infection in this boy was of a
stubborn, dangerous kind.

The floor of the fermary was strewn with herbs. Meg's work,
Hew supposed. Though women were forbidden to pass through
the college gates, her influence was plain in the comforts
Giles prescribed, though absent in the plying of emetics. Meg
approved purging only to countermand poisons. But perhaps
it was a poison that afflicted Thomas Crowe, working on his
mind?

The pungency of rosemary did not clear the air. Hew felt in
his wam a sympathetic lurch. But the old hands in the sick room
were inured to it. George Robertson finished his breakfast with
gusto, licking his fingers. It was better than the bannock served
up in the hall.

'You do not seem ill,' Hew told him.

'That is the thing about a tertian fever. It manifests itself every
other day.'

Hew knew George quite well. His fevers – tertian, quartan or
quotidian – re-emerged at intervals convenient to himself. Hew
could guess their source: flannels warmed to boiling point and
secretly applied. Kennocht was perhaps complicit in the case.

The two appeared fast friends.

'Well, I will be gone,' George Robertson said cheerfully. He thanked Cutler for the egg, and his gentle care. 'Good morrow, little friend,' he said to Thomas Crowe. 'May God requite your prayers.'

Thomas Crowe was sitting silent on his bed. He did not look up.

'Why do you say that?' said Hew. Giles Locke had left instruction that Thomas Crowe should not be left alone. Solitude was perilous in a case of melancholy. Yet Hew was not so sure. Was the ghost a trick that had been played on him? If so, then his companions must come under scrutiny.

George looked surprised at his question. 'He is sic a pious little soul.' He seemed to bear no malice for the boy.

'How are you today?' Hew asked Thomas Crowe, once Robertson had left.

Thomas Crowe replied he had the belly-thraw. The requirement to speak Latin was relaxed in the sick room, and his words were shrill and childish, causing Hew to smile.

'That is the bad stuff, swilling out,' Kennocht Cutler said. He set down a cup of green, brackish liquid, together with a basin covered with a cloth.

Thomas pleaded, 'Must I?'

'Ye want to get well, dae ye no?'

'I was well when I came,' Thomas said.

Kennocht Cutler looked at Hew and shook his head. 'Ye see how it is. It is a stubborn case.'

'Leave us awhile,' answered Hew. 'I will take care of him now.'

The fermer left them to it, glad to take his rest.

Thomas looked at Hew. His gratitude was cautious. 'Can you make it stop?'

'I expect so,' Hew said. 'Can't you?'

'I don't know how,' Thomas said. 'Except it is by prayer. The praying has not worked yet. I have not prayed long or hard enough.'

He seemed entirely earnest in his plea. Hew thought back to George: 'a pious little soul'. 'I thought you meant the medicine. I see you mean the ghost.'

'The medicine is meant to drive away the ghost,' Thomas said. 'If I tell them it has gone, they will stop the purge.' His expression told Hew that he had considered it. Who would not consider it, bent over the bowl, and the pot?

'Tempted?'

The boy's eyes were watery; frank. They carried in them a conviction Hew believed in utterly. He was used to students, to their sly omissions and their small deceits. He knew the lies they told to portion for themselves some fraction of the lives the college now controlled. The eyes of Thomas Crowe resembled none of them.

'It is meant to tempt me,' Thomas said.

'Does the ghost come still?' asked Hew.

'I have not seen it here.'

'Well then, perhaps the physic has worked.'

'I would feel it, if it had. But it was only in the chapel that it came to me.'

'Will you show me where?'

'I can take you to the place. But I do not think that it will show itself.'

Thomas Crowe showed no reluctance in returning to the chapel. He bore himself with dignity, a modest kind of pride. There were one or two students outside in the courtyard, who whispered and stared as they passed. Thomas did not shrink from them, but seemed to rise and swell a little. Liking the attention, Hew supposed.

The students were coming from the kirk itself, where the college principal had read the morning prayers. Giles came out briskly, rubbing his hands. He stopped when he saw them. 'Better, now?' he asked.

Thomas said, 'Ignosce.'

Giles looked perplexed. 'You beg my pardon? Or, I should not ask?'

Hew answered him, obliquely. 'We are returning to the scene of the crime.'

'Ah. Very good. I will leave you to it. It is cold in there.'

The restless wind picked up, snatching at the whispers in the crowd. One of the students was bold enough to step out, and address Thomas Crowe directly. A large, freckled boy. 'Salve, Corve. I am sorry that you are not well. Would you like to have my transcript of the lecture?'

Corvus was the Latin word for crow. Spoken by a friend, the words might be well meant. But Thomas gave no sign this was a friend. He shook his head, staring at the ground. The freckled boy was moved, thought Hew, by a sense of guilt. Or else he had hoped, by this pubic avowal of friendship, to allay suspicions he had bullied Crowe. If Thomas had been tricked, they would not have far to look. He asked the boy his name, and hurried his charge on. 'Is that your friend?' Hew asked. He was not surprised by the reply.

'I did not think he was.'

Thomas Crowe knelt down in the centre of the church. 'I was here, like this. I closed my eyes to pray. And when I opened them, the spirit was before me.'

Hew held up the candle to look into the boy's white face. He did not doubt his earnestness. The boy was fearful, but composed.

'Then you did not see it come?'

'I felt it. I can feel it now.'

The boy's words made Hew shiver. The kirk was cold that day. Dampness seeped across the stone, through the broken slates. The reformers had stripped out the windows, and the chasms had been stopped with whatever came to hand. Some were patched with hides, or the oiled paper sheets that were used in printers' shops, shielding off the sun. Only on a bright day, did it filter through, catching at the corners of the broken glass, sending out a scattering of violet, green or blue. This morning was not bright. The October sky hung lank, the colour of a bruise. The chapel was lit in snatches of lamplight, dim yellow pockets that seeped into gloom.

'Tell it to show itself.'

'I cannot call it, sir. And I do not think it will come to you.'

'I will go aloft, and look down from there.' Hew moved further off as the boy began to pray. He spoke the words aloud. He said his prayers in Scots, though Latin was more likely to arouse the ghost. The echo followed through the vaults as Hew moved round the church. The prayers were fast and urgent; as soon as they were done, the boy began again. The words sounded fractured, uncertain, breaking apart from the voice of a child. 'O dreadful and most mighty God . . . that . . . hast declared thyself a consuming fire . . . we have declined from thee . . . we have been polluted with idolatry . . . we have given thy glory to creatures . . . we have sought support where it was not to be found . . .'

There was something, by the place where the altar once had stood, that bore a clear resemblance to a spot of blood. Hew bent down to examine it. Not all that looked like blood was blood; and not all blood was human blood, he told himself. He took out his knife to scrape the substance up.

In the kirk behind him, Thomas gave a cry. A brief, unstructured voicing of surprise. In the time it took for Hew to turn in his direction, he had fallen to the ground. When he was lifted up, and carried to the fermary, the way that he was lying came to be remarked upon. His right arm was flung out at an angle from his body, with the palm upturned. Some said, it was shaken by the devil's hand.

II

SNELL

'God doth suffer spirits to appear unto the elect to a good end, but unto the reprobate they appear as a punishment'

Master Colin Snell had come back to St Andrews zealous in his purpose. He was on God's work.

The Lord's design for him had sometimes been obscure. In his path were obstacles, or trials. The last years had been testing ones. When God – or the devil – threw troubles in his way, Colin had not always borne them stoically. He had been hot-headed in his haste to serve the Lord. His misfortunes had begun with the student Roger Cunningham, who had daubed the college of theology with filth. Colin had attempted to drown him in the jakes, requiting like with like. He now saw that was wrong. But Roger had not faced the justice he deserved. Roger had found profit in his sins, while Colin had been pilloried for his. Colin had been forced to scrub out the latrines, for the crime of contemplating throwing Roger into them. That was the moment when his luck had changed. Ordure clung to him. He smelt it in his sleep. His colleagues at the time had refused to sit by him. Even Dod Auchinleck had wrinkled up his nose. 'We did a terrible thing.' Dod would not listen when Colin had protested that they had done nothing at all.

Now Roger had been prenticed to the surgeon to the town. Colin had discovered this just the other day. He had been tethered to the surgeon's chair, distracted by a searing soreness in his tooth, when Roger had appeared with the pincers in his hands. 'I am tooth-pick here.' Colin Snell had screamed, and broken from his bonds. He would not go back, though the toothache troubled still.

Roger, after all, might not remember him. The business with the jakes had happened years ago, when Colin was a student, training for the ministry. And Roger had been barely conscious at the time.

The year of the latrine had been a tumultuous one. The St Mary's College principal, Master Andrew Melville, and his nephew James had been forced into exile to England at the end of it, and the college of theology had fallen to decline. Colin too had left, without taking his degree. He had not thought, at first, it would hold him back. The Kirk was crying out for preachers of the faith. But it had no revenue to lend to their support. He had travelled round the country while his funds held out. Good men gave him alms, yet he found it difficult to make his message heard. In one place, he was cast out as a vagabond. Pleading his good cause, he was threatened with a whipping that would 'gar his rumpill reek', for of all the 'idle beggars', scholars were the worst. For his love of God, he was stripped and shamed. His spirit had been broken when he came back to St Andrews, seeking the assistance of his former friends. The Melvilles, by then, had returned. He had been too diffident to apply to Andrew – the master who had sentenced him to shovel up the shit – and turned instead to James. James Melville had been hesitant at first. But after he had found for him another set of clothes – Colin's were in rags – he had recommended him to a man called Crowe, who was looking for a tutor for his sons.

Stephen Crowe had asked, 'Have you taught bairns before?'

Colin had admitted he had not. But he could equip them for the university. His Latin was impeccable. 'I can teach them that, and much more besides. Under my instruction, they will be good men.'

Stephen Crowe had said the Latin would suffice.

God saw to it that Colin had the place. There were no other applicants. Stephen Crowe had engaged him, on a month's trial. He had made one condition: 'Be tender to them, sir.'

Surely, it was not because he knew of Roger Cunningham? Roger had recovered fully from the pummelling, which had been provoked. 'When I was a student, not much older than your boys, I was moved to violence more easily than now. I was young, and hot,' Colin had explained.

Stephen Crowe had stared at him, and Colin had been cowed by the expression on his face. Violence was the wrong word. '"Fervour", I should say. I was not so temperate as I am now. A wise man is one who learns from his mistakes.'

His concession was uncalled for, as it had turned out. James Melville's letter had not mentioned the assault, or Stephen Crowe would not have kept him on. It was not Colin's temper that the father was afraid of, or the lively spirit of his growing boys. It was an inherent frailty of the flesh.

At the end of that first month, the older boy had died. There was no apparent cause. Then Colin understood what God had meant for him. He had been sent there to save Thomas Crowe.

Thomas Crowe was haunted by his brother's ghost. Colin told him the ghost was the devil in disguise, and taught him how to pray to drive the devil out. The battle had been hard. There were times when he had felt almost jealous of the boy. What was so special about little Thomas Crowe, that the devil should be drawn to do battle for his soul? In time, he came to realize it was not the boy that God had meant to test. It was Colin Snell.

At first, he had believed that Thomas Crowe was one of God's elect. It was Colin's task to bring him to the light; that was God's design. Now he understood that might not be the case. God wanted him to ken that however hard he tried, there were certain souls that were lost to God. Stephen Crowe was one. Perhaps his son was too.

His work was done there now. He had his reward. When he left, Stephen Crowe had given him a gift of money, which he had added to the sum that he had saved. It was not a fortune, but it was enough.

He had looked forward to renewing his acquaintances. Not with Andrew Melville. He remained in awe of him. In a few months' time, when he had succeeded in flushing out the Jesuits, Colin's name would come up at the General Assembly. He would be admired. Andrew would approve. 'I remember Snell. A young man of great promise, and an asset to the Kirk. His training was cut short.' The savour of the stool would be forgotten then.

For now, he passed St Mary's by. The college was dilapidated, dreary in the rain. It saddened him to see how tired it looked.

Dod Auchinleck, against all expectation, had completed his training for the Kirk. He had acquired a small living, in a country parish. He had acquired a small country wife. His house was too cramped for Colin Snell to stay with him. 'If I lived alone, ye wid be mair than welcome. But ye maun see how it is,' Dod had said. His little country wife was swollen fat with child. Bulbous to the point where it was hardly decent. Colin was surprised at her. He was surprised at Dod. But he did not mind about the living, which was mean and poor, and too far away. He took lodgings on the outskirts of St Andrews, while he drew up the fine details of his scheme.

James Melville was now the minister at Kilrennie, near Anstruther. Colin had walked all the way there on foot. He had expected James to be pleased to see him, and had been received cordially enough. Arriving at dinnertime, he was asked to stay.

At dinner, he had telt him what he had in mind. James Melville had not seemed as keen as Colin was. He had stated that there were no Jesuits in Fife. 'My uncle Andro would have found them, else.'

Then he had demanded the source of his intelligence. Colin had shown him the documents of evidence, the end of his researches for the last two years. A thousand letters of inquiry had been sent, under different names, and the results had been compiled into a spider's web. He had begun with the heirs of ancient papist families, meticulously tracing all their known associates, and plotting all the names on to a charter of deceit that mapped across the land.

James had been jealous of the truth he had discovered. Therefore he had warned, 'Here you have the names of people who have made no secret of their faith, and who, in spite of it, hold favour with the King. That is not to say they harbour Jesuit priests. It is a far cry from that, and what you will accuse them of. You maun beware the wrath of powerful men.'

Colin had insisted, 'I am no feart.' He understood precisely why James was opposed to it. His uncle had been despatched, on his return from exile, to hunt for Jesuits up north, where he had found none. He had cried it vain, a wasting of his time, that kept him from the college and his proper ministry. How galling for him, if Colin had uncovered what was hidden in plain sight. He could not smell the midden under his own nose.

James would not have it, though. He had protested, 'This priest hunt is not fitting at this time.'

'It is precisely fitting at this time. The Kirk was crying out for it, fearful at the prospect of a foreign threat. More treacherous by far is the threat within.'

'Aye, but that was then. Since God has made his feeling plain, and sent the storms to rage against the Spanish ships, they know their cause is lost. Now is time to show the temper of our Kirk, merciful and generous, magnanimous in victory, proving to the world what God himself has shown, that we are better than they.'

A woman's kind of argument, Colin Snell had thought. He had made a man's: 'Our Kirk must not be gentle where there is a threat. Ye ken that yourself. Were you not troubled with witches, the now? Did you show mercy to them?'

That had blown out his bluster. 'Who telt ye that?' James had said.

'It came to me as part of the whole intelligence, which you would dispute. Do you deny it, then? Were there no witches here?'

It was Dod had written to him of the witch at Anstruther. But it did no harm for James to think he had a host of spies. The mention of the witch had vexed him, that was plain to see. Yet he could not deny he had a part in it.

'A witch and a priest are two different things,' was all that he could say.

'But neither,' Colin told him, 'can be wanted here.'

James had suggested that Colin show his document to Andrew at the college. 'He is best placed to examine the proofs. If he thinks that you have found compelling evidence, he will put it before the General Assembly.'

That was the last thing Colin meant to do. He would not have Andrew Melville take the credit for his work. When he discovered his first priest, he would bring him to the Kirk, who would make him talk. Under torments, he would tell the secrets of them all. Colin would be hailed as the saviour of the land, and be assured of a living there for life.

And so he had pretended, 'I will think on it,' tucking up the papers out of James's scrutiny. Now he regretted showing him the list.

James Melville had repeated, 'There are no Jesuits here.'

'That is what you think.' Colin had perhaps been too earnest in his passions, for he had noticed Melville flinch. 'For that is what they want you to think. They are here, among us, hidden in plain sight. I ken it for a fact, that there is one that bides at the house of Ann Balfour at the Poffle of Strathkinness. And I mean to catch him in the act.'

'My advice to you is, do not pursue this on your own.' James had eaten hardly any of his fish. He had seemed to lose his appetite. Now that Colin thought of it, it was a mean enough dinner that his guidwife had provided them, and he was not surprised.

He had urged, 'Come with me, then.'

James had said, 'I should. But the Poffle of Strathkinness is too far away. I am needed here.'

'To deal with the witches.'

Colin had intended to express his sympathy, but James had not liked that. He had not liked it at all. He had made a comment that was quite unkind: 'Some men are not called to go into the Kirk.'

Colin had asked him, 'What d'ye mean?'

James had not answered the question. Instead, he had said, 'I always thought you competent in the Latin tongue. You went to tutor boys. How did that turn out?'

It was early in the morning of the first day of November, when Colin Snell set out to snare his priest. He had been preparing for a month, hampered by the weather and the torment in his tooth, susceptible to sudden blasts of cold. The date – Allhallowday – was auspicious, he supposed, dawning to the vapour of a sluggish wind, a sky pretending to a poor attempt at day. It did not look like rain.

Colin wrapped a scarf around his face. He wore upon his head a little velvet cap, like the one the doctors wore, which had cost him more than all his other clothes. He thought it lent an air of authority and scholarship, crowned by the scarf ends tied across the top, protecting his sore tooth. His shirt was the woollen one that James had given him, for going to the Crowes. Over it he wore his old college gown, tattered now and darned, which he had gathered up and tucked into his hose, to keep the ragged edges from trailing in the mud. The hose were grey and riddled, sagging at the knees. Only his shoes were relatively new; already he had worn through several leather soles. He carried in his left hand a long shepherd's staff, which had assisted him on several of his walks. Sometimes he was troubled with a plague of bairns. A sharp swipe of the cudgel was enough to see them off. 'Dinnae fash, auld man.' Of all the insults flung at him, it was auld that stung. He was twenty-three. But they were naught but flies, buzzing round the cross.

A battered leather scrip was flung across one shoulder. In it was his bible, and a length of rope. The bible was a satisfying burden on his back. It made his shoulder ache. The bairns who mocked were fooled by his lopsided gait. He was lean and strong.

The rope was to restrain the priest, if he put up a fight. Colin would have liked something more substantial, shackles or a chain, but the blacksmith's fee had proved to be prohibitive. His pocket knife was tucked safely in his belt. A priest, though he was slippery, was unlikely to be armed, and Colin could make use of anything to hand. God would provide. But the first and most essential weapon in his armoury was that of surprise.

Ann Balfour's house was three miles from St Andrews, lying to the west, and another mile from the closest farm. In summer, it was hidden from the road by trees, its presence hinted vaguely by the wisp of smoke. Now the fields were bare, and the wind had stripped the trees of leaves, it was mantled still in holly, thistle clumps and thorns, so that Colin breaking through found his calves streaked red with blood and bramble juice. A tree branch snapped back, snatching at his scarf, and scratched him on the cheek. Smarting, he fought free and fell upon the cottage rising from the gloom. The door stood wide open, almost as though he had been expected there. Yet he saw no sign of life.

He left the door ajar, to let in the light, while he looked around. Inside, he found a panelled hall, furnished with a settle and a bed, with some kind of carpet on the walls. There were shutters on the windows, which Colin tried to open, finding that the hinges had been rusted fast, as though no one had opened them for years. On the wall were the stubs of candles, recently burnt out. The wax that puddled in the cups smelt of mutton fat. He prised a candle out, and teasing up the wick, lit it from a flint. It took him several strikes before it was alight. Blowing on his fingers, which the sparks had burnt, he held the stump in front of him, and leapt to see a shadow in the corner of the room become a sombre figure in a high-backed chair. When his heartbeat settled and he dared approach, he saw it was Ann Balfour, apparently asleep. Her face was covered with a veil of gauze, and her hands were clasped white against the lap, voluminous and dark, of her satin gown. It was the hands that captured him, before he had the chance to look up to her face. They were slender hands, the fingers long and delicate. The nails were clean and trimmed. But the skin was parched and crumpled, each blue vein pinched out.

Ann Balfour spoke. 'Who are you?' she said.

Because he had supposed she was asleep, he could not help but jump at it. Her voice was tight and quivering, an auld body's voice, distant and superior, cool in a way that irritated him. She was never meant to have the upper hand.

'I am Colin Snell, come from the Kirk.' He tried to make the words full of weight and matter, inspiring her to dread.

'Thank the Lord for that. I thought you were a ghost.' Ann Balfour did not seem the slightest bit afraid.

She was nearly blind, Colin Snell had heard. He came a little closer, holding up the candle to her face. She did not flinch from it. He saw sunken features, hollowed out with age. An aquiline nose. An old woman's whisker, white on her chin, standing proud. Her eyes, which did not see, were penetrating still, washed out to a crystalline blue. She seemed to look through him.

'The kirk of Holy Trinity?' she asked. 'I had not heard there was a new incumbent.'

'The College of St Mary,' he was forced to say.

'I did not ken there was a chapel there.'

Colin Snell was vexed that she had caught him out. Blustering, he told her, 'The Kirk kens that you are harbouring a priest. I have been sent here to apprehend him.'

The words should have filled her with terror and dismay. She should be whimpering, falling to her knees. He scarcely could believe it when he heard her laugh; a rasping, creaking sound. 'The Kirk is misinformed.'

'If the priest is here,' he told her, 'I will flush him out.'

He knew the priest was there. He could smell him in the air. The scent of incense drifted from the candles, which had been blown out. He sniffed experimentally.

'Camphor,' she said. 'It is for the moths. The tapestries are full of them.'

He knew then that the priest was concealed behind the arras. It was plain as day. He took up his staff with a cry, and began to flounder round the room, flailing at the tapestries, which fell down from the walls, scattering their dust, and clouds of moths flew out, landing on his face.

Ann Balfour said, 'Dear me. Why would ye do that?'

When the streaming in his eyes had stopped, he returned to her, brandishing the staff. He hoped she found it menacing.

Plainly, she did not. 'You have cut your cheek. Let me.' She reached out to him with a pocket handkerchief, doused in some peculiar kind of scent. Her hand touched his face, and Colin jumped back with a jolt. The brush of her fingers, papery dry, kindled the flame in his tooth. Moaning, he cradled his cheek.

'What is the matter? Poor man.'

He could not speak for the pain. When the words came, they were clumsy and thick. 'Tell me where he is.'

Ann Balfour gazed at him. 'I do not understand you. There is no one lives here but the servant Adam Cole, and his wife Grizelda. No one else at all.' She put a curious emphasis upon the final phrase, seeming to amuse her.

He saw there was a tray of breakfast by her side. The breakfast was untouched. The servants must have left it there.

'Where are the servants now?' he asked.

'If they are not about, then I cannot say. Perhaps they have gone out to the farm.'

The door was left wide open. But the farm at the Poffle was a mile away. 'And left you alone?' Colin said.

'They are good servants. They will not have gone far. Besides, they are old. They cannot go far.'

He told her that he meant to search the house. 'It will be the worse for you, if you not confess to something that I find. Better own it now.'

She declined the chance, with a gracious bowing of her head. 'I do not recommend you go into the loft. The boards are rotten there.'

He told her to stay put. 'Do not quit this place.'

Ann Balfour smiled. 'Where would I go?' She closed her eyes again and clasped her hands. He thought he saw a movement in her lips, though he heard no words. He looked around again, and noticed that the bed was stripped.

'Why do you not sleep in your bed?' he asked her. She was laughing at him, he was sure of it.

'Bless you,' she said. 'I do not sleep.'

He supposed he had found her at her papish prayers, and grimaced in disgust. He had a will to hurt her. She was old and frail, and it would be no more than the bending of a twig. But the moment was not now. It would come.

The house was not grand, and would not take long to search. The chamber where she kept had a single room behind it, serving as the kitchen and the nether hall, where the servants slept in a curtained crevice, set into the wall. Here Colin poked and prodded with his stick, but found no one underneath. The kitchen fire was cold; the ashes had been dampened down sometime in the night, and had not been kindled that day. Where were the servants, then? Had they left the house before the sun was up? A pat of primrose butter and a pot of cheese were covered with a cloth. Ale in a barrel was frothy and wholesome. He drew off a cup. There were oats in a sack, sufficient to make cakes, and haddies that were blistered to a honeyed black, hanging from a rack, yet the griddle pan was cold. There were plums and pippins, and a bowl of milk. Yesterday's bread, in a crock. In the larder he found more things to eat. A clutch of small wild birds, plucked of their feathers, packed in a dish like hatchlings in a nest. The carcase of a hare. An extravagant pie, adorned with fruits and leaves moulded from the paste.

He returned to the hall to look in on Ann Balfour.

'Your servants have not gone out for provisions. You are well supplied.'

She took a moment to answer. He did not care if he disturbed her at her prayers, or if she was asleep. Eventually she said, 'Did I say they had?'

'There is food for you. Why do you not eat?' For some reason that he could not fathom, the untouched tray offended him. It was not rational to accuse her. That he understood. And yet he felt a viciousness that spurred his questions on.

'I find,' Ann Balfour said, 'I have little appetite.'

'Then who is all the food for?' The house was full of food. The servants must intend to be away some while. Where, then, had they gone? Surely she must know.

'That is for the guests,' she said.

'What guests?' The door was left open, so that anyone who passed could easily walk in. But no one would pass. The house was not on the way to anywhere at all.

'There are always guests, at a time like this. You are a guest, and hungry, I think. You are most welcome to eat.'

He recognized at once that he was ravenously hungry, astonished that he had not noticed it before. A man who did God's service needed proper sustenance; well then, he would take the woman at her word. He returned to the kitchen and piled a plate with cheese, haddies and some pickle he had found in a jar, slathering some butter on a slab of bread. Vengeful, he carved deep into the piecrust, scooping out the meat to mash up to a jelly in the corner of his mouth. He had eaten little for the last few days, tormented by the raging in his tooth. Now, God was kind; the red volcano slept. Colin had his fill, and more; and when he looked upon the carnage he had left, the pastry coffin torn and pillaged of its flesh, the loaf smeared with butter and the butter strewn with crumbs, and remembered his excess had been visible to God, he felt a little sick. He must not lose sight of the reason he had come. He would make amends by discovering the priest.

Priests of the Catholic Church were well kent to indulge themselves. If the pie had been intended for the Jesuit priest, then it was likely that the priest was gross in size and slothful, and could not run far. Colin had no doubt that he was hiding in the loft. Perhaps at this moment, he was peering down, bleating out his rosary, fumbling at the beads, quivering with rage and indignant at the pie; the short work Colin made of it he would make of him.

Ascending to the loft, Colin reappraised this rosy view of things. The entrance to the loft, and the ladder which led up to it, had not been constructed to admit of corpulence. Any priest who hid there was of the wiry kind. He himself was lean. Yet with his staff in his left hand, and a candle in his right, and the rope and the bible banging on his back, he struggled to climb up. He needed the candle to illuminate the rafters, and the staff to subdue whatever lived up there. Colin's dread of rats equalled the revulsion he felt for Catholic priests.

The hole at the top was a squeeze. Colin set his candle down on a board in front of him, hauling himself up. The light was a drop in the pooling darkness, and Colin stretched his staff before him as a probe, prodding into chasms where the candle did not reach. This is how it must feel to be blind, he told himself, pleased at the conceit. God wanted him to see, to ken what that was like. The floorboards below were spongy to his feet; he could feel them sag. About that, at least, Ann Balfour had not lied.

He proceeded cautiously, stooping where he felt the rafters at his head. Once, he lost his footing, and fell into a pile of something soft. He wrestled for a moment, fighting his way out of what appeared to be a bundle of old clothes. Like the tapestries below, they were full of moths, and a woollen shawl fell to nothing in his hands. He satisfied himself that there was no place here to hide. Disheartened, he climbed down, missing his footing at the bottom of the steps, and landing with a thud. He felt a little flustered, certain that Ann Balfour must have heard the bump. He was followed to the ground by a cloud of dust, and brushing himself off, he found he had a cobweb caught up in his cap.

From the kitchen, he looked out to a yard at the back, where he saw some hens scratching in the dust, and a pile of wood, neatly chopped and stacked. Looking for a door that would take him out, he came upon a cupboard, four or five feet high, built into the wall. Large enough, perhaps, for a man to hide.

But when he looked inside, he saw a flight of stairs.

The steps led underground. And Colin knew at once that he had found the place.

Colin felt a thrill that he had experienced only once before, when he had smacked against the hard core of his fist the pulp of Roger Cunningham, and had conceived the plot to throw him in the jakes. His reactions then had been muddled in their heat; he now saw that was wrong, but he still believed the sentiment was sound. Evil must be carefully, thoroughly snuffed out, retribution calculating, slow. A cornered rat might fight. But Colin was prepared to take him on.

He had no need of the candle coming down the stairs. There were several lanterns lit along the way, to illuminate his path. In the vault ahead, he could hear a murmuring, he could smell the swirling of a dark, Massy scent, in the very bowel and belly of the house.

Yet he was unprepared for the thing he found. The tunnel opened out into a vaulted chamber, with a blaze of candles burning on all sides, and many others molten, puddled on the ground. The perfume he inhaled was candlewax and grease. Where he had expected to come upon an altar, a simple homemade cross was nailed up on the wall. Where he had expected the vestments of a priest were two aged servants kneeling on the floor, a man and a woman, whispering their prayers. In a kist between them Colin saw a corpse, carefully laid out.

The woman raised her eyes. 'You are not kin. Who are you?' she said.

He could not take his eyes from the body in the kist. He felt compelled to ask, yet dared not shape the question. In his heart, he knew. He answered in a whisper, 'I am Colin Snell, come frae the Kirk.'

The old man looked up at him, sorrowful and dignified. 'What kirk is that?'

Colin said, 'The right an proper one.'

The old woman sighed, while her husband said, 'Kirk or no kirk, show my mistress some respect. Tak aff your hat.'

Colin clasped his bonnet limply in his hands. 'When did she die?'

The woman said, 'Yisterday, early in the morn. The boy frae the Poffle went to fetch her folk. They will bury her. Hae the grace to leave us, sir. There is nothing here for you to do.'

'Have you kept watch here, all night?' He knew how such vigils were kept. The servants were praying for Ann Balfour's soul. He felt a cold kind of clutching, somewhere in his bowel. If Ann Balfour was dead—

'Who is it sitting up the stair?' The words were out. And his belly lurched at the glances they exchanged.

'Wha dae ye mean, sir?' Adam said.

His guidwife rose stiffly from her knees. 'Can it be the family come so soon? I will gang an see.'

Adam stayed behind to watch over the corpse. It was plain he was devoted to his mistress. It was plain he did not want to leave her side.

Colin went behind the woman up the steps. Her responses to his questions, simple as they were, brought him little hope. Ann Balfour had died in her chair early in the morning of the day before, leaving her breakfast tray untouched. Adam had left his wife to wash and dress the corpse, while he walked the mile to the Poffle farm. The sons from the farm had helped to take the body to the cellar underground, where it would be cool, until the family came.

'We have stayed by her side, ever since.'

'Did she have a priest with her, in her final hours?'

The woman was scornful. 'A priest? Where wid she hae that? There is no priest for miles, thanks to your ain kind.'

As they came through the kitchen, she caught sight of the pie. Her hand flew to her mouth. 'Mercy!' she cried. 'Go tell my husband that we have been robbed! There is a thief somewhere in the house.'

Colin felt obliged to confess. Weakly, he told her he had been asked.

'Who asked you?' she said.

'I believed it be the mistress of the house.' He withered in her gaze.

'Shame on you, sir, for a wicked lie. For a man o' the Kirk! That pie was sent this morning from the Poffle farm, for the funeral feast.'

He followed her, quailing, to the hall. The woman in the chair would put the servant right. Someone from the family, recently arrived, exhausted from the ride. So he told himself, knowing in his heart it would not be so.

The entrance hall appeared just as he had left it, except that the front door was closed. 'There is no one here, sir,' the servant said. She opened up a shutter, letting in the light. Colin was astonished at how easily it moved. The woman let slip a small mew of distress. 'Forgive me. I forgot the tray.' He sensed that the apology was not meant for him, but for someone else. In the light from the window he saw that the bread on the tray was hard. Yesterday's breakfast. Yesterday's tray. How was it he had failed to notice that before?

She had seen the tapestries. 'What happened to the cloths? Who has torn them down?'

He brushed her questions off. 'There was someone here. She has gone outside.'

She looked at him, wondering. 'Are ye sure, sir? I left the door locked.'

She showed him. It was locked still, and the key was inside.

'If it was locked,' he said wildly, 'how did I come here?'

'I thocht to ask you that,' she said.

Colin shook his head. 'There is a back door. She went out by there.'

Grief had made her dull. But she regarded him with a kind of pity, which drove him to the edge of a terrifying precipice. 'That door is locked, too. I have the key.'

That key was like a blade, cunningly slipped out, just to cut him down, paring off his reason by degrees. It glinted in her hand.

He whimpered. 'She was sitting there, just there, in the chair.'

'In that chair?' As she moved towards it, the servant gave a cry.

'She sees,' Colin thought. 'Though she will not say. Her mistress now appears to her, as she did to me.'

Relief did not last long. The woman reached her hand out to the empty armchair, finding something there. 'This was her hankercher,' she said. Her simple face had crumpled, as the tears began to spill. 'God forgive my foolishness. For though I ken that she is in a better place, and I will be there after, we three were together very many years. God bless her guid soul.' She lifted up the handkerchief, dabbing at her eyes, and Colin saw upon it spots of his own blood. His hand flew to his tooth, his mouth began to move against the searing pain, and the sound that came from it was very like a sob.

III

BALFOUR

'a counterfeit and deceiving spirit'

Hew came from his lecture on the third day of November to find Roger Cunningham waiting in his room. Roger was playing at a game of knucklebones with a silver button and a rotten tooth. He threw the tooth and caught it.

'If this is how you spend your time,' said Hew, 'I am not surprised that you persist in haunting us. Though I would remind you that you are expelled.'

'I have something for you,' Roger said. He ignored the jibe.

'Not that, I hope.'

Roger put the tooth in a pocket. 'Not this. This is a part of my collection. Something you will want.'

'Aye? And what is that?'

'News,' Roger said. 'I have brought you news. I know that it will interest you. Thank me, if you like.'

'I may thank you, or no, when you tell me what it is.'

'Do you ken a man called Colin Snell? He was a student here at the New College, who had in mind to hurl me into their latrines. I nearly died.'

'An exaggeration. But I mind the man.'

Roger grinned at him. 'I knew you would. Well, he has returned. This is his tooth.'

'I dare not ask,' Hew said, 'how he came to part with it.'

'I pulled it out myself. I never saw a man so pitifully feart. He almost shat himself. I had to let him think I had forgot the jakes. I minded it, of course.'

Hew said, 'You are a fiend.'

'That is unkind. I did not hurt him, more than necessary. Which was quite enough. Colin Snell is in a wretched state. He is presently in the care of James Melville of Kilrennie, who has brought him to his uncle at the New College. It was James who paid me to extract the tooth. He is a patient but practical man. Colin Snell is lunatic.'

'That is very sad. But I do not see what it has to do with me.'

'I though you would be interested in what has made him mad. He has seen a ghost.'

'Really? Where was that?'

A second ghost was surely more than a coincidence. Hew

wondered whether Roger had heard of Thomas Crowe, and hoped that he had not. Rumour quickly spread. Roger was by no means the common sort of gossip; he was far more dangerous than that. He kept his secrets close, waiting for the moment when they could be put to their best effect.

'At the Poffle of Strathkinness. He was on a priest hunt there, when he saw the spirit of a woman called Ann Balfour.'

'Is Ann Balfour dead, then?'

Roger said pleasantly, 'I imagine so, if she is a ghost. That is what I heard. I listen, and I hear things. Colin Snell did not confide in me. But I heard James Melville talking with his uncle, and this is what I learned. James had from Colin a precise and curious account. He had gone to the Poffle on November first. When he arrived, he found Ann Balfour sitting in her chair, with a breakfast tray beside her. The breakfast was untouched. Colin Snell made much of the breakfast. James said he was quite fixed on it. Some words were exchanged, between Colin Snell and the woman there. Then Colin went to search the rest of the house. In a vault underground, he found Ann Balfour's body, watched by her servants. She had been dead since the day before. The servants had watched, all through the night. There were no other persons in the house.

'When Andrew was informed of this, he sent a party from the Kirk. The party confirmed that Ann Balfour's body had been decently laid out. Her family had turned up, and arranged for her burial at the kirk of Holy Trinity.

'She was buried yesterday, in fact. The party found no trace of a spirit in the house. The servants were distressed at Colin Snell's suggestion that the devil had appeared to him, in the form of their mistress. They are of the superstitious kind, who believe that ghosts are the spirits of the dead. But they did not believe their mistress could have roamed abroad, as that was what their vigil was intended to prevent. They had believed a death at Halloween put the corpus under threat, yet they were convinced they had averted it. They saw and heard no ghost. The consensus is that Colin is insane. He is kept at the college, where he is asleep, silenced with a draught. Now, are you not pleased that I have brought this news?'

Hew did his best to feign indifference to it. 'I hope that you have not spread your prattle far and wide. It does not do to fright the world with ghosts.'

Roger laughed at that. 'You need not fear. I do not lightly break a patient's confidence. I saved the news for you. It is a gift, to thank you for the help you gave to Sam at Candlemas. I know it is exactly the sort of thing you like. Confess, you are agog. Now that I have telt you, we are even, are we not?'

Pulling out the tooth, he looked at it again. 'When I have gathered teeth from all my old adversaries, I will make a necklet,' he said. 'One of yours among them will look very fine.'

'When I have the toothache, I will remember that. I will not come to you,' said Hew.

'Ah, but you should. I am very good.'

'Be gone, ghoulish creature. You are very bad. Possibly the worst loun in the world.' Hew chased him out. But he was not displeased.

He went in search of Giles, and found him in the chapel. Giles appeared distracted. 'I was thinking that we should repair the roof.' Hew did not comment. He recognized the roof was not why Giles was here.

'Did you want something?' Giles said.

Hew said, 'Indeed. Did you ken that Ann Balfour was dead?'

'I certified the death.'

'You did not mention it.'

Giles replied simply, 'You did not ask.' His daily life dealt so often in such small departures, that they passed him by without report. 'Her death was unremarkable. I found her sitting peaceful in her chair.'

'Was the death expected?'

'It was not unexpected. What is your interest, Hew?'

Hew did not answer the question. Instead he asked, 'When was this?'

'It was on the morning of October thirty-first, All Hallows Eve. A boy from the farm at the Poffle came to fetch me.'

'Were there other people in the house?'

'The servants. The boy from the farm. I saw no one else there. Why?'

'A man called Colin Snell believes he saw her spirit, on November 1st. He went to her house, on a hunt for priests.'

'What? Another ghost?'

'So it would appear.'

Giles looked, in that moment, so intently troubled that Hew thought, 'He believes the spirit Thomas saw was real. That is why he came here to the kirk.' Giles Locke was a Catholic, after all.

But the doctor's mind was on another track. 'Who is Colin Snell?' he asked.

'He was once a student at the New College. He was disgraced, in the affair with Roger Cunningham.'

'Ach, I knew the name. It was in a letter that I had from Stephen Crowe. Colin Snell was tutor to his boys.'

'Then they are connected,' Hew exclaimed. 'It cannot be by chance that both have witnessed ghosts.'

'I fear an epidemic,' Giles said gloomily. 'There has been contagion here. So much must be plain. But why should it continue now they are apart? Colin Snell has had no communion with the boy. I mind now, he was absent at the start of term. Thomas telt me he had come here with his tutor. But when we looked for him, to have his own report, he could not be found.'

Hew said, 'He hid from us, perhaps.'

'Now you trouble me. I do not like to think that such a man insinuated into that poor boy.'

'Perhaps it is the boy insinuates in him.'

Giles shuddered. 'Horrible, quite horrible. I do not like to think it. He is just a bairn.'

'Do not be distressed,' said Hew. 'Whatever is the source, I will find it out. But we must be vigilant. There is more to this than we had supposed. How does the patient?'

'You had best ask Meg. He is her patient now. What use was I to him? To ply purges on a boy, who had starved himself?' Giles responded wretchedly. 'I depend on her to put right our neglect.'

Hew saw that it was conscience that had brought him to the kirk, not the fear of ghosts. He came there to atone, to make his peace with God, for the guilt he felt for failing Thomas Crowe.

Colin Snell was fettered in a fractured sleep, and unable to confirm his own account to Hew. But a word with James left him in no doubt.

'I suppose,' said Hew, 'he did not find his priest?'

'There is no priest,' James said. 'I doubt you may have heard of one called Father John, who was well kent here. He compeared before the Kirk session at St Andrews, several months ago, and was ordered to desist from holding Mass. He was sick and frail, and no action was pursued against him at that time. Shortly after that, he passed away. I tried to say as much to Colin Snell. He would not hear. He is a fanatic, Hew. There is no kind of reason to his mad pursuits. I bitterly regret I sent him to those boys. God kens what hard doctrine he instilled in them, when they came already from a tragic house.'

The story of that house had lately been disclosed, in letters to Giles Locke from the father Stephen, after Thomas Crowe had fainted in the kirk. The doctor had examined him, for the first time thoroughly, and had found his fragile body beggarly and thin. It soon became apparent he had starved himself. The regent

William Cranston was unable to recall ever seeing Thomas eat his dinner at the board. Thomas was a quiet boy, who did not draw attention to himself. In his defence, Cranston said he had never come across a boy who did not want to eat. The students in the main had ferocious appetites. They were never satisfied, but always wanted more. Which Doctor Locke would ken, if he ever stayed to supper in the hall.

Giles had blamed himself. In particular, it vexed him that he had ordered purges for a patient who was plainly ill. It was his fault, entirely, that the boy had fainted. The visions he had seen – which the purging had exacerbated, rather than relieved – resulted from his fast, for fasting was a cause of illusions in the mind. He believed the fasting had been caused by melancholy, and that Thomas Crowe had simply lost his appetite. Hew's investigations bore this out. It did not take him long to find the bits of bread that Thomas Crowe had hidden in his room. The bread was hard and stale.

The remedy prescribed was the soundest cure of all. Giles had taken Thomas home with him to Meg, trusting her to mend the harm that had been done.

Hew continued, meanwhile, to pursue the ghost. While it had a cause in Thomas Crowe's poor health, he believed its substance had a human source. It did not take him long to find it. A brisk inquisition of the first year class – who were awed by the sight of Thomas carried out – had delivered Malcom Crabbe and his pamphlets to his hands. Hew was impressed by the contents of the library.

'"A pack of Spanish lies" may be well and sound. But I like this one best: "A new ballet of the strange and most cruel whips which the Spaniards had prepared to whip and torment English men and women: which were found and taken at the overthrow of certain of the Spanish ships in July last past. To the tune of *The valiant soldier*." You cannot hum that, I suppose?'

Malcom Crabbe could not. 'It is an English song.'

'A pity. Else we might have sung it with the Gude and Godlie ballads. There are pictures too, of the different whips. I did not know they carried male and female kinds.'

Malcolm rushed headlong, mistaking for approval what was meant for irony. 'They do. This one with the barbs is to flay the women, after they have spoiled them.' He read a little late the look upon Hew's face. 'Well, that is what the verse says,' he concluded lamely.

'Although their bodies sweet and fair/their spoil they meant to make/And on them first their filthie lust/and pleasure for to take,' Hew read aloud. 'These Spaniards show no courtesy.'

'No, sir. They are vile.'

'Do you think,' said Hew, 'this filth is fit to bring into the college here?'

Malcolm Crabbe thought. 'I suppose not.'

'Why not, do you think?'

'It is not in Latin?'

'That is a small part of it. But you make a good point. You can take the "Pack of lies" and turn it into Latin. I will keep the rest.'

'Will you burn them, sir?' Understanding dawned, or more likely, Hew considered, had been lurking all the while. Malcolm Crabbe was wise enough to know to play the fool.

'I will not. For that is what the Spanish do. Where did you get them from?'

'From my father. He is a merchant, who deals in quilibets.'

'In what?'

'In what-nots, sir. It is a Latin word. I thought you would have heard of it.'

'I know the *word*,' said Hew. 'But I had not come across it in that way. He can have the pamphlets back, at the end of term, when I will want a word with him.'

'Ask for almost anything, he will find it for you,' Crabbe said with a grin. 'But his speciality is moments of the day. Mementos and remembrances. He says the Spanish wars will make our fortune yet, if they do not drive us to our graves.'

Hew had taken the pamphlets back to Kenly Green, and had read them overnight. Their lurid accounts were sufficient to cause nightmares in a time-served soldier, never mind a timid and impressive boy. Though some boys were protected by the callousness of youth, to one with a tender, troubled intellect the pamphlets were the kindle for the flame. Hew had dismissed the bloodspot in the kirk as a skew irrelevance. The source for the substance of the ghost was plain.

So he had believed. Thomas would recover, and the case was closed. But now that he had heard the tale of Colin Snell, he was not so sure.

He found Thomas Crowe sitting up in bed. Already, he could see a little colour in his cheeks. 'I do not suppose,' said Hew, 'that there are spirits here.'

Thomas Crowe agreed that there were not.

'Was it Colin Snell who taught you to fast?'

He threw out the name, randomly and carelessly, to see the boy react. Thomas clutched at the sheet, but gave no other sign. His answer was carefully staged. 'It behoveth them which are vexed with spirits, to pray especially, and give themselves to fasting,' he said. He spoke no word of Snell, but recited from a book.

'Yet you have been fasting for a while. For a long time, I would say, before you saw the spirit. Were there other ghosts? Ones you saw with Snell?'

'Will you call Mistress Meg? I do not feel well,' Thomas said, and voided the contents of his stomach down the bed.

'You have upset him,' said Meg, when Thomas was cleaned up again, and settled down to sleep. 'I will not have it, Hew. He is here to rest.'

'I have upset him?' answered Hew. 'Some who knew no better might say it was the devil made him spew.'

Meg shot him a look. 'God help him who dares to say it in this house. The truth is, his stomach cannot hold so much. He has not eaten nearly enough, over a very long time.'

'We have been derelict in our care of him.'

'That. Giles is distraught, and with cause. But it goes back much further than that. No one cared, or noticed, what he ate at home. He has starved himself, perhaps for years.'

'Why would a boy choose not to eat?' asked Hew.

'Grief does strange things.'

'From grief?' he repeated.

'It is not as simple as that.'

'Why, then?'

He wanted answers, always. Meg said, with a sigh, 'I cannot say, for sure. But I believe he does not want to grow into a man.'

For Hew, the answers were not satisfactory. He could not question either Thomas Crowe or his tutor Colin Snell in the way that he would like. Both of them were in a far too fragile state. Yet he was determined to expose the cause. 'If you are a ghost,' he promised, 'I will chase you out.' It astonished him to find he spoke the words aloud.

He resolved to begin at the Poffle of Strathkinness. That was a place where a man might find a spirit, on an ordinary day. He had been himself, to visit there at Candlemas, when Ann Balfour he supposed was already close to death. Certainly there had been a pall about the house. And Ann Balfour was the kind of woman who might well return, to haunt a man in death, just to make a point.

He dismissed the thought, as quickly as it formed. Whatever Ann's belief about the spirits of the dead, Hew did not believe their souls came back as ghosts. A spirit was a darker, more malignant thing. If it did exist, it was the devil's plaything, for it was very rare indeed that such a thing was God's. More likely though by far was that it was constructed by a human mind. Fearful men imagined fearful things.

He did not go at once to Ann Balfour's cottage, but called first at the farm a mile away. At this time of year, the land took on a melancholy hue. The harvest was coming to its close, the supple greens and golds mellowing to greys, the trees bending stark, yearning in the wind. In another week or so, it would be slaughter time, the keening mothers giving up their calves. The farmhands in the fields were raking up the dregs of summer. Winter was approaching, soft upon the storms.

The farmer's sons confirmed the doctor's tale. Early in the morning of All Hallows Eve, old Adam Cole had walked up to the farm and telt them Ann was dead. One of them had ridden to the town to fetch Giles Locke. He had taken word to the Balfour family. And they had helped the servants move the body to the laich house, where it was cooler, for the wake.

None of them had seen a stranger in the house. Ann Balfour and her servants kept to themselves. They were seldom seen about from one winter to the next. No one knew them well. 'You maun talk to Wullie,' someone said. 'Wullie brought Ann Balfour's letters from the town. He kens mair than maist.'

Wullie was the farmer's youngest son. He was nine years old. But his testimony was clearer, and far more informed, than his brothers' was. As well as the letters, he took bread and milk, and physick that the doctor had prescribed. Sometimes, he helped the servants in the house. The wifie had given him a silver penny for it. And there had been another lady staying with them, over the last months. Very auld and fine. She was Mistress Balfour's sister, and her name was Frances. It was Mistress Balfour who had telt him that herself. She had come there, he said, 'to help the leddy die. I did not speak wi' her.'

Ann Balfour's servants were sitting in the hall. Hew had little hope of making them confess. He could see by their looks – Adam Cole's in particular – that they were the stuff that martyrs were made from. Were Catholics all like that? So resolutely sure of their final end, they did not care how hard it was to come to it. Not that Hew, of course, would put that to the test.

Instead, he showed his hand. 'That was a cruel trick that you played.'

He was looking at the wife, for he thought he might have some leverage with her, if any came at all. They had met before. He had fetched her water from the well. Her suspicion at the time had overcome her gratitude. Still, it was a connection he could work upon. The husband at her side sat resolute as stone.

He saw man and wife exchange a glance. They were at an age when words were not required. The woman spoke for both of them. 'Ah dinnae ken what ye mean.'

'You let Colin Snell believe he saw a ghost, when it was Ann's sister sitting in the chair.'

'Ah niver did.'

Hew had expected that. He did not expect what she answered next, for quickly she expanded, 'Ah canna help whit was in his mind. Ah didnae tell him that it wis a ghost. He telt it to himself.'

'But you did not tell him who it was,' he pointed out. It astonished him how readily she confirmed his claim.

'Why wid ah tell him?' she replied. 'Why wis he here, but to disturb decent folk's devotions? He et the pie, and had the cheek to say my mistress telt him to. That wis a wicked lie. Nor am I sorry if he is afeart. He deserves to be.'

'Whisht, woman, will you? You have said enough,' Adam said.

'Ah will say my piece, or niver speak again. A good pie that was, sent frae the farm fer the funeral.'

Grizelda blew her nose on a spotted handkerchief.

'That was wrong of him. But why did Ann's sister not declare herself?' asked Hew.

'She was grieved, and shy. She had gone above, for a moment's sleep, and in comes this limmar from the Kirk. Whit was she to do? While he was blundering above us she slipped out. I locked the door behind her,' she explained.

Hew shook his head. 'What you have described is a counterfeit.'

'It is nothing of the kind. It was shutting in a thief, who had come into the house. Now, sir, if you will, leave us to our peace; we are mourning here.' The old man stood, with dignity, and Hew allowed himself to be ushered out.

'Where is Frances now?' he asked.

'Far from here, I doubt. Frances comes and goes, and never stays for long.'

'Will she come again?'

'That, sir, I count as unlikely, now that Ann Balfour has gone.'

There was a note of sadness in the old man's voice, prompting Hew to say, 'Forgive me, for I have intruded on your grief. I am sorry for it. And I am sorry for your old friend, Father John. I heard he had died.'

The old man's face hardened. 'Died? Aye, sir, he died. He was broken by men like Colin Snell. They couldnae let an auld man gang peaceful to his rest, but harried and pursued him till his health was gone.'

Hew responded awkwardly. 'If that is the case, it causes me regret. It must be painful to you, too, that your mistress did not have in her final hours the comfort of the sacrament which meant the most to her.'

Strangely, Adam chuckled. Grief could show itself in ways that were perverse. And Adam Cole had doubtless loved his mistress well.

The question was resolved. No ghost but a sister, punishing a man for intruding on her grief. So Hew was persuaded as he set off for the town, until he met a man who came the other way, whistling as he went, with an apple in his hand. He knew the man at once as the student Henry Balfour, from St Leonard's College, now at the beginning of his final year.

'*Salve*, Henry,' he called out.

Henry waved at him as he bit into the apple. 'Well met, and all that,' he said cheerfully.

'Not so well met,' answered Hew, 'if you are truant again.'

'I have leave,' Henry said, 'because I am bereaved.'

'Accept my doleaunce, then. Though you seem to be bearing up well.'

'My aunt and I were not close,' Henry said, biting at the apple once again.

'Was your aunt Ann Balfour?' The connection, dimly, dawned on Hew at last.

'Strictly,' Henry said, 'she was my father's aunt. Or a second cousin of some sort. I do not really ken, except my father owns the house she lived in. She was one of the papist Balfours, who have brought shame on our family. He let her live there because she was poor, and had nowhere else. He said I could have the house, and the land, if I was prepared to see to her affairs, the funeral and such. So I did. Though it is not so much of a house.'

'I have seen it,' Hew teased him. 'And I have to tell you it is full of ghosts.'

'I have no fear of ghosts. Besides, as we both ken, living folk may sometimes pass off as the dead.' Henry grinned at him. 'There are still two servants incumbent, both of them ancient and gnarled. They are living, though grimly. I am going now to see what can be done to encourage them a little.'

'The last time I saw you, you were pining for a lass,' Hew said. 'I am glad to see that you are more cheerful now.'

'The lass is still a work in hand. I hope to win her back. The house will help.'

A thought occurred to Hew. 'Were you at the funeral?' he asked.

'I was. A sad affair. I had thought the servants would complain, wanting psalms and such, but they made no fuss. I think there was a wake or something in the house. Some superstitious thing. I did not like to ask.'

Hew nodded. 'That was best.' He had the sense that Henry, for all his foppery, would be a considerate landlord.

'Was her sister there with them?' he asked.

Henry stared at him. 'What sister? She had no sister.'

'Are you sure of that?'

'Quite sure. She had a brother, though. We do not speak of him.'

'No? Why is that?'

Henry laughed. 'Well, we do. In our house, he is something of a jest. We dare to bring him up, to spite our father sometimes, for it makes him cross. But I am not convinced that he exists. He is here and there, and all about, but he is never seen. He is very old, if he is alive. Almost as old as his sister Ann.'

'What do you mean, he is never seen?'

'I suppose because he has to hide himself. When he was a bairn, he was sent away to live among the Jesuits. He became a priest, of the dreadful kind.'

'And I suppose,' concluded Hew, 'the name he took was Francis.' For, he thought, what else?

'Father Francis, aye. Though my dad would flay me if he heard me call him that. I have an idea that his given name was George.'

Hew bade him good day, and continued to the town. As he put together all that he had learned, a smile began to spread across his face.

'Will you tell the truth to Colin Snell?' asked Giles. They were sitting in the doctor's tower, away from prying eyes, and Hew had told his friend what he had found.

Hew shook his head. 'I have no proof,' he said. 'Besides, it would be cruel. To tell him that his ghost was Father Francis Balfour in a woman's gown would drive him to despair. He would be incontinent with disbelief and rage. It would send him mad.'

'Still,' said Giles, 'can it be kind, to let him go on thinking he has lost his mind?'

'He does not think it now. I spoke to James Melville. He tells me that now that Colin Snell has recovered from his fright – and the rotten tooth that Roger has pulled out – he believes the ghost was part of God's intent for him. He is very pleased with it.'

'Can that be to the good?'

'James says it is not bad. Colin Snell believes that he should now retreat to a period of contemplation, reflecting on the spirit, and what it might mean. He intends to write it all in a book. I expect his book will be condemned as heresy, by the jealous Kirk. But it will keep him quiet for a while. And his friend Dod Auchinleck has offered him a place tending to the graves in his parish kirkyard. James says it is good of him. The living he has there can barely keep him and his wife and child. But he says that Dod has a good Christian heart. If there is something to be saved inside Colin Snell, he is the man to do it.'

'Graves, though,' said Giles. 'Are graves the proper thing, for a man who thinks that he has seen a ghost? They are contradicted for the melancholic mind.'

'Surely it is choler that predominates in Colin? I should think that graves would be the perfect thing,' said Hew. 'When he is occupied among the dead, he cannot hurt the living minds of boys like Thomas Crowe, or chase about the country persecuting priests.'

Giles did not mistake the meaning in his tone. 'Then, as I suppose,' he said, 'you did not choose to tell the truth of it to James?'

'I told him,' answered Hew, 'that there was a woman staying in the house, and that Colin's fevered mind had conjured up the rest. So much I thought was necessary, to prevent further troubling of the servants at the house, who, if nothing else, are deserving of their peace. He passed the news to Colin Snell, who would not hear a word of it. He will not for the world be robbed of his ghost.'

Giles said with a smile, 'What! Hew Cullan is colluding in concealing Catholic priests!'

Hew answered carelessly, 'As I think I telt you, I have found no proof. The servants at the house will carry their secret with them to the end, and I have no will to hurry them towards it. They are weak and old. And if a person finds some comfort in their dying hours, from the ministrations of a Catholic priest, what harm has been done? They are saved, or no, with or without it, I doubt.'

Giles approved his sentiment. He was thoughtful for a while. Presently he said, 'I believe I may have seen him.'

'You have seen Father Francis?' Hew exclaimed.

'As you ken, I have attended very many deaths. I do not make distinctions for the Catholic kind. Except I have observed that Catholics die good deaths. Often, in the background, I have been aware of an old woman of the house, quiet and reserved, and yet a presence there, who tended to the patients in their final hours.'

'Did you never suspect?'

Giles shook his head. 'I never did suppose that woman was a man. Which leads me on to think that Father Francis has assumed the mantle for so long, it becomes his nature.'

'Hidden in plain sight,' said Hew. 'And in the perfect place. I almost wish I could have telt the truth to Colin Snell, just to see the fury and the horror in his face, when he understood how very close he came to proving he was right.'

'That would be quite wrong. You seem, if I may say so, pleased with this sad tale,' said Giles.

Hew said, 'I am pleased with it. For it proves a thing that I have often held, that there are no spirits walking in the night. There are disordered shades of men's imaginations, and the mischiefs played on them, but there are no ghosts, that cannot be unmasked by a rational mind.'

IV

CRABBE

'many natural things are taken to be ghosts'

The eleventh day of November was the feast of Martinmas, traditionally the time for the culling of the herd, when servants were exchanged and rents were paid. At Hew's house at Kenly Green, his wife was more observant of the rhythms of the land, more conscious of the seasons, than her husband was, and it was she who remarked of the mournful cuddochs that they knew they were going to die that day. 'They have a premonition of it,' Frances said.

Her husband would not have it. He had not spent the term laying ghosts to rest to have them resurrected here at home.

'How can they have a premonition?' he objected. 'They are dumb beasts.'

'They feel it. In the same way that they feel the coming of a storm. They are more attuned than we are to the elements.'

'That is not the same.'

'Trust me. I have lived most of my life in the shadow of Leadenhall market. Cows know when slaughter is coming.'

'They ken when they are driven to the killing place. They smell the blood, and fear, of others gone before. But they do not wake up on Martinmas morning lowing to themselves, Oh la and alas, we will die today.'

Frances said simply, 'They do.'

It was not tender sentiment that moved her. She demonstrated that by tearing off a strip from the haunch of mutton roasting at the fire and handing it to Hew. He left it on the plate.

'What? Convicted now?' She smiled at him.

'It is not that. Keep some back for suppertime. I promised I would take my dinner at the college.'

It was only half a lie. Giles had proposed they dine in from time to time, to encourage Thomas Crowe. But the dinner would be done by the time Hew came to town, unless he took his horse, which he did not mean to do.

The mutton was to feed the men who came to kill the cattle in his fields. The kitchens would be filled with clumps of salted flesh, boiling bones and candle fat when he next came home. His house would have the reek of blood, iron dark. Frances oversaw and managed everything. Brought up in the town, she had taken to the land as readily as though she had an instinct for it.

One that Hew had not. But walking through the fields he felt it, still. November was a melancholy month. The grain, what little of it had survived the storms, had been gathered in. The earth lay bare of fruits, to wait the winter frosts. In the yard by the mill, the sacrificial pig was tethered in its pen. The miller's boy, John Kintor, raised his pigs with care. When the sow was groaning with a litter in the night, he would scratch her ears. When he called to the piglets, each one by its name, they would run to take the corn husks from his hand. Was it for the sake of their tender flesh he chose the plumpest grains to fill the trough that day? Last winter, he had come shyly with a ham as a gift for Frances. English people did not shun pork like the Scots. 'This one was Jem. Sweet as a nut,' he had said.

Hew did not believe the pig that snuffled in the trough had the slightest inkling that its days were done. And what, if not the pig? 'There is no beast of the field more loyal and intelligent,' John Kintor said, 'and in that may be reckoned some that pass for men.' Did the heifer that looked up, with its lolling tongue and its doleful head turned towards the sky, harking to some secret whisper on the wind, have a premonition of its own impending death? Hew thought it did not. But he did not pretend to come to grips with nature. His heart was in the town, and with humankind.

The merchant Martin Crabbe, coming to St Andrews at the killing time, did not know that he was going to die that day. Which is not to say that he was not forewarned, but that he had chosen to ignore the signs. The first was that he woke up in the night, with a grumbling wam, to find his bedsheets sopping wet with sweat. He put it down to sleeping in an unfamiliar bed, following a long day on the road. The second was an aching in his arm and shoulder, which he thought was caused by gripping at his horse. The third was a flux, leaky and persistent, which began to trouble him the moment he got up. He blamed that on the supper he had eaten in the inn, a plate of pickled herring with a roasted egg. 'That egg was bad,' he told the lassie there. She insisted that there had been nothing wrong with it.

'It wis never fresh.'

'Ah never said it was. What do ye expect, on a Sabbath evening?' she answered with a sniff.

It did not discourage him from a decent breakfast, washed down with a flagon of the strongest ale. He enquired about his dinner, hoping there would be a pudding on the menu, boiled up with the bellox of the morning's kill. The lassie pulled a face.

'Hae what ye like, as long as long as ye can pay fer it.'

He could. He had come a long way since he was a cadger, trudging with his pack. Now he had a shop on the high gate of Dundee, and a part share in a ship. He had a son here at the university. All this he telt to the lass, as she came and went to fill his plate and cup.

'If ye hae a booth in Dondie, why are you here?' the lassie said. 'Ye ken there is no market here today? There will not be a fair afore St Andrew's day.'

Martin Crabbe was well aware of that. He had no right to trade, outside his own burgh, when there was no fair. He looked forward to the markets where his ship came in. But he was not prepared to wait until St Andrew's day. He had come ahead, to broker certain deals among the merchants in the town. Forestalling in the market place broke the burgh law. That did not mean it could or should not be done.

'What do you look to buy?' she asked.

She had been through his baggage, hussy that she was, and concluded that he had not come to sell.

'Who said I was buying?'

'Well then, what?'

He had set up several meetings in the inn that day, which would take him nicely through to dinnertime. He told the lassie he would want the finest claret wine, sack and brandy too, to keep the buyers sweet. The inn was in a vennel off the marketplace, and had a reputation for preserving secrecy. None of it came cheap. But he would recoup the cost with what he had for sale.

'Aye? An what is that?'

'Ye wad like to ken. Something all the lassies here will want. The ladies at the court will be greening for it.'

'Something bonny, then? Is it a jewel?'

He fixed her with a stare. 'Now why do you say that?'

'Because a jewel is small. And can be hidden in a pocket.'

'Been keeking, have ye, lassie?' he replied.

The lassie flushed dark. 'Ah never did. But yer bags are wee. You couldna fit in them onything of worth.'

'Now, is that a fact?'

The lassie did not like it that she was caught out. 'Ah dinna think it is onything at all. It is jist a fraud,' she said.

'Think what ye like. When the ladies clamour for it, you'll be last in line. Be sure to mak my dennar guid an hot.'

She was closer to the mark than she could know. Her interest in his empty baggage pleased him. It was his intention to instil an appetite. He had not brought the samples she was after to the town. Truth was, in themselves, they did not look like much. But it was the story that he had to tell that would prove their worth. It was all a question of creating a demand.

By dinnertime, he had drawn a crowd around him. He told them the story of the *Gran Grifon*, the flagship of the Grand Armada, which had been shipwrecked off the Orkney isles. Martin had been there on his travels at the time. He saw the ship go down. He had stood and watched, while the devils drowned, in the boiling sea that swirled them down to Hell.

'For they were monsters,' he said. Recovered from the ship, and washed up on the shore, were artefacts and tools, so cruel in their device they might have been thrown up from very Hell itself. 'Oh, it would hurt your heart to see those devils' instruments, strewn on those white sands, still wet with martyrs' blood.' To spare the feelings of the Orkney islanders, Martin Crabbe had gathered up the dreadful things, and put them in his barque, and he had brought them home. They might be seen, for the price of a copy of a pamphlet, in his shop at Dundee, or, to a most discerning and particular collector, they might be for sale.

The torments were not all. There were treasures too; cups and plates and bowls, and a hundred daggers, of the Spanish kind. Now, he drew one out, to tease them with its blade. Its owner, Martin said, had crawled out from the sea, writhing like a serpent, dying at his feet. Martin Crabbe had found the dagger buried in his breast. He had drawn it out.

'Wha stabbed him, then?' someone asked.

Martin brushed him off. He did not care for questions to interrupt his flow. 'One of his kind. They are devils,' he said. 'The blood that had flowed from the life wound was black, black as the dead Spaniard's heart. You could see right inside it,' he said. 'I looked into his face, and saw before my eyes his bright complexion fade. I could have caught it up, and put it in a glass. It was,' he said, 'a maist extraordinary thing. I have a picture of it vivid in my mind. The colour fled from him. Here, I have the ring I took from his finger. I have many others, coming in my ship.'

'Many other rings? How many fingers did the devil have?' the heckler asked again.

'Many other things.' Despite this irritation, he had made his mark. By dinnertime, his pocket book was filling up with orders. The inn was filling up with fleshers in their killing clothes, come to slake their thirst. Martin found a quiet table in a corner, and called for another stoup of wine. He was waiting for a man called Will, a customer for whom he had a special deal in mind. His shop was an essential link to Martin's chain. To please him, though, he must please his wife, which would be the key to open up the town.

Will did not seem keen. He came to the meeting late, and refused a drink. He seemed ill at ease. To make the matter worse, as soon as Will sat down, Martin was obliged to depart himself, on an urgent mission to the jakes. Outside in the yard, he found his shirt and hose again were drenched with sweat, although the damp November air was very far from warm. He could hardly breathe, but found the ruff around him choking like a chain, until he pulled it off. Struggling back inside, he found his prey was just about to leave. 'Stay, hae some dinner wi me. For you have not heard what I have to sell,' he urged.

Will sat down again. He watched, as the lass ran back and forth with bread and cheese and wine, a bowl of mutton broth, and the hot blood pudding. 'Won't you try some?' Martin said, 'It is very good.' He felt it bring a flood of colour to his cheek.

'Ah dinna think,' said Will, 'you ought to eat so quickly. Or, in truth, so much. You do not look so well.'

'I had a bad egg,' Martin said. 'The remedy for bad is to follow it with good, or so I have always found.' He dabbed his lips, unwilling to concede that at that moment he did not feel so well. He called for more wine, to wash down his queasiness.

'Show me,' Will said, 'what you have to sell.'

This had never been Martin Crabbe's intent. It was not simply that what he had to sell, without the tale to sell it, looked quite plain and dull; it was also something Will could make quite easily himself, if he put his mind to it.

'Let me first explain to you, how it comes about.' Martin told his story, which began again with the late destruction of the Spanish fleet. The lass who brought the wine appeared to be bewitched by it, but it failed to have the same effect on Will. Before it was concluded, he stood up.

'I have to go. If you have aught to show, bring it to the shop. That is the provost and the bailies over there.' This explained his nerves. The man he called the provost caught Martin's eye. Martin tipped his hat to him, annoyed. So it was the provost chased away his deals. The attention of the bailies now was drawn to him, but he would not be cowed. He would simply have to bide his time.

The lass came with the brandy. 'Oh. Your friend has gone. I will never hear the ending to the tale. What is the stuff that all the ladies like?'

Martin felt confused. A black mist had descended, and a fiery heat. He could not see, or breathe. He fumbled at his neck, to pull off the ruff, but found it was not there. His bowels turned to water, and he felt ashamed. Dimly, he saw that the provost was rising, was coming towards him. He heard the lass say 'What is the stuff' and the rest of the world became swallowed in darkness, pulling him down. Drowning, he thought, oh, I am drowning. How can it be. There is the provost. What is the stuff. His eyes were open wide, so wide he felt the weight of them. Yet he could not see. 'Dead Spaniard,' he said. That was the last thing, the sound of his words.

It was hopeless for Giles Locke, summoned to the scene, to insist that Martin's death had been a natural one. His word was overruled, by men of weight and dignity, the provost and the bailies of the town. 'With respect,' the provost said, 'ye were not here yourself, when the man went down. Ask awbody you like.' The inn was full of witnesses, many of them fresh from the killing fields. 'They are acquainted with death. And all of them ken what they saw. He was dragged down to Hell, by a ghost.'

'With respect,' said Giles, 'is any one among them trained as a medicinar? Have they ever seen an apoplectic stroke?'

'Well, sir, there is one, whose word ye maun attend to, since he is your own. And he has telt us a marvellous thing, which you have tried to keep from us. He says that the Dead Spaniard has been seen before, in your college kirk.' When the dreadful words were said a murmuring arose, with one or two among them whispering a prayer.

It was the fermer, Kennocht Cutler, who was now revealed to be a viper in their midst. He was there by chance, he said, on a sudden urgent quest to purchase aquavite, wanted at the fermary, and on no account to satisfy his thirst.

Giles fixed upon the fermer a stare full of sorrow. 'Oh, Kennocht, what have you done?'

'Ye did not it see it, sir. He wis looking at the spirit, right into his eyes, the moment that he fell. He wis trying to tell us when he died. He spake the devil's name. It was that same ghost that came into our kirk and struck that puir bairn senseless to the ground.'

'Did you see it too? Did any one of you?' Giles persisted wearily.

His protests were ignored. For it was plain to all, the Spaniard would appear only a man who was about to die.

'That cannot be the case. For no one has died at the college,' he said.

The fermer said darkly, 'No one has yet.'

Coming to the college shortly after dinnertime, Hew found himself in the middle of a storm. The provost and his bailies were gathered at the gate, demanding the right to speak with Thomas Crowe. Giles held them off; though Thomas was still safe in the care of Meg, he was now attending to the tearful Malcolm Crabbe, who had been told in a way that was brutal and abrupt that the father he had loved had been carried off by a Spanish ghost. 'It is Thomas Crowe,' he sobbed, 'who has put a curse on him,' adding fuel and fury to the swilling crowd.

Giles lit on Hew, and threw him to the wolves. 'Here is a man who can rid you of your ghosts. Ask him; he will tell you they do not exist, but are conjured up by sad and frantic minds.'

The provost, knowing Hew, fell upon him gratefully. 'Can you,' he implored, 'drive away the spirits that infect the town? For I feel the grip upon us like the plague.'

Consoling him, Hew said three ghosts were hardly an epidemy. Giles let out a groan, grim enough to muster for a fourth. The provost said, aghast, 'There has been a *third*?'

Hew, to make amends, promised he would rid the town of the Spanish ghost. 'I know what you believe happened at the inn. But I will prove to you it has a natural cause.'

It was, he thought, a mere trick of the mind, like the other ghosts. 'In the case of Thomas Crowe,' he explained to Giles, 'I thought, at first, it was a counterfeit, a trick that was played on him, by his colleagues here. It turned out that the trick was in his own imagination. In the case of Colin Snell, what we thought was in his mind, *was* a counterfeit. But both of them have an explanation, rooted in the physical or the natural world. This third ghost, surely, must be the same. Yet it is Thomas Crowe who is common to them all. His ghost lies at the heart. What made Martin Crabbe speak of the Dead Spaniard, the moment that he died? I cannot see the meaning in it. What was it killed him, Giles?'

Giles said, 'Meat and drink. Now I must go and tend to his poor boy, and leave you to confront the devil on your own.'

Hew spoke to Kennocht Cutler, to the lassie from the inn, and to several witnesses, who had seen Crabbe die. 'Did you hear him speak his final words,' he asked them all, 'or is it that you ken them from report? Were they loud and clear?' Each one said the same. The words were not in doubt.

He spoke to Will Dyer, a man that he knew well, and liked. 'Oh, he had a tale to tell,' said Will. 'A dreadful kind of tale. I wonder if he scared himself to death with it. If he robbed the graves of the Spanish as he said, no wonder that the devils came to take him at the end. He said he took the dagger from the dead man's breast. Well, the dead man came and took it back from him. I give thanks to God I did not buy from him.'

'Daggers,' said Hew, 'are hardly in your line.'

'No, they are not. He promised something finer, that was just for me, that everyone would want. He niver had the chance to tell me any mair. But I hae a notion what it was.'

'What was that?' asked Hew.

'I think it was the flag, frae the *Gran Grifon*. That was the flagship of the Spanish fleet. The flag wid be a prize, for sure. A Spanish man would gie, and tak, a life for that. I wid not want it, now, at any price.'

Returning to the college, Hew saw Malcolm Crabbe setting out for home. He called to him. 'I am so very sorry for your loss,' he said. 'And I am sorry, too, I never met your dad, to give him back the books I took from you. Next term, when you join us again, you shall have them back, to remember him.'

Malcolm Crabbe nodded. 'He would have liked you.'

'And I him.'

'You would. He was not bad. The things that he sold – the daggers and cups – were not real, you know,' Malcolm said. 'He did not really take them from a Spanish ship. There is a blacksmith makes them for him in Dundee. He never saw the wreck of the *Gran Grifon*, or took the knife from a dying soldier. It was all made up, to help him sell the things. So I do not see–' The boy broke off in tears.

'What do you not see?' asked Hew.

'I do not see why the ghost would come for him. He only told a lie. He never did it harm.'

'Nor do I see why.' Hew put his arm round him. 'I do not think it did.'

'Truly?' Malcolm looked at him. 'Then why did he cry out "Dead Spaniard"? Was it Thomas Crowe, put a curse on him?'

Hew shook his head. 'It was not Thomas Crowe. I do not know why your father said those words. But you have my promise that I will find out.'

He was late home. And though he wanted very much to discuss the case with Frances, he found her strangely cold. She would not look at him. And when he asked for Flora, she said, 'Oh, she is in bed now. Do not disturb her,' which hurt him, for she knew he liked to give a last kiss to the child, at whatever hour, before he went to sleep.

'I am sorry to be late,' he said. 'Something happened in the town.'

Frances said, 'It always does.'

He tried to make amends, with no clear understanding what his fault had been. 'I left you on your own, at killing time,' he said.

'That is of no consequence.'

'Did it not go well?'

'The slaughter is done, if that is what you mean. We have enough meat to see us through the winter. The candlemaker will come to visit us on Thursday. It is a busy week for him.'

He asked, 'What is it, then?'

'What is what?'

'The matter.'

'There is no matter, Hew.'

He took her hands in his. 'Shall we begin again? Plainly, there is.'

Frances pulled away from him. 'I went into the library,' she said.

'And?'

'I wanted to begin a new account book, because today is Martinmas.'

'Did you not find one?' he said.

The look she gave him made him thankful when she turned away. 'I do not like to tell you what it was I found,' she said. 'Oh, Hew, I had not thought of you, that you had a taste for such things.'

'As account books?' he replied, baffled at the words.

'How can you!' she cried. 'How can you make light of it, in such an unkind way. I mean, you know I mean, that cruel and vile obscenity you will say is *verse*.'

'Oh,' said Hew at last, 'you mean the Spanish scourge.'

'How can you stand and smile at it, and show no scrap of shame? I thought I knew you, Hew.'

'You do. I scarcely can believe you thought I liked that stuff. It is not mine,' he said.

Relief, and confusion, diluted her anger. 'Oh! Then it must belong to Gavan Baird. I did not think that it could be his.'

He answered, with a heavy humour, 'You did not think it could belong to the librarian. And yet you were convinced that it must be mine?'

'Do not twist my meaning, Hew. I am not a student you dispute with in your class. I did not think that Gavan Baird, being the librarian, would dare to bring such filth into his master's house. But, if he has, he must be dismissed from here at once.'

'Frances, it was not Gavan Baird. I took it from a student at the college. It has caused, to this time, more trouble than you can possibly imagine. I am truly sorry that I brought it home. I did not think, nor meant for you to see it.'

'Then it is not yours, though you brought it here?' Frances said, perplexed.

'It was never mine. And I do deplore it as a hateful thing.'

'Then I am ashamed, for thinking ill of you.'

'You should be.'

'But you should be ashamed for bringing it back home. It was not responsible. We have Flora and the servants here.'

'Flora is a babe, and the servants cannot read,' he reminded her.

'Even so, I cannot help but think it is an evil influence. It is a hateful thing. Can we burn it, please?'

'We shall. We will not have its evil come between us here,' he agreed. Could the paper be at the heart of this? Like a kind of charm that bore its own malevolence, over and above the meaning of its words? That was superstition, and Hew pushed it from his mind. He fetched the paper down and put it to the flame. And burning it, indeed, appeared to break its spell, for soon they were together, sitting in the firelight, peaceful once again. 'Are the stories of the Spanish torments true?' Frances asked.

He answered honestly. 'The Inquisition has inflicted countless cruelties. But I think also that the accounts may be exaggerated. This writing has sprung up to celebrate the triumph of the English fleet. It is more heroic when the enemy is monstrous. And people like to read that kind of stuff.'

'I do not like it,' Frances said, 'when we look for glory in a man's defeat. It should be enough, to know that we have won, and God is on our side. I think it is shameful, and small, to make foul of the tune of the good Valiant Soldier, and dress in Dead Spaniard, and such.'

Hew stared at her. 'Say what, my love? Dress in what?'

'Dead Spaniard. It is the latest colour worn in London now.'

'Dead Spaniard is the name for a kind of cloth?'

'For the *colour*,' Frances told him. 'It is all the vogue. My uncle sells the stuff. My cousin Mary has a gown of it. She writes it is a drab and dirty shade, but people like to wear it all the same. Thank God, we do not find it in Will Dyer's shop.'

'I love you, Frances Phillips,' Hew declared, and kissed her. Frances was a little pleased, and still a little vexed. 'I know you do,' she said. 'The question that remains is do I still love you? Shall we go to bed now, and find out?'

POSTSCRIPT

DEAD SPANIARD

'a proof that spirits and ghosts do oftentimes appear'

On November 26, 1588, the minister James Melville was woken from his bed and called to the harbour at Anstruther, where a ship was docked. The ship had sailed from Orkney, and the sailors aboard, who were more than two hundred and fifty, were survivors of the *Gran Grifon*, the flagship of the Spanish fleet. The men were in a desperate state, and posed no kind of threat. They were received by the civic and the Kirk authorities with civility and kindness, and responded gratefully. James Melville preached a sermon to them on their errors, which was well received. Their commander was extended every courtesy, and proved himself a credit to his rank. The rest were watched, and cared for, on their ship. The captives gave no trouble, and they wanted none. On one occasion only did they cause concern, when it was reported that one among the crew was missing from his berth. The missing man was Andres del Castillo, a young sailor born to a gentle family, who had been wounded badly in the wreck, when a piece of wood had pierced his side. If he were alive, he could not be far. A search was made, but nothing of him found. His captain thought he might have fallen overboard.

For the rest, they were quiet, honest men. If they had ever brought with them the vengeful tools of torment named in the reports, then they had gone down with the *Gran Grifon*. James Melville found them Christian, too, at heart. At St Andrews, he acquired a list of all the ships, and where they had come down, to bring back to their captain, who was keen for news. The minister was moved by how much it affected him. 'They are not monsters, at all,' he said to Hew when he met him in the street.

'But just the same as you and I.'

The college settled down for the winter term. Malcolm Crabbe had left, but promised to come back, and Thomas Crowe returned from his convalescence, with a little flesh upon his bones, and a little colour on his cheeks. The last fair in the year came on St Andrew's day. And early on that day, before the sun was up, Andres del Castillo came around the coast, looking for the town where the pilgrims used to come. The cathedral church had fallen in decline. But that was not the kirk that caught his eye. He was drawn instead to the chapel of St Salvator, with its steeple spire that towered above the town, and its aspect open to the quiet street. And there it was he chose to say his final prayers.

Hew was in the turret tower with Giles, when Thomas Crowe came bursting through the door. His eyes were shining. 'He is there! The Spaniard is there! In the chapel, now. Come, come and see!'

'You were telt,' scolded Giles, 'not to go in there.'

Hew pleaded, 'No more ghosts.'

'He is not a ghost. He is flesh and blood.' Thomas tugged his cloak. 'Come, will you, see!'

Coming to the kirk, Hew saw Andres kneeling in the place where there was an altar in the Catholic church. He rose at their approach, holding out his hands, opening his mouth as though he meant to speak. Blood began to spring from the wound on his side, and he laced his fingers, closing it again, falling to the ground. As Giles ran to catch him, Thomas said clearly, 'Now he is dead.'

There was nothing, after all, remarkable in that. Andres was the man missing from the ship, thought by his friends to have fallen in the sea. There was nothing strange in a foreign sailor, so far from his home, coming here to die in a holy place. The steeple of the chapel was a beacon to the faithful. It was meant to be. And if he did resemble someone Thomas Crowe had seen, or had once imagined seeing in a dream, that was natural too, as everyone agreed, for all the Spanish sailors looked the same.

NOTE

The epigraphs to parts 1–4, and to the Postscript, are taken from the 1596 edition of Lewes Lavater, *Of Ghosts and Spirits, Walking by Night*, with some slight modernisations.

The epigraph to 'Martinmas' is Lavater's version of the *Aeneid*, Book 4 384f. (Dido threatening to haunt Aeneas)

The 'New Ballet of the straunge and most cruelle Whippes', by Thomas Deloney, was printed in London, 1588.

BOOK V

Yule

It is easy to cry Yule at another man's cost

PROVERB

I

The old miller's son, John Kintor, at fifteen years of age, was learning to take care of Hew Cullan's land. He was followed in his work on a clear day in December by a boy of six, who helped with the grafting of the cherry and the pear trees, so there would be fruit, and blossom in the spring.

The child, Matthew Locke, took note of all he heard. 'There are grapes in the house. How is it that we have them in the winter time?' he asked.

'You maun ask your mammie,' John Kintor said, 'for that kind of alchemy. I dinna ken.'

'Alchemy is making base things into gold,' Matthew said.

'Alchemy is cookery. How are the grapes? Are they good to eat?'

'They are for the feast. I have not tried them yet. My daddie says that they are hot and moist, and an abomination at this time of year.'

John Kintor said, 'He will drink them, no doubt.'

Matthew did not understand. 'He says they puff the spleen and make it sick.'

John Kintor laughed at that. 'Best not eat too many, then. Are you not wanted at your books the day?'

'My master Gavan Baird says it is a ferie day, on account of Yule. But not to tell the Kirk,' Matthew said.

John Kintor nodded. He was learning also, at the grammar school. But he did not have to go there every day. 'Then you can help me with a special task. For it, we will want a length of strong rope. Run to the stable; they will gie you some.'

'What task is that? Is it Yule work?'

'It might be,' John said.

There was Yule work all around. Gavan Baird had taught Matthew and his sister Martha three separate songs for the nativity. They were Gude and Godlie ballads, so the minister at kirk could hardly disapprove of them, though Gavan said he would. The children were to sing at the dinner in the hall, while their aunt Frances would play on her lute.

Martha could not mind many of the words. She sang the balulalow that Minnie used to sing to her to make her go to sleep. In between it, she pulled faces, like the ones the mummers pulled at the Lammas fair. 'That will bring tears to your mither's eyes. Your daddie's too, I doubt,' Gavan Baird had said.

'Because it is so bad?'

'Because you sing so sweetly.'

The thought of his parents weeping frightened him a little. 'I do not want to mak my daddie greet.'

'The tears will be joyful ones,' Gavan Baird had said.

'Did you ken a man can greet from happiness?' Matthew asked John Kintor.

John said, 'Are you not gone yet? Run, fetch that rope.'

Matthew went back through the house. He was fond of the stables, where as an infant he had learned to ride, but he never went without an apple for the horse, and another for the boy who had to clean him out. Dun Scottis was an old and filthy-tempered nag, and since he shared his hay with others more refined, there was a danger that he might be overlooked. That was in a verse Gavan Baird had read to him, all about a horse neglected at the Yule. It had made him sad.

The apples were kept in the laich house below, where the dry air smelt leathery sweet. Matthew liked to go there, to take his time to choose a pippin from the racks. But today, a basketful had been brought up to the hall, and the pippins had been polished to a blush. The apples had been piled up in a bowl, sitting on a board. The board had been covered with a dark green cloth. It also held a bowl of apricots and nuts, and on a dish beside them, in a kind of cluster, were the pale green grapes. They had a whitish bloom on them. Matthew reached to touch.

'Don't,' said his mother behind him.

His mother's arms were filled with holly boughs. She had made a wreath to hang upon the door. The holly and the rowan trees kept away bad spirits from the house. Now she tucked a sprig into the apple dish.

'If I eat a grape, will I turn to gold?'

His mother laughed at that. 'You are gold already, in your heart. But I do not want you to eat them now. They are for tomorrow, after kirk.'

'It is fine an bonny in the house. But cauld,' Matthew said.

The hall had been swept out, down to the bare bars of the great iron grate, with its bed of ash, naked of its flame. It was cold outside; the bright winter sunshine born of the frost did not warm the ground. John Kintor blew on his hands, and his frozen breath hung in the air.

'It is warm in the kitchen,' Minnie said.

He followed her inside it, and found a blaze of heat. A great haunch of beef roasted on the spit, while several pots and kettles bubbled on the fire. In a cooler place, his aunt and Bella Frew were making coloured tarts, of saffron, plum and spinach, and of almond cream. The tarts would be frosted with a sugar crust, which the flame would fix to make it look like ice. The ice would thaw to syrup, tasting like a rose, sweet upon the tongue. It was like winter and summer in one.

Martha was here too, helping to paint the marchpanes and the gingerbread, quilting them with nuts.

The tarts would be fired in the oven in the bakehouse. Minnie had an oven made of tiles, built into the thickness of the kitchen wall. But the oven here was huge, and had a man to fuel it. The tenants of the farms brought their cakes and loaves, saving them a walk and a penny for the baxter. What the bakers did not know could not hurt them, Frances said. For six or seven days, there had been a crowd of people in the park, coming with their cold plates and going back with hot. If they had no spice or currants for their pies, Frances gave them some. And the air round about smelt of cinnamon and cloves.

Matthew and Martha had been brought here by their mother, to help prepare the Yule. Their father would join them on the morrow for the feast, which was Yule itself, or what their aunt Frances still called Christmas day.

Frances had made minchit pies. They were filled with fruits, with spice and strips of flesh, and the scent that came from them was deep and rich and savoury. She told him of a pie that she had seen in London once, in a shop belonging to a pastry cook. That pie had been shaped like the castle at Windsor. Each of its turrets was a coffin crust, and each one was filled with a different kind of meat.

Aunt Frances said in London there were pies of birds and frogs. The frogs and birds were live. And when the pie was cut, they would all fly out. The trick was that the coffin had been filled with bran, and after it was cooked, a hole was made in it; the bran was all poured out, and the animals put in. That would be a dreadful disappointment, Matthew thought. For inside the crust would be nothing to eat.

Sometimes, Frances said, they put people under it, at the English court. A jester or a dwarf. Maybe a small child. Matthew did not see why that should please the queen. It would not please a man. His father's face would fall, if Minnie baked a pie, and when it was cut open there was Martha in it.

His mother and his aunt, and Bella Frew, made cakes and biscuits for the feast of the Epiphany. The twelfth cake was vast, to feed the whole estate. Into it went pounds of raisins of the sun. Minnie made a smaller one, to share among the bairns.

That one was bound up in a dough. When it was cooked, and the pastry cut through, the plums would be plump and heavy with spice, the cake sweet and moist, Minnie said. There was a secret inside.

The big cake was to eat with a drink called lambswool, which Uncle Hew had learned to make at Leadenhall. It was a kind of spiced apple ale, with the flesh of a roasted apple on the top, whisked up in a froth, to look like the wool. It was for Uphalyday, the last day of the Yule, which Frances called twelfth night. Before then, there were other things to eat. There were all the tarts, and pies and roasted meats, the buns and biscuit bread, and the candied fruits. There were presents, too, to give out at New Year. For Frances from the children there was honey from the bees, for the infant Flora, a little silver bell, and for Hew an almanac, for 1589. 'So he can ken all that is to come,' Matthew had explained to his father at the shop. His father had declared it a very sound idea.

Minnie gave him two apples from the store, and he went out to the stables for the rope. Dun Scottis had a blanket, to keep him warm, and some hay to eat. He pretended not to know Matthew when he came, but he took the apple all the same. Matthew asked the stable boy for a piece of rope, and the boy asked a groom. That groom had a dry, cutting kind of manner Matthew did not like. He asked what John Kintor wanted with the rope, and how long it should be, and when Matthew did not ken, gave him a length 'for to hang himself'. When Matthew told John Kintor that, he laughed. He said that the groom did not like him much. He was jealous that John Kintor would be factor here.

John Kintor said the piece of rope he brought was grand. He slung it over his shoulder, and went into the wood, whistling as he went. Matthew followed him. He tried to whistle too, but he could not make the tune play between his teeth. He had no rope now to wear on his shoulder, and it had been heavy for him.

Some of the trees had been damaged by the storms. Some had been felled, and the men who worked the land had chopped them into planks, for burning on the fire or for making things. Those that remained were gathered in a clearing, where they came to now. Here John Kintor knelt, by a great block of wood, cut from the trunk of a birch tree. He tied the rope around the branches on the log. 'This is our Yule stock,' he said.

The stock was to burn in the great hall hearth. John Kintor said it came from ancient times, and the flame signified the returning of the sun, after the dark days of Yule. His dad had telt him that, when he was a bairn, and they went together, looking for a tree. Matthew knew John Kintor's dad was dead. The story made him feel sad and pleased. Sad because John Kintor had no father now, but happy still and proud that John had chosen him to help bring home the log.

They dragged the stock behind them up towards the house. Which was to say, John Kintor dragged it, for Matthew ran ahead, making clear the path, kicking over stones and skipping as he went, singing to himself a carol of the Yule. But they had not come far when they met a girl, little Jennie Kintor, coming to the mill. Jennie was the daughter of John Kintor's older brother, who was miller now. She was four or five years old, and weeping inconsolably. Not the coloured kind of crying Martha did, when she wanted folk to pet her, but with heavy tears. John Kintor asked her what was wrong, as an uncle should. Her answer took them some while to make out. At last they understood that her grandame at the mill had sent her up to Frances, for a poke of spice. They were making gingerbread for bringing in the Yule. Frances had given her some ginger in a cup, cinnamon and cloves and a little box of sugar-candied fruits, for putting on the top. She was coming home with it, joyful at her spoils, when she had met a man who took them all away. He had asked her name, and put it in a book. He had said that her parents would be fined in court, for the sin of superfluous cheer.

Matthew had not known that cheer could be a crime, though his father warned him sometimes of excess. It was, it now appeared, a very dreadful one, for John Kintor telt him he must run at once to fetch his Uncle Hew, while he would halt the man, whom they both could see before them on the path, striding in a fixed and most determined manner to the entrance of the hall. Matthew ducked down, and ran past, not daring to look back, or heeding to his call. He shot into the house.

Hew was in the cellar where he kept his wine, with his man, Robert Lachlan, choosing things to drink. Both men came at once. Robert Lachlan, who was rough and strong, lifted Matthew up to carry on his shoulders, where he felt quite safe. It gave him a clear vantage on the path ahead.

John Kintor had caught up with the man, and had kept him back, in furious dispute. He broke off as they approached, and Hew introduced himself as master of the house.

The man said, 'I ken you.'

'And I ken you, I doubt,' Robert Lachlan said. 'You are Alan Petrie, the clatterer from Kirk.'

The man was fearful now. Robert Lachlan often had that power on folk. And Matthew on his shoulders saw what Robert did. It was different, looking down from what his father said was a high perspective. He felt Robert's strength. Under his breath, he said 'clatterer'. He thought he had whispered it. But his uncle heard, for he looked at him and frowned. Hew told Robert Lachlan to set his nephew down. He told Matthew to go back to his mother in the house. And Matthew did set off. He went a little way, before his curiosity forced him back again. He wanted to hear what other things were said.

Alan Petrie said he had not come from the Kirk. He was here on behalf of the provost in the town.

Robert Lachlan said, a prier was a prier, and a clype a clype.

Alan Petrie read a paper out, which was his authority to search Hew Cullan's house, for any sign of feasting or excessive cheer, over and above the proper rank assigned to him.

Uncle Hew was not cross. He allowed the man to state his case in full, before he answered quietly that he would not give him access to his house, or to the farms and houses that were rented out to tenants on his land. He asked that Alan Petrie leave them peacefully.

Alan Petrie waved his paper all about, and said that Hew was in a thing he called contempt, and that he would be taken into ward and fined, if he did not give the access asked for here.

Hew told him calmly, it was the provost who was in contempt, for he had disturbed the peace of Yule. 'Tell him I refuse. And in defence, I invoke Yule Girth. He understands the law. You can come again, after the Epiphany, and I will let you in.'

Alan Petrie spluttered. 'After the Uphalyday, the feasting will be done.'

'That I cannot help. Your prosecutions, sir, are not lawful at this time. Tell him. He will ken.'

'I know you, sir. You are slippery, and you use the law,' Alan Petrie said, 'to your ain most subtle and perverted ends. You will not get away with it. I will come again. I know you live like kings. You treat your men like kings.'

'A pennyworth of candie for a miller's bairn is a poor treat fer a king,' Robert Lachlan said.

'Do not toy with me. I will find you out.'

Matthew did not like the man's tone of voice. He did not like menace that was meant to Hew, or the fact his uncle took it so calmly. He felt it fell to him to disarm the threat, as his father would have done. He had heard his parents say his Uncle Hew was stubborn, and that Robert Lachlan was spoiling for a fight. And so he tried to help. 'Did you say,' he asked the man, 'that it would be fine, for the king to have a feast? If a king came here?'

Alan Petrie stared at him, as though he discovered for the first time in his life that a gnat could talk, and was not impressed by it. 'It wid be,' he agreed.

Matthew beamed bright with relief. 'That is a' right, then,' he said. 'For the king will come here, at Uphalyday.'

His uncle frowned at him. 'Matthew,' he began.

Matthew said quickly, 'Did you forget, Uncle Hew? We made a cake for him.'

Then his uncle smiled. 'The bairn is right,' he said. 'The king will be among us at the twelvetide feast. It had slipped my mind.'

'Is that right?' said the man, his eyes dark with doubt. 'I had not heard it said he was expected here.'

'It is common knowledge,' answered Hew.

The man said he would put the matter to the provost, and would come again. That should have been the end of it, for he was meant to go. But when Matthew and John Kintor went back for the log they found that Alan Petrie had not left the premises. He was at the still house, peering through the lock. John Kintor cursed. 'He is still here, despite the Yule girth.'

'What is the girth?' Matthew asked.

'It is a kind of sanctuary, protecting men at Christmas, from paying for their crimes.' Suddenly, John grinned. 'Though he shall pay for his.' He took off the sling he wore around his waist for picking off the crows, and the pouch of pellets hanging from his belt. John Kintor was a sure, and a ruthless, shot. He took careful aim, and peppered Alan Petrie from his buttocks to his calves.

It did not end well. Alan Petrie bellowed, limping to the house, and the din he made brought the family out. Though Robert Lachlan sniggered, Uncle Hew did not. He paid money to the man, who hobbled back to town, promising a cold and particular revenge. Then he spoke to John Kintor, with a queer, quiet kind of anger that made Matthew want to cry, and to want his father there. He did not like to think what it felt like to be John, who was too old to cry, and whose father was dead. Hew told him it was not the behaviour that he wanted, or expected, in a factor of his house. It did not help when John Kintor mentioned the Yule girth, in his own defence. 'That is an argument I put, to protect this house, and the people in it,' answered Hew. 'You have turned it to your own wilful end, to commit a crime, that brings disgrace to us. It was an unkind and cowardly act. I am ashamed of you. And let me tell you this: though you may be free from penalty of law, you are not free from mine.' Matthew heard no more, for his mother came and took him to the house. He put his hand in hers and did not look back.

When his uncle came, he had John Kintor's sling with him. He left it in the library, next to Gavan's book. Two of the farmhands brought in the log, and settled it into the grate. John Kintor did not help, and when the tenants came to see the great fire lit, he was not among them. Matthew did not ask what had happened to him. In his bed, he imagined terrible things. He could hear, through a curtain in the closet next to him, his mother singing to Martha. Martha could not sleep. Her head was filled with Yule. She told Minnie all the songs and carols they had learned, which were meant for a surprise. Matthew wanted Giles. He wanted to sit in his lap, and to have him explain, in confounding and comfortable words, all the things he did not understand.

But his father was not there. And his mother was with Martha, soothing her to sleep. Matthew left his bed and went down in his shirt. The Yule stock was alight. But there was no one there but Frances, peaceful at its side, with Flora at her breast. Frances smiled at him. 'Can you not sleep?'

'Where is my uncle Hew?' he said.

'He has gone out. He will not be long.'

'He is at the mill.'

'Yes.'

Matthew felt a blaze of anger, burning like the log. 'It is my mill,' he said. 'My uncle gave it to me, for my christening gift.'

Frances said, 'I know.'

'Then he cannot, he should not.' He felt that there were tears, pricking at his throat, trying to spill out.

'Come and sit by me,' Aunt Frances said.

'Will John Kintor not be factor any more?'

'He will not be factor yet. He has more to learn.' It was Frances, after all, who had picked him out. 'He is not ready now,' she said.

'But he will be, soon. He wanted to protect us. He did it for you, for the house and land, and his little niece. It was not for himself.' He wanted her to see.

Frances said, 'I know.'

'But my uncle said—'

'Your uncle knows it also. But it is his job to protect us all. Because we are his family, he will keep us safe. We belong to him. John Kintor, too,' Frances said.

II

Yule day fell on Sunday, and the family went to kirk. Since the sky was clear, Hew said they would walk, to allow the horses to enjoy a holiday. But Matthew thought it was because the grooms were drunk. He had heard Bella say her husband Robert Lachlan had been drinking in the Yule, with the vicious one that Matthew did not like. They were still in bed when the rest set out. Bella stayed behind, to look after Flora and her own bairn Billy, who had caught the mumps. Or that was what she said. Really, it was to prepare the dinner board, for Bella did not care about the Sabbath much. The Kintors also stayed, to Matthew's fresh alarm. John was in the yard, tending to his pigs, when they passed the mill. He did not seem to mind, but smiled at them and waved.

The walk to town was long, and Matthew's legs were tired. When Martha girned and flagged, their uncle carried her. He could not be expected to carry Matthew too. And Matthew did not want him to. He scuffed his Sunday shoes, trailing through the dust. His mother noticed, but said only, 'You are cross today.'

Matthew fell behind, and would not take her hand. 'Why does John Kintor not come to the kirk?' he asked.

'Your uncle thought it better he should stay at home.'

Hew's kirk was the chapel of St Leonard's in the South Street. But today he came with them to the Holy Trinity, the grand kirk in the centre of the town. It was bursting full with men and wives and bairns. Some had brought their dogs. Matthew's spirits lifted when he saw his father there. He ran to his embrace, burying his head in the tippet round his neck, which was made of fur. He heard his father asking, 'Trouble?' to the air, and his mother's answer. 'Later,' she replied.

There were stools and settles brought, so no one had to stand. Frances sat with Meg, with Martha in her lap. Matthew sat on the settle next to his father, though he understood a stool was meant for him. Hew sat there instead. 'The cukstule,' he said, and winked, as though he was tickled at his own disgrace. Matthew turned his face deliberately away.

It was very rowdy in the kirk. The service began with several texts and readings by the elders of the kirk. One of those expected failed to take his place, which was unexplained, and not like him at all, Matthew heard the people say. He also heard the name, which was Alan Petrie. He peeped back to see if Hew had heard it too, but his uncle had a look of blankness on his face, almost of stupidity. Matthew saw the provost standing by the pulpit talking to the crownar Andrew Wood. That was very bad, and he had a glimpse of understanding why John Kintor had been telt to remain at home. Matthew knew the provost and the crownar well. Andrew Wood he feared. He came to the house, and never for the good, for his coming meant there was an unexpected death. His father then would have to go away, to certify the death, and explain the cause. The provost and the crownar both held courts of law. The crownar was the sheriff too, and his court was the worst. He could hang a man.

Now both men looked at Hew. And Matthew knew exactly what was in their thoughts. They were speaking of the man who had come to Kenly Green, on the provost's work, and had been shot by John. Where was Alan now?

Matthew knew his uncle must be thinking the same thing. How then could he sit so very straight and still?

His father looked at him. 'Fiddle fyke,' he said. 'You are a fidge today.'

'Dadda,' Matthew said, 'can a man be killed by a bruise on the buttock?'

'I sincerely hope not. Why, do you have one?'

Matthew shook his head.

'Well then, sit still.'

Matthew was quiet for a moment. Then he asked, 'Why has the crownar come to kirk today? He does not stay here.'

'As I understand it, he is spending Yule at his late brother's house.'

'I do not like him,' Matthew said.

His father answered sadly. 'Not many people do.'

'When kirk is over, can we go back home?'

'Not today, my love. We are going to spend the Yule with Hew at Kenly Green.'

'I dinna want to go. I want to stay at home, with you an Canny Bett.' It came out louder, and more crossly, than Matthew had intended. His father frowned, and tsked.

'What is this passion, now? You cannot stay at home. Canny will come too. What is the matter with you?'

Matthew could not say. He did not have the words for the quailing in his heart. He said what he believed came almost close to it, but was not it at all. 'I have the belly-thraw.'

It was not the sort of thing he liked to tell his father, for he never told the doctor he was feeling ill. His remedies were sore. If Matthew had a pain, his mother made it well.

But his father understood. 'That is a vulgar name for it. I do not like it much. But I do not think that that is what you mean. In my opinion, you are stomachit. That is to say, in common parlance, you are in a mood.' He lifted Matthew up, and sat him in his lap, where he found his quick heart comforted, and stilled.

He was settled there when the minister began. His sermon made no mention of the Lord's nativity, until the very end, when he looked round the kirk. 'Some of ye today, SOME OF YE TODAY,' he roared, in his usual way, 'have been out in the street, crying for the Yule. In the very kirkyard, yea, the very kirk. Now, do not deny it, I have heard ye all, and God has heard ye too. Now some of ye, in ignorance, are poor benighted bairns, and ye will not ken whence has come that cry. You think it "Jubile". It is my duty now, to put that wrang to right. It came about like this. Once there was a man that came to hang his dug on December twenty-fifth. Now that is a day, that some of ye will say is the Lord's nativity. I say fie to that. For if we mark the day our Lord was born, then why wid we not mark the day of his conception, in a Papish way? Your Christmas is but one sorry slip away. Be that as it might, he came to hing his dug upon that very day the ignorant among ye cry for Christmastide. But when he cut it doon again, the auld dug wis alive. As ye might well suppose, the devil took it then. The auld dug ran awa' and as it went, it howled, yool, yool, YOOL. And that, sirs, is the meaning of the Yule ye cry. Tis nothing in it signifies the word of Christ or God, but it is the havers of a half-deid dug. Ool, OOL, OOOOOOOOL.'

The last line of the ools, rousing up the kirk to thunderous applause, stirred the napping dogs, whose howling proved its point. The Yule day sermon ended in a pandemonium, the people and the dogs spilling to the streets. Matthew felt a reckless, giddy spill of joy. He could not still the laughter bubbling up in him. The provost and the crownar both had disappeared, and he was looking forward now to dinnertime. He dared ask Uncle Hew if John Kintor would be there. His uncle said, 'Of course.'

Both the bairns were skittish on the way back home, as though some sudden wind had been unleashed in them. People in the farms they passed bid them a guid Yule, and every time they did, Matthew and his sister rolled their eyes and howled, pretending to be dogs, until their mother warned them that they must desist, or there would be no cake or pudding at the feast. Then they sank instead into a fit of giggles, while their mother sighed, and thanked the country neighbours for their kind intent. She called out to their father once or twice for help, but he was deep in conversation with her brother Hew. Matthew did not stop to wonder what they said. He felt his heart was light, his spirits whole again.

'I am no longer stomachit,' he said.

His mother said she saw, but it was good to hear.

He did not think that anything could spoil his silly happiness, until he saw the shadow of the horse, when they were a mile or so from his uncle's house. It came upon them swiftly like a cloud. The rider overtook them, and turned the horse around. It was Sir Andrew Wood. He did not leave his mount, but looked down to Hew. 'I came to look for you.'

'You have found me,' answered Hew.

'By your leave,' the crownar said, 'I will follow to your house.'

It was Frances who replied, 'You are welcome there. If you have no friends who wait for you at home, stay and dine with us.'

'I thank you,' said the crownar. 'But the call is not a social one. I will not keep you long.'

'But surely,' Frances said, 'you do not work today.'

'I do not mark the Yule,' the crownar said.

'I meant the Sabbath, sir.'

Sir Andrew laughed. 'A strake. The lady has a point.' He turned again to Hew. 'But you are quiet, sir.'

'I am wondering,' said Hew, 'what business brings you here, when it cannot it be the business of a court, that does not sit in session in this time.'

'I have heard your argument. It amuses me. You have claimed Yule Girth. Yesterday I heard two complaints of it. First there was a man with a flesh wound in his buttock, who complained of an assault suffered on your lands, while he went about his lawful line of work. He showed to me the pellet that the surgeon had pulled out. Then he showed his arse. I dismissed them both. Next there was the provost from the town. He was somewhat vexed at what happened to his man. He does not hate your house. His hope was but to raise some money for the poor.'

'That he may have, and gladly,' Matthew's uncle said. 'I will pay to him whatever fine he likes, if he will be content to let the matter drop. His man was too officious, but did not deserve the treatment he received from us, and I am sorry for it. I have made amends. If he remains unsatisfied, he shall profit further from the hurt he got, for which I take the blame.'

'He will profit further, if he can be found. He has disappeared.' The crownar yawned. 'None of this interests me, Hew. I do not care a bean if ye keep the Yule or no. I am not the Kirk. Nor

I am concerned with these small assaults. Whip your servants soundly, if they must offend, or let them come and plead before the burgh courts, when the Yule is done.'

'I thank you for your interest, and lack of it,' said Hew. 'Why, then, have you come?'

'To have from you an intelligence, of particular concern. The provost tells me you expect a visit from the king. That is news to me. And news to all his friends. The king gives out no word he is expected here. What is the purpose of his visit?'

Matthew felt his heart leaping in his breast so tremulous and quick he thought it would break out. He thought his uncle Hew must give his part away. But Hew did not discover him, in word or in look. He said simply, and mildly, 'Oh. That.'

'Aye, that,' the crownar said.

'Well, you know,' Hew said. 'The thing is delicate.'

'I understand you. We will talk in private at your home.'

Sir Andrew Wood was satisfied. He was even pleased. He made his horse walk slow, so they could walk beside it. 'Perhaps,' he said, 'your bairns would like to ride with me.'

Matthew clasped tightly to his sister's hand, willing her to grasp the danger he conveyed. Something of it caught, for Martha shook her head.

'Neither of ye, then?'

They were coming to the mill, lying in the lea of the country tower house, next to the cottage where the Kintors lived. John Kintor was no longer outside in the yard. But there was something else, lying in the grass not far from the pen. It was not a pig, though the upper part of it was pinker than a ham.

The crownar Andrew Wood had seen it from his horse. It did not take him long to work out what it was. He was on it first, in long, forceful strides. He had left his horse tethered to a post before the others saw him beginning to dismount. He lifted up the thing that was not a pig by what looked like the flaps of a coat. 'Superfluous cheer. He found none, I doubt.'

Frances had already hurried Martha to the house. His mother tried to take him too. But Matthew pulled away.

Sir Andrew Wood called for the doctor. 'He is still limp. Warm, even. But hopeless, I think.'

Matthew's father said, 'There is blood and bruising round his nose and mouth. Something in his throat.' He felt with his hands, and something small flew out. 'That is it,' he said.

The crownar picked it up. 'It is like the pellet that was in his arse.'

Matthew cried, 'No. It is not.'

His mother had hold of him. 'Come away, Matthew.'

'He has seen it, Meg. It must be explained,' his father said. His voice held a terrible sadness. His hands had the purple thing in them, that was a man with a face.

John Kintor's brother came out from the mill. 'Jesu,' he said.

'Where is your brother? Ask him to come here,' said Hew.

John Kintor's brother said, 'You dinna think–'

Matthew cried out, 'It was not him.' He broke from his mother, and ran towards the house. He could not see for tears.

The crownar had prerogative, as sheriff of Fife, to hang a man he found in the act of murder there. In this case, with the corpse still warm and the perpetrator near, he felt there was no case for further trial. He arrested John Kintor for the redhand slaughter of Alan Petrie, and sentenced him to die on December 26.

The boy looked for mercy, not to him, but to Hew Cullan. He was afraid, but his eyes were trusting. His trust was in Hew. It was to him that he pleaded, 'I did not do this. I was in the house.'

The crownar observed, as a matter of fact but of little interest, that a man could do a murder from the safety of his house, if he had a sling.

'I dinna hae a sling. He took it from me.'

'That is true.' Hew Cullan put a hand on John Kintor's shoulder. It was not the hand that apprehends, but the hand that protects. Andrew Wood considered this. He judged each case, without sentiment or prejudice, on the basis of the evidence. His decisions were pragmatic, and his actions unreserved. He had not expected to find a murder here, but the fact he came upon one did not trouble him. He spared no pity for the age of the accused. He did not judge persons, but deeds, and he judged them as he found them, without let or pause. He dealt not in mercy, but justice.

'A sling is no more than a knotted piece of cord,' he said. 'An easy thing for anyone to make, at any time.'

'Not anyone could fire into a man's open mouth,' said Giles, covering the corpse.

'Precisely.'

'There is no certain evidence, to link the crime to John,' said Hew.

'I believe there is.' His judgment on the case was absolute. The lawyer in Hew Cullan understood this, for he played his last card.

'We claim Yule Girth.'

'I will grant you your request. But you should consider what it means. It will give this boy a stay of execution, which I permit until the seventh of January, the day after Uphalyday. On that day, the law will take its course, and you must deliver up John Kintor to be hanged. There will be no trial, and no other plea. If you think it kindness to let one of his tender years lie in dread to wait for sure and heavy justice, then do so, by all means. If it were my boy, I should want the rope to come presently, and swift,' Andrew said.

'We claim Yule Girth,' said Hew, 'upon your terms. These are ours. On January seventh, I will put forward evidence and proofs, to explain this crime. And, if I cannot . . .' He paused.

'If you cannot?' the crownar prompted.

'If I cannot, I will offer you myself, for justice in his place. For I am the master of this boy. This is my house and my land, under my protection and my jurisdiction. If there is wrong done here, I will answer to it.'

Giles Locke said, appalled, 'Think what you say.'

But Hew said, 'I know what I say.' He looked at the crownar. 'Do you accept it?'

Sir Andrew saw before him the glint of a prize. Yet he was unsure of it. 'Is this some trick of yours? Do you intend, perhaps, to come before the king?' he said.

The lawyer shook his head. 'It is an honest contract. As to the king, I cannot tell you now the confidence between us. It may not come to pass. But I will lay all before you, when the Yule is done.'

'Then,' said the crownar, 'I accept your terms.' He allowed Hew a moment to consider with his friend. 'If you are content to conclude the bargain, then it will be binding. Unless you show proof to exonerate this boy, or deliver him to the place of execution, I will take your life from you, in the place of his.'

'I am not content,' said Giles. 'I do not consent to it. Do not be a fool, Hew. Think of Frances and the bairn. This man will hang you, for sure.'

'Courage, Giles,' said Hew. 'It will not come to that.'

His confidence, his foolishness, struck Andrew as extraordinary. Never had a man placed his head so willingly in the crownar's noose. 'He will die,' he thought, 'die at my hands.' So much was a certainty, and ought to satisfy. And yet for reasons he did not quite understand, he felt uncertain of it, troubled still by doubt.

'John Kintor and Giles Locke are witness to this contract here,' he said. 'I accept your petition for Yule Girth, on the terms set out. But you maun forgive me, for my want of trust, if I place a girdle round your house. You shall have your girth, but it will confine you, your family and your household, for the rest of Yule. Justice will take place, with no let or escape, when that time is done. I shall send men to enforce it.'

'This contract is not right. It cannot bind us,' Giles demurred.

But Hew replied, 'It does.'

The crownar left for town, arranging for a guard to be placed on the house, and for Alan Petrie's body to be borne away. It was only when he came back to his brother's house, where his family gathered to enjoy the Yule, that he realized why he was not quite content: he had not found out Hew's business with the king.

III

Frances found her husband sitting in the library. He was looking at the copy of the Gude and Godlie ballads, which the bairns and Gavan Baird had left open on the desk. His smile to her was wary. 'I suppose you heard,' he said.

'I should have preferred to have heard it first from you. Or that you had consulted me, before you lost your head.'

'I know. And I am sorry for it.'

'Still,' she was bright now, and brisk, 'you will solve it, I suppose. And, if you cannot, there is the king. You will come to his will, for he is your friend.'

'Frances, the king–'

'You do not have to tell me,' Frances said. 'I know there is a reason why you did not say. I do not need to know all that's in your mind. It only hurts a little, when you do not trust me. I have English family, English friends, I see that. But you surely know by now I do not spy on you.'

'There is no one in the world I trust so much,' he assured her. 'The thing about the king, it was never meant. It came about from something Matthew said by accident.'

'Children have a way of finding out a thing, though they have no understanding what it signifies. I hope that Matthew's blurting has not put you into danger, though.'

Hew said, a little wretchedly, 'It has not. It helps.'

'Then I am glad to know that you have all in hand. I will not plague you now with questions. I came only to ask what should be done about the banquet here tonight. Though Andrew Wood has placed a guard upon the house, it does not stop our tenants from the farms from coming through to us. Since we are confined here, and we have so much, I thought we should go on with it, in spite of that poor man. His body has been taken to the town. Giles insisted it be kept in the mort house there, until the time –' Here, Frances stopped, from fear, or else from delicacy. She could not name the time. 'Till then, Giles says there is no family to contend with. He has kept the pellet here, as evidence.'

'That is good, and helpful, Frances. I do not suppose you ken what happened to the sling and pellets that were here? They were still in their places when we left for kirk.' That was on his mind, had been on his mind, ever since he came to fetch them from the library. He did not find his answer in the book.

Frances looked around. 'Are they gone from here? Does that mean John Kintor took them after all?'

'It means something, doubtless. But I am not inclined to think that it means John. A sling is something John can make himself. If he wanted to replace it he could do so in an instant. I knew that when I took it from him, and he kent it too. The confiscation was a kind of figure. It is like taking from a man the badge of his office, rather than the tools of his trade. Such a thing is not recovered quite so easily. It has to be earned. John Kintor understood that. I made sure he did. It would astonish me to find he took it back.'

'But if, as you say, he could make another one, the slinger in itself proves nothing,' Frances pointed out.

'Its presence would not signify at all,' Hew agreed, 'but its absence does. It is has been removed by someone in the house. Where is Gavan Baird today? I see he left his book.'

'He went to his sister, in Arbroath, for the holiday. But you cannot suspect Gavan Baird,' Frances said.

'I do not suspect. I admit, or reject, the possibility. When did he leave?'

'Yesterday, at noon.'

'If you saw him go, that will rule him out. That leaves us Bella, Robert, John Kintor and his family, one among the grooms, a serving lass, perhaps–'

'Robert and Bella!' Frances exclaimed. 'You cannot accuse them! They are our friends. Why, you have missed out Flora and Billy. Are the babbies not among your suspects too?'

'I do not accuse them,' answered Hew. 'I observe, merely, that they were at the house when this man was killed. They must answer questions. For if a stranger came, and passed into the library, Bella will have seen. It is also of note, that Robert had a plain dislike of the man who died. They had met before. Petrie gave evidence against him at the kirk, when Bella was with child. Robert had to marry her.'

'And?' Frances gave no quarter to that line of reasoning. She was far from pleased. And Hew began to see the perils of the path ahead.

'These are motives, Frances, that must be explored. That is how investigation works,' he said.

'Then I wish you had not chosen to investigate.'

'Would you prefer it that John Kintor was hanged, whether he is guilty of the crime or not?'

She was silent then.

'Do not fret, Frances, I will resolve this. All will work out,' he assured her. 'When did it not?'

'Well then, I trust you. I will go back to my banquet.'

'Give me leave to speak in private with Bella for a while. I will try her first.'

Frances smiled at that. 'Courage to you, then. Bella will not suffer your foolishness as I do.'

Hew smiled back at her. 'I imagine not,' he said. 'I may need some support. What is Giles about?'

'You will have to face your battleground alone. He and Meg are comforting their son. It was hard for Matthew to make sense of this.'

Hew was sobered then. 'It must have been. Then I must do without his friendly counsel too. Matthew is not pleased with me.'

'No one here is pleased with you,' Frances said severely. 'Matthew least of all.'

'He was much stomachit because I dared to discipline his beloved John. He ought to be more grateful that I save his life.'

'He does not know that yet. Matthew owns the mill. It belongs to him. And John Kintor belongs to the mill. Therefore, he thinks John is under his protection. He holds himself responsible for taking care of him.'

'Ah, that is absurd!' Hew said. 'He is six years old. Why should he believe that burden falls to him?'

'His mirror is the man who gave to him the mill,' his wife replied.

Bella Frew was a fury to contend with. The Yule bread she was making was receiving such a pummelling that Hew was thankful he was not beside it on the board. Bella had a force in her that far outstripped her size. There was sufficient muscle built in kneading buns and cakes and whisking creams and syllabubs to feed the crowds at Yule, to supply the guard.

'Ah dinna ken,' she answered him again, with so sharp a smack against the unresisting dough he almost felt a bruise. 'Ye maun pardon me, if while I wis polishing plate, and scrubbing the pots, and chopping the herbs, an washing the cups, and sweeping the flair, and hinging the clouts, and tending to Bill an wiping the airse of yer ain bonny babe, I did not keep a watch upon your lordship's library. I wis not telt I wis to be in charge of that as well.'

'Bella, you ken well that was not what I meant. Did you see anyone go up to the library, while we were out? Or could someone have done so while your back was turned?'

Bella answered plainly, 'No, and aye. I niver saw anybody climb the turret tower. I did not go upstairs. But I was not in one place all the time. I was in the nether hall, tending to the bairns, or setting up the banquet, or in the kitchen here. The kitchen door was open, to let out the steam. It was awfy warm. A person could have passed through at any time. In fact–'

'In fact, what?'

Bella gave the dough another vicious slap. 'Just what I have said. I cannot tell you more.'

Hew went to the door, which was open still. It was close by the pantry, filled up with food for the twelve nights to come. A fraction of it would be eaten at that evening's feast.

Bella came behind him. 'You will have a sour sauce, if you dip your fingers in. Niver mind ye are the master of the house; ah dinnae care.'

'Plainly,' said Hew.

'Well then, haud your hands. There is a system here, as the doctor calls it. The things to the left are all for the nicht. In the middle are the things that last another week. And to the right are things that last the longest time. Woe betide the one who dares to mix it up.'

'This is the soul of superfluous cheer.'

'It is not so much. And it is not only for us. It will feed all the farms, and those of the poor who can come to the feast, and those that your guidwife will visit at hame, if the crownar allows it. By twelvetide, it will be gone. We will want more for the king.'

'Ah. You have heard that.'

'You should have telt us,' she said. 'We have, I doubt, sufficient flour and flesh, but all of this will hae to be begun again, for some of it will spoil.'

'I do not think it will. The truth is, Bella, that the coming of the king is a secret thing, or was meant to be. Therefore, he will make do with the common ordinary, and expect no more.'

She was mollified a little. 'Will he come alone, or bring a horde with him?' she asked.

'I think it very likely he will come alone. I am sorry to have put you to more trouble over it. But do you understood why I have to ask you questions? Have you heard the news?'

She softened to him then. 'Robert said. It is a kind of game you play with Andrew Wood. He says that you have put yourself precisely in the noose where Andrew Wood has longed to have you all the while, and that he will hang you.'

'He will,' Hew said quietly. 'If I cannot find the answers to the questions. Frances does not ken. She knows, but she does not understand the set of Andrew's mind.'

'That man is a monster,' Bella said. 'And you should ken better than to play with him. Frances is too soft. If you were Robert, now, I would be blind with rage at you. Robert has a bairn, and you do too. Yet you will chance your life upon a silly game.'

'It is not a game. It is to save John Kintor.'

'Is it, now?' She sniffed. 'Tell yourself that.'

Then Bella relented. She dealt him harsh words, but offered a balm. And he knew her well enough to wait for it. 'I did not see awbody go up to the library. But.'

'But?'

'I dinnae like rats. I have never liked rats. And the trouble with a door left open by the pantry is that there is a chance that a rat may slip inside. Do you see?'

Hew believed he did. 'Did a rat come in, while you were in the hall?'

'A very large one did. It was sniffing in the pantry, when I came back in. Now when I see a rat, I chase it with the broom. Unless it is too big. Then I have no stomach for it, and I call for Robert.'

'So that is what you did.'

'That is what I did. Robert saw it out. He had it by the scruff, and I heard it squeal. That is all I ken. If you want to ken mair, ye maun talk to Robert.'

'That I intend to do. Thank you, Bella.'

'Thank me for nought. You will not hing this on Robert, Hew. He did not kill the man. And if he wanted to, he would not use a sling. Do not, in your foolishness, set your mind on that. He will not swing for John Kintor. He loves you. We both do. He has saved your life before, and you have fought for his. But fix it in your mind, he will not hang for you.'

Hew found Robert Lachlan talking at the stable with the sour-tempered groom, who had not been employed at the stable long. Both men smelt of drink. They had tried to slip the guard, Robert said, but had not succeeded. 'It wasna worth the fash of starting up a fight,' Robert said. Hew asked if he would walk down to the mill with him, to take him out of sight and hearing of the groom.

'You seem thick with that man.'

'Ach,' Robert said, 'I wasnae sure of him. I thocht to try him out.'

That was Robert's way. He was suspicious of anyone new, and an incorrigible spy. His 'trying out' involved interrogation of a subtle kind. His torture of choice was the grain. He could drink anyone into the sink. They did not know, till they woke up the next morning with their heaving bellies and their thumping brains, that they had spent the evening on the rack.

'And?'

'He can haud his drink. He has a savage wit. He is good with the horses. He likes them,' Robert said.

'But?'

'But he is a malcontent, a sour, unhappy man. You will hae no loyalty from him. He is fu' of spite. He is envious, of everything he sees. He will not start a fight, or try to steal from you.'

'That is encouraging, at least,' said Hew.

'You would think so. But ye would be wrong. A man can brawl, and steal from you, and bear ye yet no malice in the world. The man that does no ill, but bears it in his heart, is no man that ye want biding in your house.'

'You are right, and I thank you. I will bear it in mind. You have a nose for sniffing out rats. Bella tells me that you dealt with one for her today.'

'Ah, she did, did she? Well, ye will ken all about it.'

'I do not ken. Bella was tight-lipped.'

Robert roared at that. 'That wid be a first. She had some choice words to say to me of you.'

'Aye, she telt me some of them.'

'Not the half, I doubt. What possessed you, Hew, to tickle Andrew Wood? You know that he will hang you in a heartbeat.'

'Help me, then,' said Hew. 'I ken you did not kill the man.'

Robert looked at him, quizzical and humorous. His voice though had an edge to it. 'Sure of it, are you?'

'A pellet in a windpipe does not have your mark.'

Robert gave it thought. 'It has its merits though. It would stop his peep. And he was a squealer, for sure.'

'What did you do to him?'

'I will have ye ken I put no hand on him, other than to show him gently to the door.'

'You did not hurt him at all?'

Robert grinned at him. 'How should I dare, after that blast you gave the Kintor boy? He might have had a slap, on his riddled airse, to set him on his path, but I couldna hurt the man. He was jelly on a plate. There was no more fight in him than in one of Bella's custards.'

Hew and Robert Lachlan parted at the mill, where the crownar's guard stood watchful by the burn. 'You and your colleagues are welcome,' Hew told him, 'to join us tonight at our feast.' When the man looked uncertain, he said, 'Where better to watch, than where we will be?' It would be a simple thing, he thought, for Robert to disarm most of Andrew's men, through the failsafe method of the demon drink. But it would not be fair to them. And the result would be yet more blood on his hands.

The family at the mill received him with humility and a desperate gratitude. John Kintor's mother had been weeping copiously. She was an old friend from Hew's father's time, and Hew had no doubt his sister would be there to hold her hand and comfort her, as soon as she had quelled the terrors of her son. For the moment, he felt an awkwardness, for while they looked to him for hope and reassurance, he also had to question them on matters that were delicate. He must know the truth, whatever his resolve. And he must convince the mother that whatever was the truth, she would not lose her son.

In the event, his questions were pre-empted by John Kintor himself, who approached him bravely, and asked if Hew wished him to give himself up. 'For I will admit to it, if you want me to.'

'I do not wish you to, if you did not do it,' Hew said, and was persuaded quickly that the boy was innocent.

'Oh, but,' John Kintor said, 'it is all my fault. If I had never shot at him, I widnae be suspected now, and you wid not have said that you wid take my place, and you wid not be hanged. So I should be hanged now, instead of you. I am resolved.'

He looked at his mother, who wept further tears, confirming, 'He is resolved, sir. He is.'

Hew told him firmly that it was his intention that no one would be hanged. 'Or at least, not you or I, for both of us are blameless.'

'But I shot his arse. So I am the more to blame than you,' John Kintor said.

'In truth,' said Hew, 'you are the less to blame.'

'How can that be?'

'It is a question of degree. And I am of degree and a higher rank than you. So I will put to rights the trouble we are in, and you will sit there quietly and do as you are told.'

The assertion of authority worked to reassure him, as it was meant to do, and Hew was able then to continue with his questions, and to be fairly sure of the response. John Kintor had not retrieved the slinger from the library, or been up to the house. He had not seen Alan Petrie since the day before. But his brother had. He had seen him sitting by the burn, while he was at the mill. That was not so long before they found him dead. 'I swear that he was well then. He was on a hummock, wiping off his shoes. As if he'd trod in something.'

'Did you speak with him?' Hew asked.

The miller shook his head. 'Ah didn't want to draw attention to myself. I wis at the mill, on a Sunday, dae ye see?'

'Why were you there?'

'Bella thocht ye might be running short of flour. She has it in her head that the king will stay. Havers, I should think. Ye hae enough flour in the house to feed a hunerd kings. But she was on at me last night, an I thocht I'd run a sack off while ye were at kirk.'

'You did not hear him fall, or cry out?'

'I widnae if he did, for the workings of the mill.'

John Kintor and his mother had not heard a sound. But the mill house was a little further off.

John Kintor said, 'He must have had his mouth open wide enough, for someone to have lobbed the pellet in. Singing, or screaming, perhaps.'

'Or yawning,' said Hew. 'For that makes no sound.'

John Kintor looked doubtful. 'How long is a yawn? He had some aim on him, that shot the ball into his open mouth. I'm no sure I could dae it, if I tried.'

'I do not think,' said Hew, 'we will put that to the test. It may have been a happy – or unhappy – accident. We will find out when we find out who removed the sling. For I am satisfied it was not one of you.'

He told the family they should dress in all their proudest finery, and come up to the house for the Yuletide feast, where they would find good cheer, and solace from their woes. And he convinced himself that he must do the same.

Matthew opened his eyes again, to find his uncle Hew looking down at him. His uncle smiled at him. 'May I?' he asked. When Matthew nodded, he sat by him on the bed. 'I thought,' he said, 'that you might be asleep by now.'

'I tried to,' Matthew said. 'I want to be. But when I close my eyes, they are full of things. It is like a battle in my brains.'

'Mine, too,' his uncle said. 'There are days like that. This one has been hard for you. Are you cross with me still?'

'Not very.'

'Not very.' Hew repeated. It seemed to make him smile.

'Minnie telt me what you did. You have saved John Kintor. I am glad you did. For I do not think John Kintor killed that man.'

'Nor do I,' said Hew.

Matthew found a comfort in his words. He could feel his body settle, closing into sleep. 'Will you find who did?'

'I hope so,' said Hew. 'I will be in trouble if I don't.'

'If you don't, the king will put it right.'

'That is what I came to talk to you about. Our secret of the king,' said Hew.

'Should I not have said?'

'It helped me that you did. But I think we should not mention it again, until Uphalyday. For only you and I know what will happen then.'

'Only you and I,' Matthew echoed sleepily.

'That is right.'

'My father says that you and I are alike. He says it sometimes, when I have been bad. Is it not a good thing?' Matthew asked.

His uncle laughed at that. 'It is good, and bad, I think. Your daddie is not wrong.'

'I can help you, if you like. For I think I might know who it was.'

'Who what was?'

'Killed the man. It was the bad groom. The bad groom in your stable here. The one who likes to say all the sneering things.'

'I know the man,' said Hew. 'Why do you suppose that it was him?'

'He is not kind to Dun Scottis. Dun Scottis has an auld grey blanket, while all the other horses have good new coats. He is neglected, like the Yule yald in the poem.'

'I think that we can find a new coat for Dun Scottis. He is my old friend. He is the first horse that I ever bought, and ever since has proved to be the worst. But I too have neglected him. Did I give him to you, when I gave you the mill?'

'No. But you loaned him, when you were in London.'

'Then I give him to you now. He is yours, to care for here or at St Andrews as you please. I am only grateful he has had your protection, to save him from the cruelty of neglectful grooms. But though the man you mention is not always kind, that does not mean that he would kill a man.'

'But he hates John Kintor. He is jealous of him, because he will be factor, and the bad groom won't. And when I asked for the rope, to carry to John, he said he could have it to hang himself with.'

'If he said that to you, then I will have a word with him.'

'You should. If I were you, I would look in his bed. That's where I hide things. Under the pillow is a good place.'

'That is sound advice. I will think on it.' Matthew felt Hew's kiss, soft upon his forehead, as he fell asleep.

IV

In the morning Hew renewed his old acquaintance with the dun horse Scottis, who spent his summers grazing in a peaceful pasture, and his winters lazing in a stable bed. The horse showed no respect or recognition for its master, responding to his overtures with suspicious gloom.

'Do not fret, old friend. I have not come to exercise you. You are Matthew's now.'

Dun Scottis had a blanket and a fine wool coat, both of which were clean and warm and serviceable. He had fresh hay and water. His tail and mane were brushed, and he was well shod. In a pail by his stall were apples and grapes from the display in the hall. He had also a halter, for leading him out on his daily ambles round the yard. The halter was made of a long plait of cord. Hew removed it carefully, and took it to the library. He stayed there for a while, in reflective mood. He did not return to look around the stable, to question the bad groom, or to search his room. He did not have to, for it was not long before the bad groom came to him. The groom set before him the little pouch of pellets that was hidden in his bed. He was puce with rage. 'This is someone's trick, to mak me swing for him.'

Hew said with a sigh, 'They were under your pillow, I suppose.'

'How devil d'ye ken? Did ye put them there?'

'Why would I do that?'

'To save your silly skin. Well, it will not work.'

'Peace,' said Hew. 'For no one is accusing you.'

'If it is not you, then it is John Kintor. Both of you should hang!'

The groom damned them all. The worst of it, he said, was that bloody bairn; there would never be a let from his endless questions, now that Hew had given him the horse. Hew thanked him for his help, and said that he was sorry that he had to let him go. There would be, he thought, no trouble with the guard. 'For you are not one of us.'

At dinner, he asked Matthew if he could come a moment, to help him in the library. Matthew came expectantly. He saw the sling and pouch. 'Oh. You found the things. Was it the bad groom?'

'Dun Scottis had the sling, and the bad groom had the pouch.'

'Then it was just as I said.'

Matthew's uncle asked him to sit down. 'It was remarkably just as you said. The groom has gone away. He will not be unkind to you again.' Then he said some other things that were sad and serious. He said that it was wrong to try to conceal the truth, but far worse to accuse a man falsely, of a crime for which he had not been responsible. Suppose the man was hanged, because of Matthew's lie? Then Matthew cried, and asked if Hew would have to tell his father. And Hew said that he ought to, but probably would not. And he promised that whatever happened next, Matthew must not fret, for he would make quite certain John Kintor would be safe.

Once the sling had been recovered, Hew found no further evidence. He had established that Alan Petrie had returned to the house on Christmas morning, in the hope of gaining access while the family were at kirk. He had been discovered in the act of inquiry in the pantry, and despatched from there by Bella Frew. Robert Lachlan had sent him on his path, and John Kintor's brother had seen him by the mill, sitting on the river bank as though to take his rest. The pellets and the sling, as he now supposed, had remained in the library until Matthew took them, thinking in his childish way to conceal the evidence, and so had no place at all in the inquiry. But as to what happened in the brief space of time after John Kintor's brother saw him sitting by the burn, and before they came upon him lying in the grass, he could find no clue.

For the rest of the Yule, he concealed his fears. He embarked upon a cheerful, reckless kind of holiday, laughing with the bairns, and reading songs and verse. He played cards and chess, listened to the lute, and put on a play, casting John Kintor in the leading part. He drank with Robert Lachlan long into the night, and ate more than his fill of brightly coloured tarts. On handsel day, he gave out lavish gifts, and money to the farms. He encouraged Frances in her firm belief that the king would come at last to save the day, and occupied his family in a dizzy merriment, that kept them all at bay.

Only Giles suspected him. On New Year's Eve, he said to Hew, 'I feel we should perhaps prepare for the sad contingence that things may not turn out as we would like them to.'

Hew said, somewhat vaguely, that the matter was in hand.

'The matter, I suspect, is quite out of hand. Can you tell me, truthfully, that it is resolved?'

'Not, precisely, resolved,' his friend admitted.

The doctor sighed. 'I thought as much. And I do believe this business of the king is made up as a screen. Please tell me I am wrong.'

'You have been talking to Matthew.'

'I have indeed been talking to Matthew. But I have had no reason from the bairn. He has become, I may say, somewhat close and secretive since we came to stay here. It is not a good trait in a child, and one that I attribute to your evil influence.'

Hew said, 'He has a good heart.'

'That I do not doubt. My trouble is with you.'

'Oh, do not be severe with me. I am trying, Giles.'

'You are. Well then, the truth.'

'The truth is that I am no closer to solving this crime than I was when I began. And, you are right, the king is a panoply. It came up by accident. It served my purpose to allow the lie to spread. If Andrew Wood believes I have a secret worth the telling, he will let me live until he worms it out of me. That will buy me time, even after January.'

'Do you think so? He will see through it in a heartbeat, Hew. He knows your mind as you know his. I think we need another arrow in our sleeve.'

'What do you propose?'

'That we send a letter to the king, where he holds his court, and invite him here. It will be hard, but not impossible, to slip it through the girdle Andrew Wood has tied.'

'What? You think that he will quit his court and Christmas cheer, and come here at our call to sample Meg's fruit tarts?'

'Why not? They are very good tarts. He is doubtless weary of the Yule by now. He will want adventure.'

'He will not want adventure. He never does. Do we even ken where he keeps his court?'

'That,' admitted Giles, 'is a small impediment. It is hard to ken, when we are pent in. And we can hardly ask it of Sir Andrew Wood.'

'Even if we kent, and even if we could, and even if he would, it could not be done in the space of six days,' said Hew.

'You should have faith. For strange things can happen.'

'Not this.'

Giles, for all his will, had to concede the point. 'Ah, perhaps. What, then?'

'We must be still, and wait until the seventh comes.'

'Hew. You know that when it does, you must give up the boy? You cannot go yourself.'

'I will not give up the boy. He did not commit the crime.'

'Nor did you.'

'Andrew Wood will hold me to my oath. We both know that. But I will offer to defend John in a court of law, in the king's court if he will.'

'He can hang the boy, without further trial, on the existing evidence. That is his prerogative,' said Giles.

'True. But you forget I gave myself, in John Kintor's place. My hope is he will hesitate to hang me so precipitate as would hang the boy. He has not long to go before he leaves office. This may be his last case. He will want his conduct to be held beyond reproach, to snuff out my life without a stain on his.'

'I do not care for the language you choose. Snuff you out, indeed!' said Giles. 'But you argue well. The king may well have wind of it, and hearken to your cause.'

'He will never learn of it. He will be in Denmark, long before tis heard. And the case will be lost, for I have no defence. Do not tell Meg, for I have not told Frances. Let them believe that the king is to come.'

Giles shook his head. 'This is desperate, Hew.'

'They will find out soon enough. Do not let it cloud the last days of the Yule.'

Twelfth night came at last. Matthew could not contain himself at the breakfast board, though the rest of the family were listless and subdued. They had worn out their chatter and their appetites over the long days of Yule. As soon as he finished with his bread and butter, he demanded cake. His parents frowned at him, with a jointly vexed and anxious bafflement, as though they had forgotten he belonged to them. His mother said, 'Later, perhaps.'

'No, Minnie, now.'

His father cleared his throat, while his mother said, as if he were not there, 'This is what I mean. I do wish you would talk to him.'

His father said, unreasonably, 'It is your brother's fault.'

Frances said, 'The twelfth cake, he must mean. Remember that you made one, just for the bairns. He has been looking forward to it. Let him have a piece.'

Matthew did not stay for another invitation, but jumped down at once, and ran into the kitchen. Frances called after him, 'It is in the pantry, on the second shelf, covered with a cloth. Cut a slice for Martha, too.' The little girl climbed down.

Meg glowered at Giles, who said feebly, 'Twelfth day, my love.'

The adults sank once more into a weary lull, which was broken by the sound of wailing from the kitchen.

'Bella Frew has caught them in a mousetrap,' said Hew. 'Then they are lost, for she keeps no prisoners.'

'Oh dear,' said Meg.

'Bella went out to the mill,' Frances said. 'Perhaps we should see.'

For once, it was not Martha at the centre of the storm. Meg found her dizzy child standing thumb in mouth at the very edge of it, dumb and bemused at the sight of her brother, howling on the floor. Scattered all around him were clumps and crumbs of cake. He could not, at first, articulate his grief. Gradually the words came out, and they understood. There was no bean.

Meg was the first who made proper sense of it. Then she felt ashamed, and protective, of her child. 'That was wrong and silly of you, to spoil all the cake. You are not a babbie now. Look at Martha, here. She is not in tears.

'He wanted the bean in the cake, so he could be king for the day,' she explained to the others. 'I did not know he could be such a wilful boy. It is not like him. He was ay the steady one.'

'Did I not tell you,' said Giles, 'the dangers of fruits out of season? This will not do, Matthew. Stop it, at once.'

'The bean must be there,' Frances said, 'for I saw your mother put it in. And the cake was folded up inside the dough. It could not have fallen out.'

'Do not indulge him,' said Giles. 'He is petted enough.'

'By you,' said his wife.

But Matthew sobbed, 'It is not there. Do you not see? I had to find the bean, so I could be the king. I have to be the king, to pardon Uncle Hew. I must be king, to put everything right.'

The strength of the silence stoppered his tears. He took a great gulp, and stopped, scared, to gaze at the faces around him, all of them looking at Hew. Then Frances and Meg spoke at once. Frances said, 'That was the king you promised would come? A bean king from a cake?' while Meg said, 'How could you let him think that, Hew? That it fell on him, to put right your mistakes?'

'I didn't know he thought it,' answered Hew. 'At least, when he said the king would come, I knew he meant the bean king. I did not know he thought that king could do what a real king does.'

'Can he not?' Matthew whispered.

His mother hugged him, 'It is play, my love.'

Hew said, 'I am sorry, Matthew. I never did intend to put the weight of it on you. I did not imagine you would take it on yourself.'

Frances cried out, 'Why should he not? Are you so blind that you cannot see? He does what you do. You play king to the world. Why shouldn't he?'

She ran out in tears, and Meg went out after, with Martha in her arms, and a bitter glance at Hew.

Giles scooped Matthew up. He sat down on a chair, and settled the child in his lap. Matthew burrowed deep against his father's heart.

'Dear me,' said Giles. 'I fear this present tempest may rage on a while.'

'I do not have a while. Andrew Wood will hang me, and my family hates me,' Hew said peevishly.

'No cries of pity, please. And no talk of the end. You have upset the boy, already, quite enough.'

'Ach, I am sorry. Will you be my friend?' Hew said to Matthew. 'For, if you will, I can bear almost anything.'

Matthew lifted up his head from his father's breast. He nodded.

'There, all well,' said Giles. ''Tis strange there was no bean. I hope he hasn't swallowed it.'

'I didn't,' Matthew said. 'And Martha didn't. I didn't let her. We didn't eat any of the cake. It must have been in the bit that was cut out. That was not fair. The cake was for us. And Bella was to keep it safe. But someone had it first.'

'A bit was cut out?' said Giles. 'That is very strange. I wonder who it was?'

'I do not know.'

'Then it is a mystery. Perhaps Hew will investigate.'

But Hew did not have to. He already knew.

On the seventh of January, Hew left his house and went to town with Giles, coming to the tolbooth in the market place. Sir Andrew Wood received them, in a sober mood.

'You have not brought John Kintor. And, as I suppose, you are not here to accuse the doctor. Therefore, I assume that you give up yourself, for justice to be served upon you. I note, too, that you have not brought the king with you. Indeed, I assume that the visit of the king was an invention. I will not pretend to understand what madness lay behind it.'

Hew did not answer, except to give a little half smile, which by a man who did not know him quite as well as Andrew did, might have been construed as an apology.

Andrew said, unexpectedly, 'This makes me sad. I did not want this, Hew.'

Hew objected, 'You have always wanted it.'

'To hang you, perhaps. But not for another man's crime. Will you not reconsider? Bring me the boy, and the thing is done. This is wrong-minded of you. It is not noble. It is arrogant.'

'We told him that,' said Giles.

'Listen to your friends. Go home. Send the boy. And we will forget this contract. We will call it a folly of the Yule.'

'That is generous. But I cannot send the boy, because he is not guilty of the crime,' Hew said.

Sir Andrew sighed. 'You say that. But you cannot show me an alternative.'

'On the contrary. We can.'

Hew took from a pouch the pellet that was found in Alan Petrie's throat, and placed it on the board in front of Andrew Wood. 'Do you remember this?'

'Indeed. It killed the man.'

'It did. But it was not one of John Kintor's pellets for his sling. It was a bean from a twelfth cake that choked him. See.' Hew shook out the pellets from the pouch. 'They are not the same.'

Sir Andrew shook his head. 'So it is a bean. What does that signify? The boy could have shot the bean with his sling. Where was the cake, if he choked on it? We saw none by the corpse.'

'The mill is plagued with crows. That is what the sling is for. Tis likely that the crumbs were eaten by the birds.'

'In any case,' said Giles, 'you have the corpus still, in the dead house. There is likely to be cake inside the stomach.'

'You expect me to allow you to anatomize?' The crownar hesitated.

'You said he had no family.'

'Aye, but still.'

Giles appealed to one with interests near his own, and as far as possible from Hew's. 'Come now, you can watch.'

In the event, there was no need to cut the corpse. Giles found crumbs of pastry still inside the throat, and cake crumbs, oddly, in the dead man's hose. 'He must have pushed it down, when Bella Frew appeared. Then settled to his breakfast by the burn. The poor man must have bolted it,' he said. 'I wonder why he chose a piece of twelfth cake, of all the other things he could have had.'

'It was Bella's system,' answered Hew. 'It had placed the twelfth cake closest to the door.'

'Really, it was Meg that killed him,' Hew remarked, on their way back home. 'For she baked the cake.'

'If I were you,' said Giles, 'I would not mention that. The smoothing of the waters will be hard enough. The last days have been trying ones. And though I hesitate to bow down to your kirk, they may have sounder instincts when it comes to Yule. There is far too much to eat, of rich unwholesome foods, and far too much of sloth, and weariness and indolence, and nothing else to do, but fall out with family. And the whole event goes on for far too long. Still, my heart is full, and I would suffer all of it, over and again, for this happy outcome, that you are not hanged. I was sure you would be, Hew. I saw it in your horoscope.'

'What?' Hew stopped short to stare at him. 'You did not say so, then.'

'I thought it was polite to leave the worst part out. There was a chance, besides, it would not come about. The science of prediction never was exact.'

❡

we commonly say in the Prouerbe, that a man thinketh he hath founde the Beane in the Cake, when ther is some subtile mening in a thing, and he windeth himself into some companie to put forth his opinion and deuice, bearing himselfe in hande, that he hath an inuincible reson althogh it be but fond & trifling

JOHN CALVIN, SERMON ON THE BOOK OF JOB,
trans. Arthur Golding, 1574

1588: FOREVER AND A DAY

This book is an almanac of sorts, following the pattern of the early ones in which the months ahead were predicted in the stars. It begins with Candlemas, which in the Scottish calendar comes first or last among the quarter days depending on the count: officially, in 1588, the year began on March 25. Not until December 1599 did the Privy Council order that the Scottish year should conform to other countries and be reckoned to begin, 'in all tyme cuming' from 1600, on January the first. (So 1599 was almost three months short.) Properly, our Candlemas – February 2 1588 – falls in 1587, or as it is sometimes styled 1587/88. But in popular belief, reflected in the almanacs, New Year's Day had always fallen on the first of January. And since this is a book about popular beliefs, our year begins there too.

This kind of dual accounting ought not to confuse us, since we have our tax years and our school years, and in places like St Andrews academic ones. But in 1588, we have another kind of reckoning to contend with. Historians tend to date the events of the Spanish Armada according to the Gregorian calendar (adopted in Spain in 1582), then ten days in advance of the Julian one, which Scotland (and England) retained until 1752. The dates in these stories, and the weekdays they fall on, are those of the Julian calendar. Hew, though not Giles, would be appalled at anything else. And the times of the tides, the length of the days and the phases of the moon are roughly accounted to follow that calendar, which is different from the one we have today. They cannot be exact. They may, in some places, be wildly out. They do not account for differences in latitude, British Summer Time, or hours of indeterminate or of varying length. The noon or one or four o'clock is theirs; I cannot promise it's the same as ours.

Nothing of this matters to the people in the stories, whose lives are shaped by seasons – by seedtime and the harvest, by fish days and flesh days and days when rents are due – rather than by dates. And yet the almanacs are full of dates, each with an aspect and a name (February opens with St Bridget's day; Valentine is drowned in a sea of saints). They count the years since the world began (ominously, 5550, in 1588 – the world was supposed to end in the sixth millennium) and give 'everlasting tables' 'at no time to be altered' to calculate 'for ever' which sign the moon is in, on which day Sunday falls, when it is a leap year, the age of the moon 'at all tymes', the ebbing and flowing of the tides, the length of the day and the night, the dates of the moveable feasts. These 'everlasting' tables were discarded with the day, thrown away each year and like the days they represented, came round again. Of the very many thousands printed and reprinted, no more than a handful have survived. One of those is Walter Gray's for 1588, *An almanacke and prognostication, made for the yeere of our Lord M.D.LXXXVIII*, a single copy of which is in the Bodleian Library, The Vicar's Library, St Mary's Church, Marlborough. This almanac is 'rectified' for Dorchester, though it's not clear how this impacts on predictions such as: 'Februarie, the first day, darke and colde'.

The earliest existing Scottish almanac that I have come across was printed in Edinburgh in 1619, though much earlier calendars for calculating dates of religious feasts are found in psalm and ballad books. Of *A generall prognostication for ever. Fruitfullie augmented with manie plaine, briefe, chosen rules, concerning all purposes, and verie expedient for all maner of persons whatsoeuer*. 'Imprinted at Edinburgh by Andro Hart: 1619.' – 'for ever' once again – two copies have survived, one of which is in the Bodleian, and the other in the National Library of Scotland. Hart's almanac is based on earlier prognostications issued by the English astrologer Leonard Digges in various editions, dating to the 1550s. The earliest surviving one is dated 1555. Hart's 1619 version has been adapted for the market to include the Scottish fair dates, the tide times for Leith, Aberdeen, St Andrews and Dundee, and the 'readie high wayes', with the names of the towns and distances between, of which 'the whole summe is, two hundreth, and foure score of miles betwixt *Edinburgh* and *London*'. (John Taylor, the 'water-poet', who walked from London to Edinburgh in 1618, observed that 'the Scots doe allow almost as large measure of their miles, as they doe of their drink', *The Pennyles Pilgrimage*).

The almanacs together form a kind of composite of familiar themes, like the days themselves recurring year on year, with very little change. But 1588 was no ordinary year. This was the year in which the same printer who printed Walter Gray's almanac published John Harvey's *A DISCOVERSIVE PROBLEME concerning Prophesies, How far they are to be valued, or credited, according to the surest rules, and directions in Diuinitie, Philosophie, Astrologie, and other learning: Deuised especially in abatement of the terrible threatenings, and menaces, peremptorily denounced against the kingdoms, and states of the world, this present famous yeere, 1588, supposed the Great woonderfull, and Fatall yeere of our Age,* and in which James VI wrote a meditation on the Day of Judgement, in response to the threat from the Spanish fleet. This was a year in which the world was meant to end, in which 'for ever' seemed to loom perilously close. Its calendar and almanacs, and enduring histories, have shaped the stories here, which follow through the year its high days and holidays, fair days and foul, from Candlemas to Yule, where the changing of the seasons marks time to the march of human life itself, and the only constant is that every date brings death.

A LIFE SHAPED BY SEASONS: HISTORICAL NOTES

CANDLEMAS
Candilmes, February 2 1588
A term day in Scotland

Candlemas was once a festival of light, a beacon in the midst of the dark days of winter. In the early Christian Church, Candlemas was the feast of the purification of the Virgin Mary, the day on which the infant Christ was presented in the temple, and his mother cleansed of childbirth, forty days after the nativity. The story is told in the Gospel of Luke 2 22:40. The infant Jesus Christ is recognised by Simeon as the anointed one, the bringer of the 'light', which is symbolised in candles at the feast of Candlemas. It is said to have its root in the ancient Roman festival where tapers were lit to honour Februa, a double affront to the Protestant Church, compounding Roman Catholic faults with Roman pagan ones.

In the fifteenth and early sixteenth centuries, the craftsmen of Aberdeen performed, among their several pageants and processions, Candlemas 'plays', and the corporations were required to provide wax candles for the Mass. There were penalties for those who failed to take part 'in their best array'. In 1523 one John Pill was tried and convicted for not joining in the Candlemas procession, with 'his token and sign of his craft'. Compounding his offence by rudeness to the Bailies, John Pill was sentenced to appear barefoot and bareheaded at the Kirk with a candle of wax in his hand.

The Candlemas pageants, like the May folk games and Robin Hood plays, were driven out at the Reformation, when the tables turned. Sanctions were imposed on those who took part, as opposed to on those who shunned the celebrations. But the Kirk had a battle to dispel the old beliefs. In our present month of February, 1588, the General Assembly made report of Fife: 'No resorting to the Kirk in many places. The kirks ruinous and destitute of Pastours and provision. There is superstitious keiping of the Yule, Pasche, &c'. In 1591 the Kirk was still denouncing plays of Robin Hood and asking that the acts of Parliament against them be put into effect, while in Aberdeen the candlelit processions celebrating Candlemas were taken up by schoolchildren and were carried on through the eighteenth century.

The Kirk appears to have distanced itself, too, from the second part to Candlemas (if the first is the presentation in the temple of the Christ child, the bringer of the light), that is, the feast of the purification. The commentators to the Geneva Bible were careful to explain the meaning of the verse: 'And when the days of her purification, after the Law of Moses, were accomplished, they brought him to Jerusalem, to present him to the Lord' with the note 'This is meant, for the fulfilling of the Law: for otherwise the virgin was not defiled, nor unclean, by the birth of this child'. The book of Common Order – the liturgy that John Knox introduced to Scotland in 1564 – contains no service for the thanksgiving of women after childbirth, unlike the English Book of Common Prayer which it replaced. Presbyteries should be 'careful to remove superstition . . . in kirking of women after childbirth' notes the Synod of Moray in 1656. Despite this, the 'kirking' of women after childbed (and also after marriage) appears to have continued into the late nineteenth century, long after the practice in England had died out. Deep-set superstitions can be hard to shift, even for a zealous and persistent church.

CANDLEMAS LORE OF THE LAND

'As lang's the liverock sings afore can'lemas, it greets aifter't'

The liverock (skylark from Old Scots *laverok/lawrok*) should be careful not to sing too soon. Candlemas day was the point in the year at which the winter would either let go of its grip, or redouble in strength. A dark sky boded well, and a clear one ill, for:

> If Can'lemas is fair and clear
> There'll be twa winters in the year

This piece of ancient lore recurs in various forms throughout the northern hemisphere. It appears as a foolproof way to forecast the weather for the year to come, in Digges' Scottish almanac:

> If the day of Candlemas be cleare,
> The Winter shal be greater and worse that yere

According to Thomas Hill's *Gardener's Labyrinth* of 1577, 'The yearely Almanackes doe maruellouslie helpe the Gardners in the election of tymes, or sowing, planting, and grafting, but especially in obseruing the Moone, about the bestowing of plantes'.

In Meg's garden in this month, the primroses are peeping through. They will be eaten as a pot herb or boiled in white wine as a remedy 'for one that cannot make water'. A little later in the year they may be made into a 'spring tart' like this seventeenth-century recipe from *The Compleat Cook: or, the Whole Art of Cookery* (London, 1694):

> Gather what buds are not bitter, also the leaves of Primroses,
> Violets and Strawberries, with young Spinage, and boil them,

and put them into a Cullender, then chop your Herbs very small, and boil them over again in Cream, add thereunto so many yolks with the whites, as will sufficiently thicken your Cream, to which you must add some grated Naples bisket, colour all green with the juyce of Spinage, and season it with Sugar, Cinamon, Nutmeg, and a little Salt, you may bake it in Puff-paste or otherways.

Also flowering now is the lesser celandine, a member of the buttercup family that takes its name from the Greek word for swallow: 'the small Celandyne was so called, bycause that it beginneth to spring & to floure, at the comming of the Swallowes, and withereth at their returne'.

Celandines are said to be good for the eyes: 'I sau celidone, that is gude to help the sycht of the ene'.

Considered 'hot and dry in the third degree', celandine is also prescribed for toothache, haemorrhoids, jaundice, 'naughtie fleume' and 'evil humours', while the juice of the roots 'mingled with honie, and snifte or drawen vp into the nose, purgeth the brayne from superfluous moystures, and openeth the stoppings of the nose'.

In the physic garden, hellebore is flowering too. White hellebore is used with care: '*Hippocrates* in procuring a Vomit did very much use white Hellebore, which is poisonous and strangling'. As a purge in treating 'quartain' fevers: 'After meate, you must prouoke vomite (if nothing let it) with white hellebore first commixed with radishe which if it worke litle or nothing, you must minister hellebore by it selfe'. 'Quartain' fevers recur at intervals of seventy-two hours, that is, on the fourth day. Radishes, luckily, are in season too.

Also used in sneezing powders for the apoplectic patient: 'provoke him to sneezing with white hellabore' – we remember that the almanac for 1588 marked February 2 as a good day to 'purge the head by neesing' – or as a cure for lethargy. And to flush away the winter blues, the dried root of black hellebore is a 'safe remedy' for 'any infirmitie, that hath his originall, of a melancholicke cause'.

WHITSUNDAY
Quhissonday, May 26 1588

Whitsunday – 'Quhissonday' in Scots – is Pentecost, the seventh Sunday after Easter or Pasche, and a moveable feast. In 1588 it fell on May 26 in the Julian calendar.

In Scotland, it was a legal quarter day, and the term day on which tenancies were agreed or terminated. (And still is. Whitsunday was redefined for legal purposes as May 28 in the Terms and Quarter Days (Scotland) Act 1990.) The term dates also shifted year by year, according to the date upon which Easter fell, until 1690–93, when Whitsunday was fixed at May 15. 'Witsondays' are agreements going forward from that date, while the 'Whitsunday term' may be retrospective too, covering the period since the previous quarter day, or since Martinmas. A 'witsonday fee' is one due at this time.

Now was the time of year for exchange of property. The Whitsun removal day was known as 'flitting Friday', the Friday before the feast of Pentecost. The Old Scots word to 'flit' (from the Middle English, originally Old Norse), in the sense of house removal, is in use today. In early legal documents it generally appears as 'flit and remove'.

Whitsunday was also the name given to the third term in the academic year at St Andrews (until 1997, when semesters were introduced and reduced to two: Martinmas and Candlemas) and the other ancient Scottish universities, its context for the king's commission in the story here.

May was traditionally a month of revelry, beginning with the
May Day games or plays, the merry burgh pageants of misrule
and plays of Robin Hood, which like Candlemas processions
were an essential part of the early civic calendar, and were
stamped out at the Reformation by a jealous Kirk. The writing
was on the wall as early as 1555:

Concerning Robin Hood and the Abbot of Unreason:
Item, it is statute and ordained that in all time coming no
manner of person be chosen Robin Hood or Little John,
Abbot of Unreason, May Queen or otherwise, neither in
burgh nor to land, in any time to come, and if any provost,
bailie, council and community chooses such a personage as
Robert Hood, Little John, Abbot of Unreason or May Queen
within the burgh, the choosers of such shall forfeit their
freedom for the space of five years and otherwise shall be
punished at the will of [Mary of Guise], the queen's grace,
and the person who accepts such an office shall be banished
out of the realm; and if such persons as Robin Hood, Little
John, Abbot of Unreason or May Queen be chosen outwith
the burgh and other landward towns, the choosers shall pay
to our sovereign lady £10 and their persons put in ward, there
to remain during the pleasure of the queen's grace; and if any
women or others in summer tries singing, makes perturbation
to the queen's lieges in the passage through burghs and other
landward towns, the women perturbers, for the extortion of
money or otherwise, shall be taken, handled and put upon
the cukstule of every burgh or town.

Despite the law, the characters of Robin Hood and Little John,
the Queen of the May (no Maid Marian here), and the Abbot
of Unreason or Unrest, who played merry havoc in the ancient
plays, were sometimes irrepressible. At the General Assembly

for 1591, 'Profaners of the Sabbath day by Robin Hood plays' are included in a list of the vilest threats to assail the land, no better and no worse than Jesuits and murderers. Here is the plea from the Kirk to the Crown:

> It is craveit, The acts of Parliament made for suppressing of the enormities following may be put to executioun: First, against Jesuites and the receipters of them; and of excommunicats... profainers of the Sacraments; privat men and wemen givers therof; idolaters, pilgrimagers, papistical Magistrates; sayers and heirers of the mess; givers of the Sacraments according to the papisticall forme, and receivers of the same; committers of apostasie; publick mercatts vpon the Sabboth day; violent invaders of Ministers be strikeing of them or shedding of thair blood; profaners of the Sabboth day be Robein Hoodes playis; murderers and blood shedders quhilk overflow the land.

This Whitsunday story is intended for a comedy, in the gentle spirit of the merry month. But like the plays themselves, the order and disorder represented there, and the mood against them, it has darker undertones.

WHITSUNDAY LORE OF THE LAND

For Meg Cullan in her garden, May is a busy time of year. She expects to spend much of it in the still house, making medicinal waters from the morning dew. But the full moon on the last day of April means it will be later in the month before she comes to gather it, for the dew is better when the moon is waxing full. She must also choose a day when it has not rained overnight, which if the almanac is accurate, will be hard to find. When she finds the perfect day, she will slip out before sunrise and go by the light of the moon to her brother's fields, to draw off the dew with a cloth.

It is likely she will not be there alone. The dew is believed to be good for the complexion, and others will have come to wash their hands and faces in it, hoping to remove their blemishes and spots. Some of the water Meg collects will be used for cosmetics and perfumes, but most will be distilled with white wine, herbs and flowers to make the gentlest sort of medicines. It is said to be good, especially, for the eyes.

In this month, the finest kind of butter is made, with sweet new milk, delicate and fresh. It has the essence of new grass in it, the shimmer of the field, where the unripe corn is billowing in waves, and the butter has been churned into the palest primrose, speckled with crystals of salt. The butter is not only good to eat. Meg will wash it out in the morning dew, and use it as a base for all the oils and salves that require a grease. No other kind will do. Its quality has now become proverbial, so that looking as if 'butter wouldn't melt', which is a favourite grumble of the preachers, is surpassed by one. His opponents engage in such

under-hand practises, and iuggling sleights of legerdemaine . . . with such a slie and nimble conueiance, as a man would hardly imagine, that not any other but May-butter it selfe could possiblie melt in their mouthes.

Meg has made on ointment of it, mixed with oil of tartar, which Canny Bett has sworn has washed away her wart.

In addition to the still, and the herbs in her garden which are coming into flower, Meg is concerned about her bees, for this is a time when they are prone to swarm. Because it is the spring, and the weather has been cold, she gives them a little honey on a stick, 'else may they starve . . . or be out of heart'.

In the middle of this work, in blunders Lord Sempill, and the best of the bees may be lost. The physick he is using for his fundamental ailment would not be recommended by either Meg or Giles. It is a dangerous concoction of henbane which can cause unconsciousness, 'if one doe but smell often to the hearbe and flowers thereof':

> The leaues, stalkes, flowers, seede, roote, and iuice, doe coole all inflammations, cause sleepe, and swage paine, but it may not be vsed too much. Seethe Henbane in water, and wash thy forehead and feete therewith hote, to cause sleepe in the hote euill, and apply a plaster of the seedes with womans milke and vineger hote to thy temples. And so it also destroyeth the Emerods

Here is the ointment itself:

> To heale the griefes of the fundiment.
> Take of the tender leaues of Henbane, and of Purcelane, and of crummes of bread infused in wine, the yolke of an Egge rosted hard, of eche like quantitie, of oyle of Roses as much as sufficeth, braye them all: then fomentate the place with the decoction of Roses, and of Mellilot [sweet-clover plant], and laye vpon it the Cataplasme [poultice] aforesaid.

Henbane is believed to be a witch's drug, and its hallucinogenic properties may have led some to believe that they could fly. Witches could transform themselves, with the devil's help, into any form. And Lord Sempill's bird was found sitting in a hawthorn tree, which was believed to have magic properties. Hawthorn blossoms were not brought into a house, for fear they brought in death. The hawthorn has, in its chemical make-up, apparently some element that makes the dead flowers smell like rotting flesh.

As the spring brings life back to the garden and the land, and laughter and pleasure to the people who inhabit it, so it brings the regrowth of the natural world, which begins to burgeon and encroach upon the town. The world of hill and stream, of apple and of hawthorn tree, where the careless lover may yet fall asleep, is the fairy world, which threatens to disrupt and disturb the human one. And though Meg makes attempts to shape and take control of it, its lawlessness and dangers are never far behind.

LAMMAS
Lammes, August 1 1588

Lammas was a term or quarter day on which legal transactions took place, and farm hands were hired for the haymaking. In Old Scots it is sometimes written 'Lambes' or 'Lambas-tide', leading to confusion with the lamb brought to church for the ancient feast of St Peter ad Vincula, or Petermas, also August 1. But the word derives from Old English *hlaf*, meaning loaf, and the festival to which it gave its name was a consecration of the first loaf of bread from the early harvest of the grain. In Scotland, barley ripens later than the English wheat, and on the first of August, even in the Julian calendar, it might still be green. But the promise would remain. 'It is long to Lammas' is a kind of joke, said 'when we forget to lay down Bread at the Table, as if we had done it designedly, because it will be long e'er new Bread come'. In the 'old days', 'if a farmer had neglected his work and his haymaking was still unfinished on August 13 (old style) he was called in reproach a Latter Lammas man'. Latter Lammas, in the proverb, is the day that never comes; the day of reckoning too: since Lammas was a term day for the settling of accounts, Latter Lammas may be judgement day, as it turns out here.

In St Andrews, Lammas is a fair or market day, the last remaining one of five. The date of the fair moved on to the second Tuesday in the month, following the change from the Julian calendar, to accommodate the shift in the agricultural year. It now lasts for five days, beginning on the Friday of the week before, with what as children we used to call the 'shows', a funfair spilling out over Market Street and South Street, and the lanes between, in the very heart of the town. It concludes with a market of traditional traders, setting up their stalls at the west end of the South Street, supplemented latterly by food stalls on the Market Street, of the artisan and continental kind. There are motions put each year by the local merchants and residents of South Street to move it from its place at the centre of the town to the outskirts. Residents complain of the use of the machinery to operate the rides, and its risks to the structure of a street of national heritage. Merchants complain of restricted access to their shops and businesses, and the loss of customers caused by a funfair just outside their doors. Everyone complains about the litter and the noise.

No doubt they always did. At the time of a fair, in the ancient burghs, normal restrictions to trading were lifted, and the local merchants were faced with competition they did not have to contend with at other times. The influx of the chapmen and pedlars, and of foreign ships massing in the harbours, may not have been welcomed by all. For the duration of the fair, certain burgh laws and rights were suspended, old debts and grievances could not be pursued, and special courts were convened to deal with disputes at the fair itself. These were known in England as 'pie-powder' courts, from Norman French and Latin, translating literally to Scots as 'dustifute'. The allusion is to the itinerant merchant, who, in theory at least, should not be disadvantaged in the process of the law by his status as a stranger in the land. Outbreaks of violence were common at fairs, and liable to escalate, like the early racial hate crime which took place in St Andrews in 1591, and came to the attention of the Privy Council when the perpetrator failed to make amends. Robert Jackson, burgess from Dundee, had approached the servant of a London merchant at the senzie fair:

> and inquired 'giff he wes ane Englishman'. Complainer having admitted 'that swa he wes', the said Jaksoun not onlie injurit him maist maliciouslie be strykeing up of his chin with his hand and hurting thairby of his toung and mouth, bot als utterit verie mony disdainefull and contumelious speichis aganis the said complainer and his cuntrey.

Jackson later drew a dagger, and a pistol, on his victim, '"minding to have schote the said complenair through the body thairwith" which he would have done had he not been prevented by those present'. Holiday tempers are easily frayed.

LAMMAS LORE OF THE LAND

'The young goose to the old can say, see thee last at Lammas day'

Lammas is a time for the parting of the ways, as the harvest is begun and the season starts to change. The goose will be fattened up for Michaelmas, when it will prove the crowning glory of the ploughman's feast. The young goose is put to graze in the stubble fields, unaware this fortune means its life will end, and enjoys its fill.

Geese could be eaten both young and old:

there are two periods at which the goose is fatten'd for market: first, when it is very young. It is distinguished at these times by different names, the green goose, and the stubble goose

The right age for taking up the gosling to fatten it for a green goose, is at five weeks

For fattening the stubble goose . . . Taking them up soon after the harvest season is a favourable time; because in running in the stubble fields they will have got into tolerable flesh.

Green goose should be served in a sorrel sauce, and stubble goose with vinegar and mustard.

According to Giles Locke, the goose is by nature a melancholic bird, the melancholy manifest in its exceeding watchfulness, moody disposition, and blackness of flesh, making it hard to digest. Yet

taken whilst they are young, green feathered, and well fatted with wholesome meat, and eaten with sorrel sauce to correct their malignity . . . no doubt their flesh is as nourishing as it is pleasant and sweet. But of all other young stubble goose feeding itself fat in wheaten fields, is the best of all; being neither of too moist nor too dry a flesh.

The older goose he will not touch at all, unless it comes with garlic, exercise and drink.

In the meantime, for the month of August, there are two 'evil' days noted in the almanacs, the nineteenth and the twentieth. 'Not so evil' are the first (though the characters in the Lammas story may have disagreed), the twenty-ninth and thirtieth. Still, 'it hurteth not to abstain from pottage, and all hot meats, and drinks of spicerie'. Such foods are not meat for the summer months.

At Kenly Green, the cherry trees have finished bearing fruit, and Meg collects the stones. The neighbours are astonished that she grows them here, from cuttings which were brought from Balmerino Abbey, grafted onto apple trees. Giles believes the fruits are very hard and sour, but that is no bad thing, for before a meal they mollify the stomach and prepare digestion, while eaten after it, they soothe a burning heat. The sour ones are more wholesome than the sweet.

There are, at this time, a great many herbs and flowers to be cut, in both the physick and the kitchen gardens, which are in the process of a harvest of their own. In this month Meg collects most of the seeds she uses in her medicines, and the still house is filling up with seed cups and leaves, left in the sun to be dried. The apricots and plums are almost ready too, for bottling or for making into marmalades for Yule.

The fruit and the beehives must be kept from wasps, and garlic cloves are used to put them off the scent. Which goes to show, says Hew, that sauce for the goose is not sauce for the gander, after all. Soothing for the stings, Meg says, are bruised leaves of mint.

MARTINMAS
Martinmes, November 11 1588
Name given to the first term of the
university year at St Andrews

Martinmas is November 11, the feast of St Martin. It was often known as 'Martinmas in winter' to distinguish it from the feast of the translation of St Martin on the fourth of July. In Scotland it was the half-yearly quarter day when, with Whitsunday, landlords' rents were paid, and servants were contracted or discharged. It was also killing time, when cattle would be slaughtered and prepared for winter stores, and the winter's supply of candles would be made. To that end, it became a fair day in St Andrews in the nineteenth century, in place of the old St Andrew's Day and Michaelmas markets, for the hiring of farm hands to despatch the herd. A 'Martinmas coddoch' is a cow which has been fattened up for slaughter at this time; a 'ladinar-mairt' is salted to last until spring (a 'ladinar' is a larder; a 'mairt' or 'mart' is a fattened beef-cow).

A variant is 'Martlemas', shortened to 'Martel', obsolete in English since the seventeenth century. It is snatched in a song, 'Oh, Martel's wind, when wilt thou blow And shake the sear leaves off the tree?', a melancholy reference to the time of year. Engravings which depict the labours of the months show November slaughter in the midst of storms, and in 1588 it is storms at sea that define the story here, causing the destruction of the Spanish fleet, and the landing of a group of shipwrecked Spanish sailors not far from St Andrews on November 26, when the minister James Melville was woken in his bed early in the morning by the news that the Spaniards had arrived 'nocht to give mercie bott to ask' for it. Melville was presented with 'a verie reverend man of big stature, and grave and stout countenance, grey-heared, and verie humble like, wha, after mickle and vey law courtessie, bowing down with his face near the ground, and twitching my scho [shoe] with his hand, begang his harang in the Spanise toung'.

The sailor explained, through a young interpreter, that he was the commander of twenty hulks and that he and several of his captains had been driven by the storm onto the rocks at the Fair Isle of Scotland, and were shipwrecked there, where the survivors had remained for six or seven weeks in great hunger and cold. Taking a barque out of Orkney, they had come to supplicate to the king of Scotland and seek relief for themselves and their crew of 260 men, 'whose condition was for the present maist miserable and pitifull'.

After a short homily on the kind beneficence of the Scottish
Kirk, the commander and his captains were invited to come
ashore for refreshment, while the men were kept on board
the ship until Lord Anstruther arrived to entertain the officers
humanely in his own house, and to permit the crew to disembark.
The soldiers, 'for the maist part young beardless men, sillie,
trauchled [exhausted], and houngered', were given kale, pottage
and fish. Their general was Juan Gomez de Medina, who had
the charge of the flagship *El Gran Grifón*, and the command of
twenty urcas (supply ships) to the Spanish fleet.

The sailors did not know the extent of the damage that
the fleet had sustained until Melville bought a pamphlet in St
Andrews with the names of the ships and the lives which were
lost, which when it was shown to Gomez de Medina, 'O then
he cryed out for grieff, bursted and grat'.

Gomez de Medina, who had made such a great impression
in Anstruther, set out with his compatriots for Edinburgh and
was eventually repatriated in a convoy of four Scottish ships,
paid for and allowed free passage by Elizabeth. The ships were
waylaid by the Dutch, and many soldiers drowned. The general,
though, survived, and lived to return the favour, when he came
upon an Anstruther ship captured at Cadiz. He went to plead
on her behalf at court, made much of Scotland to his king, and
'tuk the honest men to his hous', where he 'inquryt for the Lard
of Anstruther, for the Minister, and his host, and sen[t] hame
manie commendations'.

His ship *El Gran Grifón* had been wrecked at Stroms Heeler,
between Orkney and the Fair Isles (on Fair Isle is a spot called
the 'Spainnarts' Graves'). The wreck was excavated in 1970 and
a full description of the site and excavation can be found online
at Canmore. In 1984 a party from the reconstructed Spanish
Orden Tercio Viejo del Mare Océano, wearing the costume of
the old conquistadors, retraced the steps of the shipwrecked

sailors from *El Gran Grifón* to Fair Isle where they planted a cross to commemorate the men who died there, and to the harbour at Anstruther where they were no doubt as warmly received as their ancestors had been almost four hundred years before them. The Anstruther manse, built for James Melville in 1590, is said to have been paid for by Spanish gold. I have heard no report that it has a ghost.

MARTINMAS LORE OF THE LAND

November take flayle,
Let ship no more sayle.

Forgotten month past,
Do now at the last.

November is the last chance to do what must be done before the winter comes. It is time to put the earth to bed, and to plan for the following year, 'contrive or forecast where and what you are to sow and plant,' prepare composts and soils, plant fruit trees and cabbages, and to gather in the seeds of holly and the yew.

In season still are onions, leeks, purslane and fresh parsnips. The apples and pears are weathering nicely, to a point where Doctor Locke, with his horror of fresh fruit, may consider they are almost safe to eat. In the physic garden, Meg is growing liquorice root, good to open up the lungs and to cleanse the phlegm prevailing at this time of year, which is cold and wet.

Phlegmatic men, her husband says, 'must abstain from meats the which is cold. And also they must refrain from eating viscous meat specially from all meats the which doth engender fleumatic humours, as fish, fruit, and white meat . . . And to beware not to dwell nigh to waterish and moorish ground. These things be good for fleumatic persons moderately taken, onions, garlic, pepper, ginger. And all meats the which be hot and dry. And sauces the which be sour.'

Meg buys ginger and pepper from the apothecary, who has replenished his stocks at the last of the fairs in November. After the end of the month, there will be no more ships until the spring. Thankfully the harbour has come through the storms, though it wants repair.

The Martinmas beef has been salted and stored, but should not be eaten in excess, or the briny flesh may lead to bladder stones. There is, at least, a remedy: 'If it do come accidentally by eating of meats ye wil ingender the stone, take of the bloud of an Hare, & put it in an earthen potte, and put therto three ounces of Saxifrage rootes, and bake this together in an oven, & than make pouder of it, and drinke of it morning and evening.'

According to Gray's almanac, this month will be filled with fogs, clouds, sleet, rain and winds. The seventeenth is bent to storms. The eighteenth and nineteenth will produce 'a pretty gale' and weather 'fit for the season'. The following three days will be 'freezing'.

The full moon on the twenty-third, near one of the clock in the morning, in Gemini, will bring in some 'good winter weather', followed by increasing winds, three days dark and changeable, until the month comes to a close with 'great winds' and 'dark air', liable to freeze.

The almanacs predict the weather many months ahead, with a breezy confidence rarely to be found in forecasts made today, though doubtless with as little, or as much, success. Richard Grafton warns in his:

November breeds rheum that will trouble the head
Beware of new wine though it be of the best

And baths of warm water are to be fled
And so is venery as well as the rest

The bright cheer of Yule still feels far away.

YULE
ȝule Day, December 25 1588

Yule, or ȝule in Old Scots, is the festive period lasting from
late December into January, of twelve or twenty days, and
sometimes longer still. It includes the twelve days of Christmas;
Yule Day on December 25; New ȝeris Day and Evin; Hansel
Monday, the first Monday in the year when the New Year's
gift or Han(d)sel was given to bring luck; and Uphalyday,
Twelfth night (and day), the Feast of the Epiphany. Rarely in
Scotland was it known as Christmas, even in the years before
the Reformation. At the Reformation itself, it ceased to be a
holiday (that is, a 'holy day') and the celebration of the nativity
of Christ was not officially restored until 1958. Many Scots
today do not remember Christmas as a childhood holiday, but
were given gifts at New Year instead.

The present giving harks back to the old Handsel day
(from Old English, to give into the hand), but the transferring
of festivities to the secular New Year, and the death of Yule,
did not begin at once at the Reformation; while the battle
persisted between Episcopalians and the Presbyterians over the
right of governance over the reformed Kirk, the old traditions
smouldered on until well into the middle of the seventeenth
century, and were kept ablaze in many parts of Scotland.

In February 1588 the General Assembly at Edinburgh
complained of the 'superstitious keeping' of the Yule in Fife,
and the Kirk Sessions were kept busy in the first month of each

year with the discipline of those who persisted in the holiday. In January 1573/4 the archbishop of St Andrews (not yet Patrick Adamson but the ailing John Douglas, who died in the pulpit in 1574) had recommended the insertion in the record books *ad futuram rei memoriam* that

> upon Sunday the xxiiii day of January Walter Ramsay, lorimar [a maker of horse bits and buckles], Walter Lathangie, cutlar, and John Smith, blacksmith, being accused and convicted . . . of observing of superstitious days and specially of Yule-Day became penitent and made open satisfaction thereof in presence of the whole congregation then being present. And therefore the minister, at command of the assembly, publicly denounced . . . that all persons within this parish, that observed superstitiously the said Yule-day . . . should be punished in like manner if they abstain from their work and labour that day, more than any other day except Sunday.

The keeping of the Yule was offensive, in particular, because it flouted the prerogative of the Sabbath day to be the single holy day of rest. The revellers were not willing to give up so quietly. On the same day Walter Younger refused to submit to the Church's discipline, complaining that 'it was unbecoming for an honest man to have to sit upon the stool of repentance', and saying that 'he is a young man and saw Yule-Day kept holiday and that the time may come that he may see the like yet; and therefore would not become obliged nor restricted in time coming to work or abstain from work that day, but at his own pleasure'. Younger was quickly brought to book, and found his place on the stool of repentance with the rest. But others would continue to offend. In the following year James Thomson, mason, accused of 'superstitious keeping of Yule last as holy day' promised that 'who would or would not he would not work on Yule day, and was not in use of the same . . . and in time coming . . . should never keep the said Yule day holiday, but would work on that day as on any other day to any man that would offer him work . . . and if no man charges him with work, he shall work some ridge stones of his own'. The key was to look busy when the Kirk dropped by.

The General Assembly had also condemned the singing of carols at Yule, despite the very lovely ones which had found their way into the Gude and Godlie Ballads, such as Luther's 'children's hymn for Christmas Eve', 'I come from hevin to tell', 'to be sung to the tune of the lullaby, Ba lula low', and 'To us is borne a barne of blis'.

The carols were still sung – and danced – and people still dressed up, women guising in men's clothes, and crying 'Zwil, Zwil, Zwil!' in loud and lewd company, while the Kirk did its best to discourage them. The story of the dog crying Yule is attributed to the preacher David Calder: 'A learned brother at a catechising told Yule-day was derived thus: There was a certain man hanged his dog on the 25th December, the creature was three hours hung, and at the end, the cord was loosed, and the dog lived; and running off, cryed Ule, Ule, Ule, and hence, says he, comes the word, Yule, Yule, Yule'. And Robert Blair of St Andrews, with a characteristic Presbyterian bluntness, is reported to have said: 'You will say, Sirs, good old Youle day; I'll tell you, good old Fool-day; you will say it is a brave Holiday; I will tell you it is a brave Belly-day; You will say, these are bonny Formalities, but I tell you, they are bonny Fartalities'. Blair had a turbulent career in the Kirk. He was nominated minister at the Kirk of Holy Trinity, St Andrews, in 1639.

It is in this spirit that the prying Alan Guthrie comes to peer into the windows of Hew's house at Kenley Green, in search of superfluous cheer. The law of which Hew falls foul was enacted first in 1552 by Mary of Guise, 'concerning the order of every man's house', ensuring that all men should eat and keep table according to their rank and status in the land. The act was the result of a dearth of food to share among the poor and a damage of excess ensuing to the gluttonous:

> because of the superfluous cheer used commonly in this realm, amongst small men as well as great men, to the great hurt of the commonwealth of the same and damage to the body, which make a man unable to perform all necessary lawful and good works

the following restrictions must apply: an archbishop, bishop or earl should have at his table no more than eight dishes of meat; an abbot, lord, prior or dean no more than six; a baron or freeholder (in which we may count Hew) no more than four; a burgess 'but three, with one kind of meat in each kind of dish'. Those who broke the law were to be punished with fines.

In those early days, already under shadow of the sharp axe of Reform, Christmas and Easter banquets were exempt, as were saints' days and marriages and entertaining strangers, and the clergy could expect a satisfying board. By 1581, when the Parliament of James VI ruled against 'superfluous banqueting and the inordinate use of confections and sweetmeats' (in the original, the more decadent 'drogges'), there were no exceptions, but 'bridals and banquets' were targeted specifically, while the Yule and Pasche already had their cards marked by the Kirk. The 'inordinate consumption' not only of native foodstuffs, but of 'sweetmeats, confections and spices brought from the parts beyond sea' was now to be deplored, for the shortage and inflation of prices it had caused, to the detriment of those who could not 'sustain that cost'.

In consequence, it was now prohibited for anyone below the rank of prelate, earl, lord, baron or landed gentleman worth less than 2,000 merks a year to have 'at their banquets or tables in ordinary cheer' any 'sweetmeats or confections' brought from overseas, such as the sweets and spices given to the farmers of Hew's lands at Yule, 'Under pain of £20 to be paid by any person doer in the contrary as well of the master of the house where the effect of this act is contravened'.

To enforce the law, the provosts and the bailies of the burghs were constrained to make use of official searchers, 'to which searchers open doors shall be made of whatsoever house they come to search, under the pains to be esteemed culpable in the transgression of this act if they refuse; and the offenders being apprehended, to be taken and held in ward until they have paid the said pecuniary pains, to be employed the one half to the benefit of the ordinary officers and searchers and the other half to the poor of the parish'.

It is an act entirely in the spirit of Protestant Reform; well-founded to assist the poor, and to curb the excesses of the rich and powerful, while it brings with it an oppressive joylessness, reflected in poor Alan's sad officious end. The king and his entourage were naturally exempt.

The law of Yule girth, invoked by Hew to take advantage of a stay of execution, was an ancient one, the remnant of which was reflected still in the justice courts. Originally, it appears to have conferred immunity from prosecution, in the sense of sanctuary, at least for a limited time. 'Girth' means immunity from harm, and to 'tak girth' means to take refuge.

When Hew invokes Yule girth, he knows it must be temporary. For the purpose of evading Alan Petrie's prying, it will serve his tenants well, allowing them the chance to consume the evidence. But justice cannot be escaped for long. In the Burgh court of Glasgow, convening after Yule, disturbing of the peace in the time of girth does not seem to remit, but almost to compound the ordinary fault. So Margaret Andro, spouse to John Anderson, cordiner (shoemaker), is called to make amends for striking and pulling the hair of Janet Taylor, daughter to James Taylor, 'within the time called of old the proclamation of Yule girth, and now of abstinence'.

And Patrick Spreull is pursued by John Boill, Chapman, for assault resulting in a bloody nose 'upon the 9th of January instant, within the time of proclamation of feriat time and abstinence'. The 'feriat' and 'abstinence' referred to here are not immunity from charges faced by the transgressors, but recognition of the fact that the courts were not in session at that time. January brings a backlog of complaints, and the Burgh sessions are as busy as the Kirk's following excessive freedom during Yule, when any sense of licence may be limited, and false.

YULE LORE OF THE LAND

Bot Yule is young, thay say vpon Yule evin.
And diuers times it hes bene hard and sene,
That efter most joy followis aduersitie.

Proverbs of the Yule do not abound in cheer. In the natural world, this is a bleak time of year. 'He is als bair as the birk in yule evin' is recorded in four versions in James Carmichaell's list of proverbs, and brings a shiver with it. Where Yule does bring joy, it will be short-lived: 'Ilk day is not yule day, cast the cat a castock'; 'a yule feast may be quit at pasche'. And mild weather at this time of year will fill up the kirkyard. Whatever the moment, the outlook is grim.

The cat who looks disdainfully upon the cabbage stalk perhaps reflects the sourness of the Scottish Kirk, sneering in the face of the festivities. James Carmichaell, who left behind these proverbs in a manuscript collection, was a student of

St Salvator's in the early 1560s, and later master at the St
Andrews grammar school. He then became Kirk minister and
schoolmaster in Haddington, and was one of the reformers
charged with the revision of (what became) the second book of
discipline in 1578. With Andrew Melville, he refused to sign a
bond accepting the authority of bishops in the Kirk, and fled to
England with Melville, Patrick Galloway and John Davidson,
poet and minister of Prestonpans, who had been a regent of St
Leonard's College, at the beginning of 1584. They were there in
exile at the same time as Hew.

Hew's yuletide celebrations would have embarrassed him,
perhaps, if he came into the company of former friends and
teachers such as these. Like the king, he is committed to the
'trew religion', in which he has been brought up since he was
a child, despite his father's – and his sister's – lasting Catholic
sympathies. But also like the king, he does not like constraint,
nor does he want his faith to hamper the festivities. He has an
English wife, and in England, where Reformation was imposed
by the Crown upon the Church, and not, as in Scotland, the
other way round, Christmas celebrations are not yet discouraged
(that was all to come).

It is not hard for Hew to justify the Yule, which is the
highlight, for his tenant farmers, of another year of hardship
in the agricultural calendar, and brings a little joy into the
darkest time. Winters at the close of the sixteenth century were
exceptionally cold, and 1588 was, on every count, an exceptional
year. That they have survived it is due to careful management,
by Frances of the land, and by Meg of the medicines and the
food stores that will see them safely through the winter months.
They deserve their feast.

Note: a full set of historical sources and suggested reading
matter can be viewed on the author's website.

GLOSSARY

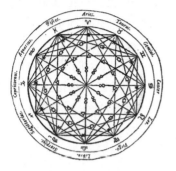

(A)feart
frightened

Ah
I

Ain
(one's) own

Allhallowday
All Saints' Day

An
and; if

Apothecar
an apothecary

Awbody
everybody

Awfy
an intensifier: very

Auld
old

Bailie
a town magistrate

Banes
bones

Baith
both

Bairn
a child

Balulalow
a lullaby

Bannock
a flat round bread or pancake
of barley or oats

Baxter
a baker

Bellox
testicles

Belly-thraw
a stomach ache

Black stane
black stone, on which students
sat during public examinations
at the ancient universities

Board
a table

Bordal-house
a brothel

Braw
fine, excellent (= brave)

Breeks
nether hose; trousers

Bumbaise
to baffle or confuse

Burn
a stream

Bursar
a student in receipt of a bursary

Buttock-mail
a fine for fornication

Butts
targets for archery practice

Cadger
an itinerant salesman

Canny
prudent, careful;
but also lucky

Cags
kegs or casks

Caquetoire
a 16th century 'gossip chair'

Cauld
cold

Chapman
an itinerant merchant, a pedlar

Chastely
chaste

Clatterer
a gossip

Clout
a rag

Clype
to tell tales (on)

Coffin
a piecrust

Coloured
feigned (of crying)

Combater
combatant

Compass
a plan

Compear
to appear before a court

Coning
a rabbit (a 'rabbit' is a young coning
or coney)

Converse
carnal conversation, i.e. sexual intercourse

Convicted
convinced

Coroner/Crownar
Crown officer responsible for
keeping peace and serving writs.
Often combined with the role
of Sheriff

Crowdie mowdie
the name of a dish made from oatmeal
and water, used (by Dunbar) as a
playful term of endearment

Cuddoch
a young cow or ox

Cukstule
stool of repentance

Dae
do

Deid
dead

Deil
the Devil

Dennar
dinner

Dinna/e
don't

Doleaunce
condolence

Doubt
to think

Dug
a dog

Economus
person in charge of the finances
of an institution

Ee, een
eye, eyes

Egyptian
a gypsy

Epidemy
an epidemic

Et tu
(Latin) 'you too'

Extremis malis extrema remedia
(Latin) Desperate times require
desperate measures

Factor
a land agent

Faither
father

Fash (oneself)
to get worked up, annoyed

Ferie day
a holiday

Fermer
person in charge of an infirmary

Fermary
an infirmary

Fey
doomed to die

Fidge
to be restless

Flankert
armour for the thigh

Flesher
a butcher

Flit
to move (house), move away

Flyte
to wrangle with aggressively

Forethocht felony
premeditated crime

Foulsum
loathsome

Flux
diarrhoea

Frae
from

Fu'
drunk (full of drink)

Futless
useless

Fyke
to fidget

Galliard
a vigorous renaissance dance

Gang
to go

Gar
to cause something to be done

Gie
to give

Girn
to grimace

Goited
bunkered

Gossip chair
a sixteenth-century conversation
chair, French caquetoire

Green
to desire, yearn for

Greet/Greetin(g)
cry, crying

Guid
good

Guidwife
a wife in her role as mistress
of the house

Haar
sea mist common on the east
coast of Fife

Hae
have

Half-deid
half-dead

Haly
holy

Hameward
homeward

Handfast
betrothed, informally wed

Handsel
a New Year gift

Havers
nonsense

Haud
to hold

Heugh
a hill

Hichty
high-spirited, courageous

Hing
to hang; to cling or hold fast to

How devil
How the devil

Ignosce
(Latin) forgive (imp.)
(lit. do not look into)

Immissa est pila in arenum
(Latin) The ball is stuck in the sand

Impressive
impressionable

Ither
more, other

Jakes
a latrine

Jougs
a type of pillory

Juglar
a magician, a conjuror

Justiciar
a judge

Keek
to peep

Ken
to know

Kirk
a church; the Reformed Church of
Scotland

Kirtle
a woman's frock or gown

Kist
a chest

Kitchins
basic provisions

Kittil
fidgety

Lade
a millstream

Laich
low

Laich house
a cellar

Laird
a smaller baron or landowner, the
landlord of a small estate, distinguished
from, and inferior to, a lord

Laik
to play (amorously) with

Lammas
August 1, one of the four Scottish term
days, and one of the five annual fair
days in St Andrews

Lammas rain
heavy rain at Lammas time, tending to
flood

Latter Lammas
never (proverbial)

Laureation
university graduation

Limmar
a villain

Loun
a member of the lower orders

Lugs
ears

Lusty
cheerful

Magistrand
student in the final year of study leading
to the degree of Master of Arts. (Henry
Balfour has taken four years to arrive at
his third (bachelor) year, on account of
the closure of the university during the
plague and of his own deficiencies.)

Magistrate
a member of the council, consisting
of provost and bailies, responsible for
commercial and civil order in the burgh

Mair
more

Maist
most

Mak shift
make shift, cope, manage

Martinmas
November 11, the feast of St Martin;
name given to the first term of the
academic year at St Andrews University

Marchpane
marzipan

Master
title given to someone who has
graduated Master of Arts

Maunna
must not

Maun
must

Medicinar
a doctor

Melee chaussee
'shat melle' – sudden affray, an
unpremeditated outbreak of violence

Mercat
a market

Milk-and-wattir
milk and water, i.e. meek and mild

Mimmerkin
a small person

Minchit
minced

Mind
to remember

Minnie
a child's name for mother

Morn
the morn = tomorrow

Mort house
a charnel house

Mow
a grimace, a pulled face

Muckle
great; much

Neb
a bird's beak; nose

Neep
a turnip

Nicht
night

Niver
never

Ordinary
a set meal at an inn, sold at
a fixed price

Pantofills
soft velvet slippers

Papingo
a painted parrot used as a
target in archery

Pavane
a courtly dance, more sedate
than the galliard

Peste
plague

Physic/ Physick
medicine

Piddling
dallying, messing about

Piker
a petty thief

Pilliewinks
an instrument designed to
crush the fingers

Pin-hippit
having narrow hips

Pintle
a penis

Plat
a dish

Ploukie-facit
having a face with blemishes; pimpled

Pocket
a smaller poke; a (detachable)
pocket worn inside clothing

Poffle
a small piece of land

Points
laces used to attach doublet and hose,
and to hold up the breeches

Poke
a small sack or bag

Port
a gate

Powder court
special court with jurisdiction
on fair days

Prentice
an apprentice

Press
a linen cupboard

Prier
one who pries

Quartan fever
a fever which recurs every fourth day

Quean
a young woman of low status

Quotidian
recurring daily, every 24 hours

Reek
to smoke; to emit; to shed blood freely

Regent
a university teacher, who took a
class of students through the four
year course in arts and philosphy

Renegat
a renegade

Richt
right

Rig
a strip, ridge or row

Rin
to run

Rumpill
hind quarters

Sair
sore

Salve!
(Latin) Greetings!

Sark
a shirt

Scunner
a cause for disgust

Sic
such

Sin
since

Slidder
slippery, not easy to control, unreliable

Sluthcroun
a slut

Snuff
indignation, a huff; to take (something)
in snuff = to take offence at

Sonsie
lucky

Sooking
sucking

Spelair
a rope dance or acrobat

Spiritus quidem promptus
the spirit is willing but the flesh is weak
(Vulgate Mark caro vero infirma 14:38)

Stoup
a tankard or pitcher

Stomachit
offended, resentful, put out

Strake
a stroke, hit

Subjectable
susceptible

Succar
sugar

Telt
told

Tertian
a third year student

Tertian fever
a fever which recurs every other day

The day
today

The gither
together

The noo
just now

Thocht
thought

Thrang
throng

Thrawn
ill-tempered, out of sorts

Thwart
from side to side

Timmerman
a carpenter

Tippet
a long narrow strip of cloth
worn as a scarf

Trauchled
worn out, exhausted

Tron
the public weighing machine in
a burgh market place

Tumbler
an acrobat

Twattle
a pygmy

Twelvetide
Twelfth Night (and Day)

Unclaithed
unclothed

Uphalyday
the feast of the Epiphany

Vacances
vacation

Vennel
an alley

Visitor
person appointed by the Crown to
investigate suspicious deaths

Vomitary
an emetic

Wam
stomach

Ward
prison

Wattir-kail
vegetable broth

Wean
a child

Wha
who

What devil
what the devil

Whisht
hush

Wi'
with

Wid
would

Widdershins
in the wrong direction

Wrang
wrong

Yald
jade, nag (horse)

Yisterday
yesterday

Yule Girth
immunity from prosecution
at Christmas

Yule stock
a yule log

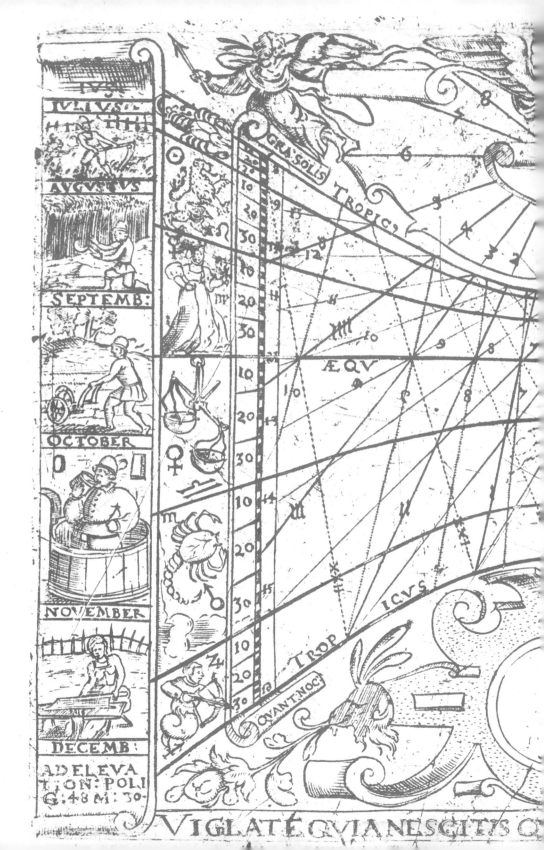

IVLIVS

IVLIVS

HIII IIII

AVGVSTVS

SEPTEMB:

OCTOBER

NOVEMBER

DECEMB:

AD ELEVA
TION: POLI
G: 48 M: 30

GRA·SOLIS

TROPIC9

ÆQV

TROP

ICVS

QVANT·NOCT

VIGLATE QVIA NESCITIS Q